MW00995615

· FATE OF THE NORNS ·

RAGNAROK

Andrew Valkauskas

DENIZENS
OF THE NORTH

© Andrew Valkauskas 2014

First Edition
Published by Pendelhaven 2014
121 Place Bourbonniere
Lachute, Quebec
J8H 3W7 Canada
www.pendelhaven.com

All rights reserved. No part of this publication may be reproduced for resale without the prior written permission of the copyright holder.

Author and Designer:
Andrew Valkauskas

Content Submissions:
Patrice Combatalade *(Hildolfr, Jolnir Puppets)*
Eric Hobberstad *(Erik the Frost Bear, Frost Mauler, Noahdher Leaf, Ravenous)*
Akira Currier *(Leif Mountain Shaker, Odur's Torc)*
Florian Hubner *(Ymir's Call)*
Mendel Schmiedekamp *(Favour of the Elf King's Daughter)*
Peter Troia *(Sagen Forandre Stones)*
Victor Ventura *(Dragvendil)*
Lawrence Huang *(Ingrid the Wanderer, Sun Stone)*
Ray Hickey, Jeff Mayo, Alex Soria, David Crowell, Lon Tatro and Joseph Soria *(Dawn of Ragnarok)*

Artists:
Helena Rosova
Richard Kane Ferguson
Sveta Sergeevna
Natasa Ilincic
Juraj Kopacka
Soni Alcorn-Hender
Nick Cragoe

Design and Layout:
Kyriaki Sofocleous
Stella Andronicou

Editing:
Sofia Moura
Mikel Matthews
Akira Currier

Proof Readers
Patrice Combatalade
Kevin Tompos
JP Rullmann
Kay Stattmueller
Doug Nordwall

Special Thanks
Sofia Moura
Jonas Zibirkstis
Davide Zanoni
Patrice Combatalade
Seth Rajakumar

ISBN# 978-0-9940240-0-8

21 Years of Viking mayhem...
Dedicated to the fans who keep the dream alive!

Table of Contents

Denizens of the North

Welcome to the magical and intriguing Viking world of *Fate of the Norns. Denizens of the North* is a lore book for the Ragnarok line of games. It takes place in the apocalyptic setting that was introduced in *Fafnir's Treasure* and continued in the *Core Rulebook. Denizens of the North* includes quests, characters and monsters that can be used in games of Fate of the *Norns: Ragnarok*. The focus of this book is the realm of mankind- Midgard, giving players and Norns additional material with which to flesh out a large evolving world.

Midgard

In the beginning, there was the great void known as Ginnungagap. Suspended in the sea of non-existence were two underived masses known as the Twin Primeval Worlds. One is known as Niflheim, a realm of absolute cold and darkness. The second is called Muspleheim and is the font of eternal fire and light. As the ice from Niflheim crept towards Muspelheim, primordial heat turned it to steam creating a crucible of life from which the cosmic tree Yggdrasil sprung forth. Currents of time would flow and cascade over Yggdrasil's bark, fostering its growth for many millenia before the first life would appear on the cosmic tree. A central world known as Midgard would come into being when the sons of Bor: Odin, Vili and Ve would slay the progenitor Jotun known as Ymir, and fashion the heavens and the earth from his corpse. When Midgard was young, all of this knowledge was old.

The sons of Bor created mankind, the first of whom were named Ask and Embla. Their children came to populate this middle world , calling it Midgard and their home. For a thousand years mankind has spread throughout Midgard, colonizing the land and carving out their destiny. Some moved to outer Midgard, forgetting their roots and adopting new customs.

The strong willed created their own dominions and gathered willing followers. When several self appointed chieftains or karls encroached on each another's land, there was war. Those that claimed to be descendants of the gods or giants exerted their influence with the most zeal. The Yngling dynasty could trace their ancestry back 1000 years to the Vanir god Frey. This dynasty birthed the greatest king of all, known as Harald Fairhair. He was the first to unite a kingdom using gifts and swords. Over a thousand petty kings bent knee, allowing Harald to create the Kingdom of Norveig.

His kingdom would be short lived as the spinners of fate called the Norns foretold of the twilight of the gods- Ragnarok! King Harald was a promiscuous man, conceiving many high-born and low-born sons. Lying on his deathbed, Harald never left clear instructions for succession. As he drew his last breath, Midgard went dark- literally! The sun and moon were devoured by two celestial wolves, plunging all of Yggdrasil including Midgard into darkness and cold.

The Sword Age

Since the death of King Harald and the coinciding extinguishing of the sun and moon, a terrible darkness and cold has fallen over the lands. This has harkened in the first age of Ragnarok known as the Axe Age. This age has seen the start of an unrelenting winter called Fimbulwinter that has destroyed any prospects of spring or summer. Society's unabashed descent into chaos and anarchy has ripped the social fabric. Farmers, hunters, and merchants have seen their livelihoods turned upside down. The scarcity of food and security has led the people down a dark road where panic and the survival instinct guide every decision. Many have perished from hunger but more lives have been extinguished by the daily violence that has claimed Midgard. The halls of the damned in Niflheim have never received so many visitors. Tales of undying corpses have become common. Whispers relate stories of Hel turning away the masses that come to Niflheim's black gates.

And so we enter the second age the Sword Age. The cold has only intensified as snow and ice have claimed land and sea. Warlords have subdued the populace and have initiated their wars for the throne. The law of Leidang, forced conscription is prevalent throughout the land. Many seek solace by fleeing westward towards Islandia and beyond. Gods and Jotuns send their emissaries on quests of tantamount importance. Order is coming, compelling chaos into capitulation. Violence is the language most common as thralls become the greatest commodity. The strong have survived and are hard at work carving up the spoils.

King Harald's many sons are vying for the throne. Amicable negotiations have been replaced with assassins and intimidation. Some go as far to align themselves with the crusaders from the south. The conquests by the crusaders in the last 2 years of Fimbulwinter have garnered them a sizeable foothold in the central Great Isles. Those looking to flee the competition for the throne have migrated westward to lawless Islandia and to the unclaimed lands even further to the west. A storm is brewing at the Cornerstone of the World, threatening to engulf all of Midgard.

In the outer realms, Jotunheim's forces have surrounded the golden city of the gods. Giants, wolves, and witches cut down anyone trying to get in or out of Asgard. In these dire times, Odin the All Father sends forth his ravens, Hugin and Munin to carry missives to his champions in the land of mankind. Plans are in motion to break the siege. Thor, lord of rage and master of storms has taken the fight to Jotunheim. He is leaving a trail of dead Jotuns as he seeks to uncover the location of Naglfar, the titanic flying ship constructed of toenails. He seeks to destroy it before the Jotuns can sail it against Asgard. In hallowed dreams, Odin's wife Frigga has witnessed the third age fast approaching. It will be known as the Wind Age. Loki is to break his imprisonment in Hvergelmir and his son Fenrir may soon break his bonds in Lyngvi.

Surt, the king of the fire giants, watches as his Sons of Muspel rise from the fiery lake. Consulting with the Norn Mogthrasir he knows that he must use Kara the Valkyrie's fury to his advantage. She, like many other disgruntled Valkyries has defected from Odin's service. She will play a pivotal role in the continuing vengeance that was started by the legendary Valkyrie Brynhild. Surt seeks champions from within Midgard as they will also play a significant role in the coming storm.

This age will be very significant as power is consolidated. Willingly and unwillingly, many will step into the mantle of leadership. Most will need to choose their champions and their cause. The battle horns have been sounded, war is now!

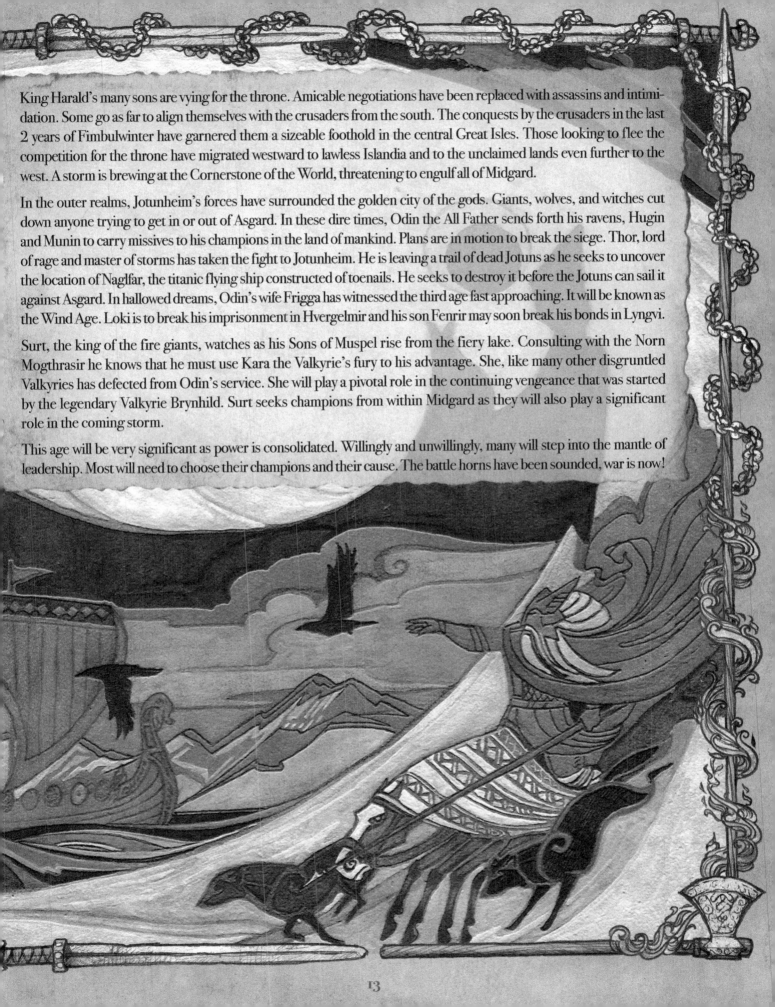

Legends and Villains

The world of Midgard is filled with interesting denizens that range from benevolent heroes to nefarious villains. Most citizens of Midgard lie somewhere in the moral grey zone in between both extremes. Herein lies a list of the most notable denizens that hold power within the realm of man.

Aethelstan, King

LEVEL 32 CRUSADER

King Aethelstan rules from his seat of power in Winchester Wessex. He is at the head of the white army that has come to the great isles from Outer-Midgard. With the great Emperor Otto's support, he is leading his crusaders in a northward expansion into Midgard. Resistance in Mercia and East Anglia has fallen, he has now set his sights on Northumbria, Hibernia and Alba.

However Aethelstan's beginnings were a lot more humble. Before Aethelstan was born, his father and grandfather faced the great heathen army of Ivar the Boneless and lost. They were driven out of the great isles and were given asylum by the Frankish king Charles the Simple. His father remarried twice, and Aethelstan had many siblings. They were raised in the various courts of Outer-Midgard. He and his half-brother Edmund were chosen to study in Emperor Otto's courts. They grew very close and gained the attention of their sire who noticed their aptitude in warfare. Aethelstan was the great tactician, and Edmund was the ideal army leader. Both were devout to the cause of the White God.

And then the darkness came. Aethelstan and Edmund were sparring in the courtyard when the sun was blotted out from the sky. Panic ensued and within days the church was rallying the kingdoms to march against the northern heathen kingdoms of Midgard. Emperor Otto rallied many kings under his banner, but all northward assaults were repelled. Otto's crusaders could not force their way past the great Danevirke. All eastern campaigns in the Baltic were halted by the Baltic tribes on land and Bjorn Eriksson's fleets oversea. A westward campaign was stalled out, awaiting negotiations with Charles the Simple.

It was one fateful afternoon that Aethelstan was sent to deliver a message to the Emperor and stumbled in during a strategic planning session that was at an impasse. While Emperor Otto read the missive, Aethelstan looked at the map and various army placements. Guided by a mysterious courage and conviction he would later attribute to the White God, he launched into an unsolicited plan on how to invade Midgard. His connections with Charles the Simple could overcome the impasse,

and his royal lineage in Mercia and West Saxony could rally the people to Otto's banner- eliminating any risk of bloody resistance to a fleet landing upon the shores of the Great Isles.

The next few weeks where a whirlwind as Aethelstan was granted a fleet of a hundred and twenty ships in order to go and reclaim his homeland as a king. As predicted Charles not only granted passage but committed to helping the new king conquer all of the northern kingdoms. With messengers heralding the return of the royal bloodline, king Aethelstan found a sympathetic army already waiting for him on the shores of Wessex. Upon hearing of his return, they had ousted their Viking king in a peasant's rebellion. Aethelstan would re-conquer his lands without a single battle, and his overwhelming force then moved into East Anglia and Mercia in order to secure Otto's crusader foothold in the Great Isles of Midgard.

Many think Aethelstan wishes to avenge his family by punishing the descendants of Ivar the Boneless, however they could not be further from the truth. Aethelstan is a master tactician whose ambitions stretch throughout all of Midgard. He will use diplomacy, intimi-

dation, marriage and war in order to secure all of Midgard as his newfound kingdom. He sees everyone as a pawn on a chess board, sacrificed if the outcome is in Aethelstan's favour. Emperor Otto is very pleased with the westward campaign led by Aethelstan, but is also weary of losing his control over the ambitious king. He has set up a Witenagemot to ensure that Aethelstan's progress follows Otto's direction. A Witenagemot is an assembly of wealthy noblemen (the ruling class) that meets to council king Aethelstan. Both ecclesiastical and secular members make up the Witenagemot.

Much like Emperor Otto using King Aethelstan, Aethelstan has begun to groom his new proxy king who will win the great kingdom of Norveig for him. A low-born bastard son of King Harald Fairhair has sought refuge in his court, and Aethelstan has adopted him like a son. Just like Aethelstan's bloodless victory in his homeland of Wessex, he wishes to capture Norveig with Hakon the Good as his emissary. For a year Hakon has studied religion and military tactics under Edmund. He is now getting ready to strike forth and reclaim his homeland from his half-brother Erik Blood Axe.

Baba Yaga

LEVEL 42 SEITHKONA, DRUID, GALDR
FYLGIA

Baba Yaga is a hermit sorceress with great talents in Seith, Rune magic and Verwandlung. She makes her home in the lands of the Baltic Tribes, but has been seen throughout Midgard. It is said that her inner sanctum is a hovel which stands on chicken legs. It can travel at great speeds, some say that it is even capable of going into other realms such as Jotunheim. Baba Yaga's other mode of transport is a Jotun's magical flying pestle which is propelled and steered by using the mortar. She has enchanted a pair of disembodied hands to act as her servants.

Baba Yaga appears as a scary gangly old crone with metal teeth. She uses her magical spells in order to stave off old age. It is said that for every year she ages, someone else lives out an entire lifetime. Her skills aren't solely magical. She treads softly, leaving no traces of her passing.

Her heart is dark, despising and begrudging mankind. This negative emotion is fuelled by humanity who has embraced evil and immorality. Those of pure heart and innocence usually find her in good favour. For those few that are paragons of mankind's goodness, she often goes as far as imparting wisdom or assistance. Whenever her magical hut settles down for an extended period of time, she uses Scorn Poles to curse all those around.

The only company she enjoys is that of her three horsemen: Bright Dawn, Red Sun and Dark Midnight.

Bjorn Eriksson

LEVEL 33 BERZERKIR
FYLGIA

Bjorn belongs to the Munso dynasty that includes the legendary Ragnar Lodbrok and Bjorn Ironside. Raiding and a healthy disdain for authority has always been in their blood. Bjorn has been no exception. He has the honour of stopping King Harald Fairhair's eastward expansion. There were many pitched battles in Gotaland and Ranrike through which both kings acquired a great deal of respect for one another. He is also very disdainful of Gorm the Old, mocking him for hiding behind a wall. Bjorn prefers taking the offence rather than a defence. He commands a great deal of respect because he will be the first one charging down a shield wall.

Bjorn's kingdom lies to the west of the Baltic sea in Svealand and Uppland. Naval battles with the Baltic tribes are fierce, but he usually comes out victorious due to his strong navy. Bjorn strives to acquire the best ships and recruit the best navigators from across Midgard. The Baltic trade contributes a great deal to his coffers so it's a market he protects with zeal. He ensures that most markets in the Baltic pay tributes to his kingdom.

Dealing with Bjorn isn't easy. He is large, loud, impulsive and boastful. Many times his decisions are based on emotion alone, but he prefers to call it instinct. Regardless, his successful track record speaks for itself. Since the onset of Fimbulwinter he has had many running battles with King Guttorm of the Ranrike. The conflicts have been so frequent that Guttorm hasn't had the time to mourn the passing of his father Harald Fairhair. Nor has he had the opportunity to engage his half brothers for the right of succession.

Bjorn Farmann, King

LEVEL 30 SKALD

Bjorn is one of many sons of the deceased King Harald Fairhair. His mother Svanhild comes from noble stock, elevating the legitimacy of Bjorn's claim to the crown of Norveig. Bjorn's love for good mead is only surpassed by his passion for song.

With his father King Harald's death, the darkness of Ragnarok has come to the lands of Midgard. His father never left no clear lines of succession, and this has caused great turmoil as King Harald has sired at least two-dozen known claimants to the throne. Bjorn's most pressing adversaries for the throne are Erik Bloodaxe the eldest son of Harald Fairhair, Olaf Geirstadalf the noble Jarl of Vingulmark (neighbouring Vestfold) and Sigrod Haraldsson the Jarl of Trondheim.

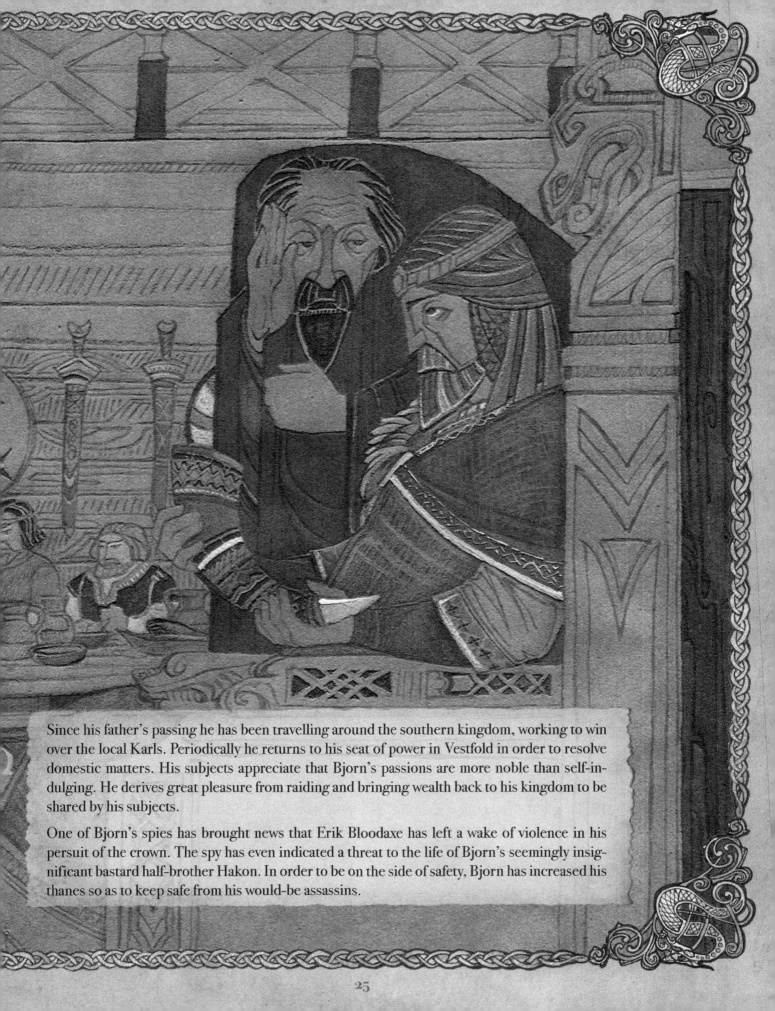

Since his father's passing he has been travelling around the southern kingdom, working to win over the local Karls. Periodically he returns to his seat of power in Vestfold in order to resolve domestic matters. His subjects appreciate that Bjorn's passions are more noble than self-indulging. He derives great pleasure from raiding and bringing wealth back to his kingdom to be shared by his subjects.

One of Bjorn's spies has brought news that Erik Bloodaxe has left a wake of violence in his persuit of the crown. The spy has even indicated a threat to the life of Bjorn's seemingly insignificant bastard half-brother Hakon. In order to be on the side of safety, Bjorn has increased his thanes so as to keep safe from his would-be assassins.

Constantine II, First King of Alba

LEVEL 27 STALO

The last Pictish king Aed inherited the throne from his brother Constantine. Aed was so very proud of his brother, so much so that he named his first born son "Constantine" (Constantine II). Constantine II and his cousin Domnall were best of friends. Since an early age Constantine II has led a life of tragedy and triumph in the tumultuous northern kingdom of the Picts. His father was pronounced king of Pictland after his brother Constantine died. He was to be the last of the Pictish kings. After assuming power, Aed chose a Gael as his right hand, a man by the name of Giric. Giric was an ambitious man and he secretly wanted Gael culture to permeate Pictland. After a series of blunders by Aed, Giric saw an opportunity to ursurp the throne. Conspiring with the rest of the ruling class, Giric murdered Aed and claimed the kingdom as his own. His first order of business was to have Domnall and Constantine II murdered to ensure no other rivals could challenge his rule.

Domnall and Constantine II fled west into Gael lands, where Giric wouldn't think of looking. They were warmly accepted by their aunt who was married to a powerful Hibernian chieftain. They were protected and raised by monks who taught them the ways of the White God. Their upbringing turned them into true Hibernian princes with a desire for vengeance. On their eighteenth birthday they sailed home under a solar eclipse and challenged Giric at the fortress of Dundern. The battle was fierce, great losses were incurred by both sides, and by the end of the conflict, both Giric and Domnall were dead. This left Constantine II as the sole beneficiary of the throne.

His unique upbringing brought new customs to the northern kingdom, and he took this opportunity to change its name, from Pictland to Alba. His coronation ceremony was something new to both the Gaels and the Picts. Monks oversaw the rituals and the Stone of Scone was introduced, a mystical stone throne that conferred special powers upon the new king. Constantine II wouldn't have much time for mourning or celebration as a new threat was moving south of his lands.

These new threats came in the form of Viking invaders from the east. Sitric, Ragnall and Gofraid defeated all of Alba's neighbours to the south, consolidating power between themselves. Constantine's only option was diplomacy, as their combined forces would overwhelm the armies of Alba. Even further south was a shrewd king known as Aethelstan. New to the great isles, he was looking to destroy any king unwilling to bend knee. Discovering Constantine II's upbringing, he sent messengers north looking to forge an alliance devoted to the White God. This alliance could then attack from both north and south, crushing King Sitric's domain. The young king Constatine II's future hangs in the balance as he is pressed for a decision.

Drifa, Queen of Svalbard

LEVEL 42 FARDRENGIR
FYLGIA

Anyone meeting Drifa will be struck by her unwavering strict moral code and honour. Reputation and one's word are sacred. In her eyes, the lowest of the low are oath-breakers. Blood is the strongest glue that binds society and family comes first. She is very cool and level headed, pragmatic to a fault. Her foes use her predictable nature against her, but even witnessing impending defeat, she refuses to waver from her code. Her weakness is also her strength, since many who admire her courage and conviction flock to her banner. She has an aura about her, that of a natural leader.

Raised in the northern reaches of Halogaland, she has always known cold and darkness. A devout Jotun follower since her birth, she has enshrined the ancient values that were set out by the Ymir: The world is divided into social classes based on the order in which the divine races emerged from the cosmic crucible. Everyone must know their place in the social stratas, and the Aesir were the blasphemers who broke this covenant.

Her enormous dislike for the Aesir and their followers as well as her devotion to the Rime Jotun cause has elevated her to unseen levels among mortals. She has been granted the northern island kingdom of Svalbard. Native portals to Jotunheim provide her with all the goods and services she needs. The Jotuns provide her with armies, food and raw materials cementing Svalbard as their launching point into Midgard. Very few non-devout Jotun followers dare to venture into her northern stronghold, even fewer return!

Edmund the Just

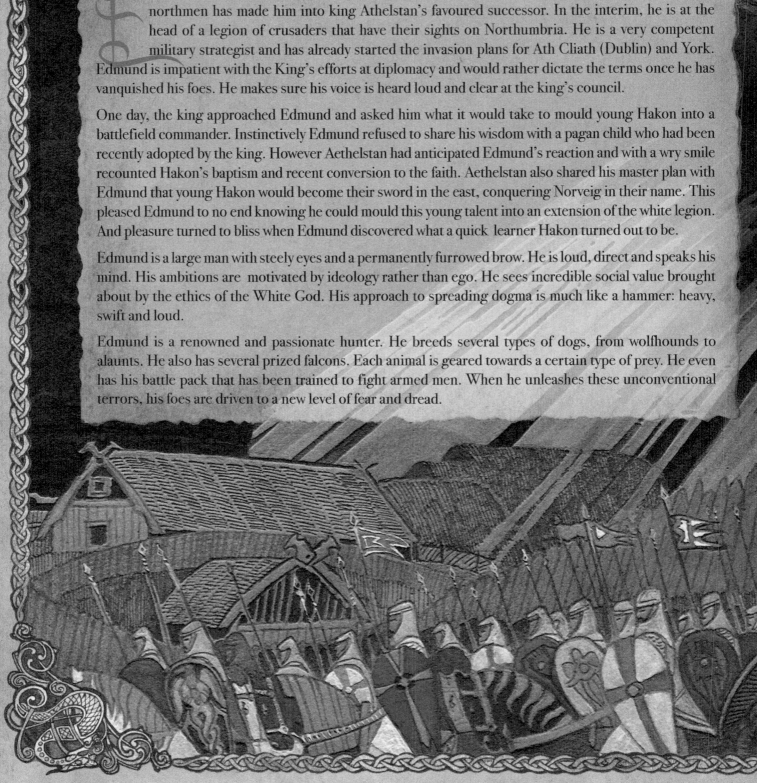

LEVEL 28 GRIZZLED WARRIOR

Edmund is the half-brother to King Aethelstan. His passion to rid the great Isles of the heathen northmen has made him into king Athelstan's favoured successor. In the interim, he is at the head of a legion of crusaders that have their sights on Northumbria. He is a very competent military strategist and has already started the invasion plans for Ath Cliath (Dublin) and York. Edmund is impatient with the King's efforts at diplomacy and would rather dictate the terms once he has vanquished his foes. He makes sure his voice is heard loud and clear at the king's council.

One day, the king approached Edmund and asked him what it would take to mould young Hakon into a battlefield commander. Instinctively Edmund refused to share his wisdom with a pagan child who had been recently adopted by the king. However Aethelstan had anticipated Edmund's reaction and with a wry smile recounted Hakon's baptism and recent conversion to the faith. Aethelstan also shared his master plan with Edmund that young Hakon would become their sword in the east, conquering Norveig in their name. This pleased Edmund to no end knowing he could mould this young talent into an extension of the white legion. And pleasure turned to bliss when Edmund discovered what a quick learner Hakon turned out to be.

Edmund is a large man with steely eyes and a permanently furrowed brow. He is loud, direct and speaks his mind. His ambitions are motivated by ideology rather than ego. He sees incredible social value brought about by the ethics of the White God. His approach to spreading dogma is much like a hammer: heavy, swift and loud.

Edmund is a renowned and passionate hunter. He breeds several types of dogs, from wolfhounds to alaunts. He also has several prized falcons. Each animal is geared towards a certain type of prey. He even has his battle pack that has been trained to fight armed men. When he unleashes these unconventional terrors, his foes are driven to a new level of fear and dread.

Einar of the Storjunkari

LEVEL 14 FARDRENGIR
FYLGIA

Einar's destiny has been emblazoned brightly into the Tapestry of Fate. Violently born in the wilds of the north western reaches of Finnmark, Einar entered Midgard with glorious distinction. His mother was dying from battle wounds, leaving his father no choice but to cut Einar out of her womb. Within days, Einar's father fell ill to a mysterious affliction and joined his wife beyond the veil. It is said the infant was then raised by the holy reindeer and protected until he was ten winters old. Einar was born deaf and mute. The handicap forced Einar to develop a very unique, soft and sublime way of interacting with the world around him.

A nomadic tribe who worship the Storjunkari (local Vaettir) found the sacred pack of reindeer who were watching over little Einar. Despite Einar's nakedness, the cold could not touch him. They adopted him, knowing that the reindeer had bestowed upon them someone of great importance. The nomadic culture slowly seeped into Einar's being, but much of his strange, wild heritage remained. He grew into a strong leader of few words, and his brethren followed him without question.

As custom in his tribe, he took many wives, and the first of which was Berga. She had always had eyes for Einar, and her interest started from the moment he was adopted by the tribe. In the usual custom, they built a shrine called a Seita to the reindeer spirits and received blessing for their union. However, on the first lay, something very strange happened. It was, as if Einar's seed imparted some magical enchantment upon his wife. Physically she remained as she was, but her mind was opened as if the night clouds parted to reveal the blazing full moon. Her soul was awakened as if it had been slumbering since her birth. She found that she could now see, commune with and interact with the spirit world. This occurred to all of Einar's wives on the night of consummation.

Einar was not without magical powers of his own. He was blessed with visions of the future. He guides his people to lands that provide for them. His direction has purpose and meaning, but even he is unsure where this road will ultimately lead him.

Erik, Blood Axe

LEVEL 28 BERZERKIR
FYLGIA

Erik was Harald Fairhair's first son. Harald would go on to having many more sons, but no more with Erik's mother Ragnhild, princess of Jutland. Erik never paid much attention to his father's grand ambitions, simply content with executing the raids his father required. The battle and the plunder were enough for Erik. On one such excursion, his fleet was lost in a storm and he washed ashore in far away Finnmark, a land of witches and monsters. Nursed back to health by a local medicine woman named Gunnhild, the two fell in love and married. Gunnhild is a highly intelligent and shrewd woman who clearly sees the potential in her husband. He is in a unique position to inherit the greatest kingdom throughout all of Midgard.

As King Harald Fairhair began to grow old, Gunnhild's grooming of Erik was paying off. He would receive more and more responsibility in running the kingdom of Norveig. But certain blunders would keep the king from declaring Erik as the true successor. Erik had a tendency to wear his emotions on his sleeve, quickly scuttling negotiations with adjoining kingdoms. As Harald's health began to deteriorate, Gunnhild redoubled her efforts in making Erik the clear choice. To her dismay, king Harald passed without any clear declaration of which of his sons would rule. This quickly devolved as Harald's many sons would begin feuding over the crown. Gunnhild had a plan, inviting them all to a wooden meadhall where they could all discuss the division of the kingdom, so long as they swear fealty to Erik as high king. However Erik's negotiating skills surfaced and soon Erik found himself standing outside a burning hall where many of his competitors burned to death. Skalds now speculate if Gunnhild summoned the spirit of Erik's ancestor Ingjald, who had performed the same treachery in order to grow his kingdom. The late King Harald's remaining sons, upon hearing this news, declared open war upon Erik.

One of the low born sons who attended the negotiaitons in the mead hall was Hakon. However he was ejected after his birthright was put into question by Gunnhild, revealing that his mother was a common serving girl in King Harald's court. His low birthright saved his life on that day, but he suspected Erik and Gunnhild's retribution and fled to the Great Isles of Midgard.

Gunnhild knows that negotiations are over, and she will now leverage Erik's strengths in defeating his challengers in the field of battle. In order to gather a large army, Gunnhild has organized a tour of Norveig, where they can meet the local Karls and secure their allegiance to Erik's banner. Erik has set his sights on Bjorn Farmann as his next victim, sending assassins to his lands.

A hulking battle-hardened figure, Erik comes across more as a rowdy Viking warrior than a son who has inherited a massive kingdom from his father. He loves to raid, feast and like his wife he has no sense of humour. His serious demeanour and short temperament make him difficult. Erik has placed his trust in Odin, and after every victory performs a blot to the All Father. Gunnhild, using her powers as a practitioner of seith, has foreseen a confrontation with a bastard son who has sided with the White God. She wishes to bestow the blessings of the gods upon Erik by organizing a coronation ceremony at Trondheim's Shrine of Kings.

Erik the Frost Bear

LEVEL: 25 BERSERKIR
FYLGIA (EMMA ROSE)
TROLL BLOODED

Erik was the only child born of a human mother and a Troll father. He was abandoned by his parents when he was but a baby so Erik was forced to grow up quickly. The only link to his past is a claw necklace that his father left in his bassinet. He learned early on how to be self-reliant, and to persevere regardless of the situation. Now a grown man, he is well built, bald and covered in tattoos. His tattoos have very personal meanings, from a Valknut on his neck for his son Noah, a tear dedicated to the memory of his daughter Emma, and snowflake tattoo representing his darkest hour. Given his size and imposing personality, he tends to intimidate those around him. His rite of passage was realized when he fought for his life against an enraged giant feral boar. Looking for an improvised weapon, he used his father's bear claw necklace to slash the boar's throat, narrowly escaping the boar's razor sharp tusks. On this day, the Norns granted him life, he pledged a life of valour, living by the standards of courage, truth, honour, fidelity, discipline, hospitality, self-reliance, and perseverance. He has managed to uphold these virtues even after Ragnarok's chaos descended upon the land. This has made him a legend, and his tale is frequently recounted by skalds.

Erik's marriage was short lived, his wife having fallen to the spears and torches of rampaging crusaders. With the onset of Fimbulwinter, keeping his children safe was his top priority. His son Noah follows in his father's footsteps, body, mind and soul consumed with the desire for high adventure. His daughter Emma Rose was the sunshine of his life, and in the trying times of the Axe Age her spirited personality is what kept the gloom away. But the Norns aren't always kind, taking Emma Rose in her prime. This sent Erik into a deep and very rage filled depression. He and his son grew apart and Erik turned inwards and focused on the unrelenting pain.

His pain led him to flee Midgard and take solace in the dark Alfar realm of Svartalfheim. There his mind found comfort in the company of nightmares and unrelenting fear. But even if his conscious wouldn't allow it, his virtues held fast. His indomitable spirit resisted and overcame not only his own failings, but even the dark oppression of Svartalfheim itself. His victory was not lost on a Svart Alfar monarch. It is said that she captured his tear in a snow flake binding some secretive enchantments upon his person.

Upon his return to Midgard, he was known as Erik "The Frost Bear", but to his son, and those who he's allowed to be called his comrades and brethren, he was called "Pappa Bjorn". They were glad to have him back, even though he had been clearly changed by his experiences in the shadow realm. But with his return a Fylgia came and bound herself to himÖ it was his Emma Rose.

Erik wades into battle with a war hammer called "Ravenous" and a gauntlet called "Frost Mauler".

Erik "the Red" Thorvaldsson

LEVEL 12 GRIZZLED WARRIOR
TROLL BLOODED

Erik is a very young man, yet his name is already stained with crimes. He has inherited his outlaw status from his father when he was exiled from Norveig for many violent and salacious offences. He and his father fled to Islandia and joined the north western villages where the most notorious criminals had been congregating. Erik's father had many accomplices hiding out there. Erik has been raised under very demanding circumstances, forcing him to assert his dominance over others his age. Already several murders have been attributed to the young lad.

Erik is very large for his young age, and even stronger than his size would infer. He also has a hard time judging his own strength which has caused some injuries to be more serious than intended. He has travelled far in his few years, and has travelled under very harrowing conditions due to Fimbulwinter's unforgiving grasp on the land. But this hasn't dissuaded the young boy from exploration. While his father forces Erik into hard labour in order to eke out a living, every free moment is spent exploring Islandia.

Gorm the Old

LEVEL 12 GRIZZLED WARRIOR
TROLL BLOODED

Gorm has always been a strong follower of Aegir. Like his father Harthacnut before him, he inherited a sworn duty to be the warden of the Danevirke. Under his watch, the provocations from the south have intensified. He had the Danevirke doubled in height and length. While King Harald Fairhair was alive, he received regular support in soldiers and gold. However, since his passing, he has had a very hard time maintaining the defenses of the great wall. The pretender kings' feuds have turned the people's attention inwards, leaving Gorm alone in his struggle against the tide of the White God.

Gorm is a no-nonsense Jarl. He has little time or interest in petty court gossip or emotional women's banter. He has been known to lose patience with those who aren't direct in their dealings with him, going so far as to throw them into the dungeons beneath the wall. His father started his training, becoming a strong military leader when he was still a very young lad. While recruiting men for his war band, his heart was captured by a young maiden named Thyra. She was adamant in becoming a shield maiden in Gorm's regiment. Her beauty was matched by her lust for battle and her direct and stubborn character set her apart from her rather banal peers. She didn't immediately return Gorm's interest or affection. If you ask Gorm's father Harthacnut, he would say that to win her over, Gorm worked hard to bring out the very best in himself.

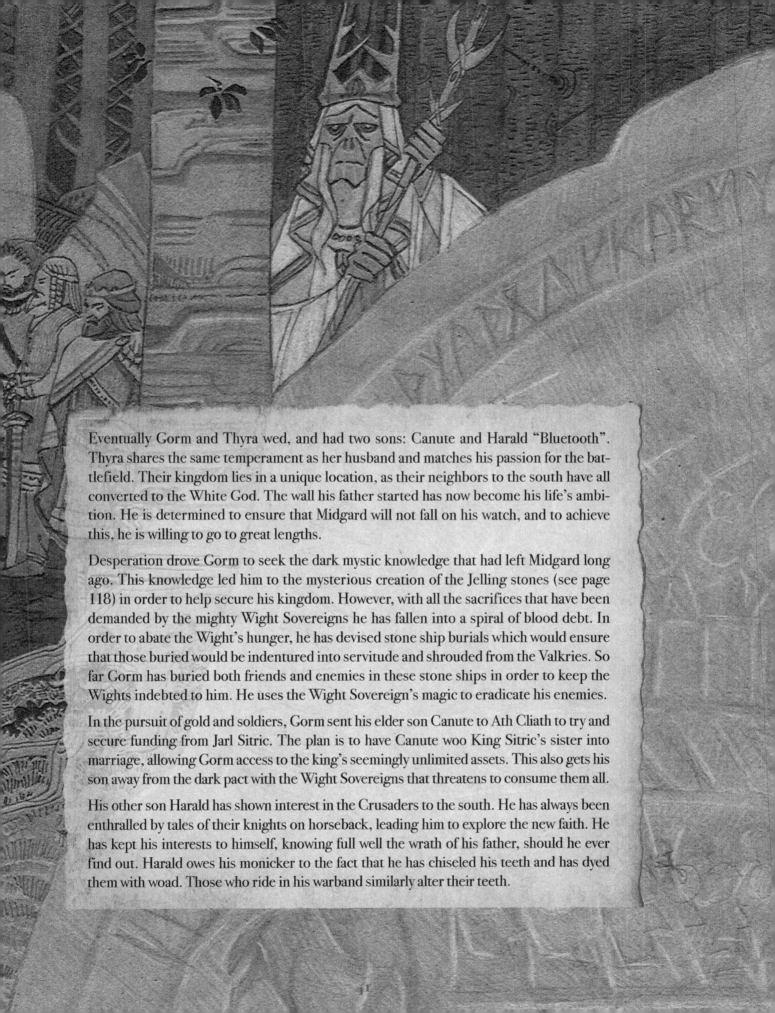

Eventually Gorm and Thyra wed, and had two sons: Canute and Harald "Bluetooth". Thyra shares the same temperament as her husband and matches his passion for the battlefield. Their kingdom lies in a unique location, as their neighbors to the south have all converted to the White God. The wall his father started has now become his life's ambition. He is determined to ensure that Midgard will not fall on his watch, and to achieve this, he is willing to go to great lengths.

Desperation drove Gorm to seek the dark mystic knowledge that had left Midgard long ago. This knowledge led him to the mysterious creation of the Jelling stones (see page 118) in order to help secure his kingdom. However, with all the sacrifices that have been demanded by the mighty Wight Sovereigns he has fallen into a spiral of blood debt. In order to abate the Wight's hunger, he has devised stone ship burials which would ensure that those buried would be indentured into servitude and shrouded from the Valkries. So far Gorm has buried both friends and enemies in these stone ships in order to keep the Wights indebted to him. He uses the Wight Sovereign's magic to eradicate his enemies.

In the pursuit of gold and soldiers, Gorm sent his elder son Canute to Ath Cliath to try and secure funding from Jarl Sitric. The plan is to have Canute woo King Sitric's sister into marriage, allowing Gorm access to the king's seemingly unlimited assets. This also gets his son away from the dark pact with the Wight Sovereigns that threatens to consume them all.

His other son Harald has shown interest in the Crusaders to the south. He has always been enthralled by tales of their knights on horseback, leading him to explore the new faith. He has kept his interests to himself, knowing full well the wrath of his father, should he ever find out. Harald owes his monicker to the fact that he has chiseled his teeth and has dyed them with woad. Those who ride in his warband similarly alter their teeth.

Hakon the Good

LEVEL 28 STALO
FYLGIA

Hakon is the bastard son of the illustrious king Harald Fairhair and a drinking wench named Thora Mosterstang. He was a handsome boy who grew up into a confident young man. His father was proud of him and stood up for him when his siblings derided his low-born status. Hakon wasn't a particularly aggressive warrior, preferring to teach the basics to young aspiring warriors. He held many administrative positions within his father's kingdom, collecting taxes and managing finances. As such there weren't any skalds willing to sing the praises of young Hakon.

When King Harald died, Hakon never expected to ascend the throne. Erik was the eldest and most likely candidate, however Hakon had his reservations. He did not trust Gunnhild and would rather see Bjorn Farmann take over the kingdom. So when Erik's wife Gunnhild organized a meeting of sons in order

to partition the kingdom, Hakon became very vocal about his opinions and his displeasure that Bjorn Farmann wasn't even invited. Gunnhild was quick to respond, inciting the sons present against Hakon due to his low-born mother's status. He was ejected from the hall and thankfully so, because a few hours later he heard that it had burnt to the ground- the only survivors Erik and Gunnhild!

Fearing the same fate, Hakon got on the first ship leaving Rogaland, and it turned out to be a ship filled with Missionaries headed to West Anglia. They advised him to seek the protection of king Aethelstan and one of them gave him a cow bone crucifix pendant. Needing all the help he can get, he accepted the gift and the advice. To his surprise the king gave him a very warm welcome, and soon he felt like one of the family. King Aethelstan dined often with Hakon, questioning him about Norveig and about all of his half brothers. Their conversations would always drift to Hakon righting the wrongs, wresting the kingdom from Erik Bloodaxe and forging an alliance with Aethelstan's growing kingdom. Slowly talk turned to action and Hakon began training in tactics and battlefield warfare with king Aethelstan's half brother Edmund.

Hakon's growing concern is the debt he has incurred with king Aethelstan. He has no idea how he could possibly repay such generosity.

Receiving news that Erik Blood Axe has tried to assassinate Bjorn Farmann has put winds into Hakon's sails. Hakon has received his fleet and is heading to Vestfold in order to help his half brother Bjorn against Erik's army.

Halfdan Ingvarsson

LEVEL 16 ULFHEDNAR
FYLGIA
TROLL-BLOODED
VAETTIR BOND

Halfdan is the son of Ingvar, the chieftain of Evingard. He is fiercely loyal to the ancient customs of his clan. As a Rager Ulfhednar, he has a very short temper and his fury is seemingly unquenchable. He recalls the old days before the riches were discovered beneath his ancestral lands. The discovery of the wealth has brought many foreigners to their land looking to extract this wealth. These foreigners have managed to convince his father that exchanging the life for a wild wolf for that of a privileged noble is a good thing... he couldn't disagree more.

Many rich merchants came to lay claim to the riches below the mountain in hopes of establishing lucrative mining opportunities. Those that did not seek Ingvar's blessing or cooperation were run off by Ingvar's feral nieces and nephews. Those that looked for a blessing were retained. One stood out due to his largesse. His name was Magnus Magnusson and he was generous enough to offer a third of the spoils for access to the mountains. Ingvar was moved by this gesture and decided to grant exclusive rights to Magnus, backed by the wolf clan's protection.

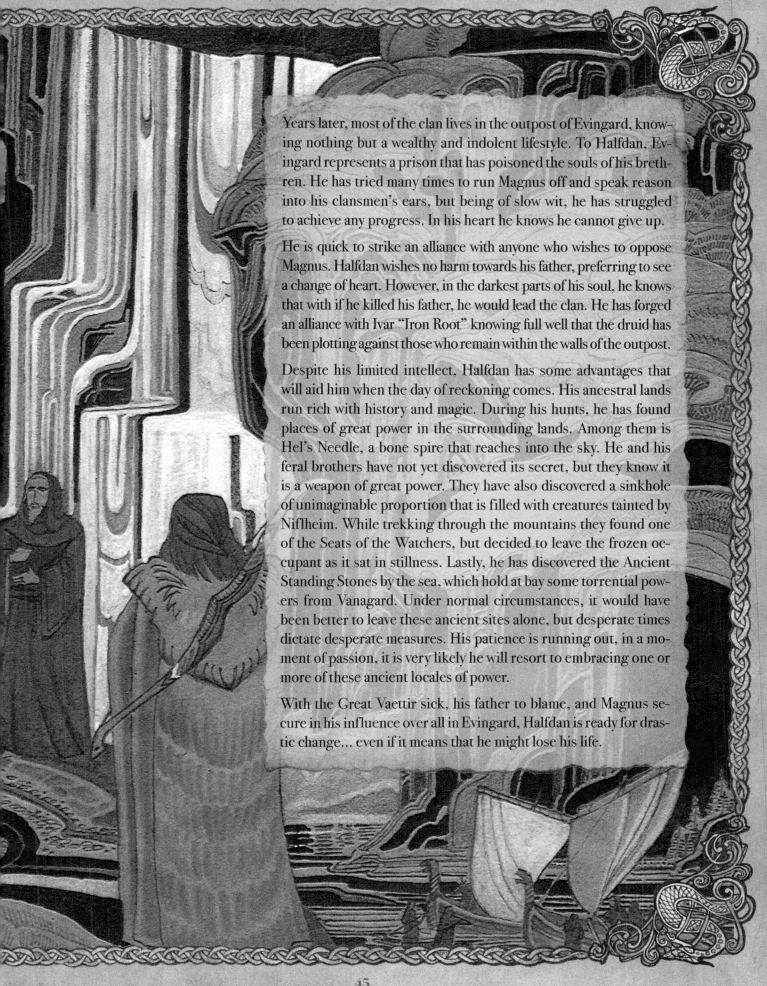

Years later, most of the clan lives in the outpost of Evingard, knowing nothing but a wealthy and indolent lifestyle. To Halfdan, Evingard represents a prison that has poisoned the souls of his brethren. He has tried many times to run Magnus off and speak reason into his clansmen's ears, but being of slow wit, he has struggled to achieve any progress. In his heart he knows he cannot give up.

He is quick to strike an alliance with anyone who wishes to oppose Magnus. Halfdan wishes no harm towards his father, preferring to see a change of heart. However, in the darkest parts of his soul, he knows that with if he killed his father, he would lead the clan. He has forged an alliance with Ivar "Iron Root" knowing full well that the druid has been plotting against those who remain within the walls of the outpost.

Despite his limited intellect, Halfdan has some advantages that will aid him when the day of reckoning comes. His ancestral lands run rich with history and magic. During his hunts, he has found places of great power in the surrounding lands. Among them is Hel's Needle, a bone spire that reaches into the sky. He and his feral brothers have not yet discovered its secret, but they know it is a weapon of great power. They have also discovered a sinkhole of unimaginable proportion that is filled with creatures tainted by Niflheim. While trekking through the mountains they found one of the Seats of the Watchers, but decided to leave the frozen occupant as it sat in stillness. Lastly, he has discovered the Ancient Standing Stones by the sea, which hold at bay some torrential powers from Vanagard. Under normal circumstances, it would have been better to leave these ancient sites alone, but desperate times dictate desperate measures. His patience is running out, in a moment of passion, it is very likely he will resort to embracing one or more of these ancient locales of power.

With the Great Vaettir sick, his father to blame, and Magnus secure in his influence over all in Evingard, Halfdan is ready for drastic change… even if it means that he might lose his life.

Harald Fairhair, King

LEVEL 49 BERZERKIR (DECEASED)
FYLGIA

King Harald had the distinction of being the very first king to unify all of the petty kingdoms into the mighty nation of Norveig. He belongs to the long standing Yngling dynasty. Their ancestral lands are in the central region called the Ranrike. His father was the infamous Halfdan the Black son of Gudrod the Hunter in turn son of Halfdan the Mild. This impressive lineage traces back over one thousand years all the way back to the Vanir god Frey. The progenitor of the Yngling dynasty is known simply as Fjolnir. He was the son of the Vanir god Frey and the Rime Jotun Gerda. Imbued with Vanir and Jotun blood, it is said that Fjolnir lived for over 200 years. His death is the stuff of legends, recounted with humour and pride that the progenitor drowned in a 30' tall vat of strong mead. Apparently he tried to bathe in this heavenly nectar.

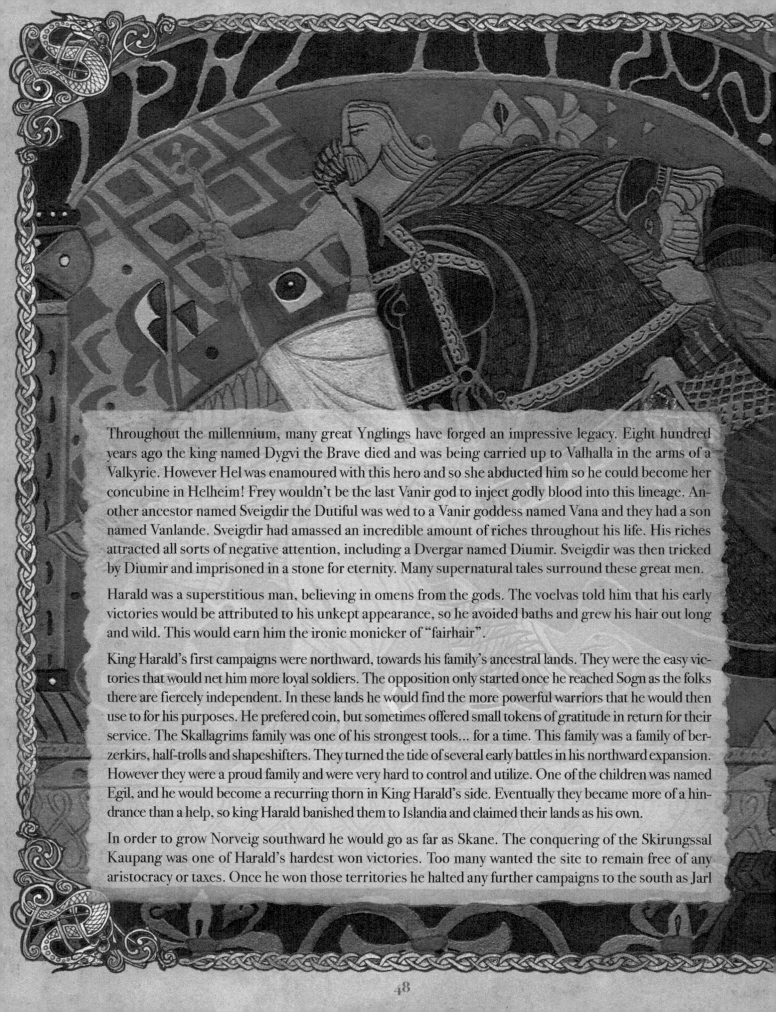

Throughout the millennium, many great Ynglings have forged an impressive legacy. Eight hundred years ago the king named Dygvi the Brave died and was being carried up to Valhalla in the arms of a Valkyrie. However Hel was enamoured with this hero and so she abducted him so he could become her concubine in Helheim! Frey wouldn't be the last Vanir god to inject godly blood into this lineage. Another ancestor named Sveigdir the Dutiful was wed to a Vanir goddess named Vana and they had a son named Vanlande. Sveigdir had amassed an incredible amount of riches throughout his life. His riches attracted all sorts of negative attention, including a Dvergar named Diumir. Sveigdir was then tricked by Diumir and imprisoned in a stone for eternity. Many supernatural tales surround these great men.

Harald was a superstitious man, believing in omens from the gods. The voelvas told him that his early victories would be attributed to his unkept appearance, so he avoided baths and grew his hair out long and wild. This would earn him the ironic monicker of "fairhair".

King Harald's first campaigns were northward, towards his family's ancestral lands. They were the easy victories that would net him more loyal soldiers. The opposition only started once he reached Sogn as the folks there are fiercely independent. In these lands he would find the more powerful warriors that he would then use to for his purposes. He prefered coin, but sometimes offered small tokens of gratitude in return for their service. The Skallagrims family was one of his strongest tools... for a time. This family was a family of berzerkirs, half-trolls and shapeshifters. They turned the tide of several early battles in his northward expansion. However they were a proud family and were very hard to control and utilize. One of the children was named Egil, and he would become a recurring thorn in King Harald's side. Eventually they became more of a hindrance than a help, so king Harald banished them to Islandia and claimed their lands as his own.

In order to grow Norveig southward he would go as far as Skane. The conquering of the Skirungssal Kaupang was one of Harald's hardest won victories. Too many wanted the site to remain free of any aristocracy or taxes. Once he won those territories he halted any further campaigns to the south as Jarl

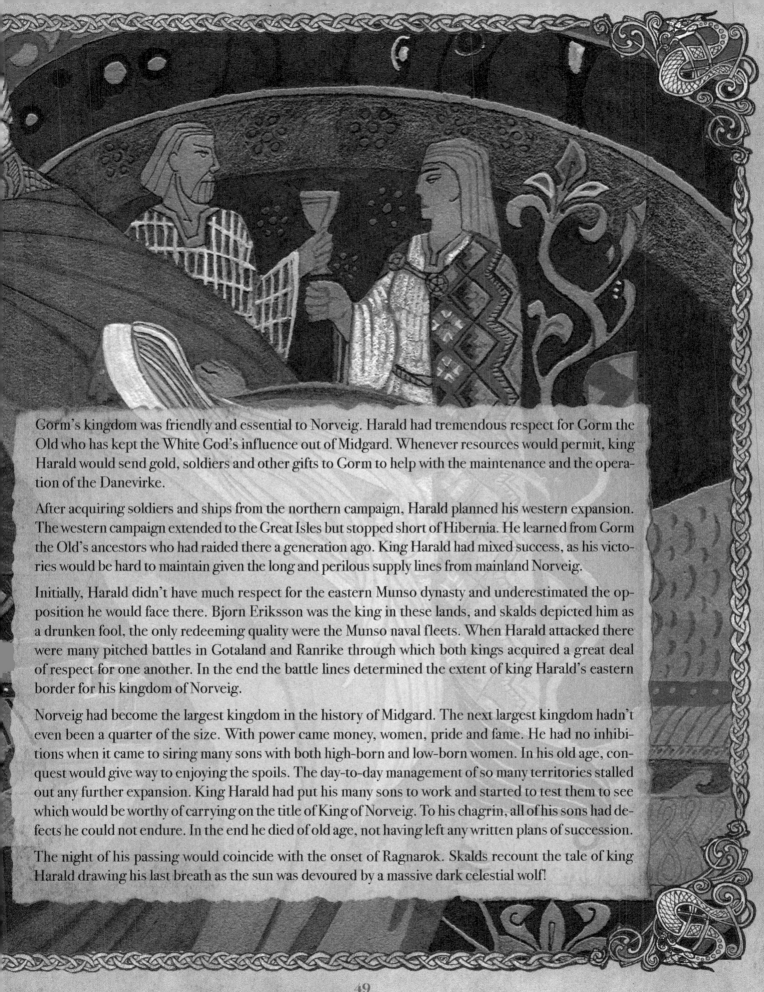

Gorm's kingdom was friendly and essential to Norveig. Harald had tremendous respect for Gorm the Old who has kept the White God's influence out of Midgard. Whenever resources would permit, king Harald would send gold, soldiers and other gifts to Gorm to help with the maintenance and the operation of the Danevirke.

After acquiring soldiers and ships from the northern campaign, Harald planned his western expansion. The western campaign extended to the Great Isles but stopped short of Hibernia. He learned from Gorm the Old's ancestors who had raided there a generation ago. King Harald had mixed success, as his victories would be hard to maintain given the long and perilous supply lines from mainland Norveig.

Initially, Harald didn't have much respect for the eastern Munso dynasty and underestimated the opposition he would face there. Bjorn Eriksson was the king in these lands, and skalds depicted him as a drunken fool, the only redeeming quality were the Munso naval fleets. When Harald attacked there were many pitched battles in Gotaland and Ranrike through which both kings acquired a great deal of respect for one another. In the end the battle lines determined the extent of king Harald's eastern border for his kingdom of Norveig.

Norveig had become the largest kingdom in the history of Midgard. The next largest kingdom hadn't even been a quarter of the size. With power came money, women, pride and fame. He had no inhibitions when it came to siring many sons with both high-born and low-born women. In his old age, conquest would give way to enjoying the spoils. The day-to-day management of so many territories stalled out any further expansion. King Harald had put his many sons to work and started to test them to see which would be worthy of carrying on the title of King of Norveig. To his chagrin, all of his sons had defects he could not endure. In the end he died of old age, not having left any written plans of succession.

The night of his passing would coincide with the onset of Ragnarok. Skalds recount the tale of king Harald drawing his last breath as the sun was devoured by a massive dark celestial wolf!

Hildolfr the Battle Wolf

LEVEL AND ARCHETYPE UNKNOWN

Hildolfr's origins are shrouded in mystery. His uncanny resemblance to the All Father Odin has some speculating on Hildolfr's true identity. Most know him for his leadership of an elite band of mercenaries known as the Battle Wolves. Adding to the mystery, those within the ranks of this elite war band will speak of Hildolfr's ability to travel at impossible speeds, seemingly appearing in two places at the same time. He is very hands off when managing his mercenaries, so he does diligent work to ensure those he recruits are the best of the best (minimum level 20 dwellers and denizens).

The reputation of the Battle Wolves is known throughout Midgard. Only the richest can afford their services, and usually only for a short time. Hildolfr has been known to substitute a monetary payment with a future favour of his choosing when the client's station may prove more valuable. Once the terms of the agreement are handled, he sets his Battle Wolves in motion and steps away until the contract is completed. Jobs include recovery of items or persons, kidnapping, assassinations, protection, information gathering, and influence.

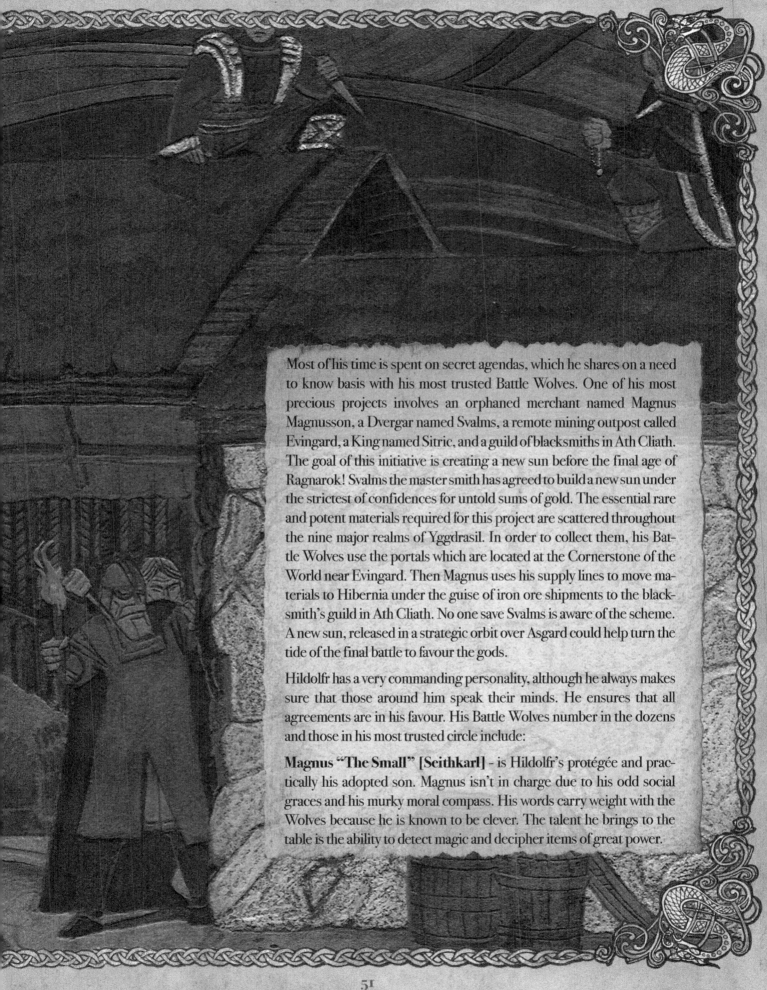

Most of his time is spent on secret agendas, which he shares on a need to know basis with his most trusted Battle Wolves. One of his most precious projects involves an orphaned merchant named Magnus Magnusson, a Dvergar named Svalms, a remote mining outpost called Evingard, a King named Sitric, and a guild of blacksmiths in Ath Cliath. The goal of this initiative is creating a new sun before the final age of Ragnarok! Svalms the master smith has agreed to build a new sun under the strictest of confidences for untold sums of gold. The essential rare and potent materials required for this project are scattered throughout the nine major realms of Yggdrasil. In order to collect them, his Battle Wolves use the portals which are located at the Cornerstone of the World near Evingard. Then Magnus uses his supply lines to move materials to Hibernia under the guise of iron ore shipments to the blacksmith's guild in Ath Cliath. No one save Svalms is aware of the scheme. A new sun, released in a strategic orbit over Asgard could help turn the tide of the final battle to favour the gods.

Hildolfr has a very commanding personality, although he always makes sure that those around him speak their minds. He ensures that all agreements are in his favour. His Battle Wolves number in the dozens and those in his most trusted circle include:

Magnus "The Small" [Seithkarl] - is Hildolfr's protégée and practically his adopted son. Magnus isn't in charge due to his odd social graces and his murky moral compass. His words carry weight with the Wolves because he is known to be clever. The talent he brings to the table is the ability to detect magic and decipher items of great power.

Brisghild [Maiden of Ratatosk] - A quick tongue and a quick blade. She speaks first and acts second; thinking is often a distant third. She has been getting into trouble despite there being few laws which remain after Ragnarok. She devotes most of her idle time to gambling and thrashing bullies. Her worth comes from her uncanny ability to bring out the worst in others, even unsettling level headed kings.

Freki [Ulfednar] - A gentle giant of a man, he is a man of few words. When he does speak, his words are woven in wisdom and eloquence. He is proficient at training new recruits and enjoys doing so tremendously. He is also slightly afraid of magic… especially Seith magic.

Volheim [Galdr & Blacksmith] - Describing him as a curmudgeon understates his surly nature. He is the Battle Wolves' quartermaster and has been in charge of accounting and supplies since before Ragnarok. Even the most ambitious newcomer will not mess with him because he truly knows where the skeletons are buried. He's also a very talented magician known to throw curses around. His ability to equip the Battle Wolves brings tremendous value.

Draugstagg [Skald] - Draugstagg is exceptionally charming and very good at verbally manipulating those around him. His role is to disassociate himself from the Battle Wolves and infiltrate organizations while earning their trust. His ultimate allegiance is to the Battle Wolves, but his act allows him to accomplish a lot more for Hildolfr.

The Battle Wolves' insignia is a wolf head superimposed over a shield. The crimson-emerald colour is very unique and almost impossible to reproduce without knowing the ingredients for the dye. To mark their membership most members of the mercenary band are given a coloured cloth that they attach to their armour to identify themselves.

53

Ingrid "the Wanderer"

LEVEL 10 GALDR

Ingrid is a beautiful young maiden with long golden hair. To those in her family, it appears as though Ingrid suffers from wanderlust. In reality, since a very young age she has been visited by many omens. She cannot help but follow where these portents lead her. Oftentimes without warning, she steals away from her home, taking ships to faraway kingdoms. Eventually she returns to a visibly shaken family. Her father King Sitric has become increasingly troubled by her escapades since the dark years of Ragnarok. Oftentimes her omens are so cryptic that all she perceives are vague locations. She has started to map out the places to which her visions lead her. Thankfully, her chameleon personality and skills in disguise have allowed her to divert unwanted attention.

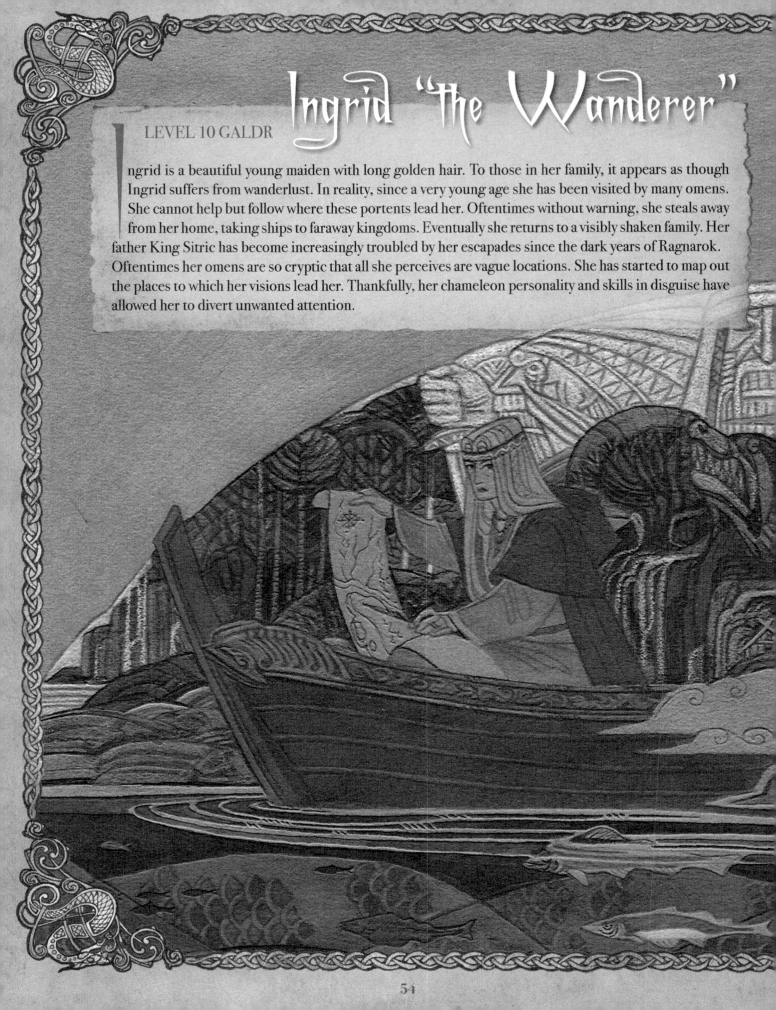

Her father is tired of making excuses as to why she only attends a few festivals a year. Her subjects have come to the conclusion that she is of fragile health… in reality each missed feast only means she is off on one of her vision induced escapades. King Sitric is seriously considering marrying Ingrid off to Canute, Gorm the Old's eldest son.

Ingrid has begun to piece together years of omens and the places they have taken her. She is getting a clearer understanding of what has occurred to the Alfar, and her conclusions are very disquieting. Mirroring the reality in Midgard, chaos threatens to engulf both the gods and Jotuns. But what most mortals do not see is the gradual disappearance of the Alfar. A parallel war is raging, a war of shadow between the Lios and Svart Alfar. It is a war of very high stakes, with the heavens of Gimli, Vidblain and Andlang hanging in the balance.

Ingvar, Lord of Evingard

LEVEL 26 ULFHEDNAR

For as far as Ingvar can recall, the north eastern lands of Islandia have been his family's ancestral stomping grounds. As his father before him, Ingvar bound himslef to Dreki, the dragon vaettir of the land. During his youth, his ambitions kept him busy ensuring that his tribe and the land were prosperous. But unlike his father and grandfather, who knew much strife and war, his reign was during a peaceful stretch of history. Unable to die young in battle, the years started to weigh on his shoulders. He started to rely more and more on his son Halfdan to manage details he didn't wish to be bothered with.

Twenty winters ago a strange band of mystics came to their lands. They were northmen, but dressed strangely, more like missionaries of the White God rather than suits of armour and weapons. They didn't seek conflict or plunder, but rather sought to setup a secluded hamlet up in the mountains. After some tense meetings Ingvar's clan decided to leave them be. The hamlet soon turned into a village and then a town as more and more mystics came to study in this remote mountain valley. After the cataclysm Ingvar concluded that they should have paid more attention to these visitors. The cataclysm came quickly and unexpectedly, creating tremors in the region that lasted a year, and releasing never-seen-before foul beasts upon the land.

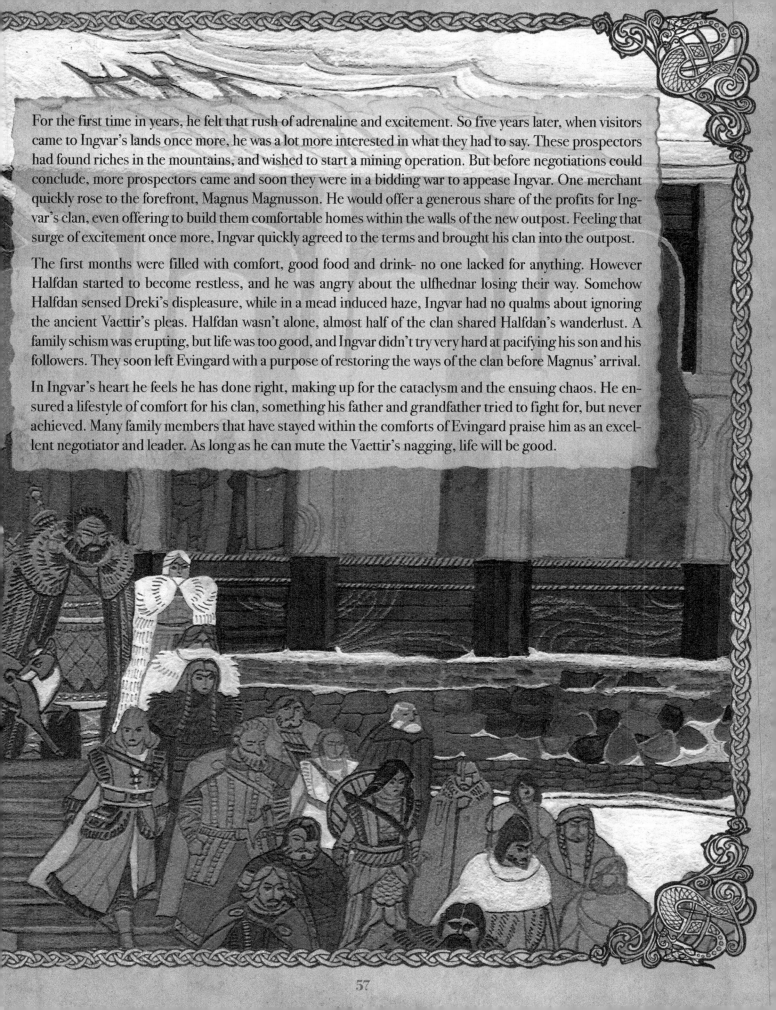

For the first time in years, he felt that rush of adrenaline and excitement. So five years later, when visitors came to Ingvar's lands once more, he was a lot more interested in what they had to say. These prospectors had found riches in the mountains, and wished to start a mining operation. But before negotiations could conclude, more prospectors came and soon they were in a bidding war to appease Ingvar. One merchant quickly rose to the forefront, Magnus Magnusson. He would offer a generous share of the profits for Ingvar's clan, even offering to build them comfortable homes within the walls of the new outpost. Feeling that surge of excitement once more, Ingvar quickly agreed to the terms and brought his clan into the outpost.

The first months were filled with comfort, good food and drink- no one lacked for anything. However Halfdan started to become restless, and he was angry about the ulfhednar losing their way. Somehow Halfdan sensed Dreki's displeasure, while in a mead induced haze, Ingvar had no qualms about ignoring the ancient Vaettir's pleas. Halfdan wasn't alone, almost half of the clan shared Halfdan's wanderlust. A family schism was erupting, but life was too good, and Ingvar didn't try very hard at pacifying his son and his followers. They soon left Evingard with a purpose of restoring the ways of the clan before Magnus' arrival.

In Ingvar's heart he feels he has done right, making up for the cataclysm and the ensuing chaos. He ensured a lifestyle of comfort for his clan, something his father and grandfather tried to fight for, but never achieved. Many family members that have stayed within the comforts of Evingard praise him as an excellent negotiator and leader. As long as he can mute the Vaettir's nagging, life will be good.

Ivar "Iron Root"

LEVEL 18 DRUID

Ivar was always drawn by the preternatural force over which the Vanir gods hold dominion. Clan Ingvarsson was never monolithic in faith, but the majority did align themselves with the cause of the Jotuns. Ivar and his sister Rin were already very close, but the Vanir faith permitted unfettered love between siblings, fostering an intimate bond between them. However, the sensibilities of the clan leadership did not condone such behaviour. Things soured between the chieftain Ingvar and Ivar's parents long before tension arose around Ivar and Rin's union. Ingvar made it clear that such a union wouldn't be acceptable to the clan, and if they were to proceed, it would result in expulsion from the clan.

Excommunicated as outlaws, Ivar and Rin were left to survive in a very hostile wilderness in the north eastern lands of Islandia. At the time, his skills were complimentary with the nomadic clan, but weren't sufficient for a life of solitude. Necessity drove Ivar to push his bounds of ingenuity, wisdom and tenacity in order to survive and keep his pregnant wife safe. Living off the land, Ivar began to uncover his unbridled talents in Verwandlung magic. Self-taught and, he would later claim, aided by Njord's watchful eye, he grew astoundingly powerful in the Druidic arts. It served him well, as he and Rin were no longer under the protection afforded by membership in the wolf clan. Drunk and vengeful clan members, wolves, polar bears, and the occasional undying not to mention the elements, threatened their way of life. A few years into the exile, Ivar made the mistake of allowing some lost, wounded clan members to seek shelter at his abode. They were youths from the new Evingard outpost who had ventured out into the wilds without proper preparation. As he tended their wounds, they abused his hospitality, pillaging his home, raping his wife and in the end beating Ivar within an inch of his life. When Ivar regained consciousness, his wife was dying. Her health deteriorated quickly and she died in his arms. He swore that he would never allow his daughter to meet the same fate as her mother. From that day on, Ivar pursued the druidic arts as a man possessed by an unquenchable fire.

Ivar's first grand accomplishment was creating his "hovel on the hill"... a magical abode that changes locations and remains shrouded from prying eyes. From a distance it appears as a small ramshackle hut, but as one enters the grounds, the real grandeur becomes apparent. A much larger longhouse that can comfortably house one hundred people is surrounded by thick spiked bramble vines. The interior is overgrown with vegetation and is home to many animals. This sanctum has granted comfort and safety to Ivar and his daughter, Rhine.

Ivar's magic allowed him to exert power over the domains of plants, animals, the land and stars. He used his powers to subjugate all manner of beasts. In an act of misguided vengeance, Ivar started to imprison many visitors who came to his home. He used his magics to slowly transform his visitors into subservient and ensorcelled women he would add to his harem. The transformation would begins within the first 24 hours and complete in 48 hours. For those he felt could be of use, he would bestow some Druidic powers, and then send them off on errands. The nature of the errands could range from simple spying and reconnaissance to more complex missions involving sabotage. With this harem of heroines, he has become a thorn in the side of Ingvar and Magnus.

He continues to despise Ingvar for the anger he cannot purge from his heart. He also blames Magnus for the harm his mines have caused the land as well as the great Vaettir's illness. He is considering a union of force with Ingvar's disenchanted son, Halfdan.

Koshchey the Deathless

LEVEL 31 FARDRENGIR, DRUID, BERZERKIR
FYLGIA
TROLL BLOODED

Koshchey is a wild man who loves to ride naked through the forest. His mount is magical, having the ability to float above the water and never tire. He is a real threat to anyone travelling the Volga trade route. His lust for fair maidens drives him to raid caravans and trading ships that carry such booty. He brings them back to his hamlet and ensorcells them into subservience.

Koshchey cannot be killed because his soul is separated from his body. His soul resides in a Death Stone, cloaked with an illusion of a mundane object that resembles a duck egg. The Death Stone effectively erases his time of death from the Tapestry of Fate. However the closer the Death Stone is to Koshchey, the weaker he gets. It is said that physical contact between the beneficiary of the Death stone and the Death Stone itself causes instant death. Until that time, Koshchey remains immortal. This makes him truly fearless in battle. On top of that, rumours abound that he is the steward of the land, having the backing of a powerful land vaettir.

Many years ago a queen whose kingdom borders the Volga was forced to deal with Koshchey's mischief. She tried to have him killed unsuccessfully. After devising a trap involving some beautiful bait, she managed to capture and imprison him leveraging his vanity as a weakness. His incarceration lasted a decade until an unsuspecting hero freed him. He has been at large ever since.

Those that have witnessed this howling marauder have described him as lanky, lean and muscled greying man. His tangled seaweed like hair frames a a pair of reptilian eyes beneath white bushy eyebrows. His large nose detracts attention from his large, misshapen and crooked teeth. His skin is mottled and dry, forever shedding like that of a snake. When he speaks, he speaks in riddles, never directly addressing a question.

More warrior than magician, Koshchey recently visited Baba Yaga in order to learn a spell that would allow him to shape-change. His favourite form is that of a whirlwind. In this new form, which he can maintain for up to an hour a day, he is able to scoop up more unsuspecting beauties for his harem. Some people mistake his disconcerting ability to mimic any voices and sounds as a magical enchantment. He does rely on divination magic in order to scry passing caravans at a distance, looking for young beautiful maidens.

However it is nothing more than an extraordinary talent that Koshchay has honed over the years. When pressed to fight, he prefers to fight unarmed and naked, as his fingernails and toenails can eject a very toxic and potent poison. His bite has been known to paralyze foes for several days. When he utters his battle-cry, he is usually escorted by a murder of crows.

He has a dozen sisters that are said to manage the hamlet which contains his harem. Those who have seen them and have lived to tell the tale, speak of hideous hags that match Koshchey's dubious charisma. They recount scenes of horror where older harem members are boiled and eaten by Koshchey's family.

Leif "the Mountain Shaker"

LEVEL 20 BERZERKIR
TROLL-BLOOD

A mountain of a man, Leif stands head and shoulders above most. His red hair is pulled into a rough braid, and his beard has been left to grow wild. Hailing from a remote village in the frigid north of Norveig, as a young man he found that he could earn more as a hired sword than by working the land, and before long, he was providing his skills to various karls for weeks or months at a time.

Leif wears a riveted chain shirt, covered on his back by a full bear skin. When asked, he gladly tells the story of killing the bear with little more than his bare hands (with only a little embellishment). He fights with a full sized maul in one hand, and a massive shield in the other, which appears to have begun its life as a tavern door. Someone went to the trouble of reinforcing it with steel bands and attaching arm straps,

but for some reason, Leif is less willing to tell the story of how he got his shield... presumably because the previous owner still wants it back.

Vicious in combat, the bearded warrior takes the form of a bear on the battle ground. His heavy strikes can be seen throwing lesser men across the field. When standing his ground he is like a rock breaking a wave, and it seems unlikely that a mortal man could move him.

Outside of battle, Leif is generally friendly and well liked. His years of travelling from village to village have instilled a wander lust which makes him restless if he stays in one place too long. With enough mead in his belly the huge man will almost always launch into tales of his exploits, many of which are too outlandish to be taken seriously by anyone not similarly intoxicated.

Louhi, Mistress of Pohjola

LEVEL 36 SEITHKONA
TROLL BLOODED

Louhi is a queen as well as a great and powerful sorceress, but in her youth things were a lot more complicated. She was born and raised in the picturesque eastern kingdom of Kalevala. Soon after birth, her parents give her up to a merchant named Alvar who raised her as his own. Louhi nor Alvar knew that her parents were of supernatural origin, being hounded by a dark and evil force bent on their destruction. They gave Louhi up for her own safety, and her first years were filled with unbridled happiness. However this quickly changed as Louhi's powers started to manifest on her 12th birthday. Not knowing what was going on, or how to control such untamed and torrential magical power, she inadvertently injured Alvar, almost killing him.

Over the years she made some close friends that understood her predicament and sympathized, but for the most part Alvar kept her hidden away from the other villagers knowing full well that their reaction would be. But the magical might within her only grew, and without proper tutelage the accidents became more and more pronounced. After a particularly horrific accident that claimed several lives, Louhi was run out of town by a blood thirsty mob. She fled north to the most inhospitable lands she could find in hopes that no one would follow her. To her surprise her true friends came to support her, and together they forged a small northern kingdom they would call Pohjola. The early years were tough, since nothing grew in this arctic wasteland. However the wide open spaces meant Louhi could practice her magic freely without hesitation and that is what she needed to hone her talents.

Unfortunately her crimes back in Kalevala weren't forgotten, and the animosity towards her only grew. Despite the vitriol, she worked hard to mend the divide. Many years passed and Louhi had become the queen of Pohjola, a mother to several children and a widow. As her children grew, age, the harsh life and magic began to wear away at Louhi's exterior, leaving her with the appearance of a gnarled crone. She resolved to craft a magical device that would provide great bounty for her kingdom. Despite her efforts at crafting a Sampo, all attempts failed.

One day, washed up upon the shores of Pohjola she found none other than the legendary sage Vainamoinen. He had taken some grievous wounds at the hands of Joukahainen. She took him in and nursed him back to health. When he recovered he was smitten by her many beautiful daughters, and asked that the youngest and fairest be his bride. In a momentary moment of weakness, she forgot about her daughter's wishes and agreed so long as Vainamoinen could provide her with a Sampo.

Vainamoinen returned with a master blacksmith named Ilmarinen. He would be creating the Sampo in exchange for the engagement. It took him three days and nights with all of the extra hands Louhi could muster to work the bellows and keep the fire hot. At last it was created and then placed within the sacred copper mountain called Sariola. The engagement proceeded as planned, but the bride and groom were at an impasse. The bride refused to leave Pohjola to a kingdom that exiled her mother. Similarly, Ilmarinen did not want to live in this desolate, cold and rocky kingdom. Vainamoinen and Ilmarinen left angry.

Feeling that they were cheated, Vainamoinen, Ilmarinen and Kaukomieli returned and using song magic, stole the Sampo. Louhi gave chase in the form of a giant ferocious eagle and the resulting battle damaged and broke the Sampo, but the majority of the artifact returned with the warriors to Kalevala. Furious, Louhi returned to her kingdom vowing the destruction of Vainamoinen and his treacherous companions. She stood atop Sariola and began a plague ritual. Winds buffet the mountain and the land grows dark and cold, something much greater than her magic is at work here- above Skoll and Hati pounce upon the sun and moon... Gazing up at the darkening skies, her grey hair flailing, Louhi had a flash of inspiration. Changing her ritual to one of beguiling, she charmed the wolves to descend and enter the caves beneath Sariola. She has captured Skoll and Hati, vengeance will be hers!

Magnus Magnusson

LEVEL 20 SKALD/SEITHKARL (MALE SEITHKONA)

Magnus Magnusson wasn't always a wealthy man. His earliest memories begin with life at an orphanage after his village was wiped out by a plague. He was one of the last children to be adopted due to his poor physical health and this helped shape Magnus' empathy for orphans.

Life wasn't easy working for his foster parents. He had several new siblings which ensured Magnus received the worst of jobs, allowing them to undertake the easier ones. This went on for most of Magnus' childhood, until one day, his trivial work resulted in him crossing paths with a man named Magnus. He was a merchant that had a tragic childhood similar to Magnus'. Magnus beseeched the merchant to take him on as an apprentice. Seeing a little of himself in the boy and some potential, he agreed to buy Magnus from his parents.

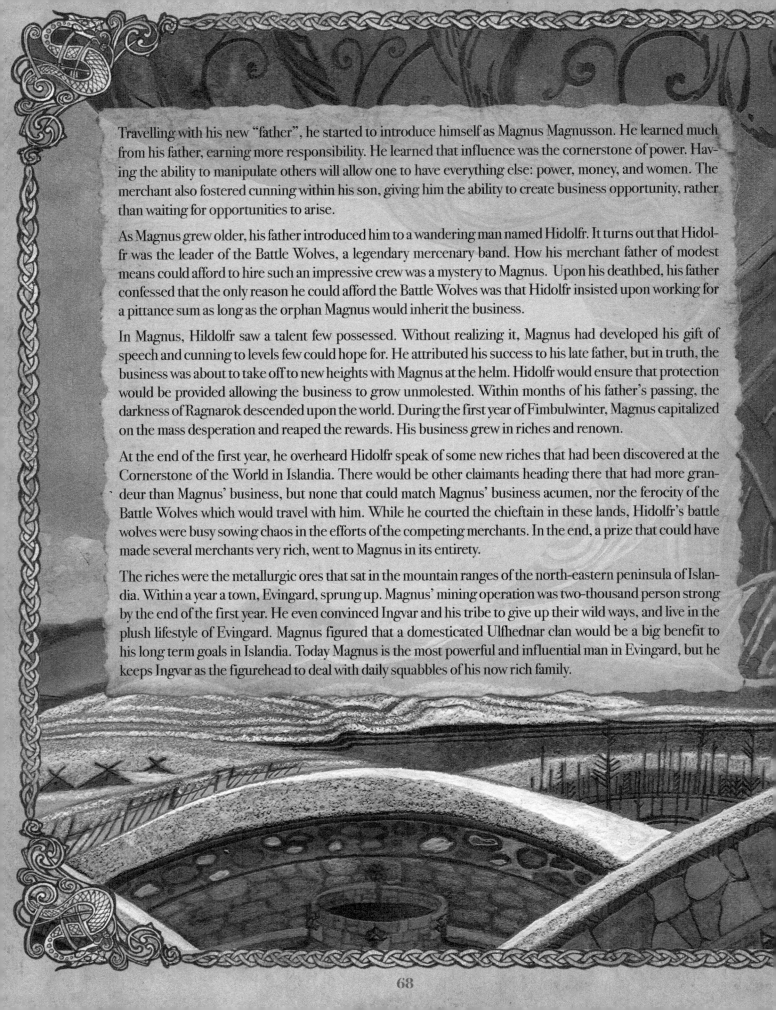

Travelling with his new "father", he started to introduce himself as Magnus Magnusson. He learned much from his father, earning more responsibility. He learned that influence was the cornerstone of power. Having the ability to manipulate others will allow one to have everything else: power, money, and women. The merchant also fostered cunning within his son, giving him the ability to create business opportunity, rather than waiting for opportunities to arise.

As Magnus grew older, his father introduced him to a wandering man named Hidolfr. It turns out that Hidolfr was the leader of the Battle Wolves, a legendary mercenary band. How his merchant father of modest means could afford to hire such an impressive crew was a mystery to Magnus. Upon his deathbed, his father confessed that the only reason he could afford the Battle Wolves was that Hidolfr insisted upon working for a pittance sum as long as the orphan Magnus would inherit the business.

In Magnus, Hildolfr saw a talent few possessed. Without realizing it, Magnus had developed his gift of speech and cunning to levels few could hope for. He attributed his success to his late father, but in truth, the business was about to take off to new heights with Magnus at the helm. Hidolfr would ensure that protection would be provided allowing the business to grow unmolested. Within months of his father's passing, the darkness of Ragnarok descended upon the world. During the first year of Fimbulwinter, Magnus capitalized on the mass desperation and reaped the rewards. His business grew in riches and renown.

At the end of the first year, he overheard Hidolfr speak of some new riches that had been discovered at the Cornerstone of the World in Islandia. There would be other claimants heading there that had more grandeur than Magnus' business, but none that could match Magnus' business acumen, nor the ferocity of the Battle Wolves which would travel with him. While he courted the chieftain in these lands, Hidolfr's battle wolves were busy sowing chaos in the efforts of the competing merchants. In the end, a prize that could have made several merchants very rich, went to Magnus in its entirety.

The riches were the metallurgic ores that sat in the mountain ranges of the north-eastern peninsula of Islandia. Within a year a town, Evingard, sprung up. Magnus' mining operation was two-thousand person strong by the end of the first year. He even convinced Ingvar and his tribe to give up their wild ways, and live in the plush lifestyle of Evingard. Magnus figured that a domesticated Ulfhednar clan would be a big benefit to his long term goals in Islandia. Today Magnus is the most powerful and influential man in Evingard, but he keeps Ingvar as the figurehead to deal with daily squabbles of his now rich family.

The main wealth comes from the exotic ores Magnus extracts from other realms that are accessible from the Cornerstone of the World. Hidolfr seems most interested in keeping these supply lines open. His warriors help guard shipments that go to Ath Cliath and keep the presence of these ores secret except from Magnus' inner circle and the Battle Wolves. The inner circle has organized the extraction of iron ore to be the cover for the much more valuable ores that are mined and moved by a select set of trusted miners. He then has a runner named Draugstagg who has a swift ship that can deliver the prized cargo to the blacksmith's guild in Ath Cliath. This entire shipment is protected by the Battle Wolves at all times.

Magnus is very hands-on in his management of the most precious parts of his business and he travels with his inner circle that includes a Galdr named Modi, Maiden of Ratatosk named Frida, and a Seithkona named Gunnlaud. Modi, Frida and Gunnlaud are orphans Magni has rescued from abuse. They are always alert and they protect Magnus with unfailing devotion.

Ingvar's son Halfdan refused to succumb to Magnus' gifts and easy lifestyle. He took a few from his clan and refused to give up their traditional ways. No matter how hard Magnus tries, Halfdan refuses to yield. If anything, the attempts have driven the relationship to levels of animosity bordering on homicidal hatred.

Olaf Hoskuldsson

LEVEL: 24 GALDR

Olaf is the son of Hoskuld Dala-Kollsson, a chieftain who lives in the Laxardal region. Laxardal is in the north western portion of Islandia, overseen by the great eagle Vaettir. Olaf is one of the richest young land owners in Islandia. However, his childhood was something else altogether.

Born to a concubine named Melkora, Olaf was a bastard. His father denied him at first but the truth came out and Hoskuld's wife, Jorunn, set out to make life as hard as possible for both Melkora and Olaf. They were cast out of the household and forced to live as thralls working for Hoskuld. The other thralls made it no easier, seeing how Olaf would get subtle benefits from his father. To complicate matters, his mother was mute, so Olaf grew up with no one that would stand up for him. This harsh upbringing forced Olaf to grow into a very strong man. Melkora gave Olaf a younger half-brother named Helgi when she became romantically involved with another thrall.

Only in Olaf's adolescence did Melkora reveal that she could speak, but chose not to in order to preserve her secret identity. It turns out that she is the granddaughter of the legendary former king of Ath Cliath named Niall Glundub. When King Sitric attacked Ath Cliath, her grandfather was killed, she was taken captive and her father Muirchertach mac Neill fled and now rules Ailech in Hibernia. She was then sold to Rus slave traders who eventually sold her to Hoskuld in one of his visits to Gotaland. On the route back, Hoskuld lay with Malkora thinking that her being a mute would keep it a secret from his wife.

Olaf's fervor in performing his labourer work, his fighting prowess, and his keen acumen caught the eye of a wealthy Godi (priest of the Aesir god Foresti) named Thord. Thord was going through a messy separation with his wife Vigdis, and he had no love for his children with her. Out of spite he wanted to arrange that Olaf become his foster-son so that he could inherit everything. Hoskuld was for the arrangement, but Melkora saw the danger in this arrangement. Vigdis would have good reason to go after Olaf, which worried Melkora tremendously. Despite her wishes, Olaf was passed onto Thord as his new foster-son.

Having ownership of the land, and riches he had never dreamed of possessing, Olaf is coping as best he can. Rangarok's Fimbulwinter has made trade difficult, and very few merchants deal in items that are not of absolute necessity. Olaf enjoys acquiring vanity merchandise such as dyes and perfumes, for both he and his mother. With the first shipment of dyes that he acquired, he managed to colour all of his wardrobe in Bifrost colours. There are those who now call him "the peacock" behind his back.

Over the last month he has been preparing to attend the very first Althing. He wants his attendance to be full of pomp and extravagance. He plans on bringing his new sword Fotbitr to the event.

Otto the Great, Emperor

LEVEL 38 CRUSADER

Otto started out as the king of Saxony, but quickly acquired stature and influence throughout Outer-Midgard. His kingdom had very close ties with the western kingdoms of Francia and Brittany, ties that had been established by his father Henry the Fowler. A generation ago, Francia had granted asylum to many royals from the Great Isles who were fleeing Ivar the Boneless. Many of these royals were accepted into various courts and Otto had the pleasure of securing a bright young West Saxon named Ahtelstan and his half brother Edmund, two bright boys that showed immense promise. With Otto's expansionist ambitions, he was always grooming new commanders.

During his eastern military campaigns into the land of the Slavs his supply lines were ambushed by an army of northmen from Midgard. It was a surprise attack by a chieftain known as Bjorn Eriksson and before reinforcements could arrive, Erik's forces plundered and made off with many slaves. Otto consulted his

chroniclers to learn more about this threat from the north. Twenty years before Otto's birth the Viking northmen laid siege to Francia. Streaming out of Midgard, they sailed into Outer-Midgard with thousands of men. Their savagery was intense and after much plunder they returned to their heathen lands.

Forgetting the Slavs, he turned his efforts north, smashing against Midgard's southern kingdoms. The Danevirke wall was immense and spanned coast to coast, forcing Otto into a naval campaign. But his efforts failed as the northmen outclassed his navy with superior ships. His efforts none the less garnered him a fan in the south, Pope John XII. Pope John XII was looking for a mighty king that could lead a crusade in his name. The crusade he had in mind was expanding the faith, the land, taxation and the influence of the Holy See. Pope John XII found his white knight in Otto and invited him to Rome. The following year king Otto's delegation arrived in Rome and he was crowned Holy Roman Emperor Otto. The agreement meant that he would bend knee to Pope John XII, be granted expanded territories in the south, be able to raise an even larger army from these new lands, and he would perform a crusade into Midgard.

Emperor Otto returned north with four additional armies he had mustered in the new territories. With high spirits his northern campaign began... but not as he nor Pope John XII would have liked. On the day of the full scale attack on the Danevirke, the sky grew dark as the sun was snuffed out. Panic descended upon his troops and what should have been a victory, quickly turned into a humiliating retreat. Dark gossip was spreading throughout the armies, sowing fear and doubt into the hearts of his soldiers. Pope John

XII's displeasure was unmistakable. The meeting with his military leaders had an unexpected breakthrough when Aethelstan surprised them with a plan that seemed foolproof. And so began the campaign for Wessex, the first foothold into Midgard. Aethelstan would be crowned king and would lead the armies through sympathetic lands. Before launching Aethelstan's armada, Emperor Otto wanted to ensure loyalty, so he married King Aethelstan's half-sister Eadgyth in order to seal the alliance. One can't be too careful when granting someone such power and priviledge.

With Wessex secured, Aethelstan set his sights on the adjoining kingdoms. Otto was preparing to send reinforcements to king Aethelstan as promised, but disturbing news from the south stayed his order. What he has heard from his southern spies is very troubling. Apparently the armies of margrave Berengar II have massed to the south of Otto's kingdom, possibly readying for attack. Pope John XII has grown silent since the failure at the Danevirke. Otto will not rule out possible treachery.

Pope John XII

UNKNOWN LEVEL AND ARCHETYPE

John was born into the Theophylact family. A family deeply entrenched in the power structure of Rome and much of Outer-Midgard. The reign of the Theophylact family is widely known as the Saeculum Obscurum (the dark age). They control both levers of power: secular and spiritual. When John was elected Pope, no one was surprised. In fact that confirmed what many already believed: that the spirit of White God had left the holy city. Many of the street rumours are based in fact. Pope John XII is a scoundrel that turned the Lateran into a brothel. He loves intrigue, gossip, war and debauchery. One of his greatest desires is to expand the Theophylact family's reach and control into Midgard. To achieve this he has recruited a mighty king whose weakness is vanity. By offering a title, he has bought his kingdom's services. However emperor Otto hasn't lived up to his expectations so Pope John XII has found a successor in margrave Berengar II. Pope John XII has dangled the title of "Holy Roman Emperor" in front of Berengar, telling him that the title will be his if he conquers Saxony and takes over the crusade. The wheels are in motion.

Sitric Cuaran, King

LEVEL 32 GALDR

Sitric hails from the legendary clan of Ivar. His ancestors are legends, started by the berserker Ragnar Lodbrok. The clan was made infamous by his grandfather Ivar the Boneless, who took great pleasure hunting down the followers of the new White God. Ivar became notorious for the use of the Blood Eagle torture, which involves cutting away the ribcage from the spine and pulling out the victim's lungs through the wounds. The banner for House Ivar is a black raven on a red field.

When Sitric was young, he was captivated by the exploits of his ancestors. Raised by a Godi of Odin, his reverence for the god is fervent and obsessive. To the shock of friends and family, Sitric performed a blot to Odin and gave up his right eye for wisdom. Since that day, Sitric's fortunes have amassed rapidly. One fateful day, his brother Sicfrith came to him beaming with pride. Apparently Sicfrith had converted to the faith of the new White God. This made Sitric sick to his core. Without a second thought, Sitric committed fratricide in the hopes it would appease Odin.

On his sixteenth birthday he received an omen from a wanderer which set him off on conquest. He asked two likeminded cousins to join him on a plunder that would know no end. Ragnall and Gofraid agreed without hesitation as all three had shared a similar dream a fortnight ago. Setting out from ancestral Jutland with three ships, each manned by 60 loyal thanes, they set forth on an expedition that would surpass all imagination. All opposition melted away as they re-took York and renamed it Jorvik. They traversed Northumbria gathering more troops under the raven banner. Lastly they sailed to Hibernia and captured Ath Cliath, one of the most central trade hubs in all of Midgard. Splitting the spoils, Ragnall took his seat of power in Jorvik, Gofraid took Northumbria as his own, and that left Ath Cliath for the new king Sitric.

His rule in Ath Cliath would face a great challenge with the onset of Ragnarok. Fimbulwinter rallied the independent chieftains of Hibernia to strike at this foreigner. However, with graces from above, Jarl Sitric held back the tide and eventually broke the opposing forces, taking them as slaves. Over the course of the first age of Ragnarok, Jarl Sitric managed to turn Ath Cliath into one of the richest and most prosperous towns, with the slave trade being no small part of this success.

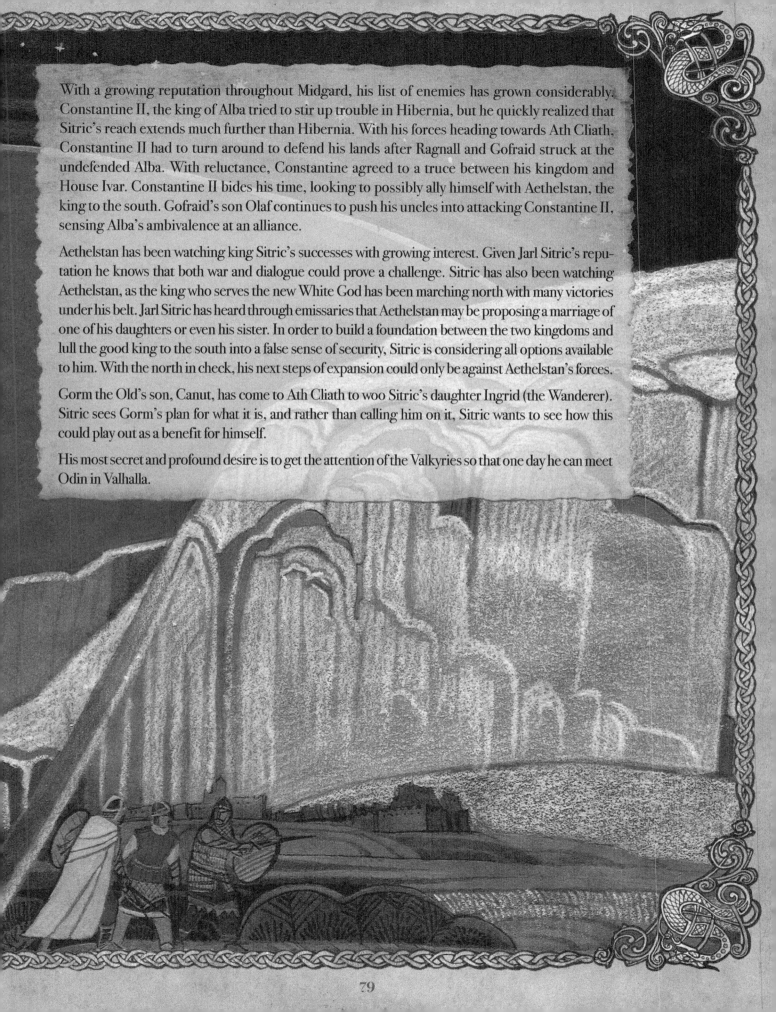

With a growing reputation throughout Midgard, his list of enemies has grown considerably. Constantine II, the king of Alba tried to stir up trouble in Hibernia, but he quickly realized that Sitric's reach extends much further than Hibernia. With his forces heading towards Ath Cliath, Constantine II had to turn around to defend his lands after Ragnall and Gofraid struck at the undefended Alba. With reluctance, Constantine agreed to a truce between his kingdom and House Ivar. Constantine II bides his time, looking to possibly ally himself with Aethelstan, the king to the south. Gofraid's son Olaf continues to push his uncles into attacking Constantine II, sensing Alba's ambivalence at an alliance.

Aethelstan has been watching king Sitric's successes with growing interest. Given Jarl Sitric's reputation he knows that both war and dialogue could prove a challenge. Sitric has also been watching Aethelstan, as the king who serves the new White God has been marching north with many victories under his belt. Jarl Sitric has heard through emissaries that Aethelstan may be proposing a marriage of one of his daughters or even his sister. In order to build a foundation between the two kingdoms and lull the good king to the south into a false sense of security, Sitric is considering all options available to him. With the north in check, his next steps of expansion could only be against Aethelstan's forces.

Gorm the Old's son, Canut, has come to Ath Cliath to woo Sitric's daughter Ingrid (the Wanderer). Sitric sees Gorm's plan for what it is, and rather than calling him on it, Sitric wants to see how this could play out as a benefit for himself.

His most secret and profound desire is to get the attention of the Valkyries so that one day he can meet Odin in Valhalla.

Svalms the Dvergar

LEVEL 50 DVERGAR

Svalms is a rarity among Dvergar. Rather than work the forges in the realms of the giant and gods where the contracts are very lucrative, Svalms has decided to setup his business in Midgard. The immediate returns may be smaller, but Svalms is in it for all four ages of Ragnarok. He sees the long-term investment into a realm whose populace may sway the war in a very profound way. As with all contracts outside of Nidavellir, he pays his tithe to King Ivaldi.

Svalms uses a magical disguise to ensure that his true nature isn't discovered. He passes himself as a short man who has become the head of the blacksmith's guild.

His import network consists of merchants who can procure ores from the outer realms such as Vanagard and Jotunheim. A constant stream comes in from a merchant named Draugstagg. He is well represented as his entourage is made up of the legendary Battle Wolves. His ships come from the west indicating a possible connection to the outlaw isle of Islandia. Draugstagg's ships carry iron as a cover, but he marks the most important cargo with the Othala rune. Within those crates, Svalms finds ores from many worlds and he makes sure his curiosity doesn't taint this lucrative relationship. Draugstagg is very good at what he does, but Svallms is

convinced that he is more of a runner than a merchant, and someone much shrewder runs the show from afar.

Svalms has recently been courted by a few of the pretender kings that seek legitimacy for their claims on king Harald's old kingdom. Erik Bloodaxe, Hakon the Good and Bjorn Farmann, as well as Gorm the Old, stewart of the Danvirke have all recently approached merchants that Svalms has sent out into Midgard looking to sell Dvergar grade wares. He is most curious about Hakon as this young man has managed to galvanize a sizeable force on the Great Isles. What talents does Hakon possess? Charisma? Is he a potent strategist? The amount of attention and support he has received is uncharacteristic of someone who is a low-born thrall. His proximity to Ath Cliath may affect Svalm's business and he is keen to know more. Knowing that Hakon's patron, King Aethelstan, is a threat to King Sitric, Svalms has decided to use King Sitric to do his dirty work. After all, the new White God must not be allowed to succeed!

Svalms has too much at stake to leave rising powers alone. His operations are too lucrative to let someone running amok whom the Norns may have woven into a pivotal role in the tapestry of fate... not that he believes in the Norns. In recent months, the Dvergar King Ivaldi has asked Svalms to investigate the market for sales to mortals. Higher powers have tremendous wealth, but during these dark times of Ragnarok, many kings are being killed and their wealth is being consolidated under increasingly fewer, but wealthier banners.

Thorsteinn Ingolfsson

LEVEL 24 SKALD

Thorsteinn comes from the Arnar dynastic clan. His father, Ingolfur, fled political and royal woe in Norveig, pledged to never again be subservient to royalty, and created his new homestead on the southern reaches of Islandia. Their life was peaceful while Thorsteinn was young, as they had very few neighbours. But, as he grew older, news of Islandia as a safe haven attracted many undesirables. Feuds became more common, and weregilds were not enough to settle some deep seated grievances.

The settlers looked to Thorsteinn for leadership. Some even wanted to elevate him to karl status, volunteering to quash any resistance to his rule. He refused, citing that Islandia should remain free of any monarchies. After a lot of thought, a plan of shared responsibility and governance came to Thorsteinn. He called it the Althing. He discussed the Althing with his thanes and found that it showed both merit and promise. So, in the second year of Fimbulwinter, when chaos was threatening the very fabric of society on Islandia, he sent messengers to all the Jarls of the island. These messengers carried news that the Althing that would occur in a few months' time. The Norns only know how this idea will play out with the others on the island.

Trondur i Gotu

LEVEL 26 BERZERKIR

Trondur is the very young chieftain of the Faroe Islands. He is a big man, red-haired and red-bearded, freckled and grim of look, gloomy of mind, cunning and shrewd towards all men, bad to deal with, and ill-natured to most folk, yet fair of speech to greater men than himself, but in his heart he is never false. He is the defender of Faroe, a small group of islands halfway between Norveig and Islandia. Many pass through her ports, and he stands between chaos and prosperity. Many have surmised that without Trondur's firm hand, the islands would have burned long ago. Too many drunken outlaws make port at Faroe on their westward journeys.

Like most small islands during Ragnarok, the forests of the Faroe Islands have been clear cut and used for fuel and shelter. This has placed a large burden on Trondur who must negotiate the purchase of fresh lumber from abroad. He has sent word that those who bring lumber to his islands will receive preferential treatment during their stay. The taxes for making port on Faroe are calculated by ship and by head. This generates a healthy income for the natives. Trondur also looks out for his kin, quashing any talk of new settlers upon the islands. All visitors must be on their way within a fortnight. Those who overstay their welcome will feel the full brunt of Trondur's wrath.

Ulfberht

LEVEL 48 STALO (DECEASED)

Ulfberht was a fabled blacksmith who invented the rare and magnificent ancestor sword. By combining the ashes of a deceased ancestor with the heated iron ingots, he raised the carbon content making the steel unbelievably sturdy and flexible... not to mention imbuing the weapon with the essence of an important ancestor. Ulfberht swords are renowned across Midgard, with warriors willing to trade their first born sons for such a fine blade. Only a few are created every year, making them scarce and valuable.

He passed on his secrets to his sons and grandsons so that the secret recipe would live on, creating an almost immortal aire around the name of Ulfberht. Over several hundred years the family has grown exponentially and now the Stalo profession's signature status symbol is the ancestor blade. The recipe is closely guarded within the family, and such a blade is rarely sold to someone outside of the family.

Vainamoinen, Son of the Wind, Hero of Kalevala

LEVEL 36 SKALD
FYLGIA

In Northern Midgard, Vainamoinen's legend precedes him. He has had a very long life filled with epic adventure and conflict. He is the son of the wind spirit Ilmatar and the sea spirit Ukko. Unlike his parents, his appearance is that of a mortal man, however he possesses wisdom only achieved by higher beings. His greatest asset is his voice which carries the magic of spell songs. His magic songs can control the elements such as moving earth and stone as well as silencing the wind. Some of his songs can even put people into a catatonic state similar to sleep. He is credited in creating the very first kantele, a harp like instrument that magnifies the intensity of spell songs.

Long ago, Vainamoinen's main rival had been the skald Joukahainen. There was a lot of jealousy and envy between the two bards. One day they decided to settle it once and for all, who is the better minstrel and scholar. The duel was to the death, and both men gave no quarter. Vainamoinen's songs prevailed, beaten, Joukahainen offered his sister as a bride in exchange for his life. The hero of Kalevala accepted.

While lucky in most pursuits, Vainamoinen was always very unlucky in love. Every romantic engagement he had over his long life has ended in ruin. It began with Joukahainen's sister Aino, who was promised in exchange for mercy. However her love for another man, and her revulsion at marrying someone old enough to be her grandfather drove her to suicide. Aino drowned herself rather than fulfilling her brother's command. Afterwards he sought out a bride in the northern lands of Pohjola, receiving one of Louhi's daughters as a possible mate. However the bride price was steep- the forging of the legendary Sampo. Vainamoinen asked his friend Ilmarinen, a mortal blacksmith with no equal, to forge it for him, but the resulting agreement meant that Louhi's daughter would wed Ilmarinen rather than Vainamoinen.

Vainamoinen has always been a champion of his homeland Kalevala. He was always ready to go to great lengths in order to ensure its safety and prosperity. Louhi, mistress of Pohjola would do much the same for her northern kingdom, so the two would be cast at odds with one another time and time again. The greatest confrontation occurred when Vainamoinen stole the Sampo away from Louhi and brought it back home to Kalevala. Even in Ragnarok, the Sampo keeps Kalevala prosperous and bountiful. Vainamoinen senses Louhi's fury and expects her coming storm.

Vargeisa the Fire Wolf

LEVEL 26 SEITHKONA/MAIDEN OF RATATOSK
FYLGIA

Known as the Fire Wolf, her pale skin and crimson hair frame an unforgettable beauty. Vargeisa is a mortal who has take it upon herself to work towards Loki's liberation. Her soul sang with joy as she witnessed the sun and moon being devoured by the outlines of fearsome celestial wolves. An omen soon followed showing her a writhing snake emblazoned with the trickster god's symbol. Vargeisa has been very active in the last two years, coaxing the followers of Loki to reveal themselves to her. She has organized their secret organization in a hierarchy with influential leaders who represent and control different areas of Midgard– they are known as the "Eyes of Loki". Her agents that travel the land following her orders are known as the "Hands of Loki". Those who hunt the Godis of Heimdal and Thor are known as the "Teeth of Loki".

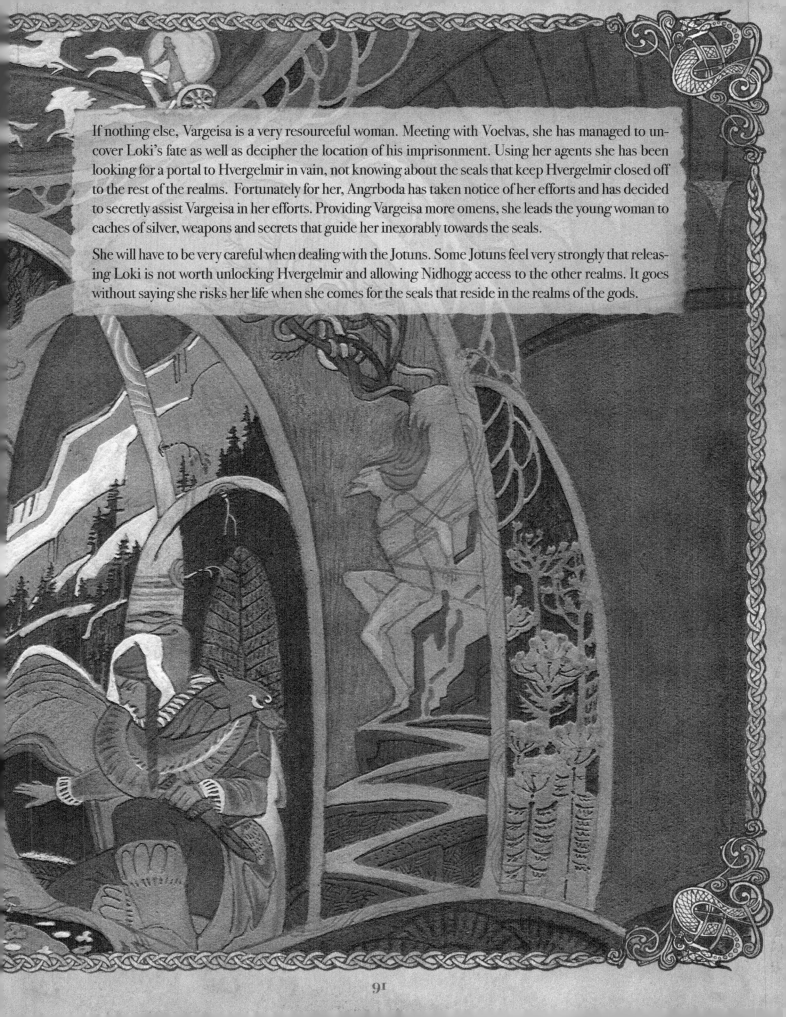

If nothing else, Vargeisa is a very resourceful woman. Meeting with Voelvas, she has managed to un-cover Loki's fate as well as decipher the location of his imprisonment. Using her agents she has been looking for a portal to Hvergelmir in vain, not knowing about the seals that keep Hvergelmir closed off to the rest of the realms. Fortunately for her, Angrboda has taken notice of her efforts and has decided to secretly assist Vargeisa in her efforts. Providing Vargeisa more omens, she leads the young woman to caches of silver, weapons and secrets that guide her inexorably towards the seals.

She will have to be very careful when dealing with the Jotuns. Some Jotuns feel very strongly that releas-ing Loki is not worth unlocking Hvergelmir and allowing Nidhogg access to the other realms. It goes without saying she risks her life when she comes for the seals that reside in the realms of the gods.

Wayland the Artisan of Grief

DECEASED?

K nown Long ago, in the distant kingdom of Lapland a Jarl named Hrim fought a losing war against the Sami tribes to the north. Hrim had three young boys named Egil, Slagfid and Wayland whom he wished to protect. He sent them south to Jamtland so they could be spared from the inevitable massacre. Some of the Sami searched for Hrim's offspring, but alas they were safe in the legendary Mirkwood. They were raised by a pair of witches, a unique upbringing that coaxed out their magical talents. Egil showed promise as a Galdr, Slagfid as a Druid, and Wayland's talents were more earthly, manifesting in Blacksmithing. The three grew up to become talented and handsome young men, and they attracted the attention of three fallen Valkyries: Hladgud the White Swan, Alvit the Strange and Olrun the Twice Born. These Valkyries had fallen out of favour with Odin and were similarly hiding in Mirkwood. However after seven years Odin had begun to close in on them, with sightings of Hugin, Odin's raven, above the haunted wood. In the eighth year they were forced to keep moving about Mirkwood because Freki, Odin's wolf, started to be seen in Mirkwood. On the ninth year, the Valkyries left their lovers in order to face their inevitable stand off with the All Father. In order to spare the men, the Valkyries left suddenly and without warning.

Egil and Slagfid resolved to follow and search out their lovers, and Wayland remained in Mirkwood in case their women returned. Alone, fueled by his loss of Alvit, he poured his grief into his forge. He made a ring for Alvit, and then he made another, and another, until he had made seven hundred. His sorrow was all consuming. It spread throughout the spirit world, crying out, he attracted the notice of the Lios Alfar. They came... They came to help in his forge... to help him forget... help him fuel his anguish into magnificence. With their guidance, within the uterus of his forge, Wayland produced works of surreal quality. Chroniclers have written about mythic swords, forged by Wayland, wielded by many famous heroes such as Roland and Arthur.

Word of his backsmithing prowess spread throughout the land and the Jarl of Narke named Nidud came looking for Wayland. Nidud simply had to own this talent like he had so many others in the past. He threw his kingdom's resources on the task, employing voelvas and diviners to find Wayland's location. He paid Wayland's ancient enemies, the Sami bounty hunters to track him down, capture and deliver him, along with his wondrous creations to Narke. Even Mirkwood's shroud could not keep Wayland safe. Captured by Jarl Nidud, Wayland had to be subdued and enslaved. To ensure he couldn't escape, his legs were broken and severed, and he was imprisoned in a forge atop a tall stone tower. He would be forced to create items of splendour for Nidud and his family.

However Wayland did not prove to be the submissive blacksmith Nidud was hoping for. His forge was the unlimited weapons arsenal he needed. He created means to trap his visitors and when they came to request something new, one by one, the royal family fell victim to Wayland's snares. In order to finally escape, he crafted a pair of wings with which he flew away. No one has heard from the legendary blacksmith ever since. Rumour has it that he has forged a magical relic that has stopped him from aging.

And thus is the legacy of Wayland the Artisan of Sorrow, Shaper of Grief.

Higher Powers

This chapter introduces more key players from the outer realms who will have tremendous impacts on the fate of Midgard.

Dreki the Great Vaettir

Level 54 Druid
Can transform into a Borghild

The Vaettir are Alfar of either disposition (Lios or Svart) who have been elevated to an illustrious duty of guardianship. Through a secretive ceremony, they cease to be Alfar and become spiritual beings that must choose a home in Midgard. The land that they choose becomes one with their essence. As a Vaettir, they are wholly spiritual in nature. They can transform themselves into a corporeal Borghild in the rare times that they need to defend their dominion. However a Vaettir would prefer to relegate these responsibilities to a human steward who could then act as their executor in the physical world. In order to have a suitable arrangement with the human steward, the Vaettir will enter into a bond with this mortal (see page 288).

The great Vaettir that oversees the north eastern lands of Islandia is called Dreki. These lands are vast, mostly primal and uninhabited. An ancient Ulfhednar tribe along with wild animals of all sorts call this their home. From the great mountain ranges to the icy coasts, this land is filled with mystery and majesty. As Ragnarok has descended upon the land, the northern sea has become extensively covered by icebergs. Dreki has been calling this part of Midgard his home for many centuries. This spirit visually assumes the shape of a great dragon when in Borghild form. Within its kingdom lies the legendary Cornerstone of the World; the location where Yggdrasil's branch holds up Midgard. Dreki has also chosen to bond with a mortal steward of the land. His name is Ingvar (see Fafnir's Treasure) and he leads the nomadic wolf clan that has called this part of Midgard their home for many centuries.

Ingvar's partnership with Magnus has resulted in a deep mine encroaching into the Cornerstone of the World. This has angered Dreki. He has made his displeasure known, but Ingvar has chosen to ignore it, putting his clan's financial well-being ahead of the land and the Vaettir. Dreki has wanted to release Ingvar from the steward bond, but it cannot be done without the consent of both parties. In his frustration, Dreki has turned to Ivar the druid for help.

To make matters worse, some sort of pestilence has been recently released into the land by the miners. They unwittingly opened an aperture into Hvergelmir, allowing Nidhogg to cast his Serpent Sigil ritual on the unsuspecting humans. Dreki awoke and went to examine the foreign taint only to be ambushed by Nidhogg's most potent sorcery. As Dreki's senses darkened he realized that he was in a struggle for his very existence. Nidhogg cast a powerful curse upon Dreki, a ritual called the Great Gloom which involves summoning an aggressive and powerful wight sovereign to feast on Dreki's very essence. Since the assault began, Dreki has been unable to oversee his dominion and it has been steadily falling apart.

The mining has also caused a disparity at the Cornerstone of the World, allowing more alkas to appear. They are flooding Midgard with the essences from foreign realms. The great sinkhole (see Fafnir's Treasure) is a result of this imbalance.

Now the great Vaettir's fate rests in the hands of Ivar. Ivar knows what needs to be done, but lacks the heroes for the job.

Nidhogg

Level 70

This primeval serpent's origin is lost to historians and scholars, but one thing is certain, the second age of Ragnarok brings this great wyrm to the forefront of events in Midgard and beyond. Nidhogg is the undisputed lord of Hvergelmir. He presides over a writhing kingdom of countless serpents, wyrms and dragons. For centuries the gods and Jotuns have been able to contain and seal off Nidhogg and his host from the other beings upon the world tree. But his venomous spittle and pestilence has caused Yggdrasil's roots to rot, and the poison is spreading.

Nidhogg is an extremely mighty being. He desires respect and awe, neither of which has been afforded to him or his brood. The gods and Jotuns fear him, and would rather quarantine him than deal with his enormous ego. With the attention of the gods and Jotuns on one another, Nidhogg is making his play. He plans to impregnate each world with his snake sigil. It is an unimaginably potent ritual that with great stealth, impregnates other species with his seed. Once impregnated, the host loses all control and reason, and lives on to be a feast for the serpents they carry within.

Serpent Sigil: takes 24 hours to cast upon an unsuspecting foe (Perception [5] to detect). Once successfully impregnated, the victim gains the Curse condition with 4 intensity. A condition removal applied on the Curse by power or skill causes an Ultimate Sacrifice +5 to both the caster and the victim. Clearing this condition requires multiple castings as a casting may never reduce the condition by more than 1 intensity.

During the second age of Ragnarok, he has released this pestilence to the 9 worlds via the Cornerstone of the World. There are 4 seals that keep Hvergelmir closed-off, one in Asgard, Vanagard, Jotunheim, and Muspelheim. He commands his newly hatched brood to melt the seals with their acidic spittle. Nidhogg has help from Angraboda, but neither is aware that they are helping one another. Angraboda wishes to have the seals destroyed in order to release her beloved Loki who has been imprisoned within Hvergelmir.

If Nidhogg is free and can exert his might over all the worlds of Yggdrasil, it is hard to predict what his actions will be. If the Norns have sway over his fate, they are careful and do not reveal it.

ASGARD

VANAGARD

ALFGARD

NIFLHEIM

MIDGARD

MUSPELHEIM

HVERGELMIR

NIDAVELLIR

JOTUNHEIM

SVARTALFHEIM

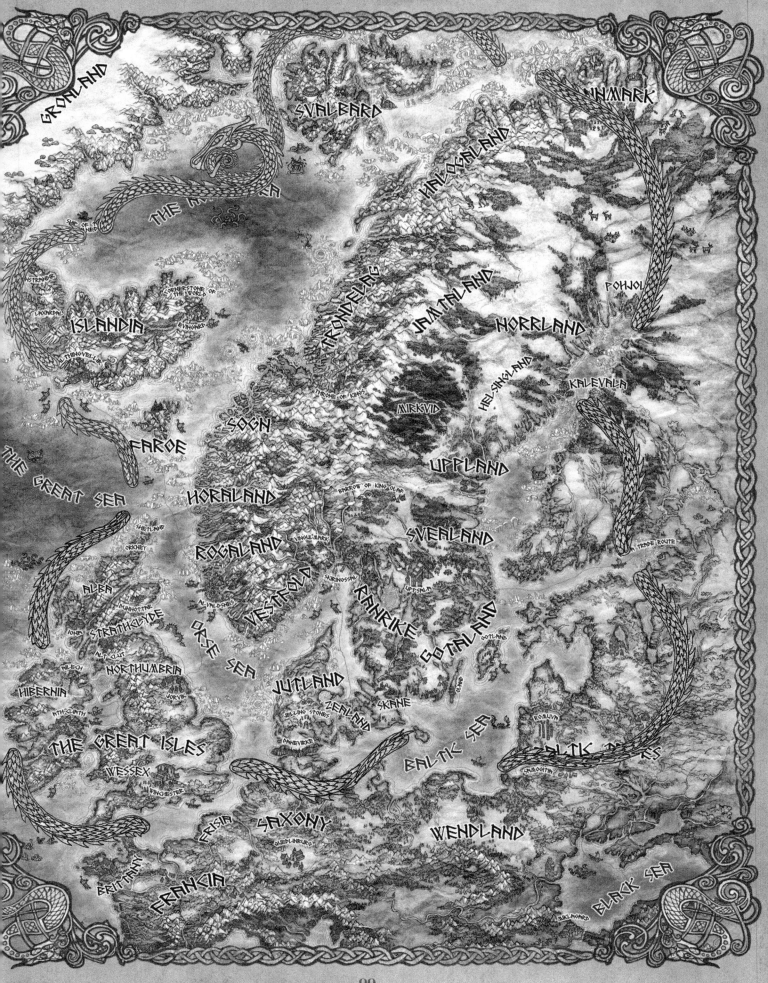

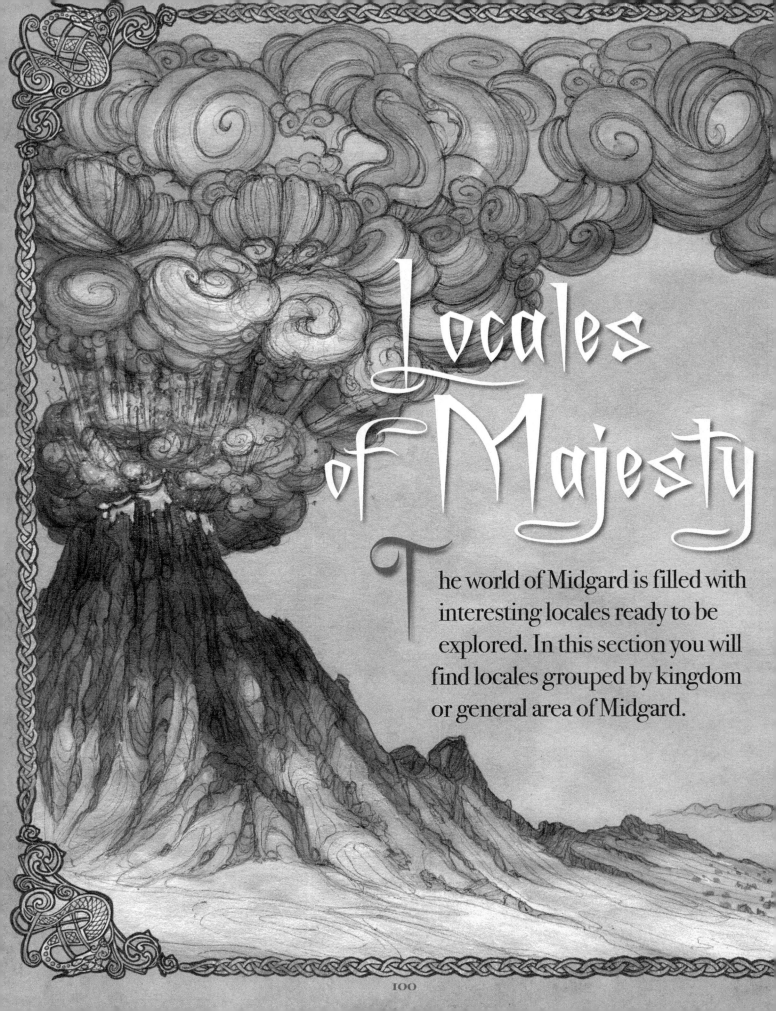

Locales of Majesty

The world of Midgard is filled with interesting locales ready to be explored. In this section you will find locales grouped by kingdom or general area of Midgard.

Islandia

Known as the island of ice and fire, it has become a popular destination for those who are fleeing the war for the crown. Its inhabitants are fiercely independent and zealously reject any settlers who wish to impose any form of monarchy on the island. Most of the settlements are on the western and southern portions of the island. The north is populated by those who are considered dangerous even by outlaws. The waters north of the island are littered with icebergs, allowing monstrosities from the north to make landfall.

Political Structure: Althing (equal representation)

Population: Tiny, Sparse

Economy: Lumber, Fishing and trade with the Skraelings

Major Hubs: Vatnsdal, Laxardal (north west), Reykjarvik, Borgarfjord (west), Drepstokk (south)

Althingvellir

Islandia is about to embark on a new form of social organization. Thorsteinn Ingolfsson has devised a central council that will manage all organizational matters and disputes. The purpose is to stay organized with laws, commerce and agreements. Independent chieftains and jarls have been invited to come together at Althingvellir, an hour trek east of Thorsteinn's fiefdom. The place was selected for its layout, allowing enough space for all those in attendance as well as offering a rather large rock outcrop to be used for speeches.

The plains that surround the rock outcrop could easily accommodate a large temporary encampment. Considering temporary structures such as tents, the Althing can be attended by thousands of visitors. Thorsteinn is inviting the leaders of their communities, but knows that any social gathering will inevitably attract merchants, skalds, spectators and other social elements.

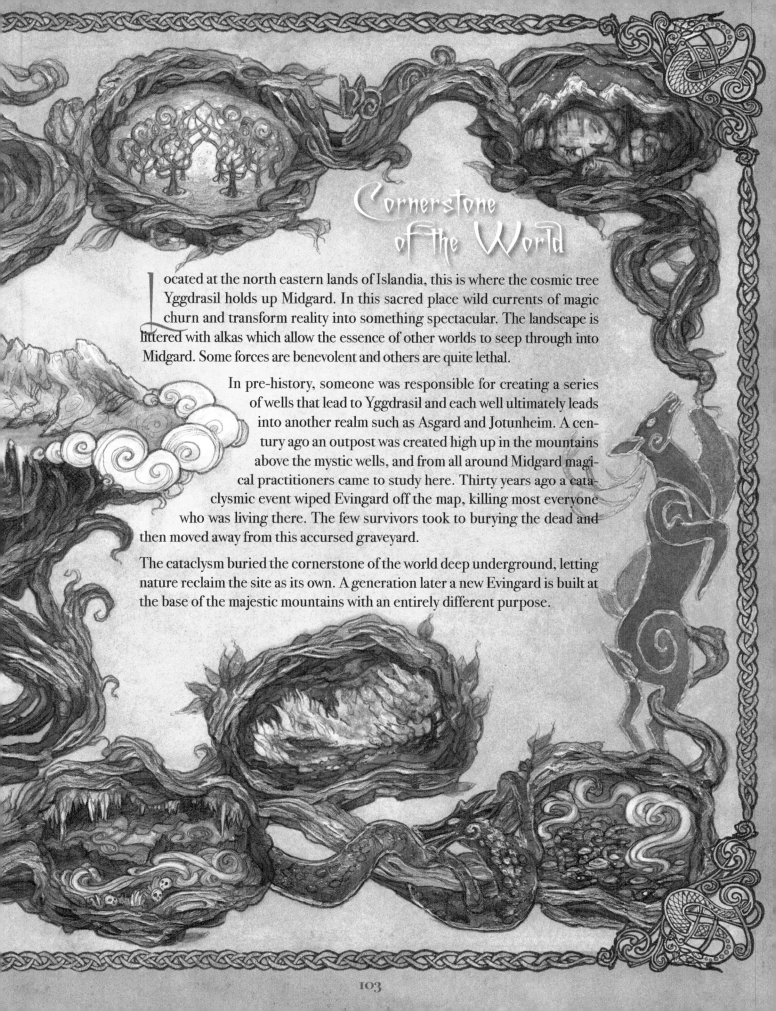

Cornerstone of the World

Located at the north eastern lands of Islandia, this is where the cosmic tree Yggdrasil holds up Midgard. In this sacred place wild currents of magic churn and transform reality into something spectacular. The landscape is littered with alkas which allow the essence of other worlds to seep through into Midgard. Some forces are benevolent and others are quite lethal.

In pre-history, someone was responsible for creating a series of wells that lead to Yggdrasil and each well ultimately leads into another realm such as Asgard and Jotunheim. A century ago an outpost was created high up in the mountains above the mystic wells, and from all around Midgard magical practitioners came to study here. Thirty years ago a cataclysmic event wiped Evingard off the map, killing most everyone who was living there. The few survivors took to burying the dead and then moved away from this accursed graveyard.

The cataclysm buried the cornerstone of the world deep underground, letting nature reclaim the site as its own. A generation later a new Evingard is built at the base of the majestic mountains with an entirely different purpose.

Evingard

The new Evingard came about as a result of prospectors finding huge deposits of wondrous ore in the region. Their claims were for naught as a wild tribe of Ulfhednar refuse to grant access to their ancestral lands without a proper tribute. Among those merchants was one named Magnus Magnusson. He differentiated himself from the others by not only offering the biggest initial tribute, but he also promised the clan a third of the profits. Such a generous offer landed Magnus an exclusivity agreement with the Ulfhednar. Ingvar the chieftain ensured that his clan would live well and had his people help build the new Evingard.

It started out humbly with only a few permanent structures, but quickly grew as Magnus imported hundreds of slaves to work the mines. Blacksmiths came to sell their wares, hunters came to feed the population and very quickly an entire local economy sprung up. Officially Ingvar is in charge, but most know that the real power comes from Magnus who prefers to leave the issues of the town to Ingvar.

Hornstrandir

Hornstrandir is the northern most peninsula on Islandia. It is overseen by the Great Eagle Vaettir and has become home to the island's more undesirable characters. Those who have committed murder and have no desire to integrate into society have made their homes in this part of the outlaw island. The most notorious is Erik Thorvaldsson whose father fled Norveig for mass murder. Erik is known as Erik "the Red" for the trail of corpses that are attributed to him... and he is but a young man.

In the last two years the ocean has frozen to the point of blocking off any naval access to the peninsula. The icebergs are so tightly packed that one can trek hours north without finding sea water. It is said that those who seek the best assassins should come here, but beware as some have never left this unsavoury den of vipers.

Baltic Amber Tribes

The Baltic tribes are a collection of barbarian tribes that live to the far reaches of eastern Midgard. There are many, but the most notable ones are the Samogitians, Selonioans, Curonians, Yotvingians, Nadraviansand Skalvians. The kingdoms of Midgard have traditionally looked at these tribes with mixed emotion. Trade with them has always been difficult, and raiding has always been risky. To begin with, their Aestii language is hard to comprehend and they have a strong distaste for dealing with outsiders. Since they are always at war with one another, their warriors are battle-hardened and raids come at a very high cost. The most revered warriors are those who have perfected horseback combat techniques.

These tribes, however, are wealthy; between the amber they collected from the Baltic, their prized horses and the fertile farm lands they maintained, the barbarians had no need to raid beyond their borders. However with Fimbulwinter ravaging their lands, the tribes set their sights on all within reach. They have struck out into the Baltic sea, attacking passing merchant vessels with impunity. The barbarian horde is rising!

Political Structure: Tribal (obfuscated social hierarchy)

Population: Large, dense

Economy: war/raiding, hunting/fishing, handicraft and trade with the Baltic kingdoms

Major Hubs: Samogitians, Selonioans, Curonians, Yotvingians, Nadraviansand Skalvians, Romuva Shrine

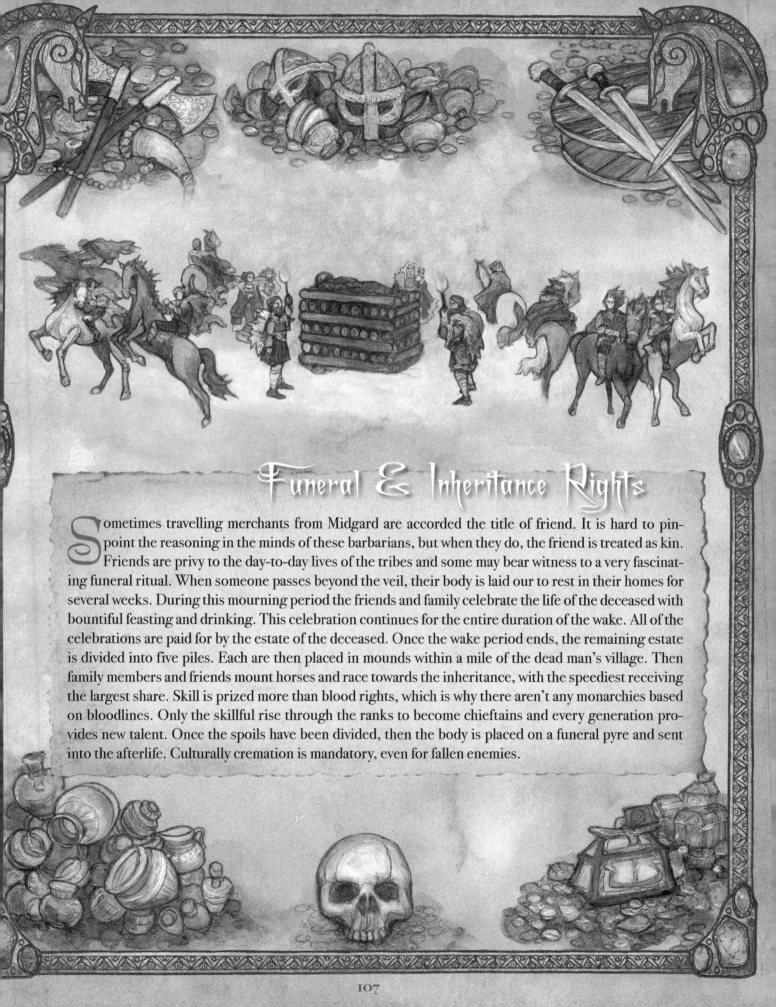

Funeral & Inheritance Rights

Sometimes travelling merchants from Midgard are accorded the title of friend. It is hard to pinpoint the reasoning in the minds of these barbarians, but when they do, the friend is treated as kin. Friends are privy to the day-to-day lives of the tribes and some may bear witness to a very fascinating funeral ritual. When someone passes beyond the veil, their body is laid our to rest in their homes for several weeks. During this mourning period the friends and family celebrate the life of the deceased with bountiful feasting and drinking. This celebration continues for the entire duration of the wake. All of the celebrations are paid for by the estate of the deceased. Once the wake period ends, the remaining estate is divided into five piles. Each are then placed in mounds within a mile of the dead man's village. Then family members and friends mount horses and race towards the inheritance, with the speediest receiving the largest share. Skill is prized more than blood rights, which is why there aren't any monarchies based on bloodlines. Only the skillful rise through the ranks to become chieftains and every generation provides new talent. Once the spoils have been divided, then the body is placed on a funeral pyre and sent into the afterlife. Culturally cremation is mandatory, even for fallen enemies.

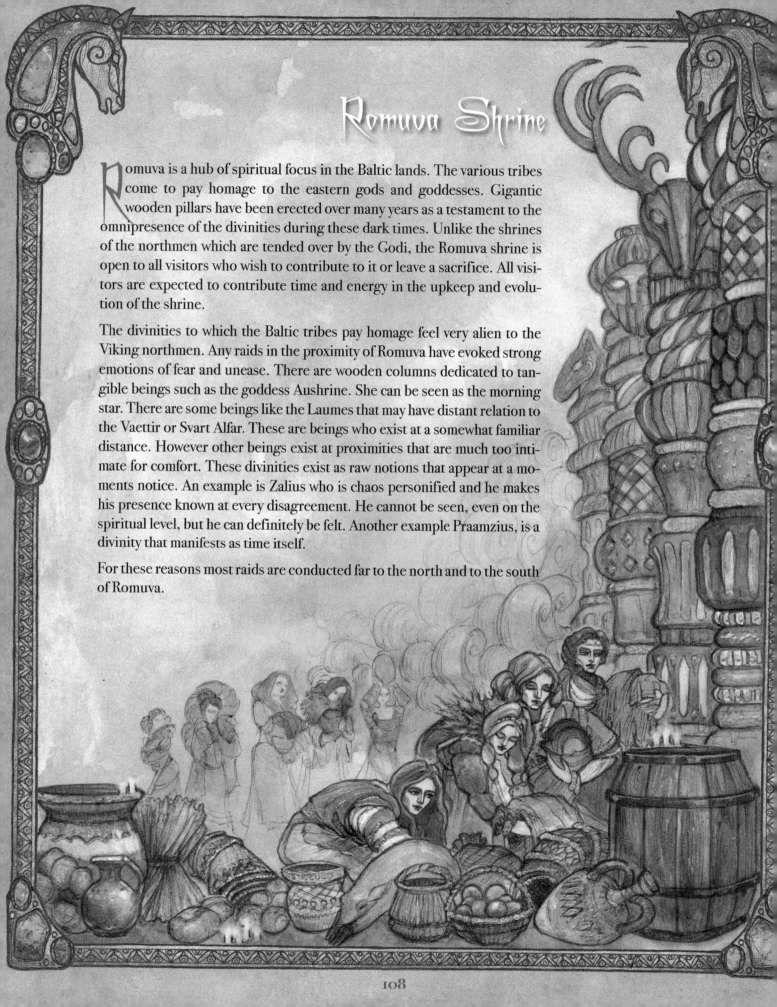

Romuva Shrine

Romuva is a hub of spiritual focus in the Baltic lands. The various tribes come to pay homage to the eastern gods and goddesses. Gigantic wooden pillars have been erected over many years as a testament to the omnipresence of the divinities during these dark times. Unlike the shrines of the northmen which are tended over by the Godi, the Romuva shrine is open to all visitors who wish to contribute to it or leave a sacrifice. All visitors are expected to contribute time and energy in the upkeep and evolution of the shrine.

The divinities to which the Baltic tribes pay homage feel very alien to the Viking northmen. Any raids in the proximity of Romuva have evoked strong emotions of fear and unease. There are wooden columns dedicated to tangible beings such as the goddess Aushrine. She can be seen as the morning star. There are some beings like the Laumes that may have distant relation to the Vaettir or Svart Alfar. These are beings who exist at a somewhat familiar distance. However other beings exist at proximities that are much too intimate for comfort. These divinities exist as raw notions that appear at a moments notice. An example is Zalius who is chaos personified and he makes his presence known at every disagreement. He cannot be seen, even on the spiritual level, but he can definitely be felt. Another example Praamzius, is a divinity that manifests as time itself.

For these reasons most raids are conducted far to the north and to the south of Romuva.

Samogitia

A tremendously stubborn people, the Samogitians trade in amber, horses and gold. Samogitians are one of the central Baltic tribes. Primitive and wild, they are tremendously xenophobic and fierce. They insist on their own language and missionaries have had no success in these lands. Even without walls or fortifications, they repeatedly defeated the efforts of Duke Mieszko's armies to bring the White God to their threshold. Their nature gods known as Laumes are as ancient as their traditions and stories. These gods are venerated atop decorated enchanted poles that house a small shrine dedicated to a particular deity. It is said that they project powerful blessings and are highly valued by the tribes.

After failing to move north through Samogitia and unable to penetrate the Danevirke, the crusaders took to the seas and managed to get a foot hold into Midgard via Wessex on the Great Isles.

Midgard, Central

Known Central Midgard is the cradle of civilization. It is said that over one thousand years ago the Aesir gods themselves ruled these lands before migrating to Asgard. Skalds tell tales of how mankind sprung up on the western shores of these lands. For these reasons, even though these lands lie to the east, it is referred to as central Midgard. It encompasses the kingdoms of Halogaland down to Gotaland. The great kingdom of Norveig consolidated all of central Midgard, making it the largest kingdom in all of history. Since the onset of Fimbulwinter, the great kingdom has started to splinter as the late king Harald's sons wage war for the throne.

Central Midgard contains the high seat of power in the city of Avaldsnes. Situated in Rogaland, it is one of the most bountiful fishing grounds in all of Midgard. Jarl Erik Blood Axe currently rules from here and King Aethelstan has set his sights on this strategic city. He believes that taking it will force all of the surrounding lands to bend knee. However as King Harald learned early in his reign, sitting in the seat of power does not obligate fealty. He was forced to contantly tour his kingdom in order to foster loyalty and obedience. Jarl Erik Blood Axe knows this all too well, resigning Avaldsnes to being nothing more than a symbol and an occasional retreat.

Political Structure: Kingdoms

Population: Large, dense

Economy: Trade, hunting/fishing, slaves, raids/war, handicraft

Major Hubs: Halogaland, Trondelag, Sogn, Hordaland, Rogaland, Jaeder, Agdir, Vestfold, Ranrike, Gotaland

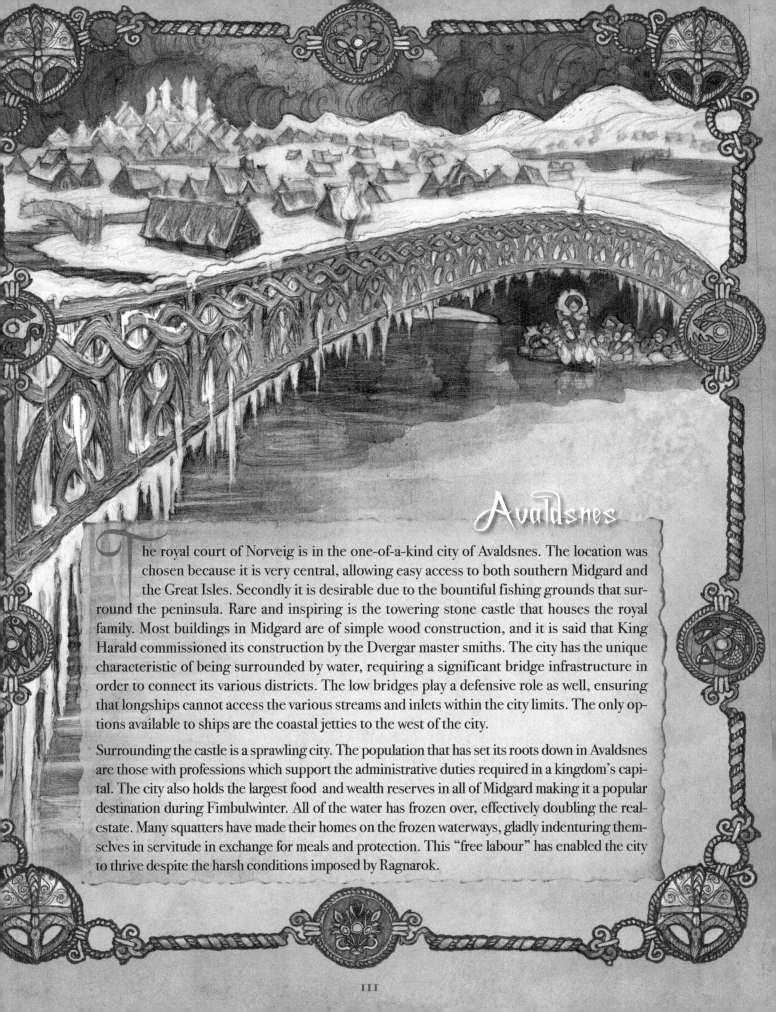

Avaldsnes

The royal court of Norveig is in the one-of-a-kind city of Avaldsnes. The location was chosen because it is very central, allowing easy access to both southern Midgard and the Great Isles. Secondly it is desirable due to the bountiful fishing grounds that surround the peninsula. Rare and inspiring is the towering stone castle that houses the royal family. Most buildings in Midgard are of simple wood construction, and it is said that King Harald commissioned its construction by the Dvergar master smiths. The city has the unique characteristic of being surrounded by water, requiring a significant bridge infrastructure in order to connect its various districts. The low bridges play a defensive role as well, ensuring that longships cannot access the various streams and inlets within the city limits. The only options available to ships are the coastal jetties to the west of the city.

Surrounding the castle is a sprawling city. The population that has set its roots down in Avaldsnes are those with professions which support the administrative duties required in a kingdom's capital. The city also holds the largest food and wealth reserves in all of Midgard making it a popular destination during Fimbulwinter. All of the water has frozen over, effectively doubling the real-estate. Many squatters have made their homes on the frozen waterways, gladly indenturing themselves in servitude in exchange for meals and protection. This "free labour" has enabled the city to thrive despite the harsh conditions imposed by Ragnarok.

Barrow of King Olaf Geirstad

King Olaf was half-brother to Halfdan the Black, making the late King Harald Fairhair his nephew. Being a king belonging to the Yngling dynasty ensured an enshrined ruling legacy- and he had a great one ruling Ranrike! His subjects remember him very fondly as a king who brought unbridled prosperity to everyone in his kingdom. Low-born or high-born, it didn't matter, everyone had unbelievable prosperity during his reign. He was also of very positive disposition, and it took much to sour his mood.

Many suspected that Olaf was half Alfar. His childhood friends suspected Olaf's father Gudrod the Hunter of laying with an Alfar named Alfhild, daughter of the illustrious Alfarin. That would be the only way to explain such marvellous fortune. In his later years, many subjects tried to worship him, but he strictly forbade it- such talk would be a sure way to incur his anger. At the time of his death, he was easily the most loved monarch in all of Midgard. He was entered in a magnificent barrow which contained a full sized longship along with his slaves and prized possessions. Among those possessions were his magical sword Besingr, an enchanted ring and a rune carved iron plated belt.

However unlike his Yngling brethren, Olaf left an even greater legacy after his death. Hard times fell upon the kingdom as it was on the fringes of King Harald's Norveig, so it saw a lot of war and tragedy. Some subjects went to visit his barrow in order to plead for better fortune, and to their surprise it started to work. Word spread and soon his barrow became a pilgrimage site.

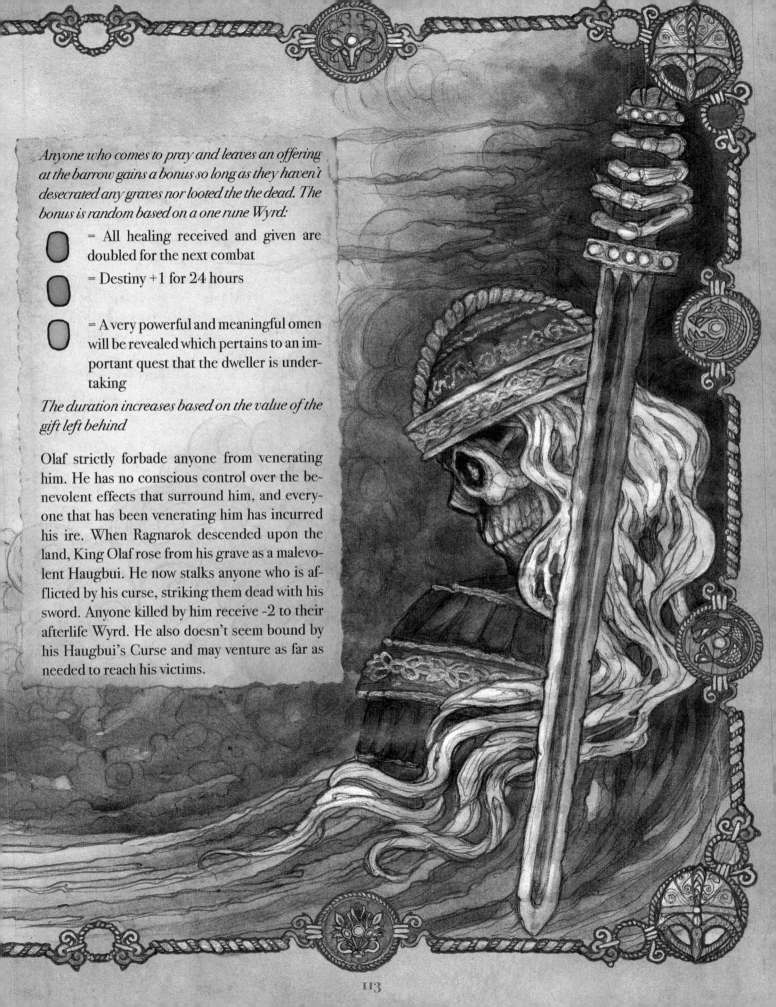

Anyone who comes to pray and leaves an offering at the barrow gains a bonus so long as they haven't desecrated any graves nor looted the the dead. The bonus is random based on a one rune Wyrd:

= All healing received and given are doubled for the next combat

= Destiny +1 for 24 hours

= A very powerful and meaningful omen will be revealed which pertains to an important quest that the dweller is undertaking

The duration increases based on the value of the gift left behind

Olaf strictly forbade anyone from venerating him. He has no conscious control over the benevolent effects that surround him, and everyone that has been venerating him has incurred his ire. When Ragnarok descended upon the land, King Olaf rose from his grave as a malevolent Haugbui. He now stalks anyone who is afflicted by his curse, striking them dead with his sword. Anyone killed by him receive -2 to their afterlife Wyrd. He also doesn't seem bound by his Haugbui's Curse and may venture as far as needed to reach his victims.

Trondheim's Shrine of Kings

Much like the Cornerstone of the World, powerful rivers of unseen magical energy course through this majestic fjord. Prior to Ragnarok, the lands to the south of this fjord were legendary for agriculture. It is said that the Vaettir and Alfar played in the winds that blow through this valley. Many children who were born in the area have grown up to be great men who performed legendary deeds. The first king of Norveig, Harald Fairhair was born in these lands and was coronated at the shrine at the head of the fjord. Erik Bloodaxe plans to follow in his father's

footsteps and be coronated there as well. The coronation, however, will have to wait until he finishes dispatching all of the other contenders for the throne.

The shrine is atop a tall stone cliff, and on this mesa is a throne carved into the stone. Twin waterfalls frame the throne and vegetation that has remaining verdant despite Fimbulwinter surrounds the shrine. It is said that only those with a benevolent and fair heart may gain the benefits of a coronation at this shrine. There are old local folk tales of the Vaettir chasing fraudulent jarls from the mountain shrine. In the darkness of the Second Age, there are very few who have the light within their heart to qualify for such a noble coronation.

Uppsala Shrine

Uppsala was a world renowned shrine dedicated to Thor, Odin and Frey. Over 1000 years ago, Frey descended from Vanagard and founded the shrine. He ensured that the surrounding land would know prosperity and peace. He placed his son Fjolnir as the first Godi of Uppsala. The shrine was situated a horse ride away from the small pilgrim town of Sigtuna and the small town grew immensely every nine years when a holy feast was organized by the local Godi. The shrine had two main sections. The first was a massive hall that housed three twenty foot tall statues made out of the wood of a sacred ash tree. The second was an outdoor grove that had many sacred ash trees which were consecrated to Yggdrasil. At the center of the grove was a great ancient ash that would miraculously remain green even throughout winter.

Before the onset of Ragnarok, the grove would be the site of a yearly blot at the spring equinox, where nine thralls would be hung as an offering to the Aesir gods. Now two years into Fimbulwinter, the trees are littered with hundreds of hanging corpses both human and animal in various states of decay. Many in Midgard feel that they have been abandoned by the gods and have gone out with great zeal in order to provide blood sacrifices to have their pleas heard.

Now only silence and the stench of death permeate this abandoned temple. Everything has been carried away by thieves and a populace in desperationÖ even the gold statue inlays have been stripped away from the icons of the gods themselves. The magic has gone out of this shrine, as even the evergreen ash has been cut down and hauled away. It is said that blacksmiths have purchased the sacred wood and transformed it into several magical artifacts.

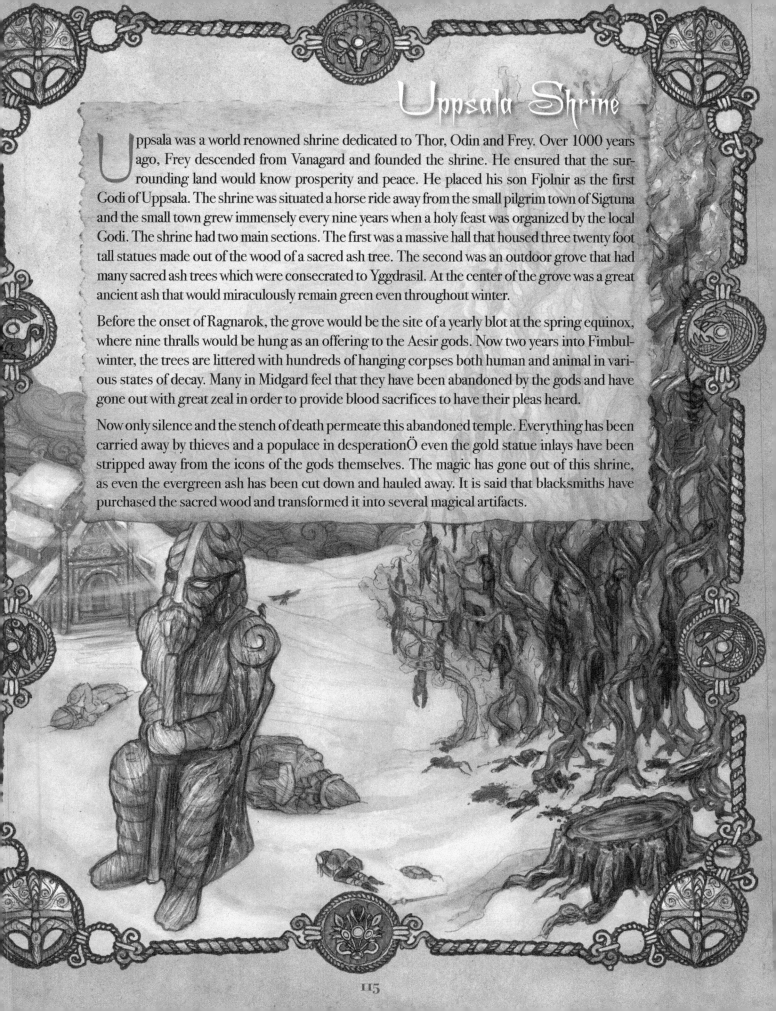

Midgard, Southern

Southern Midgard is composed of the belt-way kingdoms that press up against Outer-Midgard. Since the great exodus that created the outer world, the southern kingdoms have never known peace. Whether from attempting to seize better lands by force or defending against religious zealots, everyone in the southern kingdoms have become battle-hardened, reforged in the fires of war. The southern kingdoms also boast the most merchants per capita since all naval trade routes which connect west and east pass through the straights of Zealand.

Before the construction of the great Danevirke, the peoples of the south were forced into exile for a time. Invasions from the south forced the southerners to retreat and re-settle in the Great Isles. The generation that lived in the Great Isles were desperate and aggressive, carving out a new kingdom and imposing a taxation on the natives they defeated. Even after their later departure, this left an indelible stamp of their culture behind.

Being of strong will, they returned to their ancestral lands with a vengeance. After reclaiming their territorial integrity, they build a wall of unimaginable length and height. The new kings sank much of their wealth in forging an unbeatable navy, vowing that they would never again face exile.

Political Structure: Kingdoms

Population: Large, sparse

Economy: Trade, hunting/fishing, slaves, raids/war, handicraft

Major Hubs: Skane, Jutland, Zealand, Smaland, Oland

Danevirke

The threat from the southern kingdoms has been a painful reality since long before Ragnarok. The southern Jarls banded together and built an awe-inspiring wall that spanned from the west coast all the way to the east coast of Jutland. During the wall's initial construction its lowest point was thirty feet tall, but since then the wall has doubled in height with the onset of Fimbulwinter. In many places the wall is dozens of feet thick, with soldier barracks built right into the structure. The few gates that exist are heavily trapped and guarded. Very little wood is used in the construction to ensure that it remains resilient against fire. The top of the wall is wide enough to act as a walkway, allowing guards to patrol the length of the structure. At regular intervals fiery brazers have been set up to provide warmth and light. Other larger brazers remain unlit unless the wall is under attack. When lit, they rally the defenders around the possible breach.

King Gorm's castle is built up against the wall, like a Jotun's finger it protrudes one hundred feet into the night sky. The cunning king purposely never finished the castle, leaving it with the appearance of a work-in-progress. The wall in this section also looks rough and filled with patchwork masonry. When he receives foreign royalty and dignitaries, the decrepit appearance facilitates his requests for funds and donations in order to keep Midgard secure from the marauders in the south. His wealth is hidden away in the vast dungeon complexes beneath the castle.

Jelling Stones

orm the Old has discovered the rituals required to create stone monoliths that attract the very powerful Wight Sovereigns. These stones were erected in an abandoned village of Jelling and act as a beacon and desirable dwelling for these elite spirits. The Jelling stones are near a stone long ship which Gorm is using for sacrifice. The stone ship burial is a perversion of the standard wood ship cremation that normally assists the soul in its ascension to the afterlife. The intent of the stone ship is to allow the Wight direct access to the body and soul of the victim involved in the blot. The Wights that reside in Jelling have come to an agreement with Gorm that as long as he provides suitable souls, they will use their might to help protect the Danevirke.

The cost that the Wight Sovereigns exact from Gorm is increasingly steep. Jelling used to have a population, but he has sacrificed everyone in order to fulfill his sworn obligation. The village is now a death trap for anyone who enters.

Mounds of Skane

In the southern reaches of Skane, these ancient mounds reach a staggering 80' towards the sky. The locals call the site haunted and say that it is either a burial mound for Jotuns, ancient soulless kings, or a city for the Alfar or Dvergar. Few venture near these hills for fear of contracting some curse. There are local tales of people going mad after travelling the hills at night and witnessing things mortals should never have laid eyes on.

With the onset of Ragnarok, people have moved away, leaving this area to the ghosts who haunt them.

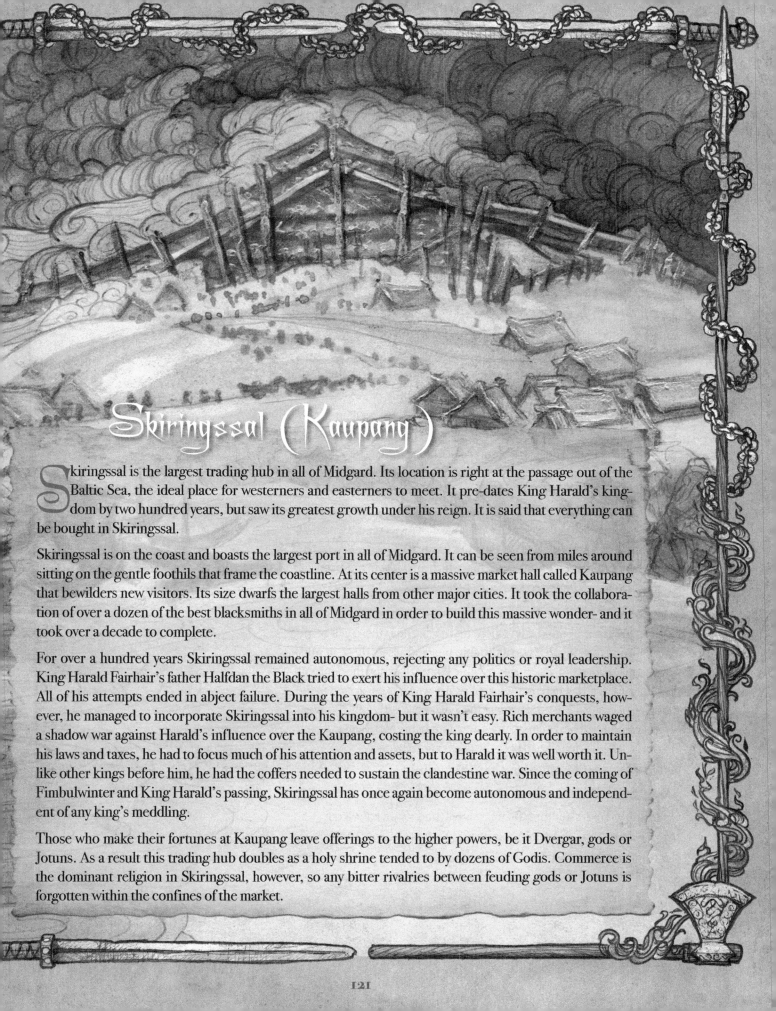

Skiringssal (Kaupang)

Skiringssal is the largest trading hub in all of Midgard. Its location is right at the passage out of the Baltic Sea, the ideal place for westerners and easterners to meet. It pre-dates King Harald's kingdom by two hundred years, but saw its greatest growth under his reign. It is said that everything can be bought in Skiringssal.

Skiringssal is on the coast and boasts the largest port in all of Midgard. It can be seen from miles around sitting on the gentle foothils that frame the coastline. At its center is a massive market hall called Kaupang that bewilders new visitors. Its size dwarfs the largest halls from other major cities. It took the collaboration of over a dozen of the best blacksmiths in all of Midgard in order to build this massive wonder- and it took over a decade to complete.

For over a hundred years Skiringssal remained autonomous, rejecting any politics or royal leadership. King Harald Fairhair's father Halfdan the Black tried to exert his influence over this historic marketplace. All of his attempts ended in abject failure. During the years of King Harald Fairhair's conquests, however, he managed to incorporate Skiringssal into his kingdom- but it wasn't easy. Rich merchants waged a shadow war against Harald's influence over the Kaupang, costing the king dearly. In order to maintain his laws and taxes, he had to focus much of his attention and assets, but to Harald it was well worth it. Unlike other kings before him, he had the coffers needed to sustain the clandestine war. Since the coming of Fimbulwinter and King Harald's passing, Skiringssal has once again become autonomous and independent of any king's meddling.

Those who make their fortunes at Kaupang leave offerings to the higher powers, be it Dvergar, gods or Jotuns. As a result this trading hub doubles as a holy shrine tended to by dozens of Godis. Commerce is the dominant religion in Skiringssal, however, so any bitter rivalries between feuding gods or Jotuns is forgotten within the confines of the market.

Midgard, Eastern

I t is said that this part of Midgard was once inhabited by the Vanir gods, specifically the Baltic sea. This is purely speculative, however, as mankind did not exist before the coming of the Aesir gods, and the Vanir gods predate the Aesir. Eastern Midgard contains many types of peoples, cultures and varying methods of social organization. The northern lands are sparsely populated and revolve around tribes. The further south one travels, the denser the population and the richer the land. Monarchies are quite common in the southernmost reaches. Prior to Fimbulwinter, the rich farmland surrounding the Baltic sea was the envy of the realm. Farming made up most of the economy and now the kingdoms can boast some of the most bountiful food reserves. The reserves contain dried grains and fruits which attract refugees who are eager to exchange their freedoms for a regular meal.

The one thing everyone shares and values is the Baltic sea. Riches from fishing and trade abound, and where there is fortune there will be piracy. Fortunately the prowess of the ship builders allows those in Midgard to maintain naval superiority over the Baltic tribes and the denizens of Outer-Midgard. There is a sense of rivalry which is enshrined in the peoples of eastern Midgard against those who live within the boundaries of central Midgard. Many battles were fought prior to Ragnarok, but Fimbulwinter has multiplied both the danger and violence.

Political Structure: Kingdoms, fiefdoms, tribal

Population: Medium, sparse

Economy: Trade, hunting/fishing, slaves, raids/war, handicraft

Major Hubs: Gotaland, Gotland, Svealand, Uppland, Hunaland, Helsingland, Jamtland, Norrland, Finnmark

Gotland

Among the thousands of islands in the Baltic Sea, the largest is Gotland. It is a very strategic island for both trade and warfare containing forests, groves, hills, inlets and coves. There are no permanent residents on this island. Most arrive for a short time to trade their wares and move on. Others use the island as a meet-up point before raiding the barbarian lands to the east. Should someone go about exploring on the island, they will find buried beneath the Fimbulwinter snow stone monoliths set about in wide circles. If they were to dig down deep enough into the ice and snow they would find blood stained stone ships.

What few understand is that Gotland is home to an evil that has been lying in wait. Anyone unfortunate enough to find themselves near the stones may never be heard from again as this evil hungers. Within the monoliths are several very hungry and malicious Wight Sovereigns. No one has offered them a blot so they feast on any souls they can catch. This partially explains why no one has successfully set up a permanent village on this damned island.

The most voracious Wight Sovereign is none other than King Siggeir. Ever since he fell to the blades of the Volsung, he has stalked this island with an unquenchable blood frenzy. Using the island's more hazardous landscape, he lures unsuspecting travellers to what would appear as an innocent accident of nature. Those that die are set upon and have little time before their souls are consumed and eradicated. Should a Valkyrie find a soul worthy of retrieval, she would have to confront the wights as they wouldn't give up the body without a fight.

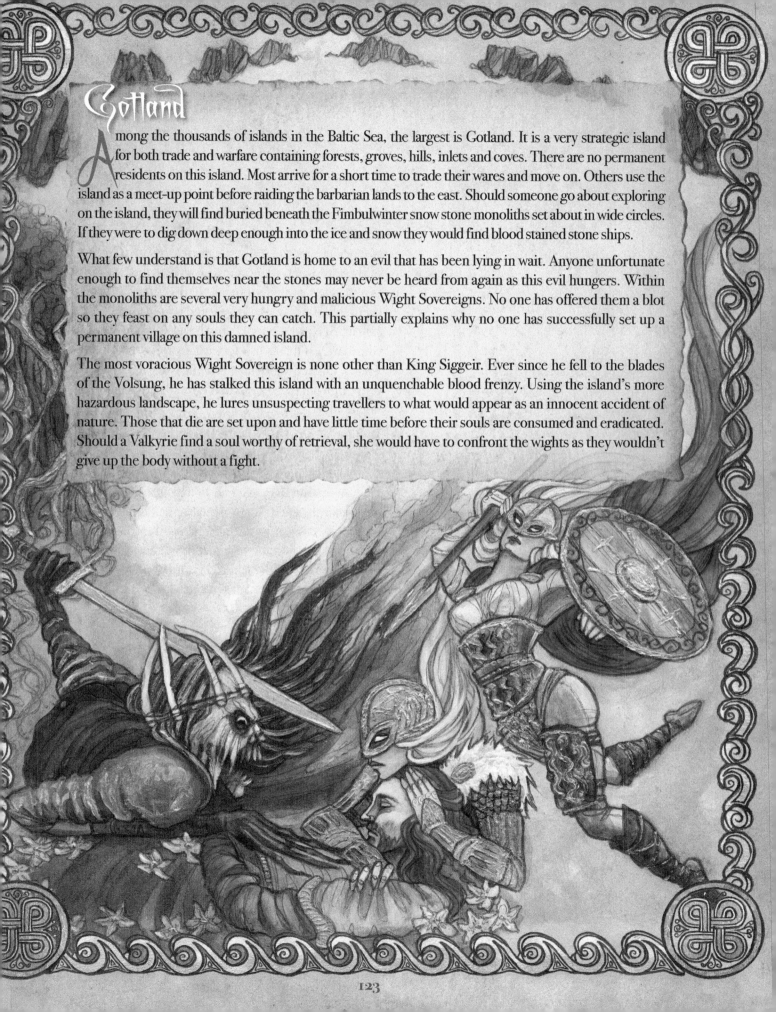

Myrkvid

Myrkvid is the legendary dark forest in the mountainous kingdom of Jamtaland. Some say that the forest is an extension of Svartalfheim, with those who venture in rarely returning. Adding to the mystique are rumours of survivors returning stark mad, raving and babbling incoherently. The hunters and trappers who live on the fringes of the forest never track any prey that runs within the shadows of this arboreal blight. It is said that even a few paces in, the largest and noisiest prey will vanish. Skalds recount tales of renegade Valkyries who have established a fortress in these haunted woods. Legend states that even the gods and Jotuns cannot pierce the shroud that envelops this hidden kingdom.

Within Myrkvid there is a misty lake on whose shores reside two Orlogs. In their thirst for deeper occult knowledge they perform many alchemical rituals attempting to create new lifeforms. On the eve of Ragnarok, one of these rituals created a twenty foot monstrosity within their giant cauldron. The foul beast cracked the iron cauldron and slithered into the waters of the lake. The Orlog sisters only caught a glimpse of a giant serpent with a cat's head.

Kalevala

Kalevala is situated on the eastern shore of the Baltic Sea. It is a small kingdom filled with rich soil, green forests and verdant valleys. Even Ragnarok has been unable to shake the economy in this part of the world as the bountiful wood from the forests is always a hot commodity. The lumberjack trade has been booming since darkness fell over the land. The natural riches are bolstered by a high concentration of land vaettirs in the area. Many of those who are born here are naturally imbued with magical talents. The people and the spirits who inhabit the land share a very close symbiosis.

Pohjola

Pohjola is a tiny kingdom at the northernmost bay of the Baltic Sea. It was founded by a renegade fleeing her homeland of Kalevala. It begins at a frothing stony coast and extends into a rocky shore and permafrost hills. There is a mountain called Sariola which has an extensive network of ancient caves rich in copper deposits. This kingdom struggled for most of its existence, making the citizens very tough and headstrong. Unlike the nomad tribes of Norrland, the people of Pohjola have set down their roots.

Great Isles

The great isles are located near the center of Midgard. They are composed of the island of Hibernia to the west, and the larger isle to the east is home to many kingdoms: Alba, Strathclyde, Northumbria, York, Wessex and East Anglia. Before the coming of Ragnarok, the forces of the White God had been blocked from northern expansion by both the Daenvike and the ferocity of the Baltic barbarian tribes. Revising their invasion plans, they decided to attack Midgard over the sea, making inroads in the eastern great isle. Otto the Great tasked King Aethelstan with the western naval invasion. Many of the northern kingdoms have been held for a time by house Ivar. However until Jarl Sitric went on his westward rampage, none of the land acquisitions had been cemented for longevity. Jarl Sitric and his cousins now exact the Danegeld on the northern kingdoms. The Danegeld is a tax levied on the occupied population and those who wish to maintain autonomy.

The fate of Midgard hangs in the balance, as an unstoppable Aethelstan means a complete obliteration of the old ways for the populace.

Political Structure: Kingdoms, fiefdoms, clans

Population: Medium, dense

Economy: Trade, hunting/fishing, slaves, raids/war, handicraft

Major Hubs: Hibernia, Alba, Wessex, Northumbria, Mercia, East Anglia, Strathclyde.

It is said that the great city of Winchester was built by the Roman giants a thousand years ago. The remnants of their awesome stonework remains in the old city. The crumbling stone buildings and sky bridges evoke a sense of mystery and awe. Many avoid the district saying that ancient ghosts haunt those cobbled streets. As a result, for hundreds of years vegetation has encroached unchallenged upon the abandoned region. Over a few centuries a new town has been built on the western bank. The location of the town on the river Itchen has allowed merchants from Brittany and Francia easy access into the markets of the Great Isles. The sizable trade has contributed to the growth of the town into a sprawling city.

King Aethelstan has made Winchester his seat of power within the Great Isles. From there he organizes his northward campaign in the hopes of conquering all of Midgard. His reinforcements from Outer-Midgard travel up the Itchen river and land in the capital, making it a veritable military stronghold. The inherent security further fosters immigration, to the point where there is no more room within Winchester's walls. The population has sprawled outside the city walls for as far as the eye can see. The most powerful Jarls of Midgard see this as a threat that needs to be dealt with sooner rather than later.

On the large island of Hibernia, the city of Ath Cliath has been a hub of trade and commerce for hundreds of years. It is the seat of power for the surrounding lands of Dyflin. Ath Cliath's location on the Liffey river bank a few miles inland has provided good protection against naval raids. The city has perimeter fortifications that keep it secure from land-based attacks. However the reigning monarch Niall Glundub did not anticipate Sitric's Viking raiding ships to be able to navigate the shallow Liffey river. The battle was brutal, and hours later a new king was crowned.

Since the onset of Ragnarok many have flocked to this city's walls for food and shelter. Jarl Sitric of House Ivar gladly let everyone into the city. This was a shrewd tactic which precipitated Ath Cliath becoming the slave capital of Midgard. Sitric put out the word to all new warlords that slave labour could be found within his walls at a cheap rate. Those refugees that had money could keep their freedom, but security within Ath Cliath would be costly. Sitric deployed many tax collectors to ensure that all goods and services would be heavily taxed.

Selling slaves and heavy taxation of the desperate refugees made Sitric a very rich king. This allowed him to buy the services of capable mercenaries who would not only guard his city, but also went on raids to get him more slaves. Everything in Ath Cliath was taxed at 100% effectively doubling all prices. Despite this, Ath Cliath attracted all sorts of persons, as anything you desired could be found within the city walls.

Hibernia

Hibernia has a long and rich history filled tales of war and magic. Bards recount the creation of the Emerald Isle when the Fomorians drew it out from the sea. It was a poisoned land on which only the ancient race could survive. This did not stop Nemed, his children, or his grandchildren from invading the land and attempting to conquer it for their own. Today, Hibernia's elder clans make boastful claims about their blood running deep with Nemed's blood.

Hibernia is the home to over two dozen fiefdoms controlled by various clans. The most valuable land in Hibernia is in the east, in a fiefdom called Dyflin. The main city is called Ath Cliath and before Fimbulwinter, the city was known for the great wealth it derived from animal husbandry and farming. With the coming of the great white death, clansmen converged on Ath Cliath in hopes of overrunning the foreign king. He offered them refuge, food and warmth, if they lay down their arms. Like lambs, they entered into a shadowy arrangement with their new shepherd.

The clans who heard about the slavery chose to stay away. However life is hard as clans turn on each other in search of resources required to survive. From his seat of power in Ailech, Muirchertach mac Neill is working hard to unite the clans against King Sitric.

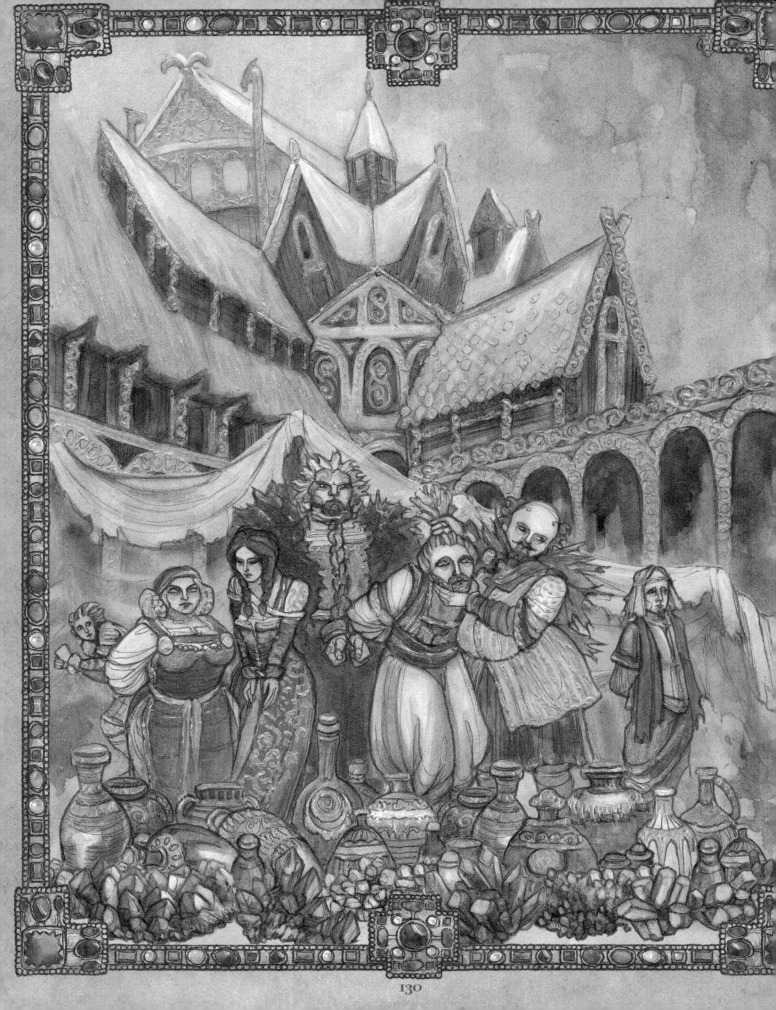

Fabled Markets of Ath Cliath

A th Cliath has become the largest trading hub in all of Western Midgard. Since King Sitric has come to power, he has used his influence to drive all trade through this hub. He taxes all commerce here, allowing him to gather unprecedented wealth. However he also looks out for Ath Cliath's residents ensuring that no competition could spoil this merchant oasis.

The largest portion of the economy within Ath Cliath is the slave trade. Foreigners that are captured in raids in outer Midgard fetch very good prices in the open air markets. Since the onset of Ragnarok, even northern slaves from Midgard can be found in the black markets in the underbelly of Ath Cliath. The amount of money that exchanges hands in the black markets is tenfold that of the regular markets. In order to facilitate vast sums, a new currency has been introduced based on gold rods rather than silver skatt. Each rod is worth 10,000 skatt and it is subdivided into 10 sections making it easy to snap off pieces worth 1,000 skatt.

There are many secretive markets operating in Ath Cliath. Some operate behind the veneer of legitimate guilds. One of the more lucrative ones is run by a Dvergar named Svalms. He runs a trade in exotic ores and wondrous items behind the front of Ath Cliath's blacksmith's guild. His undercover business is cheekily referred to as the Whitesmith's guild. Unlike common items that carry value into hundreds of skatt, these ores and items begin at tens of thousands of skatt. This clientele is made up of the elite who pull on the ropes of power throughout Midgard. The Whitesmith's guild also acts as the mint for the production of gold rods.

Ath Cliath's markets are the only markets in Western Midgard that carry items of luxury. The concentration of wealth allows for greater indulgences to feed this market.

Iona Abbey

Located on the western coast of Alba (Scotland) lies a community of missionaries that have been occupying this part of Midgard for a century or more. Hidden away no one can say for sure when they arrived, but this site has been built up for several generations at the very least. The central monastery is the main attraction. The monks have a fortified abbey with reinforced iron doors and iron window shutters that keep raiders out. There are a pair of barns with sheep as well as a large stockpile of feed for the animals. Fortunately the monks were prepared when Fimbulwinter came.

There are sixty monks with an abbot. Abbot Francis works to send the message of the White God to the denizens on the Great Isles. He sends his monks with concrete instructions on whom to convert. Unlike his brothers to the south, Abbot Francis has grown hard in the last two years. Exhausted from running to the monastic round tower (see page 244) each time raiders come by, and a significant loss in his sheep stock, he has taken up an active defense with lethal deterrence. Not all of the monks agree with his methods, and some believe he spends far too much time in the catacombs beneath the abbey.

The abbey has three floors plus a low incline roof with large cast iron tubs that can be used to pour boiling oil on anyone trying to break in. The top floor has a chapel and the study. The middle floor contains the small personal bedrooms. The ground floor houses the kitchen and the living quarters.

Interaction with the friars:

The friars will always err on the side of caution. However if the visitors come in genuine peace, they will engage in dialogue with the dwellers and denizens of Midgard. Dialogue will gravitate towards theology and faith. They will work in a non-confrontational manner to spread awareness of the new White God.

The abbey has a few sublevels of basement as well. They are behind an iron wrought door and under lock and key in order to keep raiders out. The topmost sub-level is the storage room. It has a wood plank wood floor and is filled with crates of food and barrels of wine. The second sublevel is the burial chamber. The ground is earthen and many of the more recent burials have been here. The third level drops into the bedrock and is the crypt that contains the tombs of the founders of the abbey.

A section of this hallway complex has fallen away into the depths of a natural cavern. Old rusty bars have been masoned into the stone to form a permanently closed portcullis. They have been put here to keep the dangers from below at bay.

Seas of Midgard
Longship of the Damned

It is said that there is a ship that sails the seas between Islandia and Gronland which is manned by ghosts. Those who have had a close encounter describe a tattered sail along with a crew of spectral warriors. The origin story is quite gruesome. The lord of the ship wanted to find new lands to the west and forced his crew to continue even when they were running dangerously low on supplies. Anyone who protested was run through and thrown overboard by the lord. Eventually the crew, driven by hunger and madness, mutinied and killed the captain with the gruesome blood eagle torture technique.

The lord was so driven by his desire to find land that his soul refused to leave and the intense desire transformed his body into a Haugbui. Within minutes he slayed the crew. Surprisingly the crew's desire for revenge re-animated the crew as a half dozen Haugbui. Now the ship sails, seeking land and attacking anyone they come across. The tragic irony is that the Haugbui curse keeps them in roughly the same area, and so they cannot venture far enough to actually find land. Woe to anyone who crosses their path.

Faroe Islands

The Faroe Islands are a series of picturesque islands at the midpoint between most of civilized Midgard and Islandia. Due to the recent exodus from the wars that are consuming Norveig, many find themselves bound for Islandia. Along the way, most stop at the small Faroe Islands for supplies and shelter. The young local chieftain of the Faroes is called Trondur i Gotu. He is a devout follower of Thor and opposes the incursion of the crusaders. By sword and fire, his forefathers rid the islands of missionaries who had setup a stone monastery. The stone moss covered structure rises above the land like a mole on a witch's decrepid face. It stands abandoned as many say it is haunted by a dreadful banshee.

THE NORTH SEA

SHIP OF THE DAMNED

CORNERSTONE OF THE WORLD

ISLANDIA

FAROE

Outer-Midgard

Outer-Midgard are all lands that surround Midgard and its populace. They are the peoples that exist beyond Jormundgand. They are the people who have brought war and trade to Midgard. They are also the people who make great slaves when captured on raids.

Political Structure: Kingdoms, fiefdoms, empires, tribes and clans

Population: Large, varied

Economy: Varied

Major Hubs: Brittany, Frisia, Francia, Saxony, Vedland (among many others)

Volga Trade Route

To reach the most distant and lucrative trading hubs, merchants from Midgard use the Volga trade route. The entrance to the route is from the Baltic sea and the route heads far to the east, and then even farther to the south. To reach Miklagard one must travel for months on this very perilous journey. There are many pirates and bandits on the route, ready to lighten the load of many a merchant ship. They are unlikely to kill the occupants as it is much more profitable to release them and hope they return once more with even more goods for the plunder.

Many ports have been established on this route in order to make money from passing traders. Services for coin include room and board, security, navigation and translation. Translation is very important on this long journey as many different languages will be encountered along the way. It is not uncommon for Midgard merchants to give up en route as this trek is long and fraught with danger. Many ports have seen a merchant selling off all their goods, ready to return home.

The legendary Koshchey is a menace to any traders who pass through the area. He has an eye for pretty cargo and will go out of his way to liberate the nubile goodies.

Miklagard

(the great city of Constantinople)

Miklagard is the legendary city where fortunes are made. Only the bravest, most adventurous merchants from Midgard travel to this distant metropolis. It is a once in a lifetime trip that is worn as a badge of honour among merchants. Those who make the long and arduous journey find it hard to sum up the the city using words. The populace and culture of Miklagard is beyond comprehension, and the city dwarfs the largest cities of Midgard. Goods from Midgard fetch unearthly prices and exotic goods returned from Miklagard can be sold to Jarls and Karls for exorbitant sums. A merchant can easily retire after one such return trip.

The merchants of Miklagard are not only interested in goods coming from Midgard. They are also fascinated with the people. It is said that the Emperor Basil has an elite army of six thousand Vikings. They are called the Varangians and are the pride and joy of his military. They are treated as nobility and are compensated accordingly. Since good coin can be made, warriors have accompanied merchants to this distant city in order to find adventure and riches.

SVEALAND

VOLGA TRADE ROUTE

TIC TRIBES

BLACK SEA

MIKLAGARD

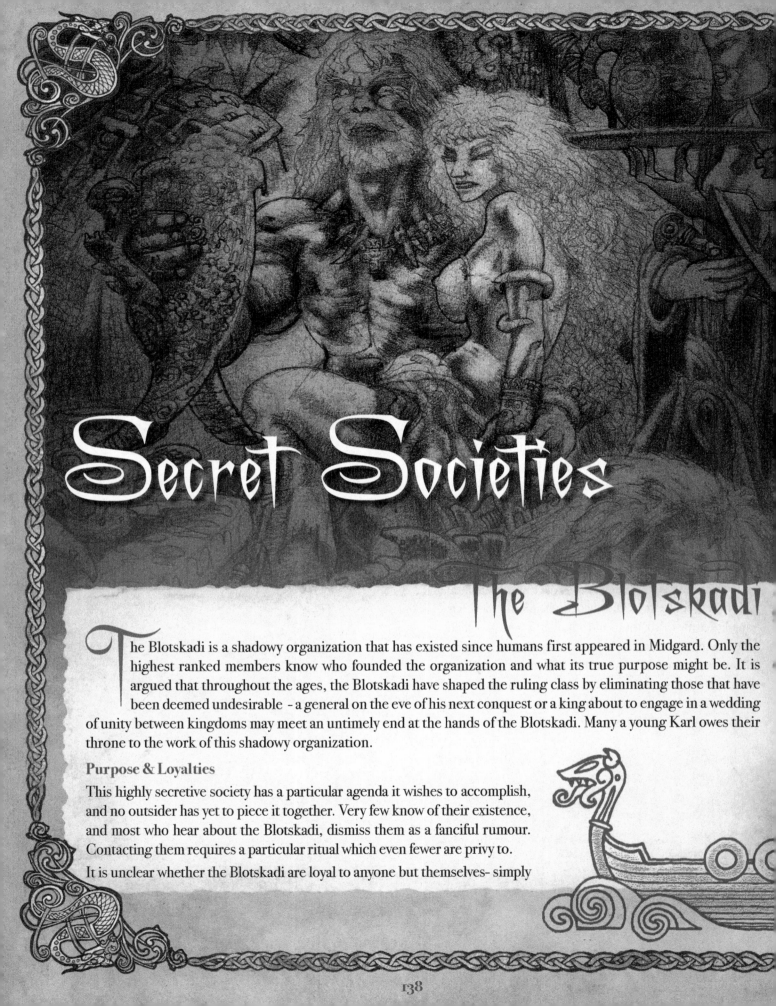

Secret Societies

The Blotskadi

The Blotskadi is a shadowy organization that has existed since humans first appeared in Midgard. Only the highest ranked members know who founded the organization and what its true purpose might be. It is argued that throughout the ages, the Blotskadi have shaped the ruling class by eliminating those that have been deemed undesirable - a general on the eve of his next conquest or a king about to engage in a wedding of unity between kingdoms may meet an untimely end at the hands of the Blotskadi. Many a young Karl owes their throne to the work of this shadowy organization.

Purpose & Loyalties

This highly secretive society has a particular agenda it wishes to accomplish, and no outsider has yet to piece it together. Very few know of their existence, and most who hear about the Blotskadi, dismiss them as a fanciful rumour. Contacting them requires a particular ritual which even fewer are privy to.

It is unclear whether the Blotskadi are loyal to anyone but themselves- simply acting as elite mercenaries. The one consensus is that they are highly effective and efficient at what they do. Even when faced with insurmountable objectives, they deliver on their contracts. Those who study this secret society are convinced that they are aided by higher powers such as the Jotuns or the gods.

Leadership & Organization

This secret society is guided by a council of elders. Blotskadi elders are said to be Voelvas- soothsayers who have direct contact with the Norns. The laws of succession are guided by destiny and are said to be preordained. Secrecy is maintained by eldritch rituals which bind the leaders who report to the council. The magic prevents them from revealing the identities of the elders, be it by speech or written word.

The organization itself is fairly clandestine, aiming to keep its activities hidden from outsiders. Each leader oversees a territory and commands a 'clique' of followers. These cliques are spread throughout the leader's territory and are further broken down into 'crews'. Crews number two to five members who have a good balance of complimentary skills. Exceptional members may even operate independently. The leaders filter information on a need-to-know basis, and often crews do not know about each other.

The Blotskadi have an interesting relationship with the beggars and orphans of the world, using them as the unlikely front face of the organization. The beggars and orphans are groomed into being unwitting representatives who do not fully understand the scope of their employers. The beggars and orphans receive initial contact from a potential client. The preferred currency are severed toes. Anyone working beneath the leadership are unaware why toes are so highly valued. It is in fact the toenails that are the strategic value that help the Blotskadi curry favour from both the gods and the Jotuns.

The Jotuns seek toenails for the construction of the mighty Naglfar, while the gods wish to acquire them in order to destroy them, ensuring they do not pass into Rime Jotun hands. This currency allows the Blotskadi to call upon higher powers whenever they need a supernatural favour such as in the assistance of a very difficult objective. The nails are also sold to both divine races for ample gold.

Objectives

Fimbulwinter has been a very busy and difficult time for the Blotskadi. In the early days, their network of beggars was nearly wiped out due to the lack of food and shelter. The Aesir and Jotuns have been actively seeking proof of loyalty. Men and women of power have been seeking favours but offering very little in return. Insular towns have been getting harder and harder to infiltrate. This has not deterred the Blotskadi from rebuilding, however territories are no longer exclusive and desperate rivalries have broken out.

Eyes, Hands and Teeth of Loki

Vargeisa the Fire Wolf is the head of this three pronged organization. She hid her love for Loki for most of her life, and has met many others who have done the same. Ever since Loki's transgressions against Baldur, his followers have had to hide their true identities. With the advent of Raganrok, Vargeisa has aimed to change the whole dynamic. Her plan has three phases, the first is to organize a secret society that has a common goal. Secondly it is to achieve the goal by any means necessary. The end game is to take the organization out of secrecy and turn it into the ultimate tool for their newly liberated god.

Purpose & Loyalties

Every decision, action and thought must bring the organization closer to Loki's revenge. The thought of his imprisonment burns Vargeisa to her core. In her mind, what the Aesir gods did to Loki and Sygin's sons was unforgivable. They turned Vali into a wolf and compelled him to rip his brother Narfi to shreds. Then they used Narfi's guts to bind Loki to the stones of Hvergelmir. Skadi ensured that snake venom would drip upon the trickster god for the duration of his sentence.

Vargeisa wishes to liberate Loki and his son Fenrir. One of the organization's goals are to establish close ties with Loki's other children, namely Jormundgand and Hel... but there has been little progress. The organization also has a secret benefactor who has been guiding Vargeisa without her knowledge. The benefactor is none other than Angrboda, Loki's mistress. Since the onset of Fimbulwinter, Angrboda has been sending gifts to Vargeisa via the nexus at Svalbard. Her emissaries are careful to ensure that all aid remains anonymous and appears to be granted by fate.

Leadership & Organization

Vargeisa has been very active in the last two years, coaxing the followers of Loki to reveal themselves to her. She classifies members into one of three sects. Influential leaders who represent and control different areas of Midgard belong to the sect known as the 'Eyes of Loki'. Her agents that travel the land following her orders are known as the 'Hands of Loki'. Those who espouse violent rebellion and hunt the Godis of Skadi, Heimdal and Thor are known as the 'Teeth of Loki'.

The organizational structure is fairly flat, with no pure administrative roles. Everyone contributes daily to the success of their sect. Information is freely disseminated across all three sects and a common sense of desperation and conviction unites all of the members. A victory for one sect is a victory for all because of the forward momentum towards the overall goal.

Objectives

The Eyes of Loki are rallying behind the Karls that are sympathetic to Loki and who wish to capture the coveted throne of Norveig. The Hands of Loki are closing in on the first seal that keeps Hvergelmir quarantined. The Teeth of Loki have been busy murdering the Godis whose gods are most responsible for Loki's torment. These relentless killings have been actively weakening the flock- turning the tables by driving those Godis into secrecy and hiding. Vargeisa is always on the lookout for more sympathetic talent.

Crusaders

The title of 'crusader' refers to many different groups throughout Midgard. While their goals are galvanized in a common belief- to unite the lands under the faith of the White God, the crusaders belong to different orders and report to different lords. They are the elite armies of Outer-Midgard, those who uphold a higher standard of quality. Originally conceived in Rome for the purpose of liberating the Holy Land, the current Pope John XII has rented out the crusaders to anyone who will further his goals. While working for other lords, the crusaders have forged their own identities and orders. The largest crusader army fight under Emperor Otto's banner, with the bravest at the vanguard in King Aethelstan's army.

Purpose & Loyalties

All of the orders swear to live a life of poverty, chastity and religious discipline. Those who truly live up to those standards are promoted into higher echelons of the organization. Those who struggle with the precepts are either allowed an extended period to better themselves, or are ejected from the order and are transferred into regular standing armies. The crusaders will only bend knee to the Pope and those kings who hold the White God above all else.

When the sun was extinguished by Skoll and Hati, the leaders (shepherds) of the various orders called a council to discuss how to deal with the coming darkness. Visions and prophesy directed their attentions to the north- towards Midgard and its heathen populace. The northern campaign moves with purpose towards different goals that must be achieved if light is to return to the world of man.

Leadership & Organization

The crusader orders are devoted to a particular holy reliquary and the cause it represents. The crusaders house the holy reliquary in their fort, and when they are on the attack, they carry it into battle. There is little doubt about the immense power that the reliquary bestows upon the order. There are many important reliquaries and orders, but only the ones engaged in northern campaigns are outlined below.

Order of the Lance of Destiny: This group of knights is devoted to the holy artifact that was used in piercing the White God while He was on the cross. They are driven by the pain and suffering that is required in order to persevere in the faith. Every member is prepared for sacrifice in order to achieve ultimate glory. This order specializes in spear warfare from horseback.

Order of the Sepulchre: Devoted to the burial site of the White God, this order welcomes the humble hearted. The Order of the Sepulchre is by far the largest group of crusaders. It welcomes the commoners who place the crusade above their daily lives. This order has so many recruits that it is impossible to issue standard issue weapons and armour. The commoners are led by seasoned warriors who train them in large scale battles.

Order of the Crown of Thorns: This military order is galvanized by the crown of thorns that rested upon the White God's head. Patience and mercy are the guiding qualities that are espoused within the order. The Crown of Thorns grant mercy to the defeated and achieve victory through patience and planning. They have a reputation for being the best of the best, so they behave with restraint and precision. Unlike the other orders, the Crown of Thorns members operate in small Warbands, executing specialized and devastating attacks on their enemies.

The Dark Order: Very little is known about this clandestine group. It is said that in his desire for victory, Emperor Otto empowered his close friend Arnolf to create a legion that would become the crusader's last stand. Their mission would be to find, decipher and use powerful heathen artifacts and magic. They would remain in the shadows, gaining power, and would be called upon only if victory over the north was in peril.

Each order has a leader known as a 'shepherd'. Their responsibility is to ensure the continued growth and success of their order. They are the ones who interact directly with the Pope and various kings.

Within an order there are some agencies. They are a smaller specialized sub-organizations devoted to a specialized set of tasks and responsibilities. Agencies exist in every order and sometimes collaborate across orders.

Missionaries are an agency that has been designed to precede the crusaders. They are the scholarly group devoted to non-violent interactions, discussions and conversions. They move into heathen lands well ahead of the crusader armies and work tirelessly to win over the population so that violent confrontation could be averted. Missionaries devote their lives to the study and worship of the White God. They learn extraordinary building techniques and erect majestic abbeys and cathedrals to honour the Saviour.

The Inquisitors are an agency that exist within each order. Their purpose is to ensure that the spirit of the White God lives within the crusaders' hearts and minds. Very special individuals are elevated to join this agency. Loyalty, unwavering character, and personal miracles are all prerequisites to consideration. The Inquisitors were founded by a virtuous Pope over one hundred years ago, but now Pope John XII uses the Inquisitors as his leash upon the crusaders. He uses the agency to ensure that the order's loyalty is to Rome above and beyond any loyalty they may have to their current king or emperor.

Objectives

The darkness that came as a result of Ragnarok has galvanized the crusader cause. There has been no shortage of recruits willing to head northward in an effort to restore the light.

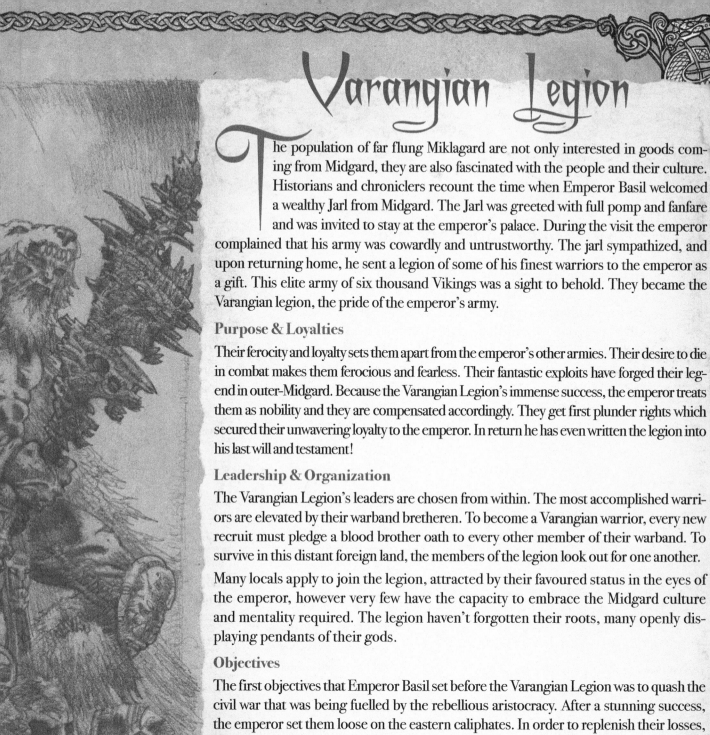

Varangian Legion

The population of far flung Miklagard are not only interested in goods coming from Midgard, they are also fascinated with the people and their culture. Historians and chroniclers recount the time when Emperor Basil welcomed a wealthy Jarl from Midgard. The Jarl was greeted with full pomp and fanfare and was invited to stay at the emperor's palace. During the visit the emperor complained that his army was cowardly and untrustworthy. The jarl sympathized, and upon returning home, he sent a legion of some of his finest warriors to the emperor as a gift. This elite army of six thousand Vikings was a sight to behold. They became the Varangian legion, the pride of the emperor's army.

Purpose & Loyalties

Their ferocity and loyalty sets them apart from the emperor's other armies. Their desire to die in combat makes them ferocious and fearless. Their fantastic exploits have forged their legend in outer-Midgard. Because the Varangian Legion's immense success, the emperor treats them as nobility and they are compensated accordingly. They get first plunder rights which secured their unwavering loyalty to the emperor. In return he has even written the legion into his last will and testament!

Leadership & Organization

The Varangian Legion's leaders are chosen from within. The most accomplished warriors are elevated by their warband bretheren. To become a Varangian warrior, every new recruit must pledge a blood brother oath to every other member of their warband. To survive in this distant foreign land, the members of the legion look out for one another.

Many locals apply to join the legion, attracted by their favoured status in the eyes of the emperor, however very few have the capacity to embrace the Midgard culture and mentality required. The legion haven't forgotten their roots, many openly displaying pendants of their gods.

Objectives

The first objectives that Emperor Basil set before the Varangian Legion was to quash the civil war that was being fuelled by the rebellious aristocracy. After a stunning success, the emperor set them loose on the eastern caliphates. In order to replenish their losses, many members of the legion sent work back home of their lucrative success in Outer-Midgard. As a result many embarked on the long and perilous Volga trade route in order to find fame and fortune among the Varangians.

Recent Days

Since the coming darkness, Emperor Basil has turned his attentions to the north and west. Messengers from Rome arrive daily and the legion has been pulled back from the East. Something intense is brewing and everyone in the legion can feel the electricity in the air.

Magic Items

Bag of Sustenance

SIZE: 4   QR: 4 (DVERGAR ENGINEERING)

This royal blue bag is embroidered with silver runes made from otherworldly thread. Anything edible placed inside this magical sack replicates itself within 24 hrs. The maximum size of an object to be placed within the magic bag is one cubic foot. This magic item may have held moderate value before Ragnarok, but since the onset of Fimbulwinter, such an artifact may start wars between kingdoms!

accessory

Bifrost Ring

SIZE: 1
QR: 3 (SINGLE TRAIT) OR 6 (DOUBLE TRAIT)

Passive Power: *PF +1 vs. Mental or Spiritual per point of Focus.*
Upon finding one, Wyrd 1 rune:

- ◖ = vs. Mental & Spiritual
- ◗ = vs. Mental only
- ◗ = vs. Spiritual only

These chromatic rings are sought after by practitioners of magic. Made from multi-coloured stone, these rings have the power to reshape themselves to the size of the finger they are to adorn.
They have been designed to protect the wearer against foul and discordant magic.

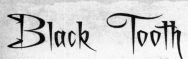

weapon

Black Tooth

SIZE: 7   QR: 20

DF: 4 I PIERCE: 8 I REACH: 3 I PARRY: 0 I FOCUS: 0 I META: SPECIAL*

* Weapon Meta: Knockdown or Knockback (2 hexes)

Dvergar Engineering: *Perform a Minor Sacrifice +1 to perform a Weak Move (no limit to how many times this is invoked during a combat round)*

Active Power: *Thundering Attack*

The head of this maul is a dead Jotun's dead tooth and the haft is forged from high quality metal alloys. This fearsome weapon is generally too large for a human to wield, and is usually found in the hands of troll and ogre champions. Within Jotunheim, it is regarded as a status symbol and within Midgard it is seen more as a symbol of Jotun allegiance. If they are fortunate enough to acquire one, a Rime Jotun Godi would use Black Tooth as the centerpiece of their shrine.

Blood Mail Coat

SIZE: 3   QR: 9

PF: 1 I PARRY: 2 I EVADE: I FOCUS: 1 I META: ABSORB

Passive Power: *Perform a Moderate Sacrifice +1 to gain a +3*

Physical damage bonus on your Attack action (applied after metas; can only be performed once per combat round)

The blood mail coat was created by the blacksmiths who worked in the service of King Harald. Equipping his most loyal soldiers, these mail coats played no small part in the success of King Harald's armies when they unified Norveig. In these dark times, these coats fetch a fair price for not only their martial powers, but for their historical collector's value. King Harald's royal seal was painted on the breast of each of these scale

Boar's Vanguard

SIZE: 3   QR: 13

DF: 0 I PIERCE: 0 I REACH: 0 I PARRY: 8 I FOCUS: 1 I META: DEFLECT

Passive Power: *Protector*

This metal shield has a bronze cast bas-relief boar on the front. This was created by the guardians of the Danevirke in order to support a shield wall defense. Some have been stolen by disgruntled defenders when they departed their service at the great wall. Finding one away from the Danevirke is a reminder of how deteriorated the defenses have become.

Book of Dreams

SIZE: 1   QR: 12

This book has 10 pages of ancient and magical parchment (consult the table below to see how many pages are blank). It is said that Mogthrasir the Norn created the parchment for this book. The ink that is drawn onto the pages unlocks a very unique effect. Any scene that is drawn becomes an enchanted vortex for anyone viewing the page. Unless they Wyrd and pull 4 Mental runes (rune morphing allowed), they will be magically transported to the scene's location. Every scene in the book save one is a real life location, some are not even in Midgard. One particular scene is fictitious and depicts an event that is transpiring. Anyone sucked through will be stuck in this dream realm until they resolve the incident that was portrayed.

WYRD	NUMBER OF BLANK PAGES
	1
	2
	4

Candle of Spirits

SIZE: 1   QR: 6

The Candle of Spirits resembles a normal candle in many regards. Only when holding the candle up to a bright light will one see the runic symbols that have been buried in the wax. These candles reveal the hidden world around them. When a candle is lit, the holder of the candle can clearly witness the world of spirits within 30′ radius. When lit, the candle grants a +1 bonus rank to 'Speak with Dead', 'Omens/Portents' and 'Lore: Arcana'. It may also be lit during a funeral pyre to reveal whether the soul has been picked up by a Valkyrie. Witnessing a Valkyrie in her glory and splendour, however, will cause the witness to perform an Ultimate Sacrifice +1. The candle may also help in 'Sense Motive' or 'Lore Personas' checks when dealing with a Haugbui (Norn's discretion) when attempting to decipher the reason for its curse in Midgard.

These candles can burn for several hours, consult the table below when one has been found:

WYRD	HOURS REMAINING
	1
	2
	4

Call of the Ancients

SIZE: 4   QR: 6

Passive Power: *Focus +1 (+2 bonus if applied to a Spell Song)*

Active Power: *Heal +6 {Spell Song}, Minor Sac +1 to add a free Area meta [Amplify Amplify Area]*

This coiled horn has been used for generations by the Sammi tribes of the north. It is created from a legendary mountain ram that is said to have gone extinct several generations ago. It is rather large and cumbersome and is tinted a very light shade of grey and ivory.

Dawn of Ragnarok

SIZE: 12   QR: 22

STRUCTURAL ESSENCE: 24   PF: 5 P

Passengers gain:
*During Upkeep Heal +3, Recover +4
Retribution- DF 1 P, Pierce +2
Parry +2*

Big battering ram / spike:
DF 9, Pierce 6, Meta: Gore

This sturdy longship was created in Evingard to protect the fishermen of the Bay of Ice from the polar kraken that lurk there. Legend has it that the crew was obsessed in hunting all predators of the sea, and having crossed paths with a kraken, they refused to back down. They worked hard at creating a ship capable of withstanding the terror of an adult kraken. Using magics and marvels of engineering, they created a ship worthy of its name. Decorated with a black kraken sail, they sailed into legend after ridding the bay of its most fearsome predator. They vowed to take to the high seas and continue their glorious hunt, which some say would only culminate in their possible encounter with Jormungand!

Death Stone

SIZE: 1   QR: 20

No one knows how a Death Stone is created. Some
speculate that Mogthrasir the Norn created them in
order to play a prank on her sisters Verdandi, Skuld and Urd.
The ritual that binds a beneficiary to the stone is also lost. The stone grants immortality to those
who are bound to it. The beneficiary's soul is removed from the body and placed within the heart
of the Death Stone., after which they cannot be killed, nor do they age. Their health remains
impeccable so long as the stone is at least 100 miles from the beneficiary. The moment it starts
to come closer, the beneficiary's health begins to degrade. Any physical contact with the stone
causes the beneficiary to die and the stone becomes receptive to a new binding ritual.

Dragvendil

weapon

SIZE: 3   QR: 19

DF: 6 I PIERCE: 14 I REACH: 2 I PARRY: 2 I FOCUS: 0 I META: HAMSTRING

Passive Power: *Afterlife Wyrd doesn't gain any bonuses for epic deeds performed while wielding Dragvendil*

Active Power: *Sundering Blow*

Taking this weapon from a grave does not incur any malice

In an era long past, Sindri was one of the best weaponsmiths and forge masters of all of the Dvergar. For the gods, he and his brother Brokk crafted many powerful artifacts. Among them, the most legendary are the gold-spinning Draupnir and the mighty hammer Mjolnir. In the years of Fimbulwinter, a shrewd Sammi Karl named Gusir wanted to become one of the greatest warriors of legend. To achieve the greatest glory he offered most of his riches to Sindri in exchange for the best blade ever created- a sword that even the Aesir would desire. The Norns smiled at Gusir and Sindri agreed. Over the years the Dvergar had aged considerably and his hands were not as steady as they once were. He required the assistance of another dwarf named Aranlad, whose ability rivaled Sindri's while in his prime.

In the final moments of the forging process, Sindri became fearful of incurring Odin's wrath and quickly decided that Dragvendil should be flawed. Sensing Sindri's hesitation, Aranlad redoubled his efforts in order to create the best artifact he could muster. The result was a paradoxical weapon with two personalities. Aranlad ensured that Dragvendil's edge would always be perfect, and no material would be able to stop its thrusts. However in panic Sindri infused Dragvendil with a shroud that would hide the wielder from the gods and some speculate that even the Norns themselves would not be able to see through the veil!

Gusir never deserved to have such a great weapon. He was never able to use it as a true warrior, and when he won battles and duels, it was wholly due to Dragvendil. The fate of the sword would become entwined with great men following Gusir's death. It began when the great warrior Ketil Hæing took it from Gusir's corpse. Ketil Hæing killed many warriors with the now infamous blade. The most famous was Framar, King of Uppland who was cut in half by Dragvendil. The sword was passed down to his son Grim Shaggy-Cheek who was also a famous warrior. The sword continued to pass from hand to hand, great warrior to great warrior. Grim gave it to Thorolf and he in turn gave it to Arinbjorn. Finally Arinbjorn gave it as a gift to Egil Skallagrmsson. Egil is the current owner of this infamous weapon.

Dreadful Antlers

SIZE: 6   QR: 24

DF: 6 I PIERCE: 4 I REACH: 2 I PARRY: 6 I FOCUS: 2 I META: GORE

Passive Power: *Thriving in the Crowd*

Active Power: *Disarming Parry, Disarm*

The Dreadful Antlers are sacred weapons to the nomadic northern Sammi. They are crafted from the antlers of a dying reindeer which has allowed someone to witness its passing. Using a special ritual, the horns are extracted to make a significant and magnificent weapon. The horns are then sharpened to points and a leather strap is attached to add a suitable grip to this unconventional weapon. In Sammi society anyone carrying this artifact elevates one's status.

Favour of the Elf King's Daughter

SIZE: 1   QR: 4

There was a very rare coupling of a Lios Alfar lord and a human woman of noble lineage. The union begat a daughter imparted with the beauty and arrogance of the Alfar and the compassion and emotion of a mortal woman. The Elf King's daughter is a beautiful, but a very capricious Fae. She enjoys disguising herself and leaving the familiarity of her kingdom in order to seek out true love. Those she meets, however, are false, vile and filled with wickedness, tainted by the desperation induced by Fimbulwinter. Invariably her affections turn to anger as she discovers the flaws of her mortal companion. Sometimes she will use her spells to taunt and drive her lover mad or she will manipulate others to exact her vengeance. Oftentimes, a willing hero is the hand of her justice, and to these she gives her Favour.

The Favour appears as a ribbon-wrapped lock of hair, which lightens and darkens with the Elf King daughter's mood. The Favor appears among the personal effects of a hero who has, knowingly or not, delivered grievous harm upon a person who has wronged the Elf King's daughter. It cannot be stolen or lost, but can be freely given to another - although the Elf King's daughter may take this as an affront.

Powers: The Favour grants its owner the ability to strike and plot revenge, not for himself, but for another. Whatever path the owner takes to achieve vengeance for another's wound he will be able to out-think, out-fight, and out-talk his foes (+1 skill ranks). This edge appears as a rush of confidence, a little more luck, and the occasional burst of energy. In addition, the owner may take the Favour and call out to the Elf King's daughter, asking or demanding of her some boon or task (see 'Beseech a Higher Power' in the *Core Rulebook* page 99). If successful she will assist within her powers, but the Favour of the Elf King's daughter will disappear forever. But care must be taken not to demand too much, lest the Elf King's daughter takes offense or feels demeaned. She might even decide to make the former owner the next target of her ire!

Frost Mauler

SIZE: 1   QR: 7

Passive Power: *Furious Cohort, Enter Rage*

Active Power: *Raging Charge, Raging Attack, Ice Aura*

This gauntlet is crafted by encrusting Rime crystals into polar bear claws. Leather straps and fur trim are added for comfort and style. The nomadic Ulfhednar clans of the north often create a set of these gauntlets to celebrate their greatest champions. To a Berserkir or an Ulfhednar, these gauntlets are a badge of honour. Anyone else that carries a Frost Mauler may be branded a thief. Be warned!

Falling Star

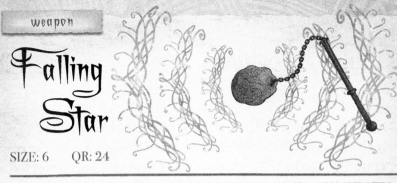

SIZE: 6   QR: 24

DF: 8 I PIERCE: 2 I REACH: 2 I PARRY: 0 I FOCUS: 1 I META: KNOCKDOWN

Realm Ore - Meteorite (Midgard): *The attack from this weapon not only attacks the space occupied by the victim, but also hits all adjacent hexes (hits friend and foe alike)*

Dvergar Engineering: *Weapon meta automatically triggers on all attack actions at +1 intensity [Counter: P]*

This flail is made from stone that fell from the night skies of Fimbulwinter. The stone looks fairly cratered with a texture that is quite foreign. There are flecks of red, gold and silver in the stone that shimmer eerily in firelight. The properties of this meteorite stone cause concussive force to be expelled when it is slammed against anything solid. The concussive force radiates out in all directions.

Fotbitr (Leg Biter)

SIZE: 3   QR: 17

DF: 4 I PIERCE: 4 I REACH: 2 I PARRY: 4 I FOCUS: 1 I META: GORE

Creature Reliquary: *It will bind the fate of the wielder with that of an innocent. The sword will ensure that the wielder crosses paths with someone noble and kind hearted.*

Active Power: *Gate Banshee {spell} [amplify range maintain] - The banshee will help ensure the premature demise of the innocent. Should anyone try and interfere, it will include them in its plans for murder. Unlike the traditional gate power where the caster controls the creature, Fotbitr's banshee is controlled by the Norn.*

Passive Power: *Curse - When the wielder least expects it, the sword will apply Possession intensity +6 on them and compel them to strike dead someone who has not warranted an early death. A Lore: Arcana skill check with 8 successes is needed to detect the curse.*

Fotbitr is a powerful but cursed long sword that drives the wielder to tragedy. It has the uncanny ability of murdering the innocent, weaving a tapestry of catastrophe in its mythology.

The sword belonged to Geirmund the Noisy, but his vengeful ex-wife Thurid stole it from him. Geirmund's last words were a curse he directed at the sword and his ex-wife... just before his death when his boat sank at sea. He swore it would 'kill the man most missed and the man least deserving of death' making the death a true tragedy. The sword has been sighted on its way to Islandia.

Golden Lockbox

SIZE: 7   QR: 24

As higher powers watch, listen and manoeuvre into positions of increasing power, it is important to keep good relations with peers. Sending gifts can be risky when a courier can easily be intercepted and robbed. The Dvergar devised expensive gift boxes for just these types of occasions. Most are the size and shape of a coffin, adorned with gold gilded edges and imagery. The quality of the box is designed to match the calibre of gift within. Anyone looking to steal such a valuable box must be willing to face divine wrath and retribution. The locking mechanism is a 3 spindle gear-set programmed with a runic combination. Picking the lock is either done through intuition or a brute force approach (difficulty 11). Destruction of the box is also near impossible as the lockbox would need to be assailed with a higher QR weapon.

Hel's Favour

SIZE: 1   QR:8

Grants a +1 to the Afterlife roll
if buried/cremated with the deceased.

These bone pendants are created and blessed by an Angel of Death. Who is worthy of such a gift is really hard to say, as these gifts have found themselves in the hands of both great heroes and unknown scoundrels alike. During these dark times, wealthy merchants and chieftains pay vast sums to acquire such a precious artifact.

Hat of Nails

SIZE: 1   QR: 9

FOCUS +2

Active Power: *Visage of Horrors*

Passive Power: *Blend into Shadow*

This morbid looking vestment grants invisibility to the wearer. It appears as a winter hat woven using thread and finger (maybe toe) nails. It uses esoteric enchantments that have been honed in Jotunheim by the witches of Jarnvid. It will magically re-size itself to its owner's head. By concentrating on the magical dweomer, the wearer may alter their facial appearnce into something truly frightful!

Hunter's Harpoon

SIZE: 4   QR:14

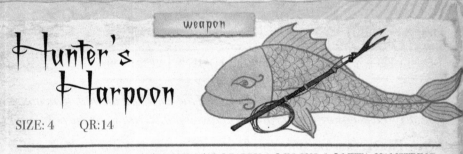

DF: 3 I PIERCE: 4 I REACH/RANGE: 3/15 I PARRY: 1 I FOCUS: 0 I META: HAMSTRING

Passive Power: *Quick Draw*

Active Power: *Chant of Skuld*

These harpoons were designed to meet the demanding needs of survivors who hunt under a moonless night sky. Ragnarok has forced most animals into borderline extinction, so hunting an animal for survival cannot be a trivial exercise. Each throw must result in a kill, otherwise the prey may get away leading to a missed meal. Too many are starving to death to leave things to chance. This harpoon is specifically crafted to inflict maximum damage while immobilizing the prey.

Jolnir Puppets

SIZE: 1 (GOD) 2 (JOTUN)   QR: 11

DF: 1 I PIERCE: 0 I REACH: 1 I PARRY: 0 I FOCUS: 0 I META: AUGMENT*

* Augment Meta: Combines the Maintain meta with the Conjure Weapon Active power. This Meta can only be evoked by one who strongly believes in the pantheon from which the puppet hails and has taken the time to craft a puppet weapon that resembles what the god or Jotun would normally wield.

Active Power: *It's Alive! {spell} [Maintain, Maintain, Maintain]* - The puppet comes to life and begins to float around under full control of the caster. It remains by your side, going no further than 3' from you. You have full control over the puppet as though it were on your hand. You have enough fine motor control that the puppet is essentially like an extra hand. Any feats of ventriloquism, or 'thrown voice' must be done with a successful Perform skill check.

Gain a +1 rank in Omens/Portents if you have crafted a weapon for your puppet and have activated 'It's Alive' in the last six hours.

Beseech a higher power (Generic action *Core Rulebook* page 99) may get a bonus if the Norn deems it appropriate. There is a Yule time tradition of children organizing puppet plays for their village. For some reason Fimbulwinter's harshness has not been able to stamp out this age old custom. Puppets are usually created by the children or their parents, but some puppets may be bought from travelling merchants.

Be it at a mysterious market stall, in a dark and foggy alley, or sitting proudly atop a pile of treasure surrounded by the corpses of dead heroes and monsters, these mystical Jolnir puppets can occasionally be found by a lucky adventurer. This line of puppets are said to hold wondrous powers, not least of which is to bring joy and laughter, or perhaps tears and trauma to a Yule night celebration. They are extremely collectible, simply because there is only one for each Aesir and Jotun. No one knows exactly where they come from or who may have made them, but one thing's for certain: No one has the complete set!

Kiss & Caress of Night

SIZE: 2   QR: 17 each

There are a pair of legendary black daggers known as the Kiss and Caress of Night. The serrated blades have a savage look to them, with an inky black finish which seems to absorb all light. These daggers are sought after by assassins and rogues. Just one of these daggers is a formidable weapon, but the pair together bring out the best in each other.

KISS

DF: 2 I PIERCE: 4 I REACH: 1 I PARRY: 3 I FOCUS: 0 I META: GORE

Passive Power: *Blend Into Shadow, Stealthy Striker*
Active Power: *Shadow Strike*

CARESS

DF: 3 I PIERCE: 2 I REACH: 1 I PARRY: 0 I FOCUS: 1 I META: HAMSTRING

Passive Powers: *Aura of Influence, Bully*
Active Power: *Shadow Step*

SET BONUS

Active Power: *Umbral Vines- Impeded and Blind Alka {Spell} [Amplify Amplify Amplify]*
Passive Power: *Render Helpless*
Disguise rank +1
The wielder may perform a Minor Sacrifice +2 to grant DF +1, Reach +1 for the next attack (no limit to the number of invocations)

Molten Rod

SIZE: 2   QR:12

DF: 1 MENTAL I PIERCE: 0 I REACH: 1 I PARRY: 0 I FOCUS: 1 I META: BLIND

Light 10' radius

Active Power: *Beckon Muspelheim*

The molten rod is an item of great use in Midgard considering the cold and darkness of Fimbulwinter. They are quite common and grow out of the ground in Muspelheim. Harvesting them is another matter altogether. The toxic air and incredible heat makes it quite lethal for folks from Midgard. When a Molten Rod finds its way into a mortal's hands, it is hidden away and guarded jealously.

Mushrooms of Dreams

SIZE: 1   QR:4

Consumable

Omens/Portents +2 Ranks

These mushrooms grow in dark and warm areas, of which there are very few these days. They are usually found in subterranean caverns that are heated by molten activity. Some more industrious individuals have used Alkas and portals to help create the proper conditions to grow and cultivate this magical fungus.

Naglfar

SIZE: 320   QR:292

Dvergar Engineering: *Flight; Shroud 4; It may be "equipped" as an accessory by all crew members*

Passive Powers: *Grants the crew every Passive power found in the Core Rulebook (140) with the exception of "summon" and "immortal" powers (as "bestow").*

The creation of this legendary longship has been prophesied by the Norns well before Ragnarok. The Rime Jotuns of Jotunheim began its construction many years ago, in a secret location so its construction wouldn't be disturbed by their enemies. The ship is 45 miles long and houses a city within its hull. The outer hull is created from toe nails which grant the ship magical invisibility. The ship has the ability of flight, and bestows dozens of benevolent enchantments upon its crew. When complete it will be a terror to behold, striking fear into the hearts of the enemy!

Navigator's Mail

SIZE: 4   QR: 10

PF: 2 I PARRY: 4 I EVADE: 0 I FOCUS: 0 I META: DODGE

Dvergar Engineering: *No swimming penalties due to encumbrance*

Active Power: *Water Shield*

This special suit of magic chain mail was created for a very successful war band of seaborne explorers. This apparently heavy armour shirt has incredible buoyancy due to the way it was crafted. After the war band was disbanded, the suits of mail started to appear on the market.

weapon

Necromancer's Vow

SIZE: 4   QR: 17

DF: 0 I PIERCE: 0 I REACH: 0 I EVADE: 1 I PARRY: 4 I FOCUS: 2 I META: DEFLECT

Passive Power: *Minor Sac +1 to grant +1 level to the gated Black Skeleton*

Active Power: *Gate Bones*

The Necromancer's Vow is a round metal shield adorned with a coiled up skeleton in the foetal position. When the terrifying magic is activated, the skeleton unwraps itself from the shield and enters the battlefield. According to scholars, there are very few of these shields remaining as they were created a long time ago and no one has managed to determine how they were made.

Noahdher Leaf

SIZE: 1   QR:14

It's said that when Odin hung from Yggdrasil for nine nights, and upon the tenth day when he removed himself from the tree, a single leaf from Yggdrasil fell. This leaf captured the essence of the biome surrounding the mighty Yggdrasil as it lay upon the ground season after season. One day a young Viking boy named Noah Ericson found this mystical leaf. With each passing season the leaf seems to take on a different appearance and with it a new set of powers:

Winter: *'Nidhogg's Breath'- Endurance rank +1*
Summer: *'Great Eagle Feather' - Athletics rank +1*
Spring: *'Dainn, Dualinn, Duneyrr & DuraprÜr's Song' - Perception rank +1*
Fall: *'Ratatosk's Message' - Animal Empathy rank +1*

The only 3 powers which are consistent from season to season are:

1.) 'Yggdrasil's Nectar' - Sweet dew drips from the leaf when placed into a drinking horn, within minutes filling it with mead.
2.) 'Magic Rivers' - Kissing the leaf in the presence of a gated creature sends it back from whence it came [Counter: S]
3.) 'Congregation of Norns' - Grants +1 rank to Omens/Portents for one vision

All of the consistent powers can be used once per day.
The seasonal powers can be used consistently as long as the season stands.

It is said that the name of the leaf 'Noahdher' sounds like 'No Other', thus villagers tales would say that once you had possession of the leaf you needed 'No Other', yet wise Vikings know better and the word 'Dher', means Support, thus the name ' Noahdher' means 'Noah Support' after the young boy that found it. In honor of this boy and his discovery, the name stands.

Odin's Noose

SIZE: VARIABLE   QR:10

Dvergar Engineering: *Extendible rope from 1' to 800'*

Indestructible: *QR +3 for purposes of being damaged*

Omens/Portents skill rank +1

+1 to afterlife roll if used as accessory during combat and then buried with it

Odin's Noose is a sacred artifact that was bestowed by Odin on his most faithful followers. This noose is to be used when performing blots in Odin's name. One of his most devout followers was a Skald by the name of Hrani. Hrani did his best to cause strife between kings in order to spark wars. He knew that war would provide Odin's Valkyries with many valiant warriors for Valhalla. Hrani was the first recorded recipient of the noose, but after his burial with the noose, it is said others had been bestowed with this sacred relic. If a follower of the Aesir were to die while carrying, but not equipping this noose, Odin will reverse the afterlife bonus!

Odur's Torc

SIZE: 1   QR:20

Absorb 5 damage from Auras per combat round

Heal +1 and Recover +2

Evade +3

Endurance rank +1

Legend says that this grand torc was commissioned from the Dvergar of Nidavellir by Freya, a gift for her husband Odur. The torc was crafted with braided silver, and capped with silver fox heads. Although given as a sign of affection, the jewelry was secretly enchanted with magics to protect her oft-absent husband.

While traveling Midgard pursuing the pleasures of the flesh, Odur wintered among the Volsung disguised as a wandering skald. Late one night he filled himself with strong mead until the room swam, and before long was heard challenging King Volsung to a wrestling match in his own great hall. Despite having little talent for the act, Odur bet his torc against a night with one of the King's maids who had caught his eye. Thinking this good sport, the king's men cheered at the brash traveller. Not far gone with drink King Volsung accepted the challenge, and a space was cleared near the head of the table. Head swimming with mead and false confidence, Odur gave a good match but was unable to get the best of the young king. True to his word Odur gave up his torc, and in appreciation of such a fine piece King Volsung granted Odur a night with the maid he so desired. The torc was passed down as a gift to Volsung's son Sigmund but years later was lost, its whereabouts unknown. No one knows Freya's response when she learned Odur had gambled away her gift, but it was many years before he travelled Midgard again.

Pelt of Golden Gate

SIZE: 2   QR:8

Passive Powers: *Unencumbered Dodger, Cornered Ferocity, Unbreakable Body, Fangs*

Curse: *During Upkeep all conditions require +1 additional rune to clear*

Animal Empathy rank +1

This pelt is specifically created for the Coming of Age challenge young Druids of Trondheim must face. Worn as a cloak, it replaces weapons and armour when facing ferocious wild beasts. Surviving the trial grants a Druid passage from initiate level to seer, opening the way for them to own a magic staff or wand. It is thought that this ritual is unique to northern Norveig and takes on different forms elsewhere in Midgard.

Pinecones of Ardour

SIZE: 1   QR:14 (20)

Consumable (+6 QR)

Generic Action: *When thrown-Deal +4 Mental damage and +4 Physical damage as well as inflict +1 intensity Possession, all in a 2 hex area [Counter: S]*

These mystic pinecones can be found on the ground of magical forests. They are rare and one must know what to look for in order to differentiate these pinecones from their mundane associates. Tossing one of these will cause all manner of ill in the vicinity where they land... physical pain, nightmares and ghosts will assail all within 10'. They are single use and disappear after they are thrown. Druids, Fardrengir and those who embrace nature use these rare objects as gifts.

Sägen Forandre Stones (Story Changing Stones)

SIZE: 1   QR:24

Possession +6 and forces a Skald to recite a corrupted version of the tale. All listeners must Wyrd at least 3 Mental runes or suffer from despair (Destiny -1). This despair lasts for several days.

The Sägen Forandre stones, or Sägen stones for short, have numerous histories and no one knows which one is true. The most common belief is that the stones can be found all along shores of the Slidr River with most deposits near the wellspring of Hvergelmir. Some believe the stones are also prevalent in the eleven riverbeds of Elivagar, but that is a lesser held belief. It is a mystery how Sägen stones can be found in the known lands of men, but those who claimed to have escaped from Hvergelmir or have bartered with Nidhogg himself are the same ones that are often in possession of such stones. Sägen stones are never bigger than a sling stone, and appear to be made from a smooth black mineral often mistaken for onyx. The stones however have a clammy feel to them (like holding the hand of someone on their deathbed), and when shaken, give off a faint but eerie rattle. It is the feel of the stone and the sound of its rattle that gives away their true nature. The stones truly have a nefarious reputation to them, Sägen stone is a slayer of stories with no runic markings evident to have infused such magic. No self-respecting Norsemen would carry such stones, and they are thought of as a weapon for cheats and tricksters. They are most prized in secrecy by witches, rogues, and those that follow Loki.

When a Skald is struck by a hurled Sägen stone while reciting a magical poem, the stone's power is unleashed in the following manner. The Skald will be unable to stop reciting the poem and the story will become immediately corrupted on the lips of the Skald. The stone will change the very fabric of the story in such a manner that the result will be an unfavorable outcome for both the Skald and its intended listeners within ear shot.

Ravenous

SIZE:2   QR:9

| DF: 6 | PIERCE: 0 | REACH: 3 | PARRY: 0 | FOCUS: 0 | META: KNOCKDOWN |

This maul's head is in the shape of a feral boar, with its snout as the blunt side and its tail as a spike on the other side. Its feet draw in towards the handle. This unique item was created by Eric the Frost Bear, to whom it holds deep personal meaning. He is unlikely to part with it as it feels like an extension of his arms.

Sampo of Prosperity

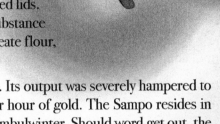

SIZE: 6 (2 FOR EACH MILL)   QR:15

The Sampo was forged by Ilmarinen, a blacksmith with immense talent. Over three days the talisman was fashioned from one swift quill, milk of the fertile cow, a grain of barley and the fleece of a summer lamb. The talisman appears as three mills joined back to back. The top of the artifact has 3 multicoloured lids. It has a flour mill, slat mill and gold mill. One must pour any common substance (such as dirt or snow) in through the top and as the mill grinds it will create flour, salt or gold. Ten pounds per hour may be created.

The Sampo was damaged in the fight between Vainamoinen and Louhi. Its output was severely hampered to 8 pounds per hour of flour, 3 pounds per hour of salt and 1 pound per hour of gold. The Sampo resides in Kalevala, whose residents keep the artifact a secret since the onset of Fimbulwinter. Should word get out, the citizens could expect unending raids by those who seek the immeasurable value of the Sampo.

Shield of the White Stag

SIZE:3   QR:21

DF: 1 I PIERCE: 0 I REACH: 1 I PARRY: 6 I FOCUS: 0 I META: BLIND

Sheds light as a bonfire (40')

Passive Powers: *Aura of Influence, Fellowship of the White Hare, Fellowship of the Silver Shields, Fellowship of Hel's Ice Hand, Protector*

This legendary shield belonged to a Maiden of Ratatosk named Ljosa. How she came to acquire such a great artifact makes for a great skald's tale. Ljosa was the illegitimate daughter of a chieftain who ruled an ancient kingdom near the Baltic sea. Her father sold her into slavery while negotiating a deal with a Dvergar smith of dubious moral character. He intended her to be his play thing, but never counted on her dexterity in avoiding his clutches. Being more trouble than she was worth, he offered her up as tribute to King Ivaldi. In Ivaldi's court she was to be a distraction, a dancer to help pass the time. Her dance moves, however, were so unbelievably graceful that she quickly won the king's affections.

Many who recount tales of the Dvergar halls of Nidavellir will speak of legendary Ljosa's dances. Despite being human, Ivaldi doted over her like his firstborn. She would affectionately call Ivaldi her "White Stag". She managed to extract all manner of gifts from the forges of the underdark and figuratively got away with murder. Ivaldi would muse that her soul was too grand for the confines of Nidavellir. The Shield of the White Stag was a parting gift when Ivaldi set her free. It would always remind Ljosa of the bitter sweet memories of the dwarven realm where she grew up.

Singing Beard of the Axelord

SIZE: 1 TO 2   QR:15

Passive Power: *Price of Progress, Warrior of Song, Bastion, Precision, Alabaster Magician, Thriving in the Crowd, Misery Loves Company*

Active Power: *Night of the Long Knives*

Always +1 to Possession (minimum 1) while worn

> In combat, possessed runes are treated as in Rage (Rage starts at 1 and cannot go below 1)

> Out of combat, spiritual skill checks will always use Price of Progress

Graft: *To put on the beard one must pay an Ultimate Sacrifice +1; To remove the beard one must pay an Ultimate Sacrifice +5*

Very little is known of the fabled Mountain King. It is said he lived hundreds of years ago in the mountain ranges of Jamtaland. He was an incredibly powerful and charismatic warrior skald who had a very short temper but a great love for song. It is unclear whether he ruled a people or simply a kingdom of one, but what is clear is the legacy he has left behind. His biggest asset was a spectacular golden beard. It was his most prized possession and he composed many ballads about its magnificence. Some speculate that this beard was created by Dvergar, or that he was a Dvergar, while others say he naturally grew this incredible specimen. After his death, it is said that after his funeral pyre all that remained in the ashes was a pristine magical golden beard.

If someone were to put the beard near their chin, it will magically graft itself to the face [Counter: P]. While worn, the wearer will hear non-stop singing as the spirit of the Mountain King comes and inhabits the body.

Staff of Serpents

SIZE:5   QR:17

DF: 1 I PIERCE: 0 I REACH: 4 I PARRY: 2 I FOCUS: 2 I META: KNOCKDOWN

Major Sacrifice +1 to rearrange the Metas in a spell active power (remap the Traits to the Metas)

Active Power: *Gate (Familiar-Snake) {Seith Spell}* [Amplify Amplify Amplify]

The Seithkonas who have debased themselves to Nidhogg and his realm of Nidavellir are granted a token of his appreciation. These staves are not only a sign of their allegiance, but also a very potent weapon in Nidhogg's cause to spread his will upon the worlds of Yggdrasil.

Stone of Scone

SIZE: 6   QR: 4

This stone throne looks rather simplistic, crafted from three stone blocks, each roughly six cubic feet. The throne, however, is imbued with a very special enchantment backed by the White God. When a new king is crowned on it, he gains a "curse" condition with intensity 1. While this condition is in effect, any deed performed for the good of the kingdom gains a +1 skill rank. This effect dissipates if the king ever turns his back on the White God or his kingdom.

Sun Stone

SIZE: 1   QR: 1

Navigation rank +1 to anyone with a Mental Trait of 3 or more.

This ivory white smoky crystal comes in shards that can be as small as a finger to as large as a plate. These tools of navigation have always been useful to the adventurous sailor, but with the sun devoured, they have become quite useless. Their magnificent power was to allow a sailor to see the sun even on cloudy days. Peering through the crystal would allow one to see the sun, even obscured by an overcast sky. There are rumors that some blacksmiths have created a variant that works by homing in on the distant and subtle glow of Muspelheim or the shimmering Bifrost Bridge.

Sun Bow

SIZE: 6   QR: 24

DF: 5 I PIERCE: 4 I RANGE: 20 I PARRY: 0 I FOCUS: 2 I META: SEE BELOW

Meta: *Gore or Alka of Fire (+4 tokens) that deals +4 Physical damage and applies the Degeneration condition with +1 Intensity*

Active Power: *Penetrator Stance - ranged attack actions strike everyone in a straight line (similar to 2 range metas creating a "beam" effect)*

Passive Power: *Die Hard, Tap the Source (Fire)*

This bow shines with the light of Alfgard and has the fiery properties of Muspelheim. Outside of combat, the bow resembles a beautiful Alfar maiden that shines like a hundred torches (100' radius of light). The maiden is a beautifully rendered effigy of Dvergar design. It floats over the ground and follows her owner until she is needed in combat. Once combat breaks out she transforms into a fiery bow and floats into her owner's hand during the Upkeep phase.

This is a very noticeable weapon. Those who would be brave enough to own one will need to be just as mighty so as to not fall prey to the undesired elements that would be attracted by it.

Thistle Wolf Claws

SIZE: 1   QR:6

Passive Power: *Fangs, Unarmed Power, Unencumbered Dodger*

This is a very popular paw or hoof fitted manopele that increases a pet's feral factor. Those with quadruped thanes will attach these to the paws in order to make claw attacks more vicious in nature. This magic item will also add more dexterity to the said beast.

Torc of the Jotuns

SIZE: 3   QR:13

Passive Power: *Fangs, Unarmed Power, Unencumbered Dodger*

Passive Power: *Giant Size, Feral Transformation, Enter Rage, Raging Cohort, Bestial Heart*

Active Powers: *Blood Wolf Form*

The items thrown during a combat round return to the thrower during Cleanup

Since the portents of Ragnarok have become prevalent, these magical torcs have been handed out to many ogres, ettins and trolls who reside within Jotunheim. More Dvergar have been commissioned to duplicate these torcs so they could be more widely utilized by the Rime Jotun armies.

Tyrfing

SIZE:3   QR:17

DF: 10 I PIERCE: 10 I REACH: 2 I PARRY: 0 I FOCUS: 0 I META: IMMOLATE

Curse: *Every round during Upkeep, 2 ranks of Possession are applied to the wielder [Counter: S per intensity] and 2 ranks of Rage are applied to the wielder [Counter: S per intensity] forcing the wielder to slay the closest combatant (friend or foe).*

Curse: *Every harmful spell that targets the wielder also applies the Vulnerable condition [Counter: S].*

Curse: *Attempting to detect the curses applies a difficulty +3 to the skill check.*

Svarfrlami was the grandson of Odin, and the one who commissioned the creation of this magnificent sword. It wasn't so much a commission as a coercion of two Dvergar named Dvalinn and Durin. The two Dvergar weren't pleased with the arrangement and decided to add a few curses to Tyrfing. When unsheathed, Tyrfing's blade is coated in flames, causing opponents to immolate. It always strikes true and has unearthly sharpness. However it also carries several curses. The first is that it will cause a fatality each and every time it is unsheathed. Secondly it was destined to cause 3 great evils (which have already occured). Lastly the sword eventually ensures the death of its owner.

The Immolation weapon meta always triggers, causing Degeneration. If the Weapon meta is activated with an Active power that ultilizes the sword, then an additional intensity of Degeneration will be applied.

Visage of Blood

SIZE: 1   QR:6

Passive Power: *Arcane Reach, Penumbral Ring, Niflheim's Boon*

This iron mask magically attaches itself to the wearer. The mask fully covers the face with only 3 slits revealing the appearance below: the eyes and mouth. This iron mask has signs of rust which streak downwards, hence the appearance influencing the name. To remove the mask, the wearer must pay an Ultimate Sacrifice +1.

Wayland's Swords - Almance

SIZE:3   QR:22

DF: 4 I PIERCE: 4 I REACH: 2 I PARRY: 4 I FOCUS: 2 I META: GORE

Passive Power: *Alabaster Magician*

Set Bonus: *Bestow Conviction, Bestow Wisdom, Companion in War*

Almance, Curtana and Durandal were crafted over 100 years ago by the legendary blacksmith Wayland. They were commissioned for the legendary crusader named Roland of Francia. They operate as a set, as long as three warriors take up the swords and fight within 50' of each other, the set bonus is unlocked. Almance has been designed for a warrior with some magical capabilities.

Wayland's Swords - Caliburn, Sword of Kings

SIZE:3   QR:27

DF: 5 I PIERCE: 2 I REACH: 2 I PARRY: 5 I FOCUS: 3 I META: BLIND

Passive Power: *Resistance to Degeneration (x2)*

Dvergar Engineering: *It will only allow itself to be wielded by one who is destined to lead great men. It will find a way to get lost if acquired by someone who is unworthy.*

The legendary blacksmith Wayland was approached by a great Voelva with a request for a sword which will define future kings. Caliburn was designed to seek out those who have a potent destiny which has been emblazoned on the Tapestry of Fate. It has been wielded by the infamous king Arthur, lord of the Britons.

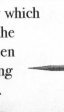

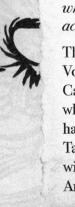

Wayland's Swords - Curtana

SIZE:3   QR:22

DF: 4 I PIERCE: 4 I REACH: 2 I PARRY: 10 I FOCUS: 0 I META: GORE

Passive Power: *Untouchable*

Set Bonus: *Bestow Conviction, Bestow Wisdom, Companion in War*

Almance, Curtana and Durandal were crafted over 100 years ago by the legendary blacksmith Wayland. They were commissioned for the legendary crusader named Roland of Francia. They operate as a set, as long as three warriors take up the swords and fight within 50' of each other, the set bonus is unlocked. Curtana is a balanced sword designed for defense.

Wayland's Swords - Durandal

SIZE:3   QR:22

DF: 7 I PIERCE: 10 I REACH: 2 I PARRY: 4 I FOCUS: 0 I META: GORE

Passive Power: *Favour Offence*

Set Bonus: *Bestow Conviction, Bestow Wisdom, Companion in War*

Almance, Curtana and Durandal were crafted over 100 years ago by the legendary blacksmith Wayland. They were commissioned for the legendary crusader named Roland of Francia. They operate as a set, as long as three warriors take up the swords and fight within 50' of each other, the set bonus is unlocked. Durandal has been designed to penetrate armour and defences.

Wayland's Swords - Mimung

SIZE:3   QR:21

DF: 6 I PIERCE: 2 I REACH: 2 I PARRY: 4 I FOCUS: 1 I META: KNOCKDOWN

Active Power: *Sundering Blow*

Creature Reliquary: *Jarnvid Wolf Fang - automatically applies +2 Vulnerable per attack*

Wayland purposely designed this weapon so its reputation would precede the warrior, instilling fear in the hearts of his foes. The weapon is notorious for destroying weapons and armour, making it a terror on the battlefield.

Ymir's Call

SIZE:6   QR:40

DF: 8 I PIERCE: 4 I REACH: 4 I PARRY: 0 I FOCUS: 0 I META: HAMSTRING

Active Power: *Raging Attack*

Passive Power: *Enter Rage, Drive Back, Constitution, Frenzy, Giant Size, Unstoppable Aggression, Unstoppable Carnage*

This axe is a mighty status symbol that will add +2 ranks to Verbal Manipulation when dealing with denizens from Jotunheim

It is said that Ymir himself forged this mighty Axe for his children and while this is probably not true, nobody can deny that it's truly a masterpiece weapon. Ymir's Call contains very rare crystals that formed only when the sun shone upon Jotunheim. It has been many millennia since this realm has felt the sun and its denizens long for justice. These memories fuel the aggression of the wielder to blood curdling summits. Many powerful Jarls wielded this axe of conquest, unifying tribes to crush their opponents. The huge axe was obviously not built to be wielded by humans, though the strongest and largest of them can still make good use of it by holding it in both hands.

Woads (Tattoos) of Power

SIZE: 1 (CONTAINER)   QR:6

Consumable

Blue - Focus +2

Black - Afterlife Wyrd +1

Red - DF + 2 and Evade +1

Green - Upkeep Heal +6

This special pigment is meant for temporary tattoos that confer some magical effect. The effect lasts for 1 hour. The number of applications available is based on a rune pull:

physical 1

mental 4

spiritual 9

Denizens

Banshee

Banshees appear as frightening ghostly women with a dark and alien psyche. They are the supernatural emissaries of the Norns, and sisters of the Fylgias. It is said that to hear a banshee's song, one will bear witness to someone's demise. In many ways, the consequence of the song may be more frightening than witnessing this nether spirit. Their native realm is Niflheim and they are drawn out of Niflheim by the Strands of Life as they are woven into the Tapestry of Fate. Banshees are drawn to the victim as their Strand of Life approaches its end. Usually victims with Fylgias get these dark visitations in their final minutes. Banshees have been known to snuff out the lives of those around the one who's been destined to die at the preordained time.

If your campaign is rooted heavily in pre-ordained destiny, then introducing a Banshee into play means you must kill-off a persona of great importance (either a dweller or a denizen). This has strong consequences on the gaming group, so it must be used judiciously and after careful deliberation!

Base Powers: None
Base Level: 0
Size/Move: 4/4
Equipment Type: None

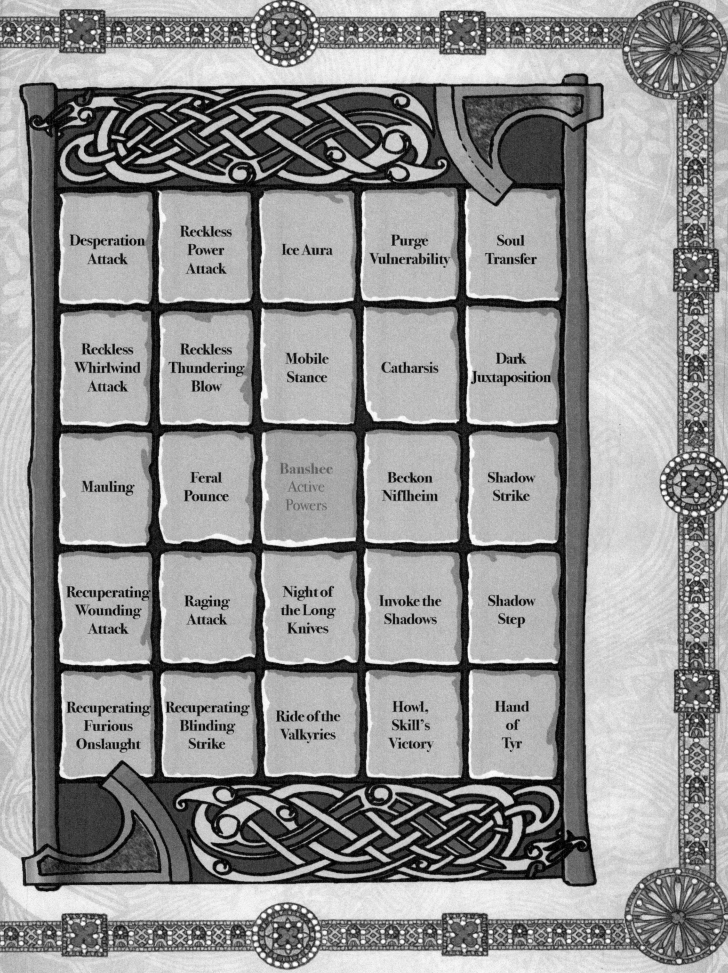

Desperation Attack | Reckless Power Attack | Ice Aura | Purge Vulnerability | Soul Transfer

Reckless Whirlwind Attack | Reckless Thundering Blow | Mobile Stance | Catharsis | Dark Juxtaposition

Mauling | Feral Pounce | Banshee Active Powers | Beckon Niflheim | Shadow Strike

Recuperating Wounding Attack | Raging Attack | Night of the Long Knives | Invoke the Shadows | Shadow Step

Recuperating Furious Onslaught | Recuperating Blinding Strike | Ride of the Valkyries | Howl, Skill's Victory | Hand of Tyr

Keen Aptitude	Dance of Spring	Agility	Dance of Summer	Keen Aptitude
Spirit Domination	Sadist	Hover	Unencumbered Dodger	Aura of Influence
Fangs	Enter Rage	Banshee Passive Powers	Tap the Source	Running Jab
Spiritual Conduit	Misery Loves Company	Essence of the Ghost	Tactical Advantage	Alka Mastery
Keen Aptitude	Giant Size	Angered Spirit	Dance of Winter	Keen Aptitude

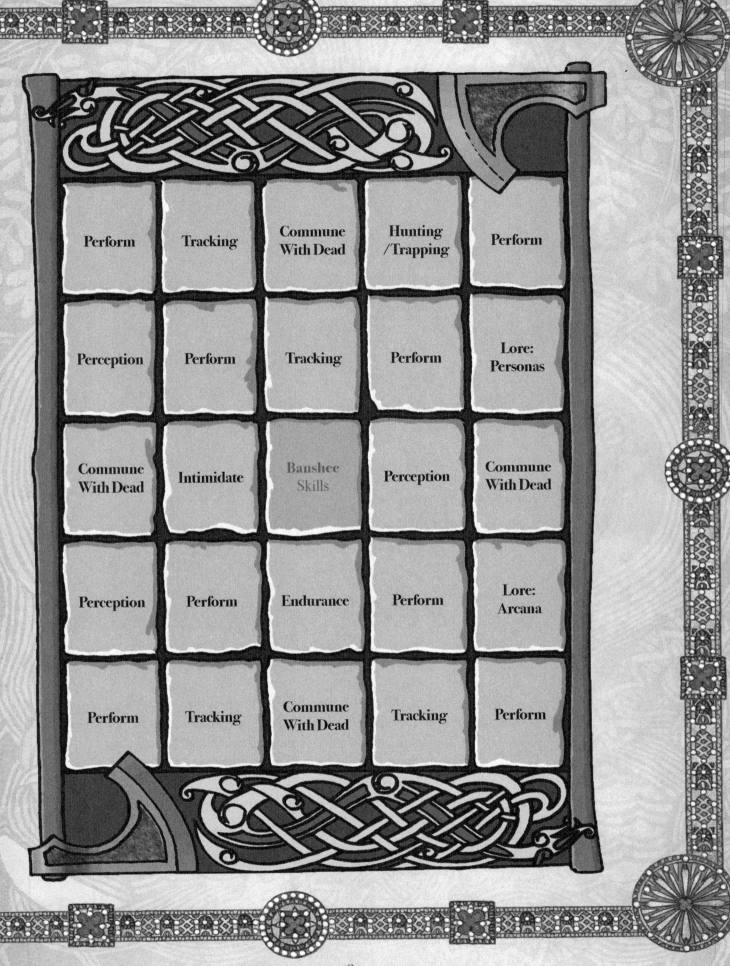

Perform	Tracking	Commune With Dead	Hunting /Trapping	Perform
Perception	Perform	Tracking	Perform	Lore: Personas
Commune With Dead	Intimidate	Banshee Skills	Perception	Commune With Dead
Perception	Perform	Endurance	Perform	Lore: Arcana
Perform	Tracking	Commune With Dead	Tracking	Perform

Borghild (Land Vaettir)

(Land fortification violent battle)

A Borghild is a physical manifestation of a Vaettir. When a Vaettir needs to assume material form so it can bring order to its land, it will rise up as a gigantic monstrosity. It appears as half land and half beast, as if a beast rose up out of the ground and ended up carrying a mountain or other biome on its back. The creature in this form is considered to be shapechanged/transformed.

Base Powers: Quadruped
Base Level: +3
Size/Move: 6/12
Equipment Type: None

Recuperating Furious Onslaught	Regenerating Attack	Run Away Laughing	Spirit Bastion Stance	Spiritual Abortion
Recuperating Wounding Attack	Cleansing Attack	Gate Hrokkvir	Apples of Idunn	Stitch Destiny
Sudden Blizzard (Beckon Jotunheim) {Manoeuver}	Magma Eruption (Beckon Muspelheim) {Manoeuver}	Borghild Active Powers	Catharsis	Howl, Hati's Victory
Attack from Above	Swallow	Trample	Channeling	Howl, Skoll's Victory
Destroyer of Crowds	Aggressive Assault	Aggressive Stance	Defensive Stance	Shake Off (Power over Wind) {Manoeuver}

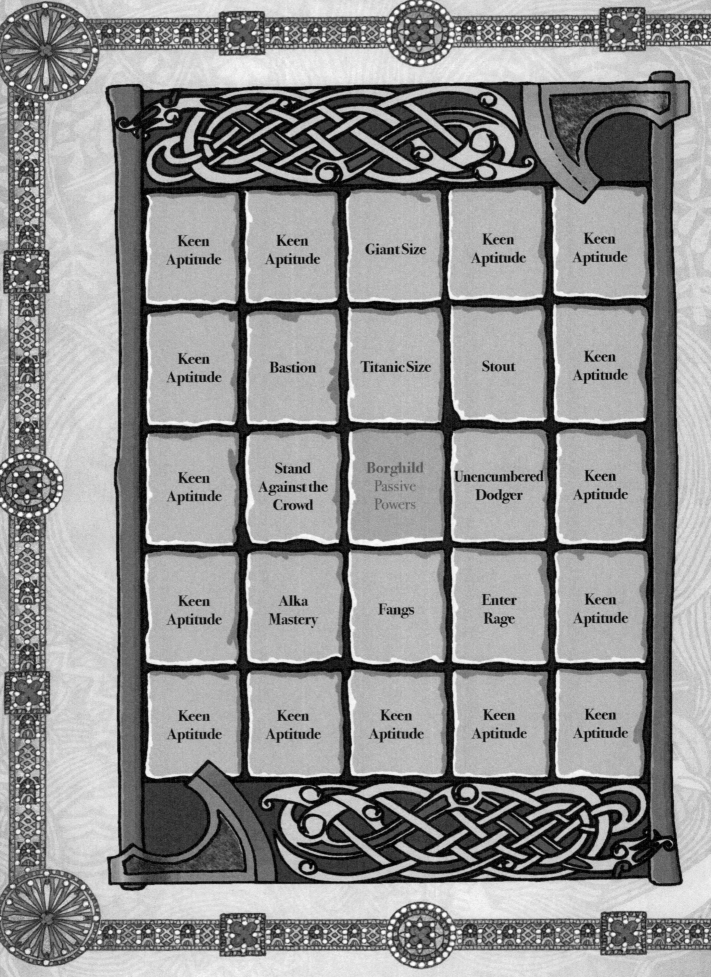

Keen Aptitude | Keen Aptitude | Giant Size | Keen Aptitude | Keen Aptitude

Keen Aptitude | Bastion | Titanic Size | Stout | Keen Aptitude

Keen Aptitude | Stand Against the Crowd | Borghild Passive Powers | Unencumbered Dodger | Keen Aptitude

Keen Aptitude | Alka Mastery | Fangs | Enter Rage | Keen Aptitude

Keen Aptitude | Keen Aptitude | Keen Aptitude | Keen Aptitude | Keen Aptitude

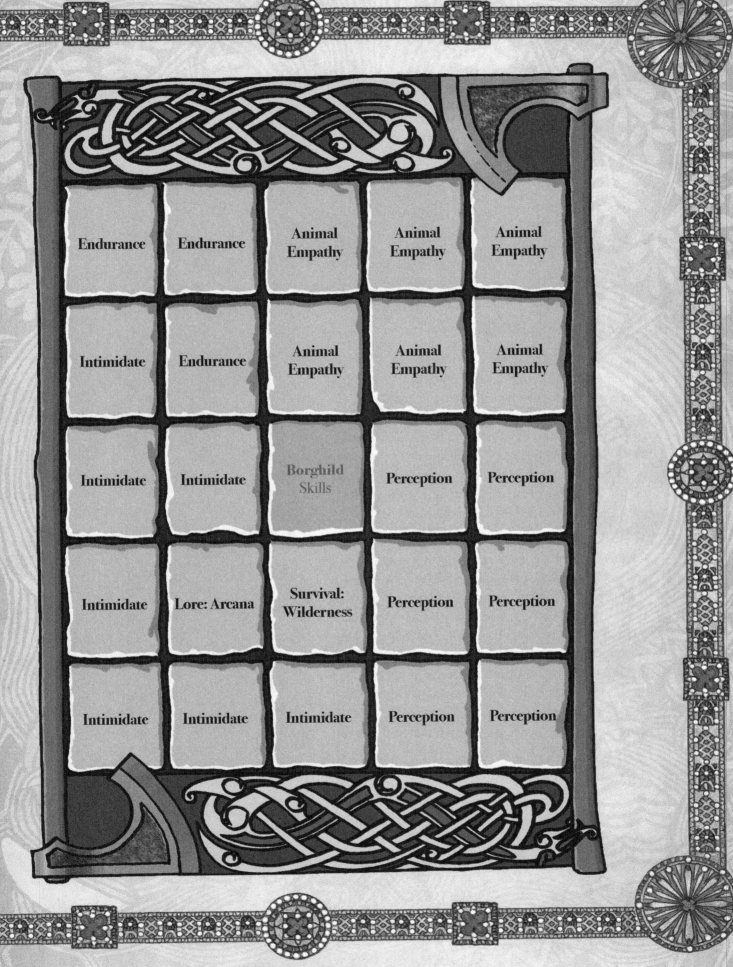

Endurance	Endurance	Animal Empathy	Animal Empathy	Animal Empathy
Intimidate	Endurance	Animal Empathy	Animal Empathy	Animal Empathy
Intimidate	Intimidate	Borghild Skills	Perception	Perception
Intimidate	Lore: Arcana	Survival: Wilderness	Perception	Perception
Intimidate	Intimidate	Intimidate	Perception	Perception

Doppelgangr

There are many whispered tales that speak of the mysterious Doppelgangr. Someone is accused of having an adult twin sibling that actually died in childhood... Engaging in a conversation with someone and as they leave through one door they enter through another and claim to have never met before... A reflected image which has no pupils. The perplexity remains high since no one has even seen a Doppelgangr in true form, let alone had a meaningful exchange with one about its origins.

These double walkers have the mighty power to assume the form of another. They can mimic apperance, sound and smells perfectly, but sometimes have issues mimicking mannerisms. Their pupils also fail to register when viewed through a reflection. In a world where one's reputation is worth more than gold, a mischievous Doppelgangr's actions may bring the downfall of even the greatest of Karls. While not all Doppelgangrs are hostile, having their identity compromised usually results in a fight or flight reaction. Many believe that the sight of a Doppelgangr is perhaps an omen of things to come.

Base Powers: Can assume the form of any being regardless of size or shape (power restrictions removed)

Base Level: +2

Size/Move: 4/4

Equipment Type: None (body dissolves at death)

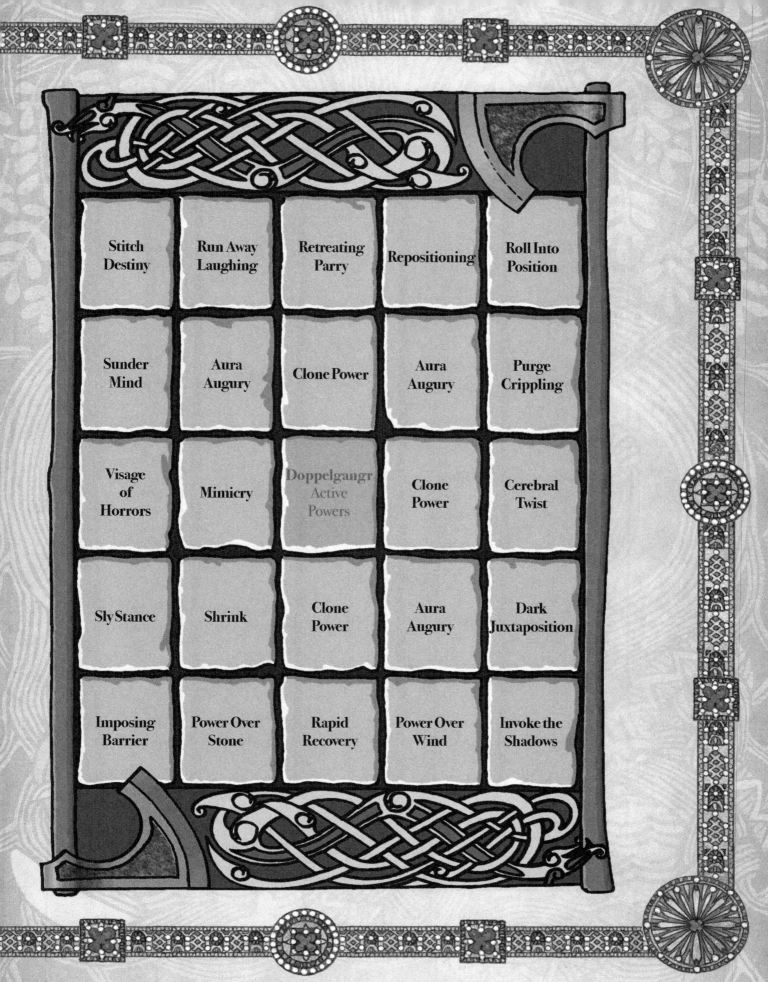

Stitch Destiny	Run Away Laughing	Retreating Parry	Repositioning	Roll Into Position
Sunder Mind	Aura Augury	Clone Power	Aura Augury	Purge Crippling
Visage of Horrors	Mimicry	Doppelgangr Active Powers	Clone Power	Cerebral Twist
Sly Stance	Shrink	Clone Power	Aura Augury	Dark Juxtaposition
Imposing Barrier	Power Over Stone	Rapid Recovery	Power Over Wind	Invoke the Shadows

Keen Aptitude	Keen Aptitude	Agility	Keen Aptitude	Keen Aptitude
Keen Aptitude	Blend into Shadow	Unbreakable Mind	Stout	Keen Aptitude
Rune of Fate	Rune of Scrying	Doppelgangr Passive Powers	Tactician	Constitution
Keen Aptitude	Fae-Kin	Nimble	Resistance to Possession	Keen Aptitude
Keen Aptitude	Keen Aptitude	Insight	Keen Aptitude	Keen Aptitude

Disguise	Escape	Lore: Arcana	Lore: Personas	Capture Memories
Etiquette	Disguise	Capture Memories	Lore: Locales	Disguise
Endurance	Capture Memories	Doppelgangr Skills	Capture Memories	Feather Fingers
Disguise	Lore: Locales	Capture Memories	Disguise	Sense Motive
Capture Memories	Lore: Personas	Lore: Arcana	Escape	Disguise

Draugar

Draugar are corpses of the dead that have reanimated with a lost soul because Hel has rejected their entry into Niflheim. They act as Hel's army in the lands of the living. Draugar corpses take on the appearance of charred black bodies, with glowing blue eyes and who move with exceptional speed and agility. High ranking Draugar will carry weapons and armour made out of Niflheim ore called Death Bone. These weapons can be detected by Draugar within 100 miles. They will do anything in their power to reclaim such a weapon if it were to fall into non-Draugar hands. Draugar receive a bonus on Perception checks when trying to locate Draugar equipment. The bonus is equal to +5 per piece at that location (if a group is carrying 3 pieces, the Draugar receive a +15 Perception bonus).

Draugar are very cunning and will seek out their brethren in order to gain strength in numbers. They will avoid a conflict if victory isn't in their favour. Of course Hel may direct them as she chooses and they are powerless to object.

Base Powers: None
Base Level: 0
Size/Move: 4/4
Equipment Type: Special- 3 to 4 equipped items with individual QR equivalent to half the denizen's level

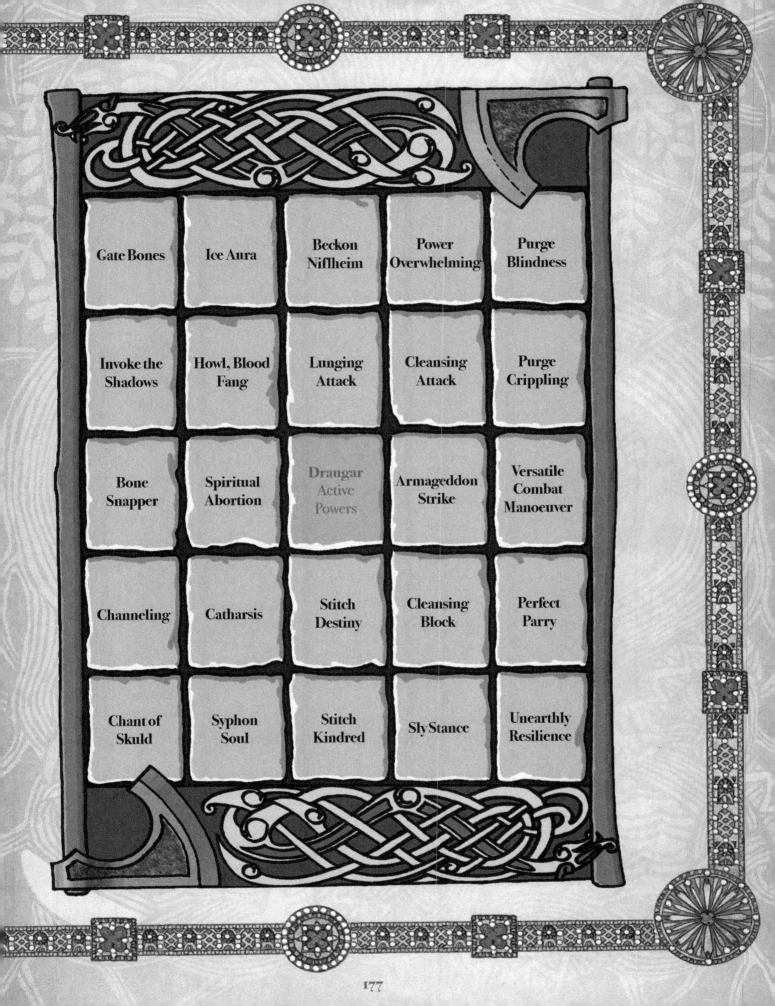

Gate Bones	Ice Aura	Beckon Niflheim	Power Overwhelming	Purge Blindness
Invoke the Shadows	Howl, Blood Fang	Lunging Attack	Cleansing Attack	Purge Crippling
Bone Snapper	Spiritual Abortion	Draugar Active Powers	Armageddon Strike	Versatile Combat Manoeuver
Channeling	Catharsis	Stitch Destiny	Cleansing Block	Perfect Parry
Chant of Skuld	Syphon Soul	Stitch Kindred	Sly Stance	Unearthly Resilience

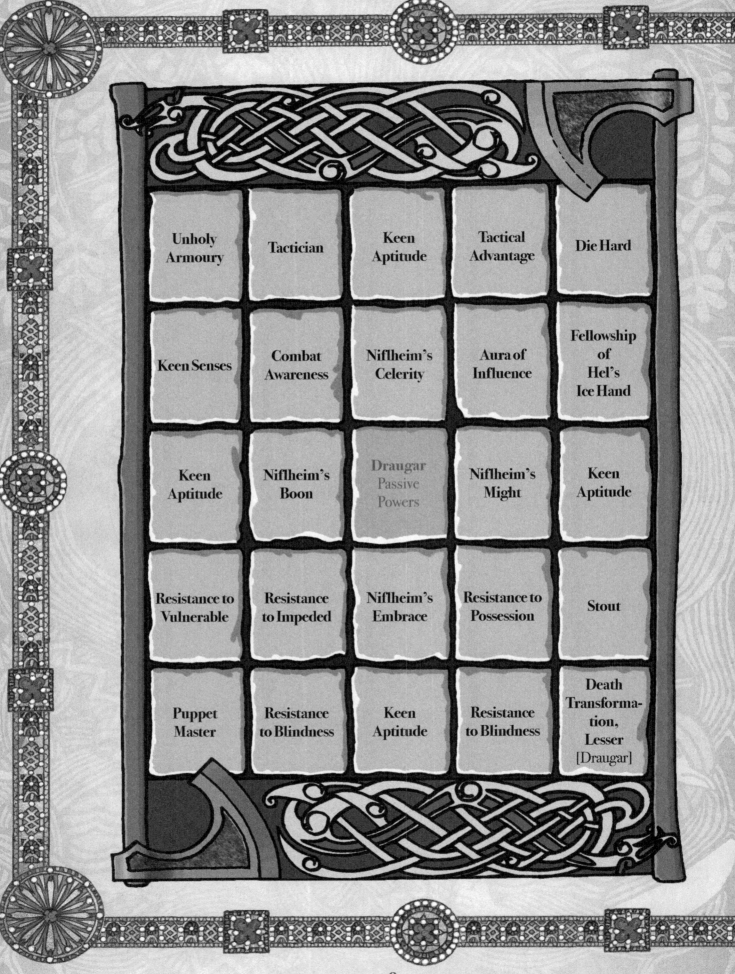

Unholy Armoury	Tactician	Keen Aptitude	Tactical Advantage	Die Hard
Keen Senses	Combat Awareness	Niflheim's Celerity	Aura of Influence	Fellowship of Hel's Ice Hand
Keen Aptitude	Niflheim's Boon	Draugar Passive Powers	Niflheim's Might	Keen Aptitude
Resistance to Vulnerable	Resistance to Impeded	Niflheim's Embrace	Resistance to Possession	Stout
Puppet Master	Resistance to Blindness	Keen Aptitude	Resistance to Blindness	Death Transformation, Lesser [Draugar]

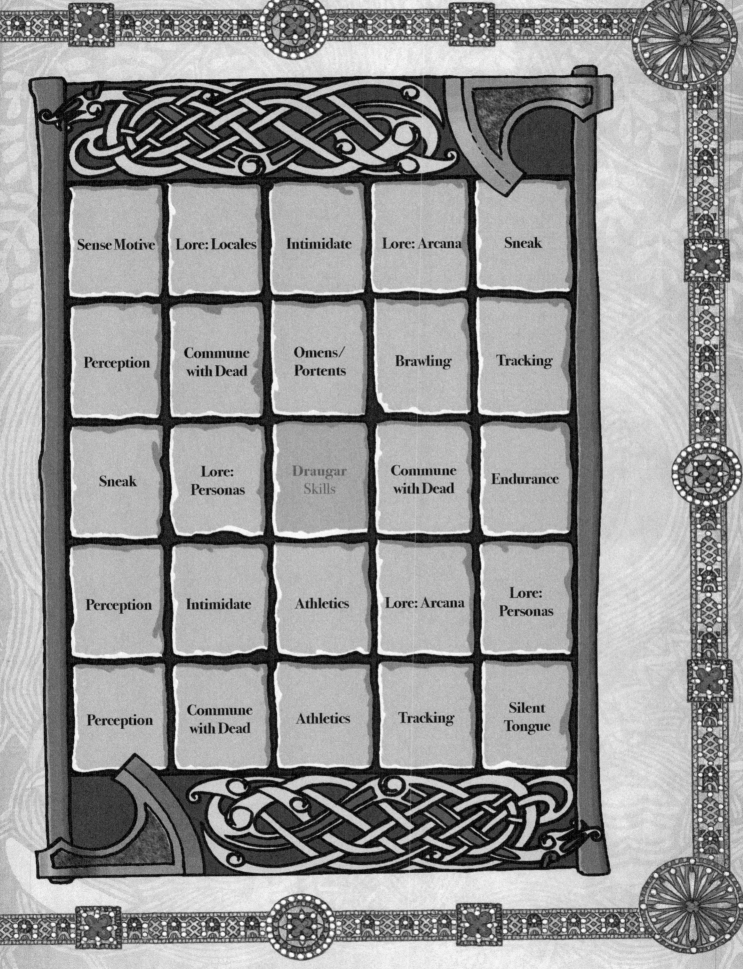

Sense Motive	Lore: Locales	Intimidate	Lore: Arcana	Sneak
Perception	Commune with Dead	Omens/Portents	Brawling	Tracking
Sneak	Lore: Personas	Draugar Skills	Commune with Dead	Endurance
Perception	Intimidate	Athletics	Lore: Arcana	Lore: Personas
Perception	Commune with Dead	Athletics	Tracking	Silent Tongue

Dreyri

Dreyri are very large blood drinking bats who come from Vanagard and have a taste for human blood. Unlike their mundane brethren, they have fully functional eyes and are cunning predators. Dreyri have gotten a lot more aggressive since the onset of Fimbulwinter, some say in order to assert themselves at the top of the food chain. They are drawn to light and shiny objects.

Base Powers: Flight, Move +2

Base Level: +1

Size/Move: 4/4

Equipment Type: None

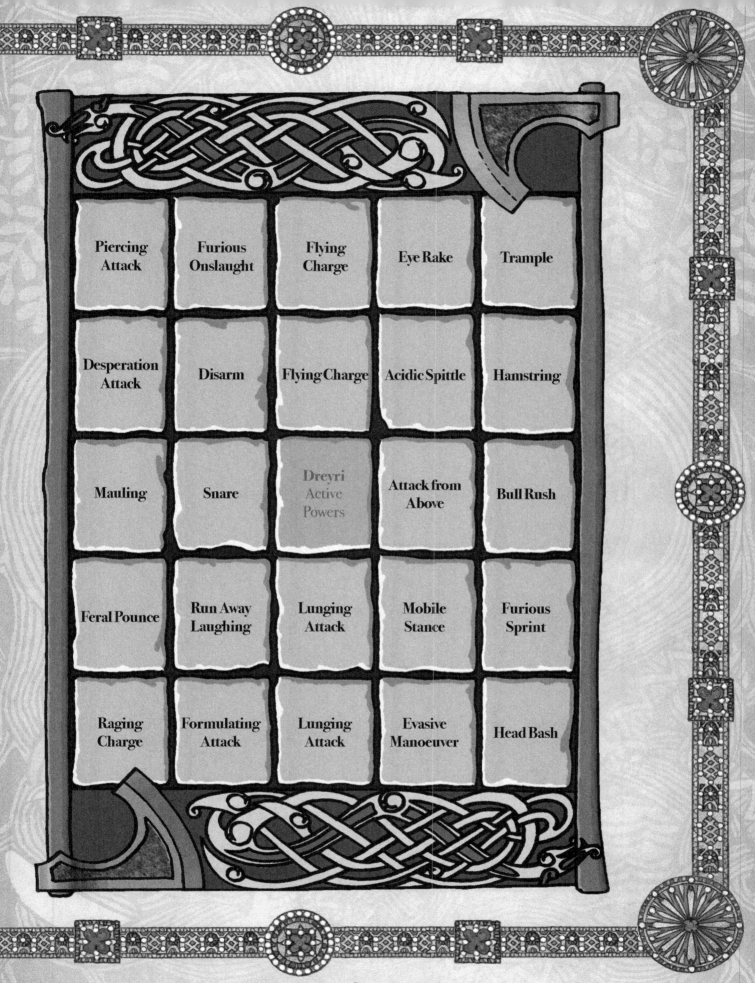

Piercing Attack	Furious Onslaught	Flying Charge	Eye Rake	Trample
Desperation Attack	Disarm	Flying Charge	Acidic Spittle	Hamstring
Mauling	Snare	Dreyri Active Powers	Attack from Above	Bull Rush
Feral Pounce	Run Away Laughing	Lunging Attack	Mobile Stance	Furious Sprint
Raging Charge	Formulating Attack	Lunging Attack	Evasive Manoeuver	Head Bash

Keen Aptitude	Desperation	Giant Size	Precision	Keen Aptitude
Drive Back	Stout	Fleet Footed	Die Hard	Render Helpless
Giant Size	Agility	Dreyri Passive Powers	Running Jab	Giant Size
Dance Away	Unencumbered Dodger	Combat Awareness	Fangs	Sadist
Keen Aptitude	Frenzy	Giant Size	Keen Senses	Keen Aptitude

Athletics	Sense Motive	Sense Motive	Sense Motive	Survival: Wilderness
Sneak	Intimidate	Sense Motive	Perception	Athletics
Sneak	Silent Tongue	Dreyri Skills	Perception	Survival: Wilderness
Sneak	Lore: Locales	Survival: Wilderness	Lore: Personas	Tracking
Perception	Athletics	Survival: Wilderness	Perception	Survival: Wilderness

Forge Beast: Lilliputian

Lilliputians are tiny humanoids from the realm of Asgard. They have an incredible passion for creating things and will easily make friendships with those who have talents in said passion. Asgard's most magnificent feats of architecture are thanks to Lilliputian talent and passion. They know no borders and will travel to other realms should creative opportunities lead them abroad.

Base Powers: Perfect vision in darkness
Base Level: 0
Size/Move: 1/1
Equipment Type: None

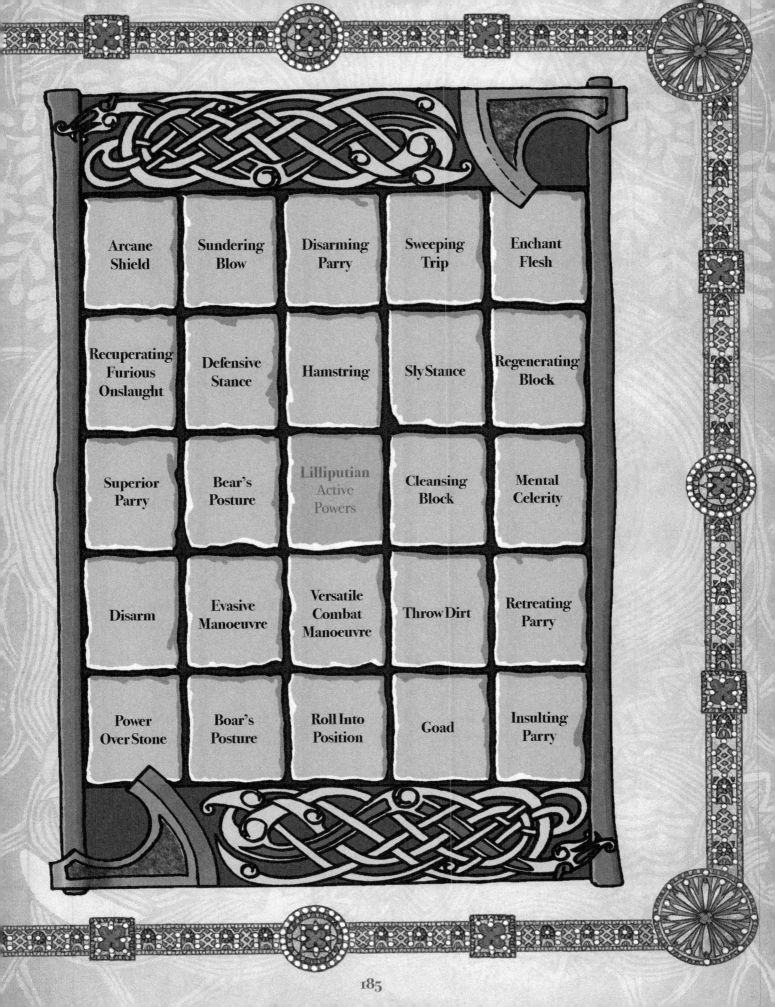

Arcane Shield	Sundering Blow	Disarming Parry	Sweeping Trip	Enchant Flesh
Recuperating Furious Onslaught	Defensive Stance	Hamstring	Sly Stance	Regenerating Block
Superior Parry	Bear's Posture	Lilliputian Active Powers	Cleansing Block	Mental Celerity
Disarm	Evasive Manoeuvre	Versatile Combat Manoeuvre	Throw Dirt	Retreating Parry
Power Over Stone	Boar's Posture	Roll Into Position	Goad	Insulting Parry

Keen Aptitude	Cornered Ferocity	Companion in Destiny	Dance Away	Keen Aptitude
Fleet Footed	Favour Defence	Agility	Cerebral Warrior	Fellowship of the Silver Shields
Companion in War	Nimble	Lilliputian Passive Powers	Bastion	Companion in Life
Protector	Spirit Warrior	Combat Awareness	Bestow Wisdom	Fuelled by the Crowd
Keen Aptitude	Defy the Crowd	Companion in Death	Mob Mentality	Keen Aptitude

Repair Equipment	Bestow Skill: Infuse	Appraisal	Bestow Skill: Infuse	Repair Equipment
Bestow Skill: Infuse	Bestow Skill: Miniaturize	Bestow Skill: Infuse	Sneak	Bestow Skill: Infuse
Bestow Skill: Craft	Silent Tongue	Lilliputian Skills	Bestow Skill: Silent Tongue	Bestow Skill: Craft
Bestow Skill: Miniaturize	Bestow Skill: Craft	Bestow Skill: Miniaturize	Bestow Skill: Craft	Bestow Skill: Miniaturize
Bestow Skill: Craft	Bestow Skill: Miniaturize	Bestow Skill: Craft	Bestow Skill: Miniaturize	Bestow Skill: Craft

Forge Beast: Nanus Drake

Nanus Drakes are tiny dragons that herald from the fiery realm of Muspelheim. They grow to 6' in length as adults, and are considered insect sized within the realm of fire giants. Nanus Drakes have a hunger for meta ores and are easily befriended by Blacksmiths. They have a peculiar shape, with small wings and a rather large head. The drake's fire creates a musical song as if the flames are licking over the strings of a harp.

Base Powers: Flight, Move +2
Base Level: 0
Size/Move: 1/3
Equipment Type: None

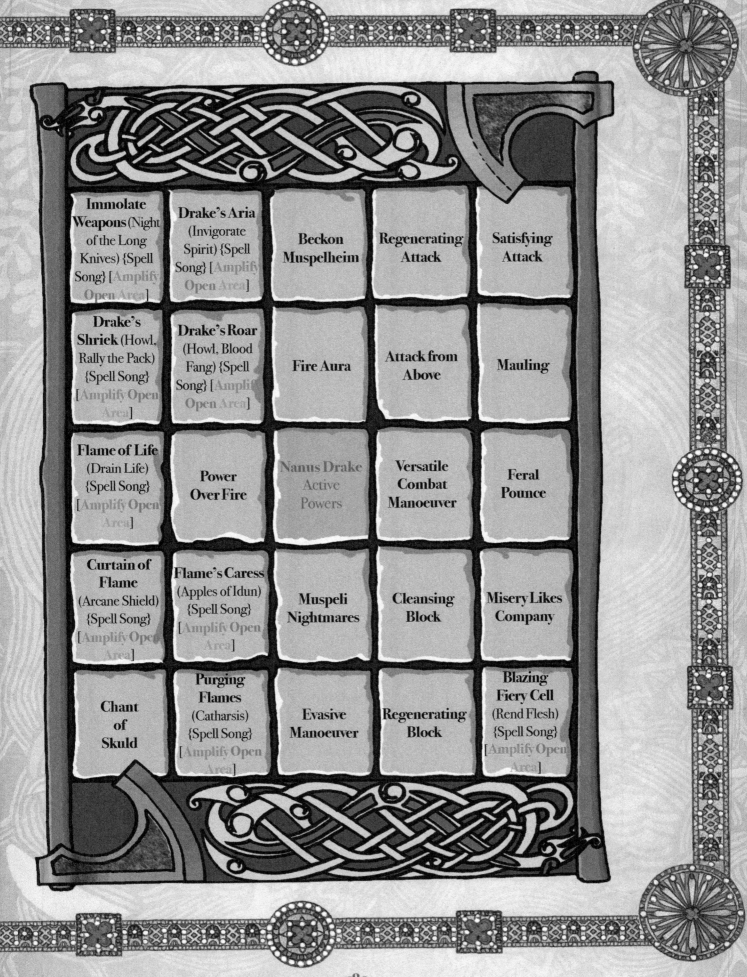

Immolate Weapons (Night of the Long Knives) {Spell Song} [Amplify Open Area]	**Drake's Aria** (Invigorate Spirit) {Spell Song} [Amplify Open Area]	**Beckon Muspelheim**	**Regenerating Attack**	**Satisfying Attack**
Drake's Shriek (Howl, Rally the Pack) {Spell Song} [Amplify Open Area]	**Drake's Roar** (Howl, Blood Fang) {Spell Song} [Amplify Open Area]	**Fire Aura**	**Attack from Above**	**Mauling**
Flame of Life (Drain Life) {Spell Song} [Amplify Open Area]	**Power Over Fire**	**Nanus Drake** Active Powers	**Versatile Combat Manoeuver**	**Feral Pounce**
Curtain of Flame (Arcane Shield) {Spell Song} [Amplify Open Area]	**Flame's Caress** (Apples of Idun) {Spell Song} [Amplify Open Area]	**Muspeli Nightmares**	**Cleansing Block**	**Misery Likes Company**
Chant of Skuld	**Purging Flames** (Catharsis) {Spell Song} [Amplify Open Area]	**Evasive Manoeuver**	**Regenerating Block**	**Blazing Fiery Cell** (Rend Flesh) {Spell Song} [Amplify Open Area]

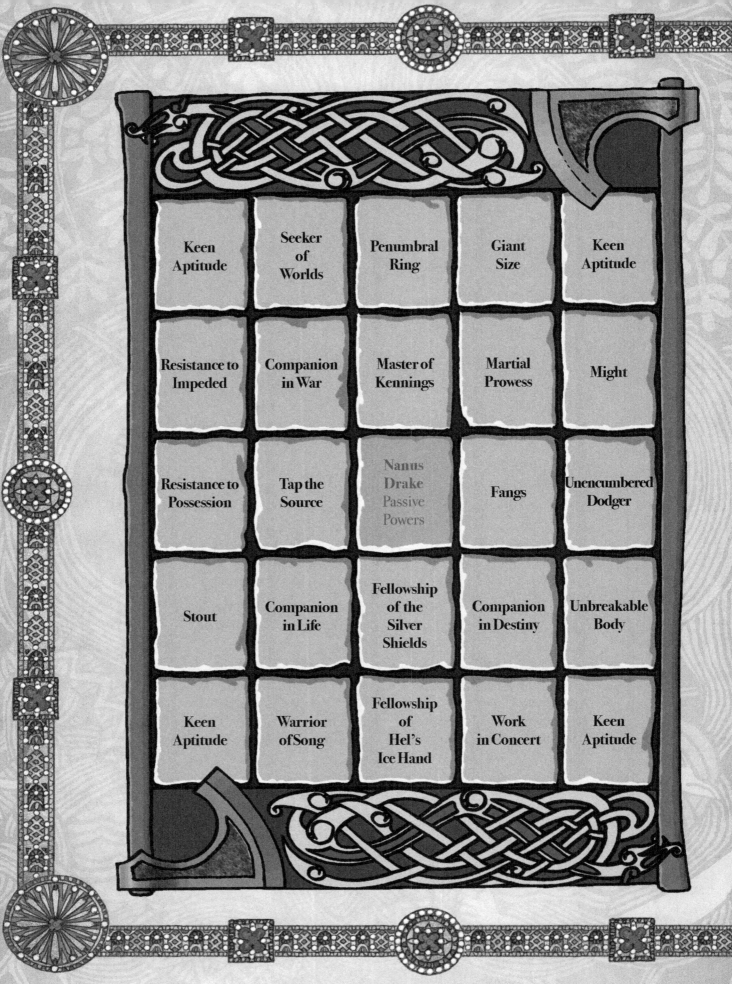

Keen Aptitude	Seeker of Worlds	Penumbral Ring	Giant Size	Keen Aptitude
Resistance to Impeded	Companion in War	Master of Kennings	Martial Prowess	Might
Resistance to Possession	Tap the Source	Nanus Drake Passive Powers	Fangs	Unencumbered Dodger
Stout	Companion in Life	Fellowship of the Silver Shields	Companion in Destiny	Unbreakable Body
Keen Aptitude	Warrior of Song	Fellowship of Hel's Ice Hand	Work in Concert	Keen Aptitude

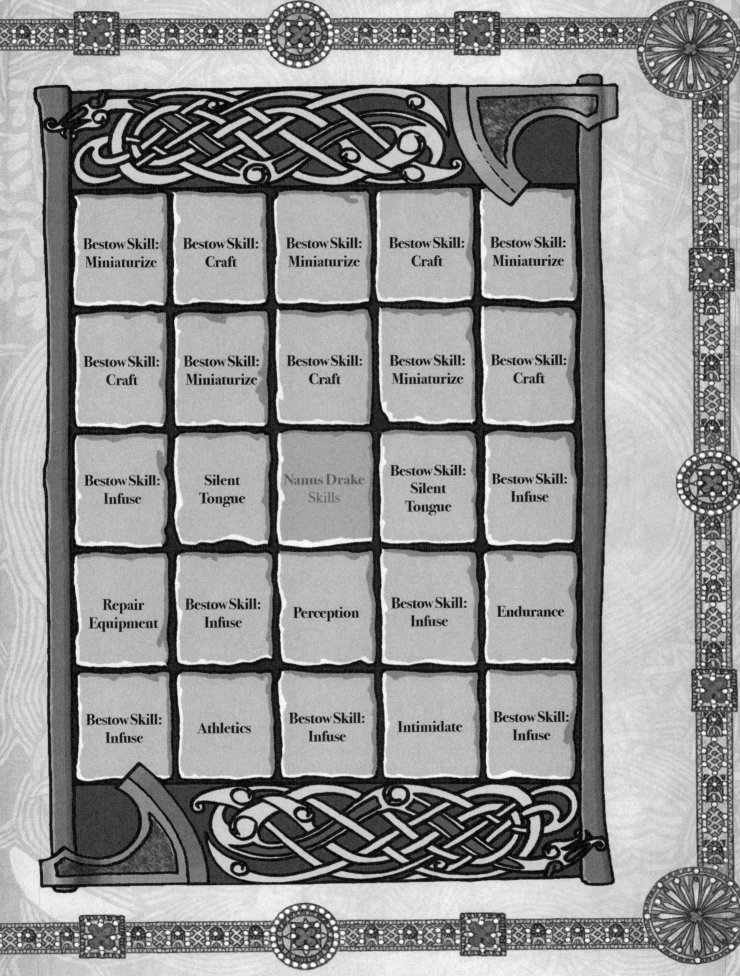

Bestow Skill: Miniaturize	Bestow Skill: Craft	Bestow Skill: Miniaturize	Bestow Skill: Craft	Bestow Skill: Miniaturize
Bestow Skill: Craft	Bestow Skill: Miniaturize	Bestow Skill: Craft	Bestow Skill: Miniaturize	Bestow Skill: Craft
Bestow Skill: Infuse	Silent Tongue	Nanus Drake Skills	Bestow Skill: Silent Tongue	Bestow Skill: Infuse
Repair Equipment	Bestow Skill: Infuse	Perception	Bestow Skill: Infuse	Endurance
Bestow Skill: Infuse	Athletics	Bestow Skill: Infuse	Intimidate	Bestow Skill: Infuse

Gargangjolp (Snake Shriekers)

Those who get infected with the blight, be it human or animal, become twisted by Nidhogg's magic and are transformed into "snake shriekers" (Gargangjolp). These twisted beings have been transformed on a mental and spiritual level, leaving only their bodies as a glimpse of their former selves. They run on all fours, slither and bound towards their prey hooting and howling as they go. Their final purpose is to impregnate as many others with the Snake Sigil as possible. They have no fear of death as the death of their bodies will liberate the serpentine spawn that lives within.

Base Powers: None
Base Level: 0
Size/Move: 4/4
Equipment Type: Martial

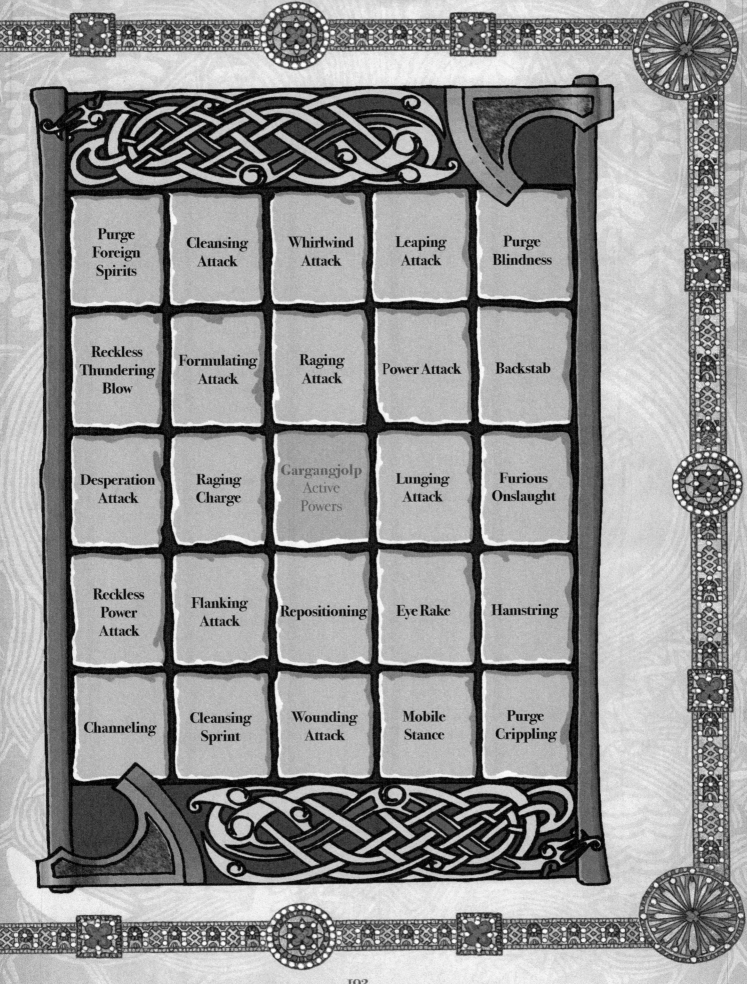

Purge Foreign Spirits	**Cleansing Attack**	**Whirlwind Attack**	**Leaping Attack**	**Purge Blindness**
Reckless Thundering Blow	**Formulating Attack**	**Raging Attack**	**Power Attack**	**Backstab**
Desperation Attack	**Raging Charge**	*Gargangjolp* Active Powers	**Lunging Attack**	**Furious Onslaught**
Reckless Power Attack	**Flanking Attack**	**Repositioning**	**Eye Rake**	**Hamstring**
Channeling	**Cleansing Sprint**	**Wounding Attack**	**Mobile Stance**	**Purge Crippling**

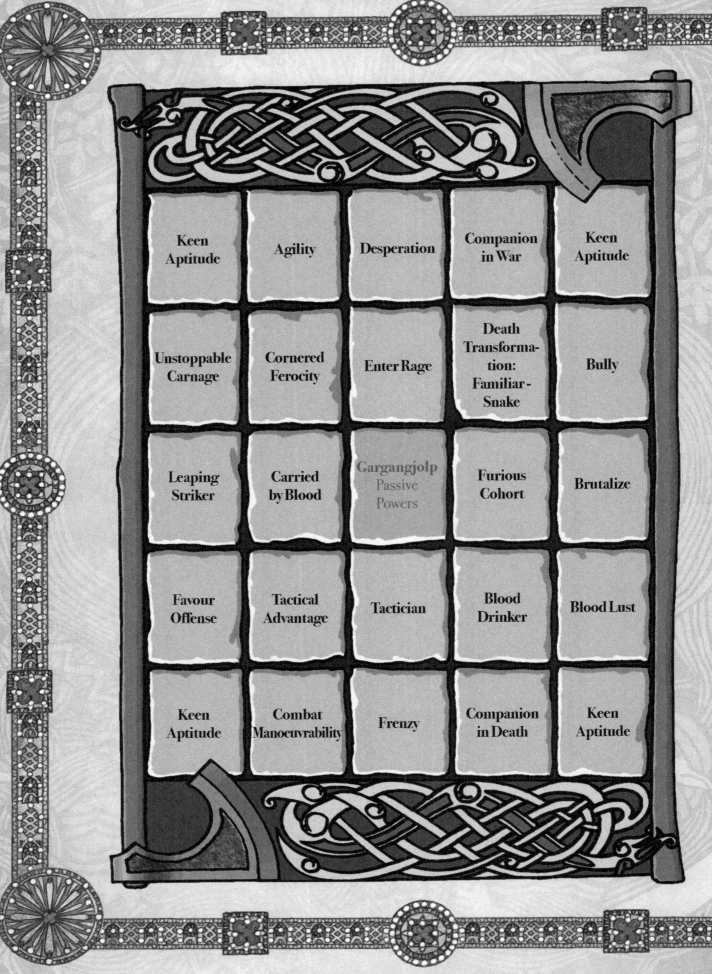

Keen Aptitude	Agility	Desperation	Companion in War	Keen Aptitude
Unstoppable Carnage	Cornered Ferocity	Enter Rage	Death Transformation: Familiar - Snake	Bully
Leaping Striker	Carried by Blood	Gargangjolp Passive Powers	Furious Cohort	Brutalize
Favour Offense	Tactical Advantage	Tactician	Blood Drinker	Blood Lust
Keen Aptitude	Combat Manoeuvrability	Frenzy	Companion in Death	Keen Aptitude

Brawling	Brawling	Brawling	Brawling	Brawling
Brawling	Brawling	Brawling	Brawling	Brawling
Sense Motive	Perception	Gargangjolp Skills	Endurance	Intimidate
Survival: Wilderness	Survival: Wilderness	Survival: Wilderness	Survival: Wilderness	Survival: Wilderness
Survival: Wilderness	Survival: Wilderness	Survival: Wilderness	Survival: Wilderness	Survival: Wilderness

Giant Spider

Similar to their much smaller brethren from Midgard, giant spiders herald from Jotunheim. They have similar physiology, however their size is a thousand fold. Giant spiders prefer cold and darkness, so since Ragnarok, they have made their way into the other realms. Their webs are very potent, almost indestructible (QR: 10+ denizen level) and have an adhesion that can effortlessly hold a polar bear securely snared. Extremely quiet, they usually ambush their prey, using an already well-established web. Giant spiders are very smart and use their webs to disarm opponents and pull their weapons well out of reach.

Base Powers: The web Alka also hinders Attack actions, while Impeded is greater than 1 intensity, only Weak Attack actions are possible. The Web can be burned off by any fire related power dealing more than 5 points (every 5 points of fire damage dealt to the snared victim reduces the Impeded condition by -1). At Intensity 4 Impeded the generic action of spinning to change facing orientation is not possible.

Base Level: 0

Size/Move: 4/4

Equipment Type: Lair

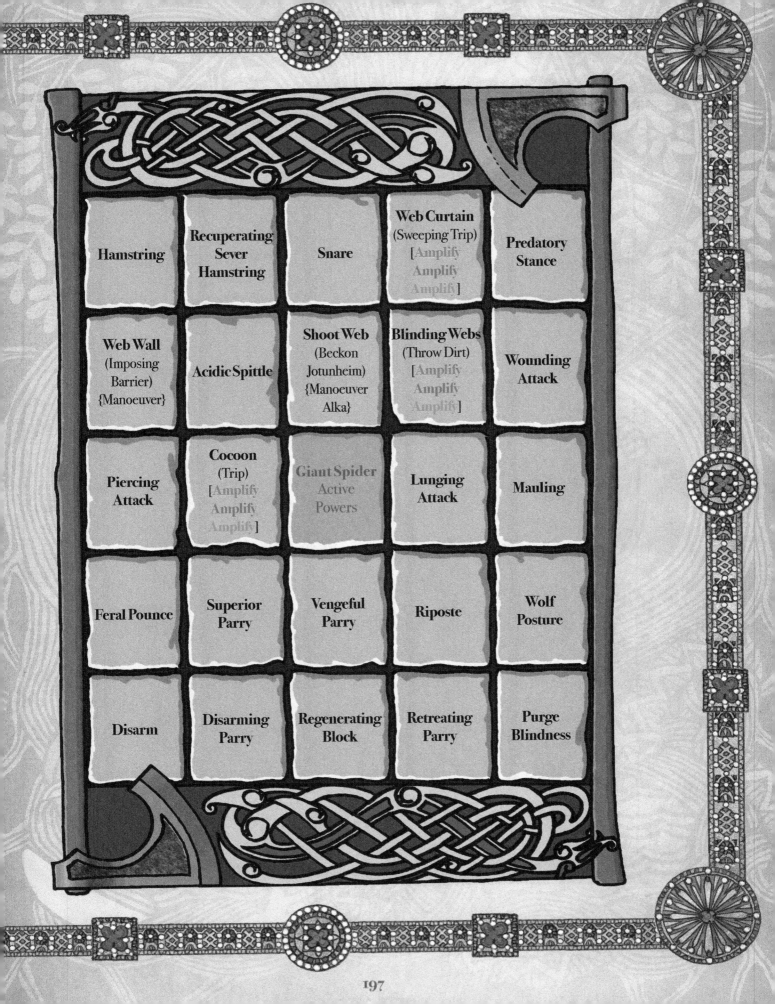

Hamstring	**Recuperating Sever Hamstring**	**Snare**	**Web Curtain** (Sweeping Trip) [Amplify Amplify Amplify]	**Predatory Stance**
Web Wall (Imposing Barrier) {Manoeuver}	**Acidic Spittle**	**Shoot Web** (Beckon Jotunheim) {Manoeuver Alka}	**Blinding Webs** (Throw Dirt) [Amplify Amplify Amplify]	**Wounding Attack**
Piercing Attack	**Cocoon** (Trip) [Amplify Amplify Amplify]	**Giant Spider** Active Powers	**Lunging Attack**	**Mauling**
Feral Pounce	**Superior Parry**	**Vengeful Parry**	**Riposte**	**Wolf Posture**
Disarm	**Disarming Parry**	**Regenerating Block**	**Retreating Parry**	**Purge Blindness**

Keen Aptitude	Render Helpless	Alka Mastery	Precision	Keen Aptitude
Untouchable	Giant Size	Trail Blaze	Giant Size	Might
Unarmed Power	Fangs	Giant Spider Passive Powers	Unencumbered Dodger	Stout
Brutalize	Giant Size	Tactical Advantage	Giant Size	Leaping Striker
Keen Aptitude	Pounce	Unbreakable Body	Keen Senses	Keen Aptitude

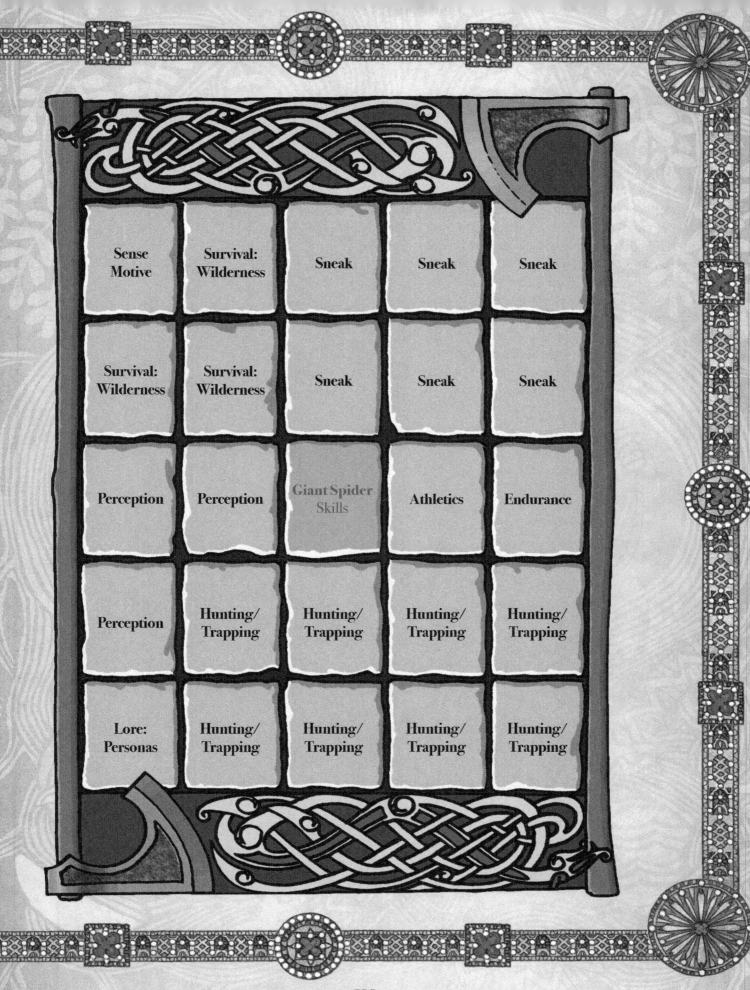

Sense Motive	Survival: Wilderness	Sneak	Sneak	Sneak
Survival: Wilderness	Survival: Wilderness	Sneak	Sneak	Sneak
Perception	Perception	Giant Spider Skills	Athletics	Endurance
Perception	Hunting/ Trapping	Hunting/ Trapping	Hunting/ Trapping	Hunting/ Trapping
Lore: Personas	Hunting/ Trapping	Hunting/ Trapping	Hunting/ Trapping	Hunting/ Trapping

Hrokkvir (Ent)

Hrokkvir are the most ancient trees (or shrubs) of the forest. They are wildlife that has matured over centuries and has blossomed into wild consciousness. This gift allows these Hrokkvir to move, walk, talk and see. Ents are usually very large and ancient. Slow to anger, once they get hostile it is almost impossible to pacify their wrath. Hrokkvir have been made restless by Fimbulwinter, becoming an arboreal menace to pockets of civilization that require wood for survival. Druids have been placed in the middle of such conflicts trying to resolve the need for wood and the Hrokkvir's duty to their forest.

Base Powers: Extra limbs- Deal an extra +1 P damage per rune in Essence

Base Level: +1

Size/Move: 4/4

Equipment Type: None

Catharsis	Strangling Vines (Beckon Jotunheim) {Alka Manoeuver}	Trample	Chant of Skuld	Cleansing Block
Cloud of Pollen (Beckon Svartalfheim) {Alka Manoeuver}	Mauling	Whirlwind Attack	Defensive Stance	Pinecone Bombardment
Feral Pounce	Attack From Above	Hrokkvir Active Powers	Life Overwhelming	Apples of Idun
Needle Storm	Disarming Parry	Disarm	Aggressive Assault	Purge Blindness
Violent Slap (Power of Wind) {Manoeuver} [Amplify Multi Amplify]	Destroyer of Crowds	Hamstring	Purge Foreign Spirits	Invoke Rage

Favour Defence	Keen Aptitude	Keen Aptitude	Keen Aptitude	Keen Senses
Turn the Blade	Striker	Giant Size	Stout	Drive Back
Protector	Unencumbered Dodger	Hrokkvir Passive Powers	Fangs	Nature's Child
Untouchable	Resistance to Possession	Verdant Size	Resistance to Blindness	Bastion
Nimble	Keen Aptitude	Keen Aptitude	Keen Aptitude	Cornered Ferocity

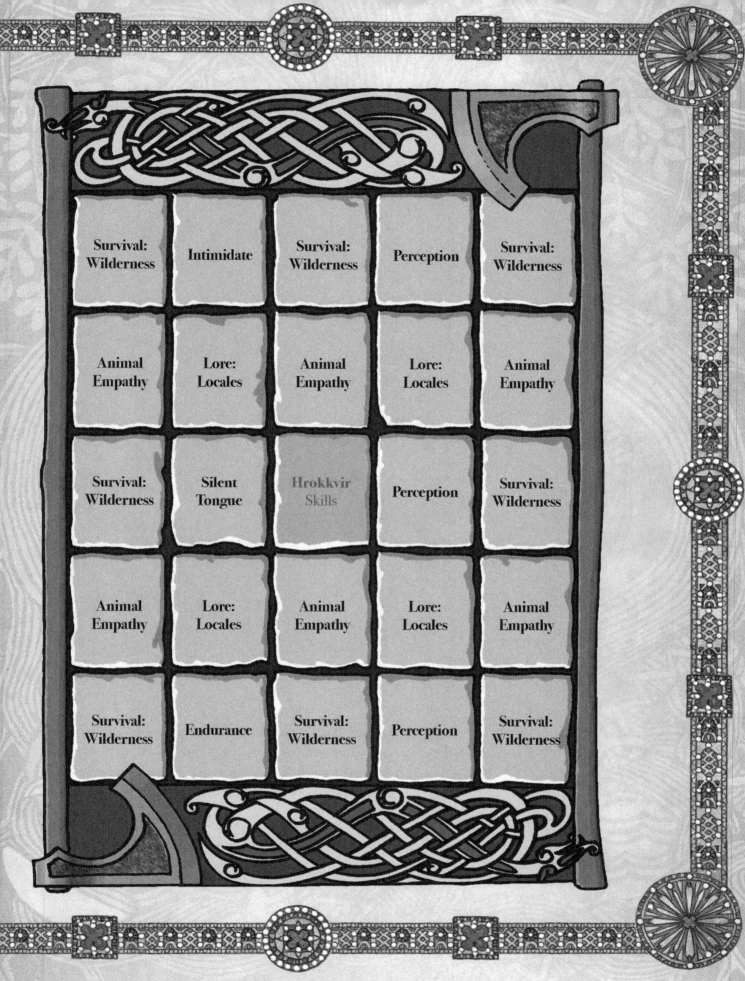

Survival: Wilderness	Intimidate	Survival: Wilderness	Perception	Survival: Wilderness
Animal Empathy	Lore: Locales	Animal Empathy	Lore: Locales	Animal Empathy
Survival: Wilderness	Silent Tongue	Hrokkvir Skills	Perception	Survival: Wilderness
Animal Empathy	Lore: Locales	Animal Empathy	Lore: Locales	Animal Empathy
Survival: Wilderness	Endurance	Survival: Wilderness	Perception	Survival: Wilderness

Leader

The leader template can be added to any denizen the Norn feels needs to be harder to beat. This template will make the leader harder to shut down when it has to face multiple opponents alone or outnumbered. These power and skill boards are there to compliment any other boards the Norn has assigned to the big bad evil guy (BBEG).

Base Powers:	None
Base Level:	0
Size/Move:	N/A
Equipment Type:	None

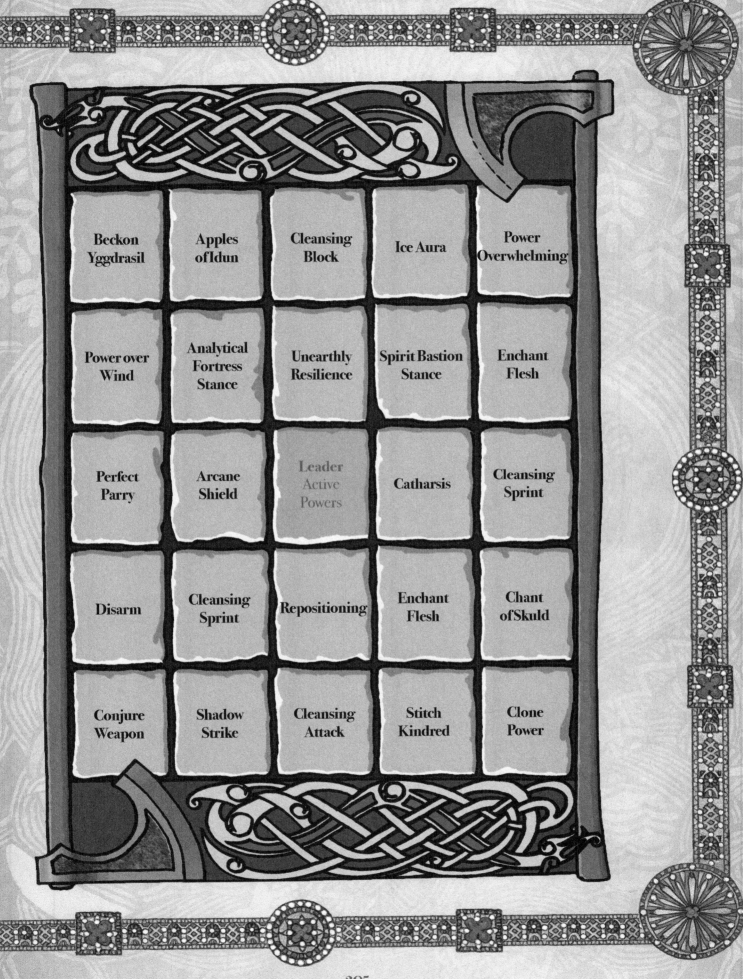

Beckon Yggdrasil	Apples of Idun	Cleansing Block	Ice Aura	Power Overwhelming
Power over Wind	Analytical Fortress Stance	Unearthly Resilience	Spirit Bastion Stance	Enchant Flesh
Perfect Parry	Arcane Shield	Leader Active Powers	Catharsis	Cleansing Sprint
Disarm	Cleansing Sprint	Repositioning	Enchant Flesh	Chant of Skuld
Conjure Weapon	Shadow Strike	Cleansing Attack	Stitch Kindred	Clone Power

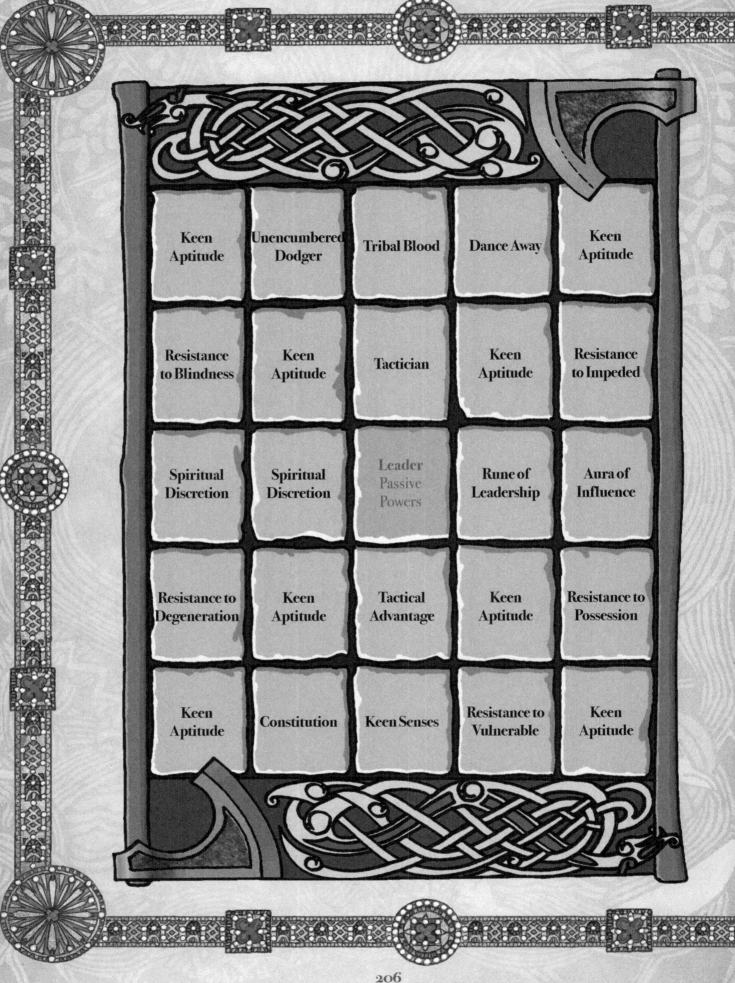

Keen Aptitude	Unencumbered Dodger	Tribal Blood	Dance Away	Keen Aptitude
Resistance to Blindness	Keen Aptitude	Tactician	Keen Aptitude	Resistance to Impeded
Spiritual Discretion	Spiritual Discretion	Leader Passive Powers	Rune of Leadership	Aura of Influence
Resistance to Degeneration	Keen Aptitude	Tactical Advantage	Keen Aptitude	Resistance to Possession
Keen Aptitude	Constitution	Keen Senses	Resistance to Vulnerable	Keen Aptitude

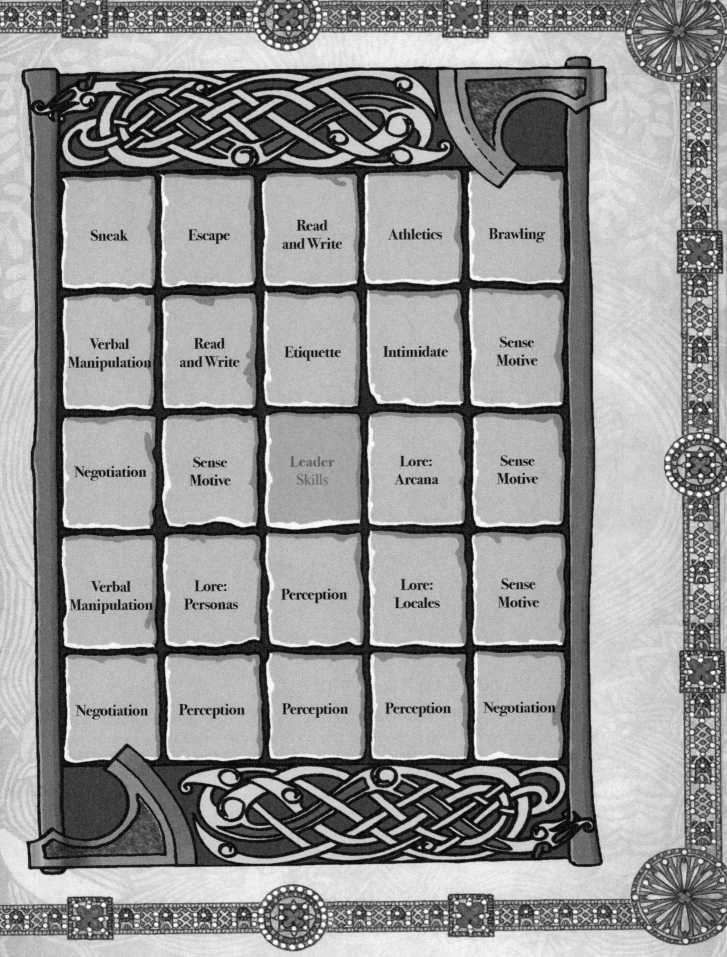

Sneak	Escape	Read and Write	Athletics	Brawling
Verbal Manipulation	Read and Write	Etiquette	Intimidate	Sense Motive
Negotiation	Sense Motive	Leader Skills	Lore: Arcana	Sense Motive
Verbal Manipulation	Lore: Personas	Perception	Lore: Locales	Sense Motive
Negotiation	Perception	Perception	Perception	Negotiation

Mount: Golden Boar

The Golden Boar are giant beasts that may bond with worthy humans. No one knows from which realm they evolved. It is said that over 1000 years ago they made their home in Vanagard, Midgard and Asgard, now they can be spotted in most other realms as well. They have incredible resilience and adaptability, which has made them the hardy species they are today. They can grow to 4000 pounds and yet they have more agility and speed than their diminutive Midgard brethren. Some learn to ride these mythical creatures, but usually it is the boar who chooses its rider. They get their name from the glittering golden boar bristles which adorn their form.

Base Powers: Quadruped
Base Level: 0
Size/Move: 5/10
Equipment Type: None

Bull Rush

Flying Charge

Regenerating Attack

Satisfying Attack

Trample

Aggressive Assault

Mobile Stance

Mount's Synergy

Lunging Attack

Attack From Above

Run Away Laughing

Furious Sprint

Mount: Boar
Active Powers

Mauling

Feral Pounce

Superior Parry

Regenerating Block

Versatile Combat Manoeuvre

Defensive Stance

Vengeful Parry

Perfect Parry

Evasive Manoeuvre

Cleansing Block

Retreating Parry

Boar's Posture

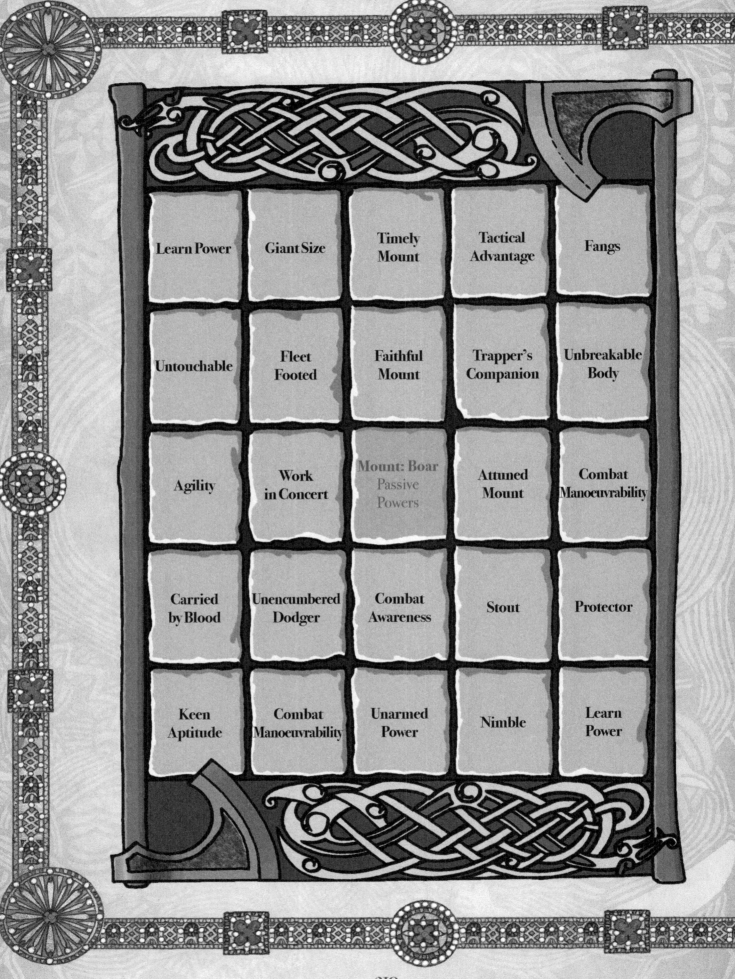

Learn Power	Giant Size	Timely Mount	Tactical Advantage	Fangs
Untouchable	Fleet Footed	Faithful Mount	Trapper's Companion	Unbreakable Body
Agility	Work in Concert	Mount: Boar Passive Powers	Attuned Mount	Combat Manoeuvrability
Carried by Blood	Unencumbered Dodger	Combat Awareness	Stout	Protector
Keen Aptitude	Combat Manoeuvrability	Unarmed Power	Nimble	Learn Power

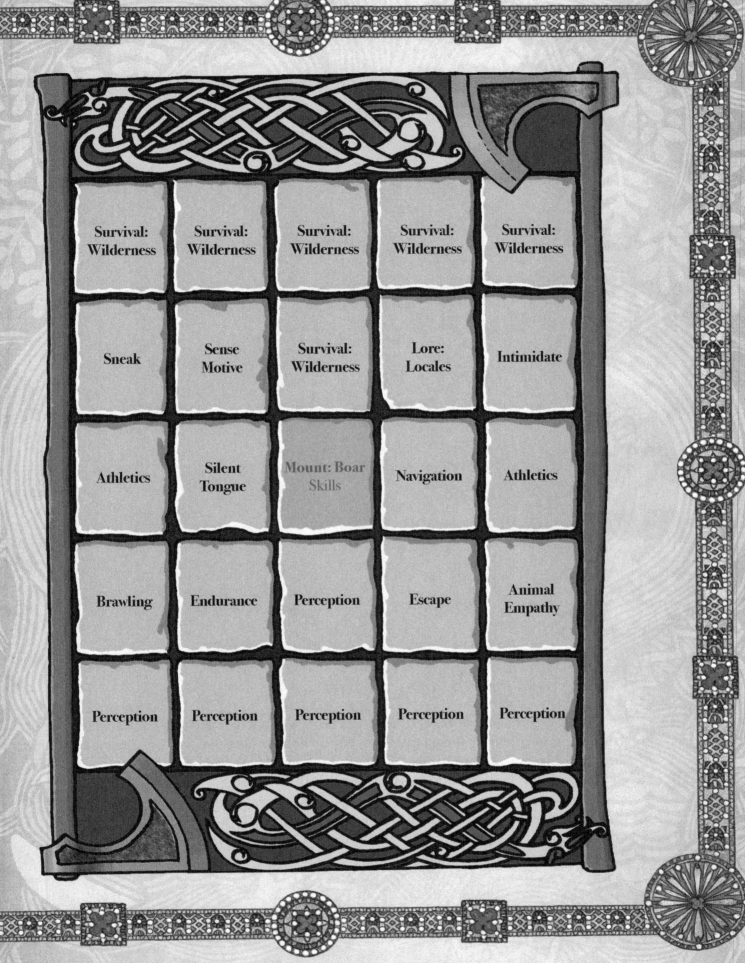

Survival: Wilderness	Survival: Wilderness	Survival: Wilderness	Survival: Wilderness	Survival: Wilderness
Sneak	Sense Motive	Survival: Wilderness	Lore: Locales	Intimidate
Athletics	Silent Tongue	Mount: Boar Skills	Navigation	Athletics
Brawling	Endurance	Perception	Escape	Animal Empathy
Perception	Perception	Perception	Perception	Perception

Mount: Silver Stag

The Silver Stags are majestic magical beasts that possess incredible intellect. Originating from Vanagard, over many centuries these beasts have migrated throughout the worlds of Yggdrasil. Despite their bestial nature, they are capable of forging incredible bonds with more evolved species. Their communication at an empathic level is very nuanced. The Silver Stag has magic coursing through its being, and it has magical capabilities that surprise many who interact with these legendary creatures. If a bond of trust and loyalty is forged, the Silver Stag will become a companion and agree to serve as a mount.

Base Powers: Quadruped
Base Level: 0
Size/Move: 5/10
Equipment Type: None

Purge Crippling	Superior Parry	Power over Wind	Sun and Moon	Stitch Kindred
Cleansing Sprint	Mobile Stance	Mount's Synergy	Catharsis	Invigorate Spirit
Run Away Laughing	Furious Sprint	Mount: Stag Active Powers	Apples of Idun	Boar's Posture
Unearthly Resilience	Regenerating Block	Versatile Combat Manoeuvre	Defensive Stance	Vengeful Parry
Perfect Parry	Evasive Manoeuvre	Cleansing Block	Retreating Parry	Enchant Flesh

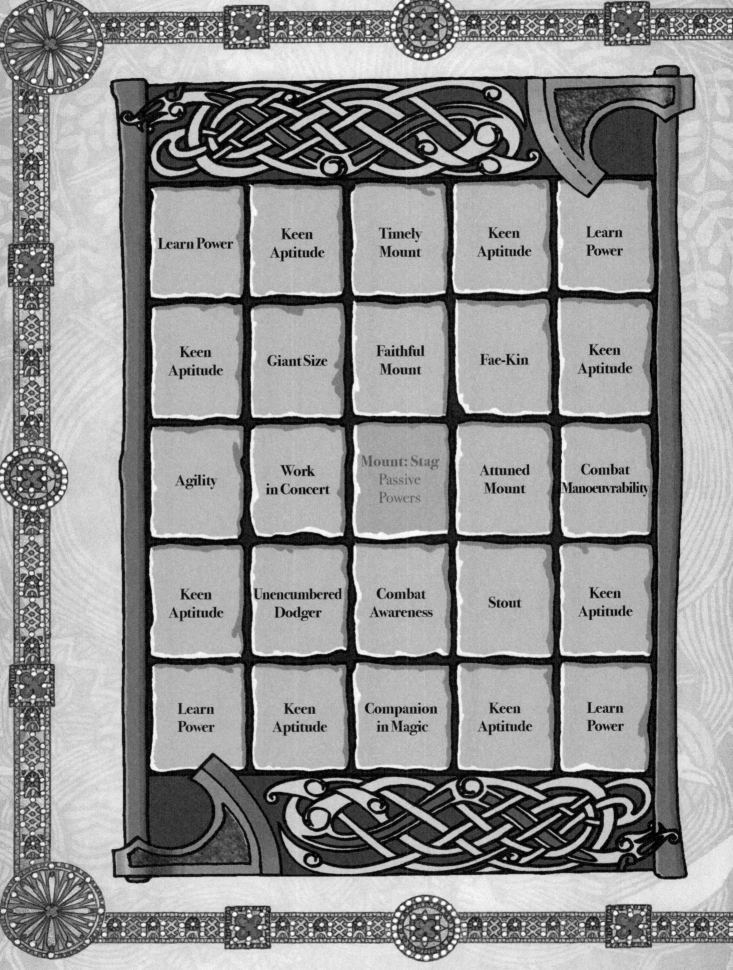

Learn Power	Keen Aptitude	Timely Mount	Keen Aptitude	Learn Power
Keen Aptitude	Giant Size	Faithful Mount	Fae-Kin	Keen Aptitude
Agility	Work in Concert	Mount: Stag Passive Powers	Attuned Mount	Combat Manoeuvrability
Keen Aptitude	Unencumbered Dodger	Combat Awareness	Stout	Keen Aptitude
Learn Power	Keen Aptitude	Companion in Magic	Keen Aptitude	Learn Power

Survival: Wilderness	Survival: Wilderness	Survival: Wilderness	Lore: Personas	Lore: Arcana
Sneak	Sense Motive	Survival: Wilderness	Lore: Locales	Intimidate
Athletics	Silent Tongue	Mount: Stag Skills	Navigation	Athletics
Brawling	Endurance	Perception	Escape	Animal Empathy
Swim	Perception	Perception	Perception	Tracking

Skraeling Angakkuq (Shaman)

The Skraeling shaman is the medicine man and magical practitioner of the Skraeling peoples. They derive their knowledge and power from the spirit world. Entering a spirit trance is achieved through drumming, singing, dancing, sweat lodges, fasting and vision quests. Sometimes they utilize herbs and mushrooms to assist in the voyage of consciousness. To them knowledge is power, and the spirit world contains untold lore. Skraeling Shaman magic is a blend of Seith and Verwandlung. Rather than dealing with lost souls, the shamanic magic reaches out to the spirit of ancestors, animals and plants.

The most powerful shaman can shape change into different types of animals and beasts. They usually dress in brightly dyed leathers, bird plumage, bones and body paint.

Powers are granted based on the type of spirit that possesses the Angakkuq.

Base Powers: If Possessed on home soil, spirits are always benevolent

Base Level: +1

Size/Move: 4/4

Equipment Type: None

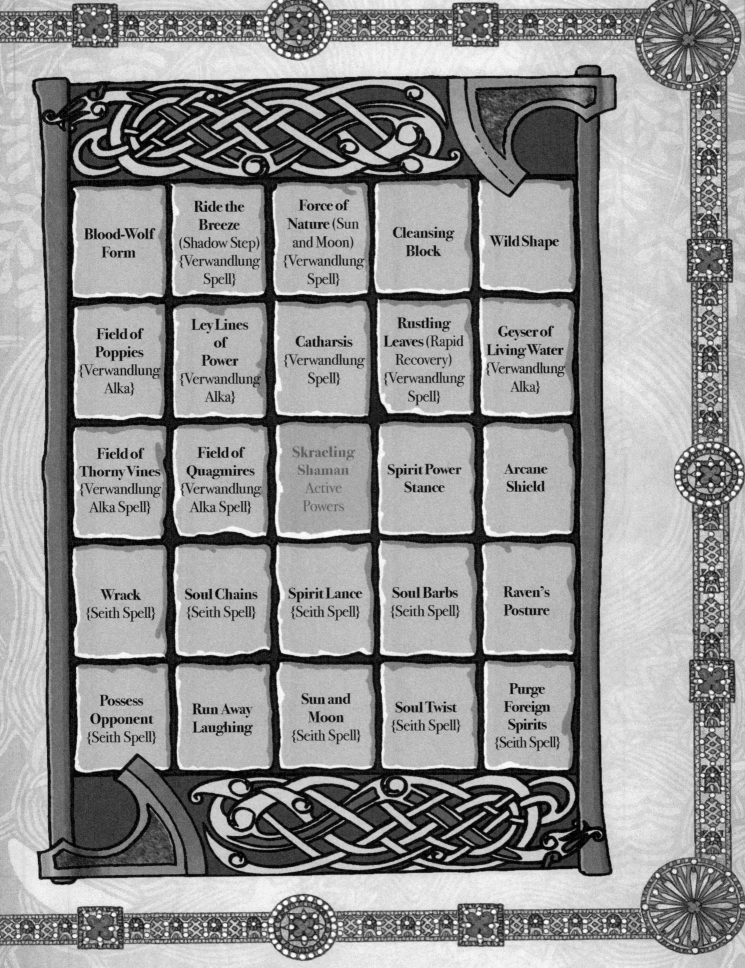

Blood-Wolf Form	**Ride the Breeze** (Shadow Step) {Verwandlung Spell}	**Force of Nature** (Sun and Moon) {Verwandlung Spell}	**Cleansing Block**	**Wild Shape**
Field of Poppies {Verwandlung Alka}	**Ley Lines of Power** {Verwandlung Alka}	**Catharsis** {Verwandlung Spell}	**Rustling Leaves** (Rapid Recovery) {Verwandlung Spell}	**Geyser of Living Water** {Verwandlung Alka}
Field of Thorny Vines {Verwandlung Alka Spell}	**Field of Quagmires** {Verwandlung Alka Spell}	Skraeling Shaman Active Powers	**Spirit Power Stance**	**Arcane Shield**
Wrack {Seith Spell}	**Soul Chains** {Seith Spell}	**Spirit Lance** {Seith Spell}	**Soul Barbs** {Seith Spell}	**Raven's Posture**
Possess Opponent {Seith Spell}	**Run Away Laughing**	**Sun and Moon** {Seith Spell}	**Soul Twist** {Seith Spell}	**Purge Foreign Spirits** {Seith Spell}

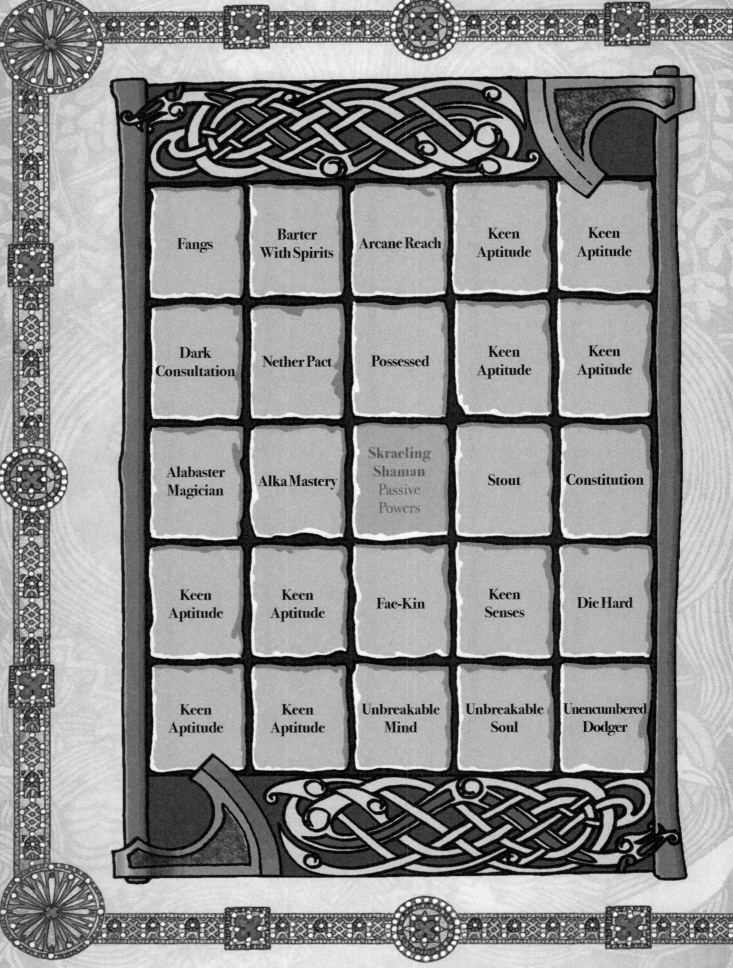

Fangs	Barter With Spirits	Arcane Reach	Keen Aptitude	Keen Aptitude
Dark Consultation	Nether Pact	Possessed	Keen Aptitude	Keen Aptitude
Alabaster Magician	Alka Mastery	Skraeling Shaman Passive Powers	Stout	Constitution
Keen Aptitude	Keen Aptitude	Fae-Kin	Keen Senses	Die Hard
Keen Aptitude	Keen Aptitude	Unbreakable Mind	Unbreakable Soul	Unencumbered Dodger

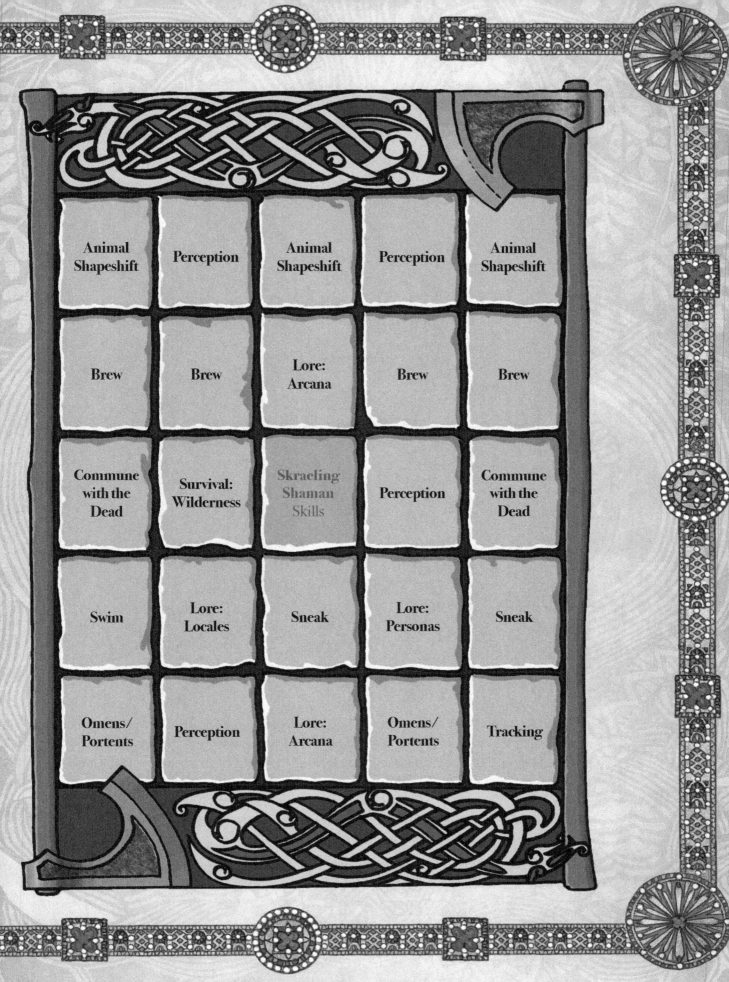

Animal Shapeshift	Perception	Animal Shapeshift	Perception	Animal Shapeshift
Brew	Brew	Lore: Arcana	Brew	Brew
Commune with the Dead	Survival: Wilderness	Skraeling Shaman Skills	Perception	Commune with the Dead
Swim	Lore: Locales	Sneak	Lore: Personas	Sneak
Omens/ Portents	Perception	Lore: Arcana	Omens/ Portents	Tracking

Skraeling Warrior

The Skraeling warrior is brave and doesn't fear confrontation or death. They are masters of the land, moving unheard and unseen. Some may even commune with animals as easily as they do with with their brethren. They do not take life indiscriminately, as all life is sacred. Each and every kill must be justified and the appropriate spirits thanked. Warriors are capable with many types of weapons: bows, stone axes and spears. They are also well versed in snares and traps as well as how to best use terrain to their advantage. Rarely wearing armour, the Skraeling warriors possess great speed.

They personalize their look with distinct hair-styles, war paint and wear trophies obtained on the hunt.

Base Powers: None
Base Level: 0
Size/Move: 4/4
Equipment Type: None

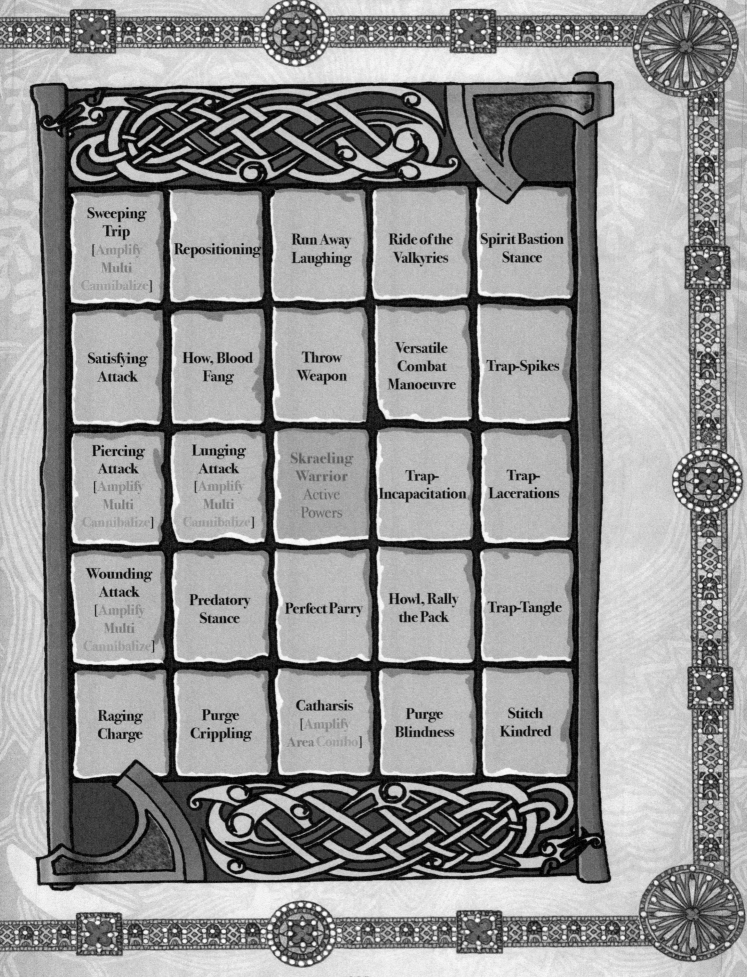

Sweeping Trip [Amplify Multi Cannibalize]	**Repositioning**	**Run Away Laughing**	**Ride of the Valkyries**	**Spirit Bastion Stance**
Satisfying Attack	**How, Blood Fang**	**Throw Weapon**	**Versatile Combat Manoeuvre**	**Trap-Spikes**
Piercing Attack [Amplify Multi Cannibalize]	**Lunging Attack** [Amplify Multi Cannibalize]	**Skraeling Warrior** Active Powers	**Trap-Incapacitation**	**Trap-Lacerations**
Wounding Attack [Amplify Multi Cannibalize]	**Predatory Stance**	**Perfect Parry**	**Howl, Rally the Pack**	**Trap-Tangle**
Raging Charge	**Purge Crippling**	**Catharsis** [Amplify Area Combo]	**Purge Blindness**	**Stitch Kindred**

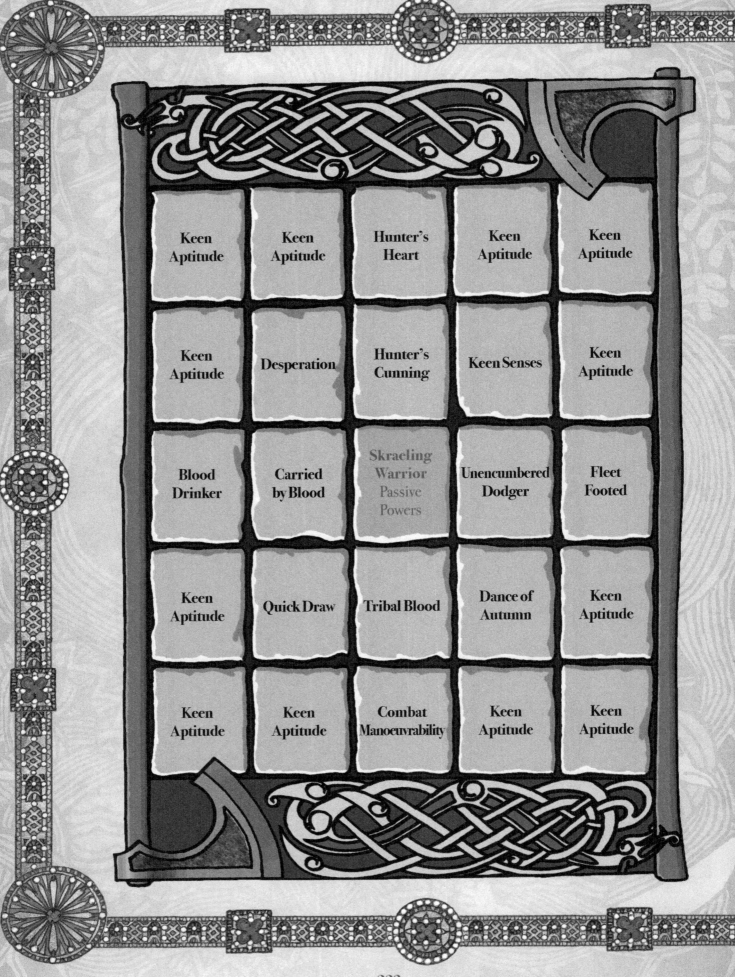

Keen Aptitude	Keen Aptitude	Hunter's Heart	Keen Aptitude	Keen Aptitude
Keen Aptitude	Desperation	Hunter's Cunning	Keen Senses	Keen Aptitude
Blood Drinker	Carried by Blood	Skraeling Warrior Passive Powers	Unencumbered Dodger	Fleet Footed
Keen Aptitude	Quick Draw	Tribal Blood	Dance of Autumn	Keen Aptitude
Keen Aptitude	Keen Aptitude	Combat Manoeuvrability	Keen Aptitude	Keen Aptitude

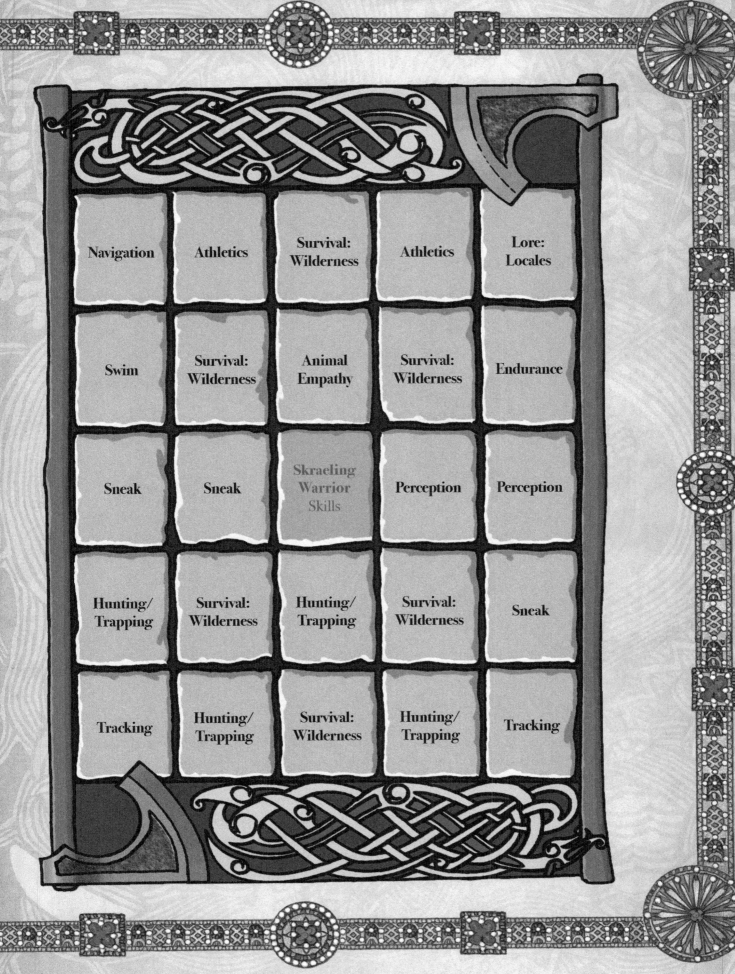

Navigation	Athletics	Survival: Wilderness	Athletics	Lore: Locales
Swim	Survival: Wilderness	Animal Empathy	Survival: Wilderness	Endurance
Sneak	Sneak	Skraeling Warrior Skills	Perception	Perception
Hunting/ Trapping	Survival: Wilderness	Hunting/ Trapping	Survival: Wilderness	Sneak
Tracking	Hunting/ Trapping	Survival: Wilderness	Hunting/ Trapping	Tracking

Snow Serpent

Snow serpents are highly intelligent and fearsome snakes that can grow to 40' in length. Most of their body is covered in white fur allowing them to blend into their surroundings. The most disconcerting feature of the snow serpent is its ability to speak in any language. They used to be confined to the upper reaches of Nidavellir, but with the onset of Ragnarok, they have begun to migrate into other realms. Snow serpents are as at home underground as underwater or under the snow. They hunt prey that is human sized and smaller. Most would believe that they use a combination of venom and constriction to immobilize and kill, but few count on their magic which they use as a nasty surprise.

Base Powers: None
Base Level: 0
Size/Move: 4/4
Equipment Type: Lair

Versatile Combat Manoeuver	**Wounding Attack**	**Run Away Laughing**	**Attack From Above**	**Whirlwind Attack**
Tail Whip (Power Over Wind) {Manoeuver} [Amplify Amplify Amplify]	**Recuperating Wounding Attack**	**Constrict** (Swallow)	**Power Attack**	**Mauling**
Flying Charge	**Lunging Attack**	**Snow Serpent** Active Powers	**Venomous Bite**	**Feral Pounce**
Retreating Parry	**Vengeful Parry**	**Ride of the Valkyries** {Spell Song}	**Cleansing Block**	**Superior Parry**
Evasive Manoeuver	**Riposte**	**Disorienting Ballad** (Cerebral Chains) {Spell Song} [Amplify Area Maintain]	**Regenerating Block**	**Water Shield**

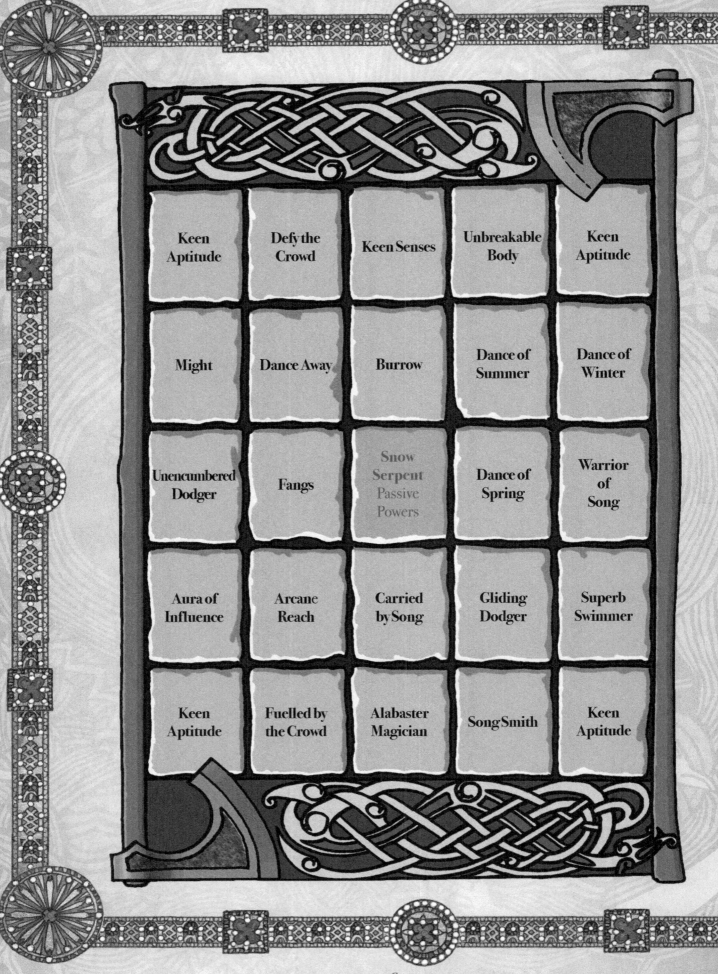

Keen Aptitude	Defy the Crowd	Keen Senses	Unbreakable Body	Keen Aptitude
Might	Dance Away	Burrow	Dance of Summer	Dance of Winter
Unencumbered Dodger	Fangs	Snow Serpent Passive Powers	Dance of Spring	Warrior of Song
Aura of Influence	Arcane Reach	Carried by Song	Gliding Dodger	Superb Swimmer
Keen Aptitude	Fuelled by the Crowd	Alabaster Magician	Song Smith	Keen Aptitude

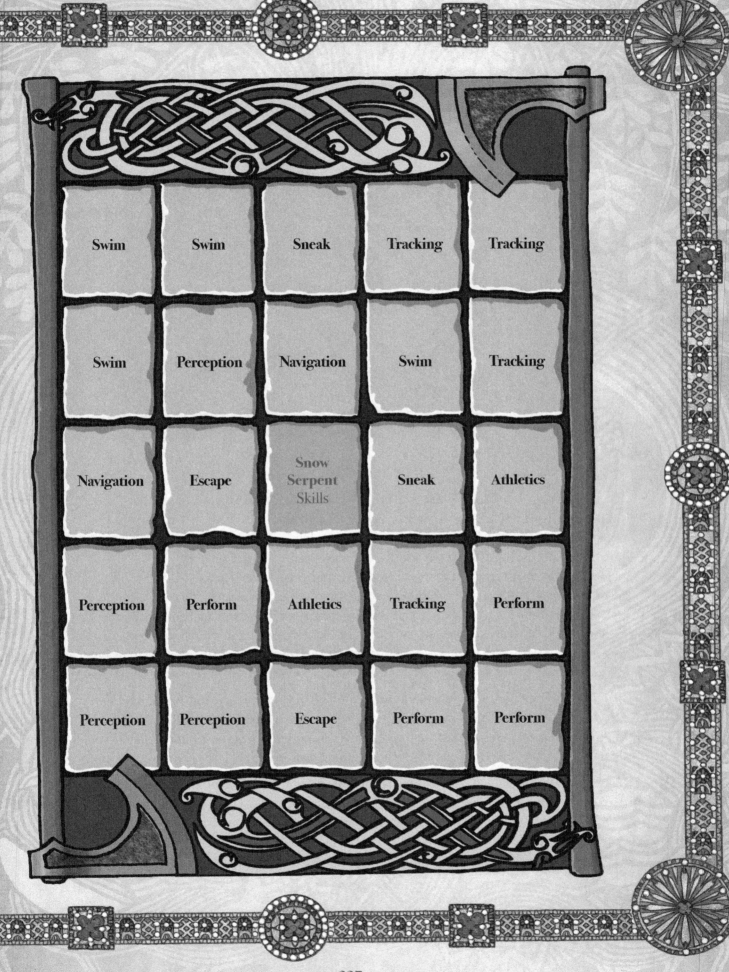

Wight Sovereign

Wight Sovereigns are lost souls that have mastered the state of limbo within which they have been left. They cannot proceed to the heavens, nor to Niflheim, and have abandoned all hope for resolving their unfinished business in Midgard. They are souls that have replaced anger with appetite. Hunger and ambition drive them to master this very unique predicament they suffer. They have discovered how to create a dwelling (a stone that reshapes into a runic monolith) and how to feed on the soul energy of the living; some can even assume corporeal form! They are the harbingers of tragedy, as they sometimes devour souls of legendary heroes before the Valkyries can get to them. Some mortals have been known to seek esoteric lore which would permit them to create stone monoliths that would be suitable for Wight Sovereigns. The foolish and the desperate then enter a bargain with these malevolent and powerful wights.

While the Wight Sovereign inhabits a runic monolith, it is very hard to kill. Sometimes the creature will leave the monolith in order to assume physical form (see powers and skills below). During this time, the runic monolith is more susceptible to destruction. A Wight Sovereign can spent 1 entire round to enter or leave their home. If they are "killed" in physical form, they must wait an hour before once again assuming corporeal form.

The monolith is completely immune to Mental and Spiritual damage. It has an Essence of 10x the level of the Wight Sovereign and a PF vs. Physical damage equal to the level of the creature. The PF is cut in half when the Wight Sovereign assumes corporeal form. While in the stone, it cannot be affected by any powers or skills. The runic monolith accords every Wight Sovereign one specific spell that they can cast while within their home. They may spend their entire Destiny on meta tags for that spell.

Base Powers: Flight; Move +2
Base Level: 0
Size/Move: 2/4
Equipment Type: None

Gate Seith Aberration	**Invigorate Spirit** {Seith Spell}	**Beckon Yggdrasil** {Alka Seith Spell}	**Winds of the Barrows** (Power over Wind) {Seith Spell} [Area Multi Amplify]	**Conjure Troll Illusion**
Invoke the Shadows {Seith Spell}	**Dredge Up Nightmares** (Cerebral Shroud) {Seith Spell}	**Beckon Niflheim** {Alka Seith Spell}	**Darkness Comes** (Catharsis) {Seith Spell}	**Possess Opponent** {Seith Spell}
Devour Mind (Devour Thought) {Seith Spell}	**Arcane Stance**	**Wight Sovereign Active Powers**	**The Nightman Cometh** {Seith Spell}	**Death Chant** (Howl, Skoll's Victory) {Seith Spell}
Raven's Posture	**Tendrils of Deceit** (Channeling) {Seith Spell} [Area Range Amplify]	**Soul Transfer** {Seith Spell}	**Blade of Lies** (Conjure Weapon) {Seith Spell} [Amplify Maintain Maintain]	**Shrink** {Seith Spell}
Shadow Step	**Seith Frenzy**	**Unearthly Resilience** {Seith Spell}	**Spiritual Abortion** {Seith Spell}	**Dark Juxtaposition** {Seith Spell}

Keen Aptitude	Combat Awareness	Possessed	Blend Into Shadow	Keen Aptitude
Alka Mastery	Aura of Influence	Fangs	Fae Kin	Barter with Spirits
Puppet Master	Essence of the Ghost	Wight Sovereign Passive Powers	Tactician	Dark Consultation
Nether Pact	Tactical Advantage	Unencumbered Dodger	Niflheim's Boon	Devour Faith
Keen Aptitude	Spirit Domination	Haugbui's Curse	Unbreakable Mind	Keen Aptitude

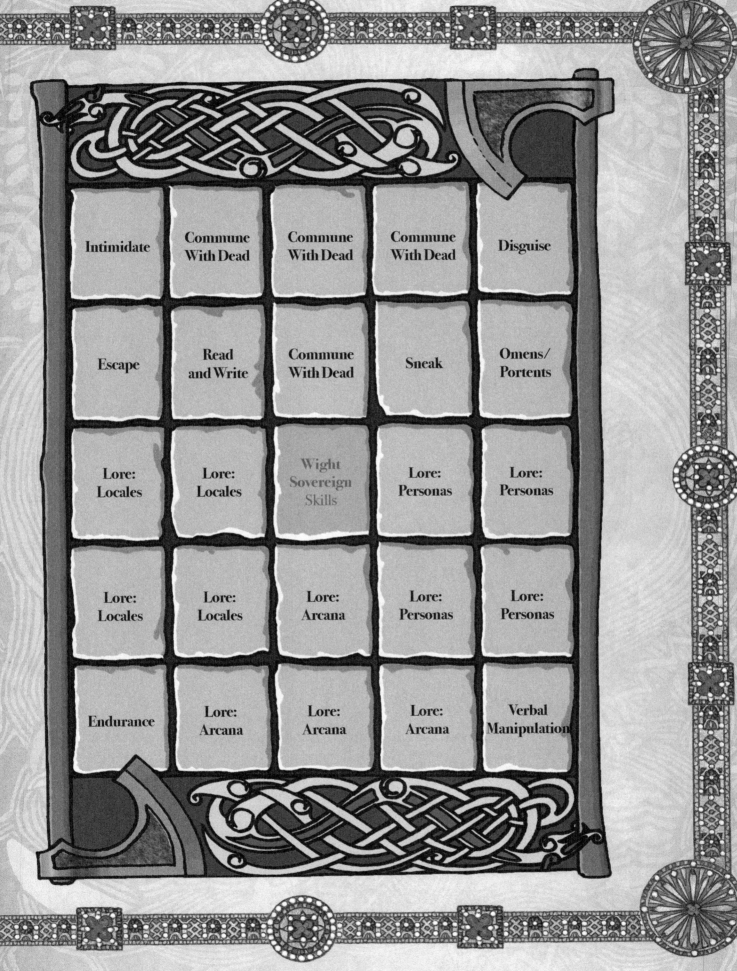

Intimidate	Commune With Dead	Commune With Dead	Commune With Dead	Disguise
Escape	Read and Write	Commune With Dead	Sneak	Omens/ Portents
Lore: Locales	Lore: Locales	Wight Sovereign Skills	Lore: Personas	Lore: Personas
Lore: Locales	Lore: Locales	Lore: Arcana	Lore: Personas	Lore: Personas
Endurance	Lore: Arcana	Lore: Arcana	Lore: Arcana	Verbal Manipulation

Willow Wisp

Willow Wisps are flying balls of light that shift in colour and appearance to intrigue and draw in their prey. A voracious predator of Vanagard, the Wisp is an enigmatic being. Many from Vanagard do not understand the Willow Wisp's ways. Usually solitary, it leads both voluntary and involuntary victims into very treacherous terrain. They subsist by feasting on the last living breath of a sentient being. Willow Wisps can create a cursed domain that reduces the skills of all those within it. Bringing prey into this kind of harsh terrain can see drownings, lethal falls and other seeming accidents take the lives of those within this accursed land.

Base Powers: Flight; Move +2
Base Level: 0
Size/Move: 2/4
Equipment Type: None

Analytical Power Stance	Mental Celerity	Beckon Muspelheim	Syphon Soul	Stitch Destiny
Purge Foreign Spirits	Imposing Barrier	Beckon Yggdrasil	Soul Twist	Evasive Manoeuver
Unearthly Resilience	Flare	Willow Wisp Active Powers	Rend Flesh	Purging Tirade
Purge Crippling	Evasive Manoeuver	Ride of the Valkyries {Spell Song}	Cleansing Block	Insulting Parry
Raven's Posture	Vanaheim Bond (Catharsis) {Spell Song} [Amplify Maintain Amplify]	Revitalize (Rapid Recovery) {Spell Song} [Amplify Maintain Amplify]	Regenerating Block	Insulting Parry

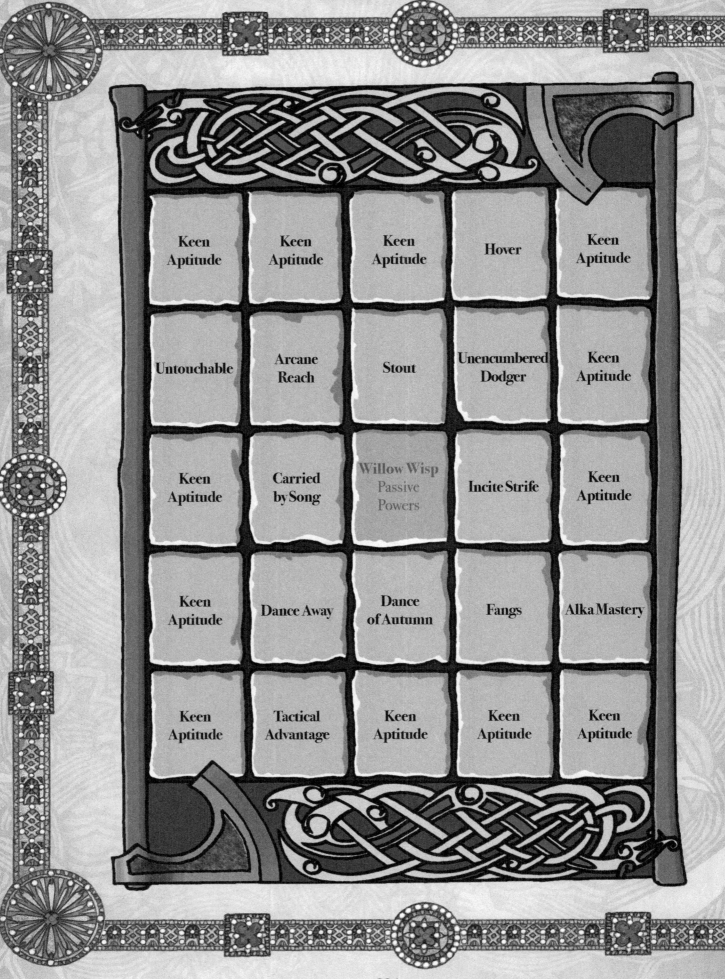

Keen Aptitude	Keen Aptitude	Keen Aptitude	Hover	Keen Aptitude
Untouchable	Arcane Reach	Stout	Unencumbered Dodger	Keen Aptitude
Keen Aptitude	Carried by Song	Willow Wisp Passive Powers	Incite Strife	Keen Aptitude
Keen Aptitude	Dance Away	Dance of Autumn	Fangs	Alka Mastery
Keen Aptitude	Tactical Advantage	Keen Aptitude	Keen Aptitude	Keen Aptitude

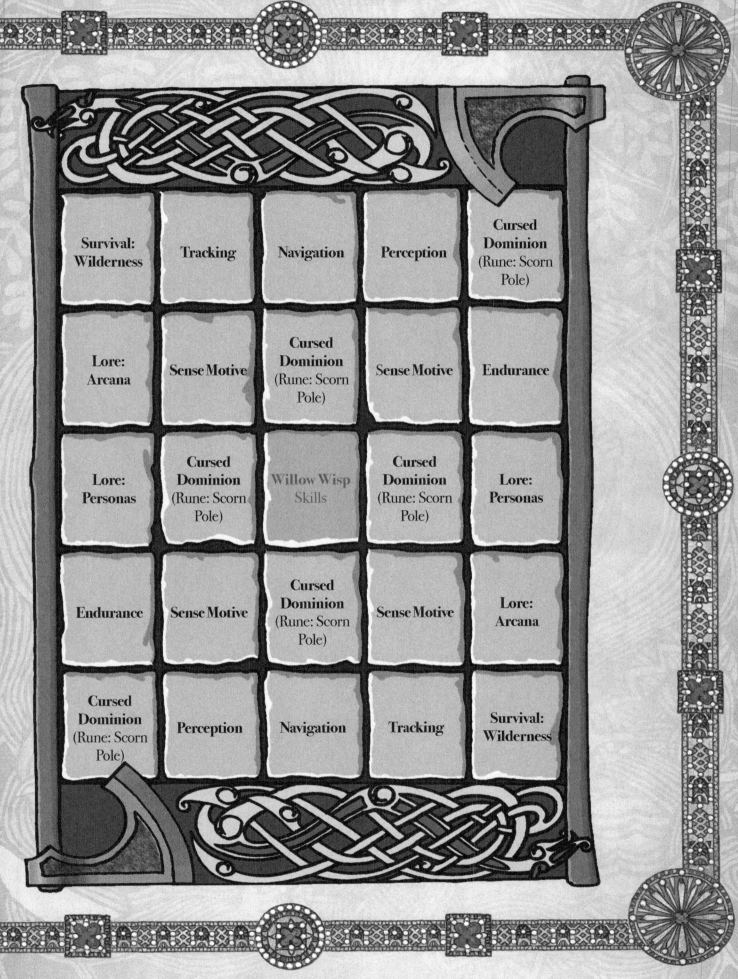

Survival: Wilderness	Tracking	Navigation	Perception	Cursed Dominion (Rune: Scorn Pole)
Lore: Arcana	Sense Motive	Cursed Dominion (Rune: Scorn Pole)	Sense Motive	Endurance
Lore: Personas	Cursed Dominion (Rune: Scorn Pole)	Willow Wisp Skills	Cursed Dominion (Rune: Scorn Pole)	Lore: Personas
Endurance	Sense Motive	Cursed Dominion (Rune: Scorn Pole)	Sense Motive	Lore: Arcana
Cursed Dominion (Rune: Scorn Pole)	Perception	Navigation	Tracking	Survival: Wilderness

Viking Life

Althing

From the planning notes of Thorsteinn Ingolfsson:

"We must gather all persons in positions of power from across the island. Runners will go to the four corners of Islandia spreading the word about the Althing that is to occur in a month's time. Every jarl, godi and chieftain will receive an invite to the Althing and we will ask them to bring supplies that are sufficient for not only the travel, but for a few days stay in the Althingvellir. The supplies should be enough for them and their entourage. Their entourage may consist of any freemen and thralls, but only the freemen will be allowed into the Althing. I will supply the closing feast, but for future Athings, every attendee should be encouraged to contribute.

I will be organizing the proceedings of the Althing, assuming the role of "Althing speaker". The speaker's seat will be upon the Logberg outcrop where everyone will be able to hear the speaker clearly. The speaker's role is to keep the meeting organized on the agenda:

- Ensuring that all Karls of Islandia may address the attendees with introductions and news
- Election of the Logretta
- Making sure the Logretta members are efficient in creating, modifying and annulling the common laws of Islandia
- Election of the Lawspeakers
- Agreements for the next Althing
- Celebration feast

Each agenda item may take a few hours to a few days. The speaker should work diligently to ensure no agenda item takes more than 2 days.

The speaker will ensure that 39 members are elected to the logretta council. Each Jarl of Islandia must put forth at least one nominee from their fiefdom. For all who set foot on Islandia, we will establish common laws that everyone must adhere to. No law may place one freeman above another- equality must be maintained.

We will then elect 39 judges that will be able to resolve disputes that arise throughout the year. We will call them "Lawspeakers" and ensure that they are neutral and fair in their enforcement of the laws. All future grievances regarding property boundaries and annexation, status of thralls and outlaws, grievances that involve members from different homesteads and other objections should all be brought before the elected Lawspeakers.

Before we end the assembly, we will need to decide when the next one should occur. I will propose that we create an annual cycle for this very important meeting. We will also need to nominate a new speaker that will sit upon the Logberg outcrop. We should avoid having the same person assigned more than once. Anything that would place one representative in a more authoritative position over the others risks Islandia slipping into an autocracy.

As a final note, I must extend the invitation to Njall Thorgeirsson personally. His insights into legal issues will be invaluable for the first Althing."

Arm Rings

Within Midgard there is a universal method of displaying one's wealth and status. It is accomplished by openly wearing arm bands of silver and gold. They are also used as generous tokens of appreciation. They are generous because an arm-ring could easily be worth 1000 skatt simply on weight alone. A chieftain may bestow an arm-ring to a warrior who distinguished himself by turning the tide of battle. When Ragnarok broke out, many took their rings off to try and avoid getting robbed. But now as we enter the second age, the strong have begun to flaunt their authority by making the arm rings fashionable once more.

Blood Brothers

A pledge of sworn loyalty is a common custom in Midgard. When a man's word is his reputation, swearing an oath of blood carries much weight. To seal such a pact, is to perform the blood ritual that leads to a blood brother bond. The blood ritual necessitates that both members must self inflict a bleeding wound, and then the two wounds are pressed together and bound, signifying that each person's blood now flows in the other participant's veins. Then both members recite oaths of loyalty and unbreakable friendship before sealing the deal with a drink from a communal drinking horn.

Usually warriors that spent time together in a warband will forge a battle bond of trust they wish to take to the next level. The ritual will make their friendship and trust official in the eyes of men and gods. Blood brothers have an understanding that any offence levelled at one of them is also levelled at the other. They also share plunder and spoils equally. Forgiveness must also come unconditionally, albeit without forgetting justice and atonement.

Calendar

The days of the week are: Manadagr, Tys-dagr, Odinsdagr, Thorsdagr, Frjadagr, Lau-gardagr, Sunnudagr. The translations behind each day are as follows: Moon day, Tyr day, Odin day, Thor day, Freya day, Washing day, Sun day. To those who worship the Jotuns, the names of the week are slightly different: Manad-agr, Lokdagr, Surtrdagr, Bergelmrdagr, Laufdagr, Laugardagr, Sunnudagr. These translate similarly to: Moon day, Loki day, Surt day, Bergelmir day, Laufey day, Washing day, Sun day. The months are as follows: Morsugur, Thorri, Goi, Ein-Manudr, Harpa, Skerpla, Sol-Manudr, Heyannir, Tvi-Manudr, Haust-Manudr, Gor-Manudr, Frer-Manudr There are many feast days and celebrations, but under the eternal night of Fimbulwinter, many have been over-looked or completely forsaken. The most im-portant feast days are as follows:

Date	Feast/Celebration
Winter Solstice (December 21)	Yule - celebrates the zenith of the Wild Hunt as the longest night consumes the world.
Vernal Equinox (March 21)	Ostara/Summer Finding (Vaetrblot) - It is no longer celebrated but a Vaetrblot is still performed by those who seek the land's blessings. The blot is performed in honour of the local Vaettir in expectation of luck and good fortune.
Summer Solstice (June 21)	Midsummer - No longer celebrated
Autumnal Equinox (September 21)	Winter Finding - An offering is made to the Rime Jotuns in hopes of a gentle winter.
Night of the Dead (October 31)	Vetmaetr (Disablot) - An offering is made to Odin/Surt, Hel and the Disir in honour of the deceased. This is the period of the year where the veil between the worlds of the living and the dead is at its thinnest. It is when Odin rides out on the Wild Hunt in search of Lost Souls.

Crannog

When security is paramount, a water fortress known as a crannog is built. It is a dwelling that has been built upon stilts (approximately 12' above water) and the only means of access is via a long narrow bridge (usually 50' long). The choke-point on the bridge allows for excellent defence when outnumbered, allowing a much smaller force to keep a larger one at bay by forcing one-on-one combat. Access from the water requires a water borne vessel and would necessitate climbing up onto the deck surrounding the dwelling. Warriors attempting to breach in this manner would suffer many casualties inflicted by the defenders, who would be in a much better fighting position.

With the advent of Fimbulwinter, many crannogs on freshwater lakes have become useless. Innovative blacksmiths now create coastal crannogs over bodies of saltwater. The design has been altered to account for storms, waves and icebergs. Foundations of stone eliminate structural failure due to erosion. Only those in positions of power can afford the high-priced blacksmiths who can construct such a marvel.

Drink Recipes

Despite the cold and darkness of Fimbulwinter, the denizens of Midgard have found ways to keep the gloom at bay. Few things are a more effective remedy than a good horn of mead. After all honey doesn't spoil, and there are plenty of stockpiled dried herbs and grains that could be plundered for ingredients!

Note: Yeast is always present in the brewer's jugs and tools. Only modern brewers need to add yeast to stimulate fermentation.

Jutland Braggot Recipe:

- 10 lbs Wildflower honey
- 6 lbs Dry wheat malt (preferably smoked)
- 2 lbs dried blackberries
- 2 oz. Dried heather
- 2 oz. Dried meadowsweet
- 1 oz. Dried chamomile
- 1 oz. Dried yarrow
- 1 pinch of dried bog myrtle

DIRECTIONS:
Put the malt and dried herbs n a cauldron. Add 2 gallons of water and bring to a boil. Boil for 45 minutes to an hour. Then remove from fire and add honey. Stir frequently for 20 minutes until honey is fully dissolved. Add frozen berries to cool the mixture down to room temperature. Move entire contents to fermentation barrel and cover with cloth.

The mixture is left to ferment for three to four weeks. Solids that rise to the surface should be mixed and pushed back down on a daily basis. After 2 weeks the solids may be removed from the fermentation barrel. Once fermentation is complete, the mead is ready for consumption. However it may be strained through a cheese cloth, poured into sealed containers and allowed to settle and age. The ageing duration is entirely subjective and will vary from brewer to brewer.

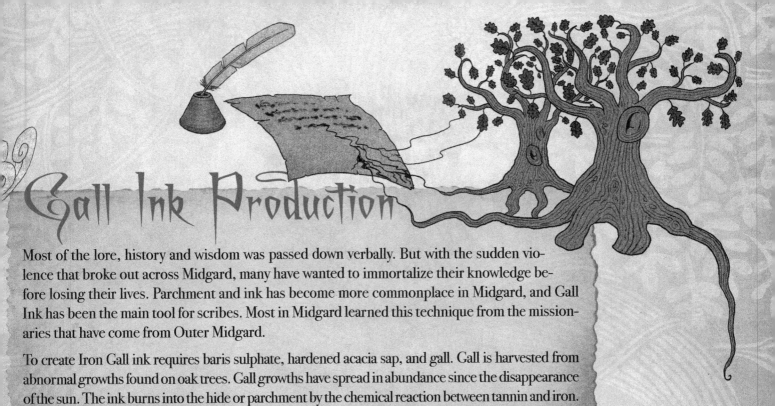

Gall Ink Production

Most of the lore, history and wisdom was passed down verbally. But with the sudden violence that broke out across Midgard, many have wanted to immortalize their knowledge before losing their lives. Parchment and ink has become more commonplace in Midgard, and Gall Ink has been the main tool for scribes. Most in Midgard learned this technique from the missionaries that have come from Outer Midgard.

To create Iron Gall ink requires baris sulphate, hardened acacia sap, and gall. Gall is harvested from abnormal growths found on oak trees. Gall growths have spread in abundance since the disappearance of the sun. The ink burns into the hide or parchment by the chemical reaction between tannin and iron. This ensures that the script that was captured is effectively secured onto the writing surface.

Game of Shadows

Despite the harrowing effects of Fimbulwinter, the exuberance of youth cannot be discounted. In perpetual winter and darkness, between wars and robberies, children find time to indulge in some recreational fun. One of the most popular games played that utilize the new weather is the "game of shadows". It requires no more than a light source such as a lantern and some trees. Children go off into a glade and light the lantern. The oldest child is the light elf and the other children are the dark elves in the game. The light elf closes their eyes and sings a song. For the duration of the short melody, the dark elves go and hide in the shadows cast by the tree trunks. They aren't allowed to leave the area lit by the light source. Once the light elf finishes the song, he or she looks at the tracks made in the snow and they run after the dark elves, trying to spot them. The first one spotted is eliminated and must now stand at the edge of the light and act as a shade. They cannot speak, but may throw snowballs at the dark elves. The game continues until all of the dark elves have been found.

Despite being simple and fun, it can also be dangerous. Many children have been abducted or killed by hungry animals while playing the game of shadows. None the less, the game seems to be gaining popularity as Fimbulwinter drags on.

Justice

The justice system within Midgard is relatively uniform, but has some small variations from place to place. As a rule of thumb, the local chieftain or Godi holds council once a week to hear of grievances. The accused are sent summons to appear at their trial, usually by messenger, and failure to appear means receiving a conviction. For urgent policing matters, alleged criminals are captured and rounded up by the local militia. They are then placed under arrest until the next council of grievances.

Oaths & Reputation

For those living in Midgard, your reputation is extremely important; it is perhaps your most important attribute. Having someone question or tarnish another's reputation means that person must defend it, at all costs. Besmirching another's reputation is not done lightly, as if the accusation is proven to be false the accuser's reputation is diminished.

Reputation is also influenced by a person's circle of friends. Sometimes reputation may increase or decrease depending on the company someone keeps. If a close friend's reputation becomes tarnished, it will impact your own.

In a culture where oaths are the stitching in the fabric of society, being known for keeping your word is one of the defining aspects of reputation. It is important to keep one's word, so most agreements are sealed with an oath. Failure to uphold one's oath could brand one an "oath breaker". This is a damning title that could cost someone many social day-to-day advantages people take for granted. They may be refused a job or some form of hospitality, or prices may be inexplicably marked up. Life can become very tiresome for an oath-breaker. News of someone's reputation has a way of preceding them in their travels. It is best to keep up one's legend or infamy.

Justice: Killer vs. Murderer

The Viking justice system within Midgard has a very important distinction between "killer" and "murderer". Violence is endemic in Fimbulwinter wrought society and disputes usually lead to violence. So long as both aggrieved parties engage in an honourable face to face fracas, death and injury incurred in such a manner carry a lesser sentence. A fair fight isn't a requirement here. Someone killing an wary armed defender will usually be accused of the lesser crime of being a "killer". These types of tragedies are usually settled via a weregild, sometimes without ever necessitating a court trial. A trial would involve witnesses and a recouting of the grievance that resulted in the unfortunate loss of life. In most cases a conviction would damn the killer to lesser-outlawry. That is the reason most would prefer to settle out of court with a payment of a suitable weregild.

However if someone sets out to harm another via subterfuge and surprise, then the assault is categorized as a "murder". There is no honour in murder, and the ramifications on the victim's chances at a glorious afterlife are greatly hampered. A conviction after a trial almost always results in the maximum sentence of outlaw.

Justice: Outlaw vs. Minor Outlawry (Skoggangur)

Someone subject to full outlawry is banished from society. His property is confiscated. He cannot be fed or sheltered. Wherever he goes, he could be killed without penalty by anyone who sees him. Lesser outlawry differs in that the guilty party is banished for only three years. His property is not confiscated, making it possible for him to return to a normal life after the three years is over. Lesser-outlawry sentence also creates safe zones of imprisonment where the convicted may remain safe from being murdered. Usually these reservations of the damned would be set in desolate and remote locales, allowing them to fend for themselves. Sometimes one would be forced to leave the kingdom for the duration of the sentence. Anyone found in violation of their lesser-outlawry terms would be upgraded to full outlawry.

Outright executions were rare prior to Ragnarok, and were instituted only in extreme cases such as regicide. Since cruel warlords have taken hold of the Sword Age, inevitably, the Blood Eagle has become more prevalent as a means of execution. The Blood Eagle involves breaking open the victim's ribcage at the spine and pulling out the lungs so that they resemble bloody wings.

Languages

Most regions in Midgard share a common tongue called Orse. It has two dialects, the East Orse and the West Orse. West Orse is spoken in the regions bounded by Trondelag, Zealand and Gronland. East Orse is prevalent in the regions surrounding the Baltic Sea. Conversations are possible between both dialects, but some nuances are lost in translation.

Alba, Hibernia, Wessex, East Anglia, Finnmark and Svalbard all have their own distinct languages. The Pictish language predominates in Alba. Hibernia's many clans use the Gaelic tongue. Folks from Wessex and East Anglia speak Anglic. The northern people in Finnmark and Svalbard speak the Sami language.

Outer Midgard regions such as Brittany, Frisia, Flanders, Saxony, Vedland, Helluland, Markland and Vinland have languages that sound very different from the languages of Midgard. Latin is used extensively throughout the Outer Midgard lands belonging to the crusaders (Brittany, Frisia, Flanders, Saxony, Vedland). There hasn't been much successful communication in the western Skraeling lands, however those that have successfully setup trade are forced to learn the Aleut language.

Given that there are linguistic shards within Midgard, many of its denizens are multilingual. One would be hard pressed to find someone in Midgard who doesn't have a semi-functional understanding of either of the Orse dialects.

Leidang

Leidang is the law across Norveig that warlords use to enlist the commoners into their warbands. This forced conscription is commonplace among the pretender kings that vie for King Harald's throne and is also gaining popularity among local chieftains and warlords who look to carve out their own fiefdoms. Commoners are coerced by being told it is their duty to protect their homelands, and that they should enlist in their chieftain's warband. Some that are desperate for food or shelter are easily bribed, and those that refuse are sometimes taken by force, and reduced to thralls. This practice is one of the main reasons why most are trying to flee Norveig. The exodus takes many to Alba, Hibernia and the distant Islandia.

Monastic Round Towers

Most Vikings were pretty confrontational when it came to the new White God and his servants. Monks and missionaries who wished to conquer using the word rather than the sword would try to avoid violent confrontation as much as possible. They would build a stone tower that was between 80 and 100 feet in height. The door to the tower would be raised 15' off the ground and a ladder would be required to climb up to the door. The interior of the tower would have platforms every 20' connected by ladders. If the monks felt threatened by Viking marauders, they would take supplies into the tower and retract the first ladder. This would make a violent confrontation very difficult for the raiders, so rather than molesting the monks, the raiders would just pillage the monastery.

Monickers & Titles

There is a Midgard fashion that assigns persons in positions of power certain nicknames. Sometimes those nicknames are literal, other times they are sarcastic or ironic. For example Erik "Blood Axe" refers to his literal desire to slay all opponents. Applying some sarcasm to a moniker, Gautrek "the Generous" was in fact extremely frugal. Players may wish to name themselves or perhaps each other with colourful nicknames. Below is a list of a few inspirational ideas that covers names based on habits, physical characteristics, temperament, etc...

Monicker	Reason
"the Red"	Tendency to leave a trail of blood in their wake
"the Dwarf"	Actually a very large individual
"Sealed Breeches"	Someone who is romantically challenged
"Fork Tongue"	A pathological liar
"the Vigilant"	Great perception due to rather large and comical ears

The Walking Dead

Midgard's dead aren't resting in peace as they had in the past. Since the onset of Fimbulwinter, an alarming number of dark and sinister tales have emerged about burials and barrows. It is said that Niflheim is full and Hel has started to turn the dead away. The reasons are unclear, but what is clear is that the dead are restless. A growing number of burials are followed by hauntings. Many falsely believe that a cremation will avert a revenant, but Lost Souls are just as terrifying as a Draugar or Haugbui. In order to avert a cursed funeral, one must follow the proper burial procedures. The local Angel of Death is the final authority on proper burial and cremation that will ensure that the dead rest and leave the living in peace. However many local superstitions have created home made rituals that claim to be effective, such as the following:

A pair of open scissors must be laid upon the dead person's chest, and small pieces of straw laid crosswise under the shroud call upon the local Vaettir spirits. The large toes must be tied together so that the legs cannot be separated. Needles must be run into the soles of the feet, so that the dead cannot rise and walk the earth. Then the coffin is carried out, the bearers, just within the threshold of the door, must raise and lower the corpse three times in different directions so as to confuse the dead. When the coffin has left the house, all chairs and stools on which it had rested must be turned over. When the deceased reaches the barrows, everyone sends prayers to the higher powers, binding the dead to the afterlife with magic words.

Tattoos & Woads

The process of permanent and temporary tattoos is said to have come from an ancient civilization called the Picts. The name attributed to these people actually means "design" or "picture". The Vikings adopted tattoos for many reasons, ranging from serious reasons such as religious or magical, to frivolous reasons like aesthetics or style.

The pigment from tattoos would be created from something as mundane as charcoal ash to something as exotic as plant dyes such as woad (blue), weld (yellow) and madder (red) and resin from the rubber tree (imported from Out-Midgard through trade or raids). A temporary tattoo would require nothing more involved than painting the dyes on the skin. For the more permanent tattoo, a bone needle would be used to pierce the skin and deposit the pigment.

Taverns

Taverns and inns were very uncommon in northern Europe during this period of history. Tradition in Midgard required home owners to provide hospitality to travellers. However in the Fate of the Norns setting, Midgard during Ragnarok is filled with danger and paranoia. Travellers are turned away from most homes and halls, so a new business opportunity has sprung up. Inns and taverns employ security to ensure that the guests do not decide to rob the establishment. These establishments facilitate food and lodging for travellers at a reduced risk to both parties.

Town Denizen Creation

Sometimes a Norn will need to populate a town or city with some interesting personalities. In order to assist the Norn in producing some denizens on the fly, a quick table is provided that has names, professions and dispositions. Just Wyrd 3 runes (4 if you need an archetype or denizen template).

Rune	Name	Profession	Disposition	Archetype
↑	Bruni	Thrall	Suspicious	Grizzled Warrior
⋃	Durnir	Bondi	Apathetic	Grizzled Warrior
ᛒ	Gapi	Jarl	Predatory	Grizzled Warrior
◇	Grettir	Merchant	Conniving	Grizzled Warrior
ᛗ	Gusir	Town Guard	Friendly	Zealot
ᛗ	Helga	Bar/Innkeeper	Drunk	Zealot
ᛗ	Hildir	Bounty Hunter	Opportunist	Mugger
ᛦ	Idi	Beggar	Amorous	Mugger
ᚾ	Ima	Merchant	Curious	Blacksmith
ᚵ	Imr	Town Guard	Annoying	Galdr
ᚼ	Kraka	Traveller	Jovial	Ulfhednar
ᚵ	Leif	Artisan	Entrepreneur	Skald
ᛁ	Lutr	Merchant	Pessimist	Seithkona
ᛉ	Mjoll	Town Guard	Adventurer	Berserkir
ᛦ	Nati	Traveller	Carousing	Maiden of Ratatosk
ᛊ	Regin	Artisan	Meek	Druid
ᚠ	Sivor	Outlaw	Secretive	Fardrengir
ᚱ	Skalli	Whore	Obnoxious	Orlog
ᚢ	Stumi	Conman	Boastful	Rogue
ᛉ	Svadi	Orphaned Child	Empathic	Son of Fenrir
ᚦ	Svava	Tax Collector	Social	Stalo
ᛪ	Thiazi	Labourer	Evasive	Godi
ᚠ	Thjosnir	Tavern Wench	Violent	Angel of Death
ᛈ	Valdi	Missionary	Confrontational	Missionary
○	Viparr	Karl	Neutral	Einherjar/Son of Muspel

Trade

Life doesn't exist without commerce. Even with Fimbulwinter wreaking havoc with world economies, everyone is trying hard to eke out a living. There is little supply and much demand for all goods that permit survival. Items such as furs, torches, lanterns, oil, food, weapons and armour have seen prices soar. Decorative items, dyes, perfumes and other vanity items which used to hold the most value are now worthless in most markets. Large trading hubs such as Skiringssal Kaupang and Ath Cliath still have buyers for vanity items because some have grown very rich as a result of Ragnarok.

The general rule of thumb is that an item's worth increases the further it travels from where it was manufactured. Be it an animal skin, a weapon or a type of food- the further it travels before entering the sellers market, the greater the potential for price markup. For Norns, the formula could be stated as follows: Every 48 hours of seaborne travel away from the site of manufacture will raise the value by +10%. After a week's travel, the value jumps +10% per 24 hours. That is why travel via the Volga trade route, or the distant markets of Miklagard offer such amazing rewards. Everything is measured in seaborne travel as overland has been made near impossible with the advent of Fimbulwinter.

Travel by Longship

Longships have an average speed of 10 knots (given a favourable wind and a good navigator onboard). This translates to roughly 11.5 mph (18.5 km/h). A world renowned navigator may get another 2 knots out of a longship while the general populace probably travelled between 6 and 8 knots.

To put things into perspective for someone wishing to travel between Islandia and Norveig, the distance is roughly 745 mi (1200 km). The Faroe Islands would be a fair halfway mark. It would take a master navigator 33 hrs to get to the Faroe Islands and 66 hours to get to Norveig. Weather permitting, a decent navigator could travel that route in 200 hours (8 days).

Obviously in the dark times of Ragnarok, sea travel is filled with peril. Dangerous naval encounters can prove fatal. The unbearable cold of Fimbulwinter has filled the oceans with icebergs, and Jormungand's thrashing has a tendency to cause massive one hundred foot waves. Luckily the stars remain in the sky, allowing travel to still be relatively accurate. For those who know how to use a sunstone and are lucky enough to get a hold of one, the distant dim lights from Muspelheim can also help guide the way (reducing travel time by 20%).

Navigation skill check		
Result	**Speed Adjustment**	**Chance for a Dangerous Naval Encounter**
0 to 1	A few wrong turns- Double the time	66%
2 to 3	+50% time	33%
4	Average travel speed	0%
5	Get to your destination 10% faster	0%
6	Get to your destination 20% faster	0%
7	Get to your destination 25% faster	0%

Any Norn feeling adventurous with a group of high level dwellers (level 35+) may consider an encounter with Jormundgand. Definitely not a direct confrontation (unless dwellers are level 50+) but rather being thrown about by his immeasurable wake.

Surviving Fimbulwinter

Once the sun and moon were devoured by Skoll and Hati, Midgard would never be the same. It's always dark and cold, and when the snow falls, it never melts. Surviving the thus far 3-year long winter has been a lethal affair for the populace of Midgard. Farmers have lost their way of life with the onset of Fimbulwinter. Only stockpiles remain, and those are either dwindling quickly, or they act as magnets for raiders. All the freshwater bodies of water have frozen solid making fishing in the interior quite impossible. Bodies of salt water aren't without peril, with the copious presence of icebergs clogging up waterways as far south as the coast of Brittany. The temperatures have dropped by at least fourty degrees (20 degrees Celcius) in the interior, making it deathly cold to all forms of life. Many who were unprepared died in the first year, but as Fimbulwinter shows no signs of abating, the strong and stout are rising. Common decency has been replaced with well founded paranoia making life feel like an insurmountable struggle.

Successful adventurers will always carry ample food, never knowing when their next meal may be. Furs and lanterns are necessities that cannot be overlooked. Travel by land is more dangerous than travel by sea, but when it's necessary, snow shoes and skis will be indispensable.

Economic Devastation & War

The economy has been turned upside down, and prices for essentials have risen tenfold. Most forests that surrounded villages and towns have been clear cut for heat, light and shelter. Trade negotiations usually end in desperation as violence becomes the final offer. The wares in the highest demand are: food, furs, light sources, weapons and armour... in that order of priority. Some have seen this as an opportunity for immense profits and have acted quickly after the cataclysm. They now hold positions of power, using their riches to control the flow of good, and in turn control their new subjects. Slavery was always reserved for those from Outer-Midgard, but the new social support structures are turning the denizens of Midgard into thralls- sometimes without them even realizing it.

With the dawn of the second age, raids have turned into full scale wars over resources. Some petty Karls battle for the throne of Norveig, but deep down it is a desire for resource acquisition and control. One would be hard pressed to find a corner of Midgard that hasn't known violent struggle in the past three years. Many join a banner eagerly, knowing that there is power in numbers. Others see such a conscription as slavery and would rather strike out on their own. Compounding the wars in Midgard are the crusaders from the south. Their leaders have blamed the darkness upon the "heathens" to the North. The war campaign has spilled even more blood in the Great Isles as the crusader's momentum of slaughter accelerates.

The most troubling of conflicts come from the Einherjar and Sons of Muspel that are increasingly more prevalent within Midgard. The gods and Jotuns send them on missions of paramount importance and they usually leave turmoil in their wake, as they care very little for their former homeland. Their transformations imbue them with an altered consciousness that re-orders their priorities. They use their inhuman might to get what they want. In the very rare cases when these powers meet, the inevitable clash usually leaves miles of devastation, within which hopefully there wasn't any life to begin with. They travel with their quest in mind, and the troubles of mortals are but mere distractions.

Religion and Devotion

Since the onset of Fimbulwinter, the religious convictions of most have waned tremendously. For a very few zealots, the events of the last three years have inflamed their passion and reverence. But for the general population, survival has been their primary concern. Faith has never been monotheistic, with prayers directed at the appropriate divinities for any given hurdle life may throw. Gods, Jotuns, Vaettir, one would choose the divinity that embodied the aspect with which one needed divine assistance. With the waning enthusiasm, many cross their reverence between gods and Jotuns without second thought. This has made life much harder for the Valkyries who must bring the devoted to the right destination. As a result it isn't uncommon for Valkyries to fight over a fallen hero's soul.

Life as Usual

Despite the insanity that Fimbulwinter has brought, the population still knows how to have a good time. A good sense of humour is as important as a sturdy blade. Songs and dance can still be found throughout the realm. Boasting of one's exploits has never been so enthralling as everyone has epic tales to share over a horn of mead. Everyone knows one's end will come sooner or later, and the truly heroic ensure that their lives will have been lived to the fullest!

The Mysterious Skraelings

Some folk flee Midgard due to personal troubles or as a result of being branded an outlaw. Others are optimistic traders, willing to skirt the uncharted edges of Midgard. Most of these stalwarts and survivors head west to Islandia. Other more adventurous types, some may call them foolhardy, head past the isle of ice and fire and into the violent and dark north sea. These expeditions, if not met by ruin, lead the explorers to lands shrouded in exotic mystery.

These lands are unlike anything in Midgard or even the southern kingdoms. The peoples of the far west have strange appearances and customs. Their languages sound strange and their villages and towns are very different from those found in Midgard. Homes are made out of ice and animals skins since much of their northern lands are devoid of trees.

Should an expedition successfully negotiate with the Skraelings of Gronland and Helluland, managing to navigate the rocky waters of another culture's etiquette and customs, then they are granted passage further west. The further one travels west, the more bountiful the land becomes. Still under the darkness of Fimbulwinter, the icy barren landscape gives way to vast forests. The Skraelings of Markland and Vinland speak yet another language and are less hospitable to newcomers. Their curiosity and desire for trade is mostly trumped by their xenophobic tendencies.

Skraeling Society

The Skraeling peoples are nomadic hunter gatherers by nature. Their lives follow the rhythms of the physical and spiritual world around them. They inhabit harsh landscapes and travel with the seasons, following the migration patterns of their prey. A few Skraeling choose to follow a more spiritual path and eventually become the wise elders and revered shamans known as the Angakkuq.

To become an Angakkuq, one must learn from an elder shaman and go on a Vision Quest. The first step of the learning process is a unique and secret language of the Angakkuq. A shaman in training must learn about various plants, animals, weather patterns, spirits and history. Some tribes burn special plants in order to connect with the spirit world. In order to ascend, the Vision Quest must be completed. This is a process which involves both discomfort and sensory deprivation. The ritual varies from tribe to tribe, but multi-day hikes without food or water or prolonged seclusion in a darkened sweat tent are common examples.

Once the initiate graduates into a full Angakkuq, a spirit called a Tuurngait comes to them and becomes their spirit guide for life. Tuurngaits have the ability to bestow supernatural powers upon their liege.

TUURNGAIT- If the Norn wishes to involve a Angakkuq's Tuurngait in battle, the following abilities may be applied:

- If the Skraeling is of higher level than the dwellers, then all adjacent Fylgia ring powers are useless while within 10' of the Tuurngait (temporarily unbind Active powers and ignore Passive powers in the grey outer ring).
- The Angakkuq may allow their Tuurngait to possess them. If they do, treat the effect identical to Seith Magic. All of the Angakkuq's spells gain the {Seith Spell} descriptor.

Every tribe has their own sacred land and animal spirits. Some tribes erect totem poles to pay homage to those spirits. The poles are made from the trunks of sacred trees and can be as tall as thirty feet. The spirit imagery is carved into the wood and the poles are finished using consecrated paint. It is believed that erecting such a tribute brings good fortune to the tribe.

TOTEM POLE- The continuous benefits granted are equivalent to a +1 bonus to skill checks. During battles, if a sacrifice is made, then a continuous Catharsis is cast on all tribe members within 200' of the Totem Pole.

If a Generic action is used to Beseech a Higher Power, it gains a benefit when invoking very receptive higher powers (spirits of the Skraeling lands) within sight of the Totem Pole. A bonus rune may be drawn from the bag.

The best way for young men to win the respect and admiration of other warriors and attract the attention of women is to distinguish themselves in battle. This is one of the primary catalysts for the unending wars between Skraeling tribes. Marriage is not limited to the union of one man and one woman. Depending on local customs, union with more than one partner or even unions with animals are possible. Once universal rule is that one cannot marry someone of the same tribe.

Transportation and Housing

With little to no wood to be found in the far north, the Skraeling use stone, bone, ivory and animal gut/skins for their crafting. Albeit primitive materials are used, the skill of the craftsmen results in the creation of truly spectacular items. When wood is not available arctic moss, leather straps, dried feces and dung are used for kindling.

Prior to the coming of Ragnarok, eight person canoes were the preferred choice for nautical travel. These lightweight leather skiffs enabled swift movement over small bodies of water and were light enough for long portages over land. Since the onset of Fimbulwinter, most freshwater bodies of water are frozen and so the use of these boats has been relegated to the far north where travel between Helluland and Gronland is perilous, but necessary for some tribes.

The Skraeling pride themselves on being in harmony with their surroundings. As a result, their villages are built in such a way as to blend in with the surrounding landscape. This skill is honed and refined since it is invaluable when at war with other tribes. As a result any foreigners from Midgard would have a very hard time discerning a Skraeling village. Conversely a foreigner's beachhead would stand out like bonfire in the night.

War and Weaponry

The Skraeling warrior caste rely on stone axes and spears. The Angakkuq tradition introduces some more exotic weapons such as the bone death rattle as well as the staff sling. The staff sling uses very unique ammunition. The projectile is comprised of a sewn hide bladder filled with special stones that produce a high pitched grating noise when jostled. When hurled through the air, the contents in conjunction with the shape of the projectile produces a frightful shrieking sound. Impact causes the special stones to violently shatter into shards that pierce the leather casing.

> Due to the materials and processes used, these weapons are crafted using the "Survival: Wilderness" skill rather than "Craft" skill.

A Skraeling warband has no hierarchy. Every member receives the same training and is autonomous on the battlefield. Pre-planned strategy is replaced with real time coordination. This creates a very different dynamic on the battlefield in comparison to traditional roles of war leaders at the head of Midgard armies. Engaging the Skraeling in war is a dangerous proposition as their tactics seem chaotic and they never fail to surprise.

Monsters and Spirits

The Skraeling world is filled with spirits, both benevolent and frightful. Day to day life is shaped by the spirit world, and finding success in life means navigating a relationship with many types of spirits. When dealing with the spirit world, Angakkuq never use people's real names for fear that the spirits will be able to hunt them down. Every one is referred to by their spirit names when asking for guidance, victory or protection.

Skaelings foster a relationship with sympathetic personal and tribal spirits while appeasing and avoiding evil ones. However there are a rare few who seek out the nefarious spirits in order to learn how to harm or exact revenge. In both cases the Skraeling folk treat spirits with tremendous respect.

Some spirits are beyond the scope of human interaction, and some believed that this aloofness was tied to their immortal nature. At Ragnarok, this myth has been clearly dispelled with the destruction of the sun spirit Akycha and the moon spirit Igaluk. The greater raven spirit Tulungusaq, who is said to have created the world from the abyss, was once aloof, but now is active within the lives of the Skraeling people.

In the darkest recesses of the Skraeling lands one may find truly terrifying monsters such as the Adlet. The Adlet are five blood drinking monsters who were born from the union between a woman and a shape-shifting dog. They have tremendous strength, speed and hunger, and their appearance is that of a man crossed with a wolf. They have been seen throughout the lands to the west, migrating with their prey.

Nanook is the great polar bear spirit and while at one time he was a minor spririt, he has grown more powerful and aggressive since the coming of Fimbulwinter. Nanook is not alone. Akhlut is a spirit which can take the form of an orca or a wolf. Since the eternal darkness began, he has become ravenous for human flesh.

Spirits, Birth and Death

When the Skraeling die, the corpse is washed and groomed. It is then wrapped in caribou skins and buried under a cairn. The body remains, but the soul moves into the spirit world, taking a path pre-ordained by their living deeds. Those who led decent lives are returned once more to their people as a newborn. The wicked go to a frightful realm in the deepest depths of the cosmos while the enlightened may remain and become timeless spirits.

Adlivun is the Skraeling underworld. This cold and dark existence beneath the north seas was reserved for those who led lives of wickedness. Anguta is the caretaker spirit of Adlivun and those whom she deems worthy, she sends to Adliparmiut- a darker and deeper afterlife where the souls are permitted to hunt.

When a child is born, they are given the name of an ancestor following Pittailiniq tradition. The tradition rituals ensure that the name is indeed the spirit which has returned. Henceforth the newborn is then treated with the same amount of respect as the elder after whom they were named. The matron spirit known as Pukkeenegak is invoked to ensure that the birth is safe and successful.

First Contact

The Skraelings of Gronland do not take kindly to intruders upon their land. They are, however, by far the most tolerant of the Skraeling tribes. The further one goes west and south, the more xenophobic the Skraeling become. A first encounter with Skraelings may result in trade, but more often than not it ends with violence. If an Angakkuq is present, his wisdom will drive the encounter towards a mutually prosperous one involving trade rather than bloodshed.

Skraelings use a bone staff to signify their intent. If they spin it sunwise then they wish to parlay peacefully. If their intention is violent, then the staff is spun counter-sunwise, helping to gather the war spirits to their side. Very strong etiquette skills are essential if someone from Midgard wishes to seek trade with the Skraeling. A minimum of three successes are required to simply understand the basics of their alien customs.

There is a chance that physical contact with the Skraelings will result in an expedition becoming infected with the White Plague. Many Skraelings are carriers of a disease that does not affect them, but is terribly debilitating and lethal to those from Midgard. Should the disease make its way to Islandia and further east, the damage it could cause is of cataclysmic proportions.

> **THE WHITE PLAGUE-** Should the dwellers meet a Skraeling group, there is a 33% chance that they are carriers of the White Plague. Wyrd 1 rune, a Physical rune indicates potential for contagion. Transmission of the disease requires physical contact and each time physical contact is made the Norn should check to see if the disease has been transmitted (66% chance- Physical or Mental rune). If infected, the Curse condition should be raised to intensity 1.
>
> Every hour the victim must perform an Ultimate Sacrifice equal to the Curse condition intensity. Every week, the intensity will automatically increase by +1. Within Midgard there is no known cure for this plague, magical or mundane. The Norn may choose to create a means by which the White Plague can be slowed or even reversed within the lands of the Skraeling. Perhaps a pilgrimage to a sacred spring or unique vegetation could achieve some level of relief.

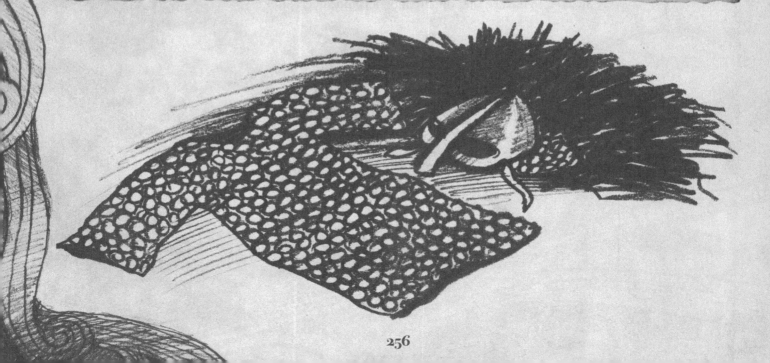

We present a host of
new player archetypes
in *Denizens of the
North*. These arche-
types were introduced in the *Core
Rulebook*, but within this tome you
will find them fully fleshed out and
playable. These new player options
open the door to some signature
roles portrayed in Viking myths of
legend.

Archetypes

ARCHETYPES	TOP-LEFT	TOP-RIGHT	BOTTOM-LEFT	BOTTOM-RIGHT
Galdr	Blacksmith	Skald	Druid	Seithkona
Maiden of Ratatosk	Sceadugengan	Skald	Seithkona	Stalo
Seithkona	Sceadugengan	Skald	Galdr	Berserkir
Skald	Ulfhednar	Galdr	Berserkir	Stalo
Ulfhednar	Galdr	Berserkir	Sceadugengan	Fardrengir
Berserkir	Ulfhednar	Fardrengir	Druid	Blacksmith
Blacksmith	Druid	Maiden of Ratatosk	Galdr	Stalo
Druid	Ulfhednar	Fardrengir	Skald	Blacksmith
Fardrengir	Druid	Stalo	Maiden of Ratatosk	Ulfhednar
Sceadugengan	Maiden of Ratatosk	Fardrengir	Seithkona	Skald
Stalo	Maiden of Ratatosk	Fardrengir	Blacksmith	Sceadugengan

Berserkir

A Berserkir is a warrior who is blessed with the anger of the gods. In this rage, he loses all control and becomes a killing machine, striking down foes with the strength of twice four men. They have no need for armour, since neither iron nor fire can touch their skin while in this feverish rage. People have tried calming the fires within a Berserkir consumed with Modr by pushing them into vats of ice-cold water, but the water was turned to steam by the fiery anger of the Berserkir's breast. Throwing naked women in the path of a Berserkir has also failed to calm the heavenly rage.

In some cases, a Berserkir has been known to transform himself into a mighty bear. After the rage wears off, the warrior is in a weakened state for a time. It is said that a king sent five Berserkirs to conquer a neighbouring kingdom and they accomplished their task, slaying all of the opponent's armies.

This rage is spiritual in nature, since it is a lesser form of what the god Thor possesses.

Juggernaut

Berserkirs that personify the oncoming storm are known as Juggernauts. They are a purely destructive force that believe the best defence is a strong offence. Most will utterly decimate an opponent before they can mount an effective attack. Those that survive the initial onslaught find themselves on their heels, facing an aggressor that will eventually spell their doom.

Dreadnought

Berserkirs that are blessed with rage cannot be touched by fire or steel. Dreadnoughts strive to become the most indestructible forces of nature. Their resolve is unwavering and their body is immovable. Most foes retreat knowing that killing a Dreadnought is an almost insurmountable challenge.

Ursen

Berserkirs that embrace their bear form choose to follow the path of the Ursen. They use their form to gain every advantage over their opposition- size, speed, power and ferocity. Ursen use their tremendous reach to great advantage, swatting opponents about the battlefield.

	JUGGERNAUT	DREADNOUGHT	URSEN
Trait	Physical	Mental	Spiritual
Active	Defying Leap	Armoured Reflex	Unleash the Beast
Passive	Iron Fist	Iron Hide	Iron Beast
Skill	Athletics	Endurance	Brawling

Cross-Archetype Active Powers: Ulfhednar	Howl, Hati's Victory [Amplify Cannibalize Amplify]	Fylgia's Scorn (Cleansing Attack) [Amplify Cannibalize Weapon]	Reckless Wounding Attack	Invincible Sprint	Reckless Bull Rush	Cross-Archetype Active Powers: Fardrengir
Howl, Heart of Fury	Stand of Punishment	Reckless Whirlwind Attack	Lunging Attack	Reckless Power Attack	Stand of Presence	Obliterating Blow
Reckless Raging Attack	Pained Strike	Whirlwind Attack	Raging Charge	Power Attack	Wounding Attack	Reckless Lunging Attack
Reckless Aggressive Assault	Cleansing Attack	Raging Attack	ACTIVE POWERS	Satisfying Attack	Regenerating Attack	Protective Impulse
Fylgia's Splendour (Throw Dirt) [Amplify Amplify Echo]	Desperation Attack	Vaulting Attack	Thundering Blow	Frenetic Charge	Piercing Attack	Improvised Attack
Furious Bestial Mauling	Stand of Impunity	Leaping Attack	Reckless Thundering Blow	Aggressive Assault	Stand of Domination	Fylgia's Fury (Formulating Attack) [Amplify Cannibalize Weapon]
Cross-Archetype Active Powers: Druid	Lead the Charge	Reckless Feral Pounce	Fylgia's Rallying Strike	Snare	Armageddon Strike	Cross-Archetype Active Powers: Blacksmith

Cross-Archetype Passive Powers: Ulfhednar	Desperation	Brawler of Spring	Temper Rage	Zerkir Weapon Toss	Pounce	Cross-Archetype Passive Powers: Fardrengir
Unarmed Power	Furious Cohort	Fleet Footed	Drive Back	Combat Manoeuvrability	Stout	Unencumbered Dodger
Unbreakable Mind	Die Hard	Agility	Raging Bear	Bastion	Constitution	Champion of Summer
Unbreakable Body	Spirit Warrior	Enter Rage	PASSIVE POWERS	Harbour Grudge	Leaping Striker	Silence the Crowd
Unbreakable Soul	Cerebral Warrior	Blood Lust	Zerkir Chest Bump	Carried by Blood	Unstoppable Carnage	Quick Draw
Resistance to Degeneration	Running Jab	Might	Unstoppable Aggression	Resistance to Blindness	Bestial Heart	Resistance to Vulnerable
Cross-Archetype Passive Powers: Druid	Resistance to Possession	Untouchable	Frenzy	Seeker of Winter	Resistance to Impeded	Cross-Archetype Passive Powers: Blacksmith

Cross Archetype Skills: Ulfhednar	Drinking/ Wenching	Athletics	Brawling	Peak Performance	Swim	Cross Archetype Skills: Fardrengir
Lock Bash	Lore: Locales	Lock Bash	Brawling	Endurance	Omens/ Portents	Athletics
Endurance	Short Fuse	Peak Performance	Intimidate	Swim	Brawling	Lock Bash
Short Fuse	War Tactics	Brawling	SKILLS	Short Fuse	Athletics	Repair Equipment
Omens/ Portents	Drinking/ Wenching	Short Fuse	Athletics	Repair Equipment	Brawling	Endurance
Athletics	Survival: Urban	Endurance	Intimidate	Craft	Short Fuse	Lock Bash
Cross Archetype Skills: Druid	Endurance	Omens/ Portents	Survival: Urban	War Tactics	Craft	Cross Archetype Skills: Blacksmith

Blacksmith

The Blacksmith has talents that many envy. He can create items not only out of metals and stones but also out of wood.

He is a master warrior thanks to his knowledge of weapon creation. Blacksmiths are one of the clan's most valued subjects due to religious taboos around looting corpses. Many blacksmiths worship Dvergar, since their crafting skills are the envy of all.

Some master blacksmiths have created artefacts that clans and kingdoms have gone to war over. They are not bound by their forges: once they surpass apprentice levels, they gain the ability to summon a forge beast to their side, allowing them to craft while travelling.

Creating items, ranging from the mundane to the magical, follows a simple set of rules. The process uses the skill system, and may be attempted by those with no ranks in the required skills. The two principal skills are: Craft and Infuse. Craft allows one to create mundane items of great quality, and infuse allows one to add magical properties to an already crafted item.

Exemplar

The Exemplar Blacksmith enjoys time in the forge, but enjoys testing and showing off their creations even more. The exemplar judges his creations on the battlefield against items created by other smiths. He pushes himself to ever higher standards and ideals.

Artificer

The Creator Blacksmith enjoys nothing more than spending as much time and effort in the forge. The focus of an artificer's efforts are to create the most awe inspiring items, far surpassing anything shop owners may be peddling.

Alchemist

The Alchemist Blacksmith is one who explores the esoteric pleasures of imbuing items with magical properties. These items are sought after as they expand and greatly increase the power of the wielder.

	EXEMPLAR	ARTIFICER	ALCHEMIST
Trait	Physica	Mental	Spiritual
Active	Weapon Stance	Soul-bound Strike	Infused Strike
Passive	Builder's Glory	Crafter's Promise	Invoker's Charity
Skill	Repair Equipment	Craft	Infuse

Cross-Archetype Active Powers: Druid	Fylgia's Scorn (Cleansing Attack) [Amplify Cannibalize Proficiency]	Purging Tirade	Wolf's Dreadnaught (Wolf's Posture) [Amplify Maintain Area]	Misery Loves Company	Fylgia's Fury (Specialized Formulating Attack) [Amplify Cannibalize Proficiency]	Cross-Archetype Active Powers: Maiden of Ratatosk
Fylgia's Sanctuary (Unearthly Resilience) [Area Maintain Area]	Aggressive Stance	Specialized Whirlwind Attack (Whirlwind Attack) [Amplify Multi Proficiency]	Predatory Stance	Specialized Formulating Attack (Formulating Attack) [Amplify Multi Proficiency]	Specialized Hamstring (Hamstring) [Amplify Multi Proficiency]	Fylgia's Splendour (Throw Dirt) [Amplify Amplify Echo]
Specialized Trip (Trip) [Amplify Amplify Echo]	Specialized Flanking Attack (Flanking Attack) [Amplify Multi Proficiency]	Specialized Power Attack (Power Attack) [Amplify Multi Proficiency]	Specialized Lunging Attack (Lunging Attack) [Amplify Multi Proficiency]	Specialized Precision Attack (Precision Attack) [Amplify Multi Proficiency]	Specialized Disarm (Disarm) [Amplify Multi Proficiency]	Snare
Narwhal's Dreadnaught (Narwhal's Posture) [Amplify Maintain Area]	Healing Stance	Specialized Sundering Blow (Sundering Blow) [Amplify Multi Proficiency]	ACTIVE POWERS	Versatile Combat Manoeuver	Mobile Stance	Boar's Dreadnaught (Boar's Posture) [Amplify Maintain Area]
Repositioning	Presence of the Weapons Master	Specialized Regenerating Attack (Regenerating Attack) [Amplify Multi Proficiency]	Regenerating Block	Superior Parry	Cleansing Block	Run Away Laughing
Fylgia's Touch (Channeling) [Combo Range Amplify]	Presence of the Ultimate Warrior	Presence of the Invincible Shield	Defensive Stance	Disarming Parry	Perfect Parry	Fylgia's Shadow (Cleansing Block) [Amplify Cannibalize Proficiency]
Cross-Archetype Active Powers: Galdr	Fylgia's Destiny (Stitch Destiny) [Multi Range Maintain]	Fylgia's Grace (Purge Vulnerability) [Area Amplify Area]	Bear's Dreadnaught (Bear's Posture) [Amplify Maintain Area]	Insulting Parry	Fylgia's Kiss (Catharsis) [Range Combo Amplify]	Cross-Archetype Active Powers: Stalo

Cross-Archetype Passive Powers: Druid	Bestow Wisdom	Summon Forge Beast	Companion in Destiny	Constitution	Bestow Conviction	Cross-Archetype Passive Powers: Maiden of Ratatosk
Nimble	Summon Forge Beast	Might	Summon Forge Beast	Favour Offense	Equipment Mastery	Summon Forge Beast
Summon Forge Beast	Stand of Haste	Artisan's Pride	Mob Mentality	Spirit Warrior	Combat Awareness	Fellowship of the Silver Shields
Defy the Crowd	Summon Forge Beast	Stand of the 4 Winds	PASSIVE POWERS	Protector	Favour Defense	Aura of Influence
Summon Forge Beast	Stand of Victory	Drive Back	Tactician	Cerebral Warrior	Precision	Companion in War
Work in Concert	Summon Forge Beast	Stand of Deliverance	Tactical Advantage	Quick Draw	Attuned Weapon	Summon Forge Beast
Cross-Archetype Passive Powers: Galdr	Resistance to Blind	Summon Forge Beast	Resistance to Vulnerable	Bastion	Resistance to Impeded	Cross-Archetype Passive Powers: Stalo

Cross Archetype Skills: Druid	Miniaturize	Craft	Miniaturize	Infuse	Miniaturize	Cross Archetype Skills: Maiden of Ratatosk
Dvergar Engineering	Infuse	Miniaturize	Craft	Miniaturize	Infuse	Realm Ores
Craft	Repair Equipment	Craft	Appraisal	Craft	Repair Equipment	Craft
Dvergar Engineering	Sense Motive	Survival, Urban	SKILLS	Repair Equipment	Read and Write	Realm Ores
Infuse	Repair Equipment	Infuse	Appraisal	Infuse	Lock Picking	Infuse
Dvergar Engineering	Craft	Omens/ Portents	Infuse	Negotiation	Craft	Realm Ores
Cross Archetype Skills: Galdr	Creature Reliquary	Infuse	Creature Reliquary	Craft	Creature Reliquary	Cross Archetype Skills: Stalo

Druid

Druids follow the way of the woods. Wood is sacred and has a spirit: knowing how to interact with it is a hidden art that goes by the name of Verwandlung and is the sacred property of the druid. Verwandlung involves a hierarchy of different wood that must be fashioned into wands and staves. Wielding the wand or staff made from that wood gives the druid powers associated with that grade of wood. Powers involve and encompass interactions with vegetation as well as with wild animals.

The mightiest of druids become one with the land and have the awe-inspiring power of terra-forming: a druid can change desolate tundra into a verdant mountain range as easily as one dresses in the morning. Druids shun civilization and prefer to dwell in pure nature.

Warden of the Woods

The Warden of the Woods specializes in verdant magic that is both restorative and benevolent. The Druid strives to understand the land and the spirits that dwell within. He understands that he is the drop that wishes to reunite with the sea.

Child of the Stars

Some Druids have the gift of foresight granted to them by their attunement to the heavens. The Child of the Stars gains insight from the constellations and can easily share his knowledge with his allies. He is also an expert brewer of potions and ointments.

Animist

This particular Druid has specialized in the ability to assume animal form. This bestial form is a kindred spirit for the Animist. The special affinity allows them to exemplify the very best from that species.

	WARDEN OF THE WOODS	CHILD OF STARS	ANIMIST
Trait	Physical	Mental	Spiritual
Active	One With the Land	Beckon Vanagard	Wild Shape
Passive	Nature's Child	Bestow Illumination	Giant Size
Skill	Sacred Wood Binding	Brewing	Animal Shapeshift

Cross-Archetype Active Powers: Ulfhednar	Invigorate Spirit {Verwandlung Spell}	Chant of Skuld	Possess Opponent {Verwandlung Spell}	Fylgia's Destiny (Stitch Destiny) [Multi Range Maintain]	Fylgia's Grace (Purge Vulnerability) [Area Amplify Area]	Cross-Archetype Active Powers: Fardrengir
Fylgia's Sanctuary (Unearthly Resilience) [Area Maintain Area]	Land's Caretaker (Power Overwhelming) {Verwandlung Spell}	Power Over Stone {Verwandlung Spell}	Force of Nature (Sun and Moon) {Verwandlung Spell}	Geyser of Living Water {Verwandlung Alka}	Field of Poppies {Verwandlung Alka Spell}	Fylgia's Touch (Channeling) [Combo Range Amplify]
Life Overwhelming {Verwandlung Spell}	Rustling Leaves (Rapid Recovery) {Verwandlung Spell}	Oyenstikker	Swords to Snakes {Verwandlung Spell}	Field of Thorny Vines {Verwandlung Alka Spell}	Ley Lines of Power {Verwandlung Alka Spell}	Imposing Barrier {Verwandlung Spell}
Fylgia's Scorn (Cleansing Attack) [Amplify Cannibalize Weapon]	Cleansing Block	Forest's Gaze (Apples of Idun) {Verwandlung Spell}	ACTIVE POWERS	Field of Quagmires {Verwandlung Alka Spell}	Stitch Kindred {Verwandlung Spell}	Arcane Shield {Verwandlung Spell}
Narwhal's Posture {Verwandlung Spell}	Catharsis {Verwandlung Spell}	Regenerating Attack	Versatile Combat Manoeuvre	Superior Parry	Gate Hrokkvir {Verwandlung Spell}	Cleansing Sprint
Fylgia's Fury (Specialized Formulating Attack) [Amplify Cannibalize Weapon]	Recuperating Furious Onslaught	Snare	Cleansing Attack	Power Over Wind {Verwandlung Spell}	Perfect Parry	Fylgia's Kiss (Catharsis) [Range Combo Amplify]
Cross-Archetype Active Powers: Skald	Fylgia's Children (Howl, Rally the Pack) [Amplify Cannibalize Amplify]	Leaping Attack	Lunging Attack	Fylgia's Cloak (Enchant Flesh)	Fylgia's Pride (Vengeful Parry) [Amplify Cannibalize Amplify]	Cross-Archetype Active Powers: Blacksmith

Cross-Archetype Passive Powers: Ulfhednar	Companion in Destiny	Resistance to Degeneration	Fellowship of the Silver Shields	Resistance to Blindness	Favour Defense	Cross-Archetype Passive Powers: Fardrengir
Companion in Magic	Alka Mastery	Agility	Unbreakable Body	Gliding Dodger	Die Hard	Misery Loves Company
Unwelcome Motivation	Keen Senses	Stout	Alka Kinship	Alka Tenacity	Seeker of Worlds	Protector
Companion in War	Unencumbered Dodger	Nature's Child	PASSIVE POWERS	Fae-Kin	Unbreakable Soul	Work in Concert
Price of Progress	Superb Swimmer	Channel the Unseen River	Constitution	Resistance to Possession	Bestow Conviction	Rallying Pack Howl
Companion in Life	Cornered Ferocity	Bestow Wisdom	Unbreakable Mind	Arcane Reach	Combat Awareness	Enchanted Prowess
Cross-Archetype Passive Powers: Skald	Companion in Death	Resistance to Impeded	Insight	Resistance to Vulnerable	Companion in Blood	Cross-Archetype Passive Powers: Blacksmith

Cross-Archetype Skills: Ulfhednar	Sacred Wood Binding	Lore: Locales	Brew	Lore: Arcana	Sacred Wood Binding	Cross-Archetype Skills: Fardrengir
Brew	Inner Sanctum	Navigation	Sacred Wood Binding	Riding	Inner Sanctum	Brew
Omens/ Portents	Perception	Brew	Omens/ Portents	Brew	Athletics	Animal Empathy
Inner Sanctum	Sacred Wood Binding	Survival Wilderness	SKILLS	Animal Empathy	Sacred Wood Binding	Inner Sanctum
Survival Wilderness	Swim	Brew	Hunting/ Trapping	Brew	Tracking	Animal Empathy
Brew	Inner Sanctum	Lore: Locales	Sacred Wood Binding	Lore: Arcana	Inner Sanctum	Brew
Cross-Archetype Skills: Skald	Sacred Wood Binding	Navigation	Brew	Wilderness Survival	Sacred Wood Binding	Cross-Archetype Skills: Blacksmith

Fardrengir

The Fardrengir is a travelling soul and a seasoned hunter. She will not stay in a town too long. Her need for adventure, exploration and nature will keep her on the move. The Fardrengir is a master of the wilderness. Many travellers seek the Fardrengir's guidance in their trek. She can safely navigate even the most difficult terrain. She works towards harmony with all beasts of nature, but that does not diminish the hunter inside her heart.

Fardrengir usually travel with animal companions that are possessed by the realm spirits of Yggdrasil. The companions have consciousness far more evolved than a regular animal. They serve as mounts allowing the Fardrengir to cover vast distances in very little time.

Farvaldr

The Farvaldr is consumed with wanderlust. They cannot stay in one place for long and through their travels, they have become masters of the wild. Their survival instincts are second to none. Farvaldr are trap specialists, having the ability to rig a lethal trap from almost anything found in the wild. The most successful bounty hunters are the Falvaldr, also known as Striders. Their competition affectionately call them "spiders" rather than "Striders".

Dyrvaldr

An animal lover at heart, the beast master attracts special mounts with whom they forge an unbreakable bond. They train with these loyal thanes in order to hone their mesmerizing and synchronized manoeuvres. What they achieve together is much more astonishing than what they muster on their own. Depending on the Dyrvaldr's goals, they will choose the right mount that will compliment the skills and powers they require.

Geirvaldr

The Geirvaldr is the spear master. A hunter who specializes in bows and thrown weapons. The celerity and dexterity of their arms shocks and astonishes onlookers. Besides their uncanny accuracy, the Geirvaldr has the ability to draw and launch an astonishing number of projectiles- be it with bow or javelin.

	FARVALDR (TRAP MASTER)	DYRVALDR (BEAST MASTER)	GEIRVALDR (SPEAR MASTER)
Trait	Physical	Mental	Spiritual
Active	Trapper's Stance	Rider's Synergy	Projectile Ricochet Technique
Passive	Trap Master	Summon Mount	Archer's Third Eye
Skill	Hunting/Trapping	Riding	Survival: Wilderness

Cross-Archetype Active Powers: Druid	Satisfying Attack [Amplify Multi Piercer]	Stitch Kindred	Flanking Attack [Amplify Multi Piercer]	Thundering Blow [Amplify Multi Piercer]	Sundering Blow [Amplify Multi Piercer]	Cross-Archetype Active Powers: Stalo
Fylgia's Sanctuary (Unearthly Resilience) [Area Maintain Area]	Misery Likes Company [Amplify Multi Piercer]	Flying Charge [Amplify Multi Piercer]	Lunging Attack [Amplify Multi Piercer]	Formulating Attack [Amplify Multi Piercer]	Cleansing Attack [Amplify Multi Piercer]	Fylgia's Scorn (Cleansing Attack) [Amplify Cannibalize Piercer]
Apples of Idunn	Backstab [Amplify Multi Piercer]	Trap-Tangle	Throw Weapon	Trap-Incapacitation	Attack from Above [Amplify Multi Piercer]	Weapon Stance
Throw Dirt	Piercing Attack [Amplify Multi Piercer]	Cleansing Sprint	ACTIVE POWERS	Hamstring [Amplify Multi Piercer]	Regenerating Attack [Amplify Multi Piercer]	Versatile Combat Manoeuvre
Trip	Defensive Stance	Trap-Lacerations	Presence of the Wind Warrior	Trap-Spikes	Mobile Stance	Recuperating Sever Hamstring [Amplify Multi Piercer]
Fylgia's Touch (Channeling) [Combo Range Amplify]	Run Away Laughing	Precision Attack [Amplify Multi Piercer]	Arcane Shield	Power Attack [Amplify Multi Piercer]	Repositioning	Fylgia's Kiss (Catharsis) [Range Combo Amplify]
Cross-Archetype Active Powers: Maiden of Ratatosk	Sweeping Trip	Recuperating Wounding Attack [Amplify Multi Piercer]	Wolf Posture	Wounding Attack [Amplify Multi Piercer]	Howl, Blood Fang	Cross-Archetype Active Powers: Ulfhednar

Cross-Archetype Passive Powers: Druid	Summon Mount	Mob Mentality	Companion in War	Agility	Summon Mount	Cross-Archetype Passive Powers: Stalo
Nature's Child	Aura of Influence	Untouchable	Tactician	Resistance to Blindness	Stout	Leaping Striker
Keen Senses	Fleet Footed	Summon Mount	Tactical Advantage	Summon Mount	Resistance to Impeded	Drive Back
Summon Mount	Combat Manoeuvrability	Quick Draw	PASSIVE POWERS	Striker	Mighty Arm	Summon Mount
Work in Concert	Martial Prowess	Summon Mount	Rider of Lightning	Summon Mount	Drive Back	Favour Offence
Defy the Crowd	Archer's Sight	Rider of Thunder	Attuned Weapon	Hunter's Heart	Hunter's Cunning	Rallying Pack Howl
Cross-Archetype Passive Powers: Maiden of Ratatosk	Summon Mount	Companion in Life	Blend into Shadow	Companion in Death	Summon Mount	Cross-Archetype Passive Powers: Ulfhednar

Cross-Archetype Skills: Druid	Hunting / Trapping	Survival: Wilderness	Sneak	Swim	Riding	Cross Archetype Skills: Stalo
Perception	Riding	Lore: Personas	Athletics	Silent Tongue	Hunting / Trapping	Navigation
Survival: Wilderness	Repair Equipment	Lore: Locales	Navigation	Perception	Survival: Wilderness	Sneak
Riding	Endurance	Hunting / Trapping	SKILLS	Riding	Animal Empathy	Hunting / Trapping
Tracking	Swim	Sneak	Tracking	Sense Motive	Tracking	Survival: Wilderness
Navigation	Riding	Intimidate	Survival: Wilderness	Omens / Portents	Hunting / Trapping	Perception
Cross Archetype Skills: Maiden of Ratatosk	Hunting / Trapping	Animal Empathy	Navigation	Survival: Wilderness	Riding	Cross Archetype Skills: Ulfhednar

Sceadugengan

Sceadugengan are known as the "dark walkers". They begin their lives as rogues, living a life of theft, fraud and murder. Life's ambition drives the rogue to obtain the most for the least amount of effort. Their motto is "when all else fails, steal and backstab". But while in pursuit of increasingly better concealment, pilfering and assassination techniques, they eventually fall upon the dark lore of the Svart Alfar. This pursuit takes them down a dark road where their psyche and spirit erode and are replaced with greed, envy and lust. Their growing powers are fed by the shadows and darkness, encouraging a penumbral existence. This lore and techniques transform the rogue into a Sceadugengan. The darkness becomes their play-thing. The general population of Midgard is easy prey for seasoned dark walker. Many seek out the Sceadugengan for their clandestine talents and offer lucrative contracts. The Sceadugengan's powers stem from the dance of light and dark. Despite an adoration for the Svart, the powers of shadow also require the Lios. Some of their powers will take on a life of their own, transforming their very nature to capitalize on the surrounding light and darkness.

Thief

The Sceadugengan that is driven by greed seeks the path of the thief. Wealth is a motivator, but the thrill of the score is what truly excites her. It is said that in Svartalfheim you can have your sword plucked right out of your hand without even knowing it. The Thief studies the techniques that allow her to secretly pilfer personal effects, even in the heat of combat. No one's possessions are safe when a Sceadugengan Thief is around.

Assassin

Most Sceadugengans' actions are beholden to their shady moral compass. However the darkest of those belong to the assassins. They are the ones who have embraced their talent and bliss when choking out the flame of life. The combat style that they bring back from the shadow involves the least amount of strikes in order to murder their quarry. Those who are the best in this discipline also melt away after the deed is done, so as to avoid any blame.

Scoundrel

While the other Sceadugengan pride themselves at stealth, the scoundrel prefers to hide in plain sight. Their mightiest power is their disarming charisma. Replacing the need for nimble fingers and instead relying on flattery, charm and pure presence, the Scoundrel can spin almost any situation into a favourable one. The Svart lore they covet has trained the scoundrels in the art of using others to do their dirty work.

	THIEF	ASSASSIN	SCOUNDREL
Trait	Physical	Mental	Spiritual
Active	Pilfer	Death Strike	Mesmerizing Gaze
Passive	Quick Draw	Assassin's Reflexes	Deflect Aggression
Skill	Feather Fingers	Sneak	Verbal Manipulation

Cross-Archetype Active Powers: Maiden of Ratatosk	Fylgia's Pride (Vengeful Parry) [Amplify Cannibalize Amplify]	Shade of Whispers	Sly Stance	Shade of the Dark Mother	Fylgia's Scorn (Cleansing Attack) [Amplify Cannibalize Weapon]	Cross-Archetype Active Powers: Fardrengir
Fylgia's Sanctuary (Unearthly Resilience) [Area Maintain Area]	Shade of the Treasure Hoard	Cerebral Shroud	Backstab	Cleansing Block	Shade of Night and Day	Fylgia's Kiss (Catharsis) [Range Combo Amplify]
Shade of the Darkening Sky	Beckon Svartalfheim	Shade of the Blustering Blizzard	Shadow Strike	Shade of the Darting Fox	Run Away Laughing	Shade of the Abyssal Current
Purge Blindness	Boar's Posture	Cleansing Attack	ACTIVE POWERS	Stance of Darkness	Formulating Attack	Precision Attack
Shade of the Endless Mind	Dark Juxtaposition	Shade of the Toxic River	Run to Shadow	Shade of Malevolence	Lunging Attack	Shade of the Enveloping Miasma
Fylgia's Splendour (Throw Dirt) [Amplify Amplify Echo]	Shade of the Lost Ship	Invigorate Spirit	Shadow Step	Invoke the Shadows	Shade of the Fallen Jarl	Fylgia's Rallying Strike
Cross-Archetype Active Powers: Seithkona	Fylgia's Touch (Channeling) [Combo Range Amplify]	Shade of Piercing Eyes	Power Overwhelming	Shade of the Enraged Serpent	Fylgia's Grace (Purge Vulnerability) [Area Amplify Area]	Cross-Archetype Active Powers: Skald

Cross-Archetype Passive Powers: Maiden of Ratatosk	Aura of Influence	Companion in War	Untouchable	Shadow of Hvergelmir	Nature's Child	Cross-Archetype Passive Powers: Fardrengir
Die Hard	Shadow of Illicit Deeds	Combat Awareness	Dance Away	Leaping Striker	Shadow of Faith	Resistance to Impeded
Shadow of the Ice Raven	Tactical Pause	Agility	Defy the Crowd	Combat Manoeuvrability	Render Helpless	Misery Loves Company
Silence the Crowd	Fueled by the Crowd	Fleet Footed	PASSIVE POWERS	Tactical Advantage	Constitution	Bully
Resistance to Blindness	Keen Senses	Aura of Influence	Blend into Shadow	Precision	Brutalize	Shadow of the Ice Wolf
Bestow Wisdom	Shadow of Memory	Running Jab	Stealthy Striker	Stubborn	Shadow of Youth	Drive Back
Cross-Archetype Passive Powers: Seithkona	Insight	Shadow of Niflheim	Martial Prowess	Stout	Desperation	Cross-Archetype Passive Powers: Skald

Cross-Archetype Skills: Maiden of Ratatosk	Feather Fingers	Athletics	Disguise	Perception	Lore: Poison	Cross Archetype Skills: Fardrengir
Sense Motive	Sneak	Omens/Portents	Negotiation	Lore: Personas	Sneak	Verbal Manipulation
Feather Fingers	Survival: Urban	Drinking/Wenching	Verbal Manipulation	Sense Motive	Feather Fingers	Athletics
Escape	Lock-Picking	Feather Fingers	SKILLS	Sneak	Disguise	Escape
Lore: Poison	Intimidate	Perception	Escape	Silent Tongue	Verbal Manipulation	Lock-Picking
Sneak	Verbal Manipulation	Lore: Locales	Athletics	Lore: Arcana	Feather Fingers	Sneak
Cross Archetype Skills: Seithkona	Omens/Portents	Sense Motive	Lock-Picking	Verbal Manipulation	Lore: Poison	Cross Archetype Skills: Skald

Stalo

The Stalo is the master of controlled combat manoeuvres. It is said that Odin himself taught the first warriors the ways of the Stalo, and throughout the centuries these skills have been passed down through the chosen bloodlines. The Stalo arts are deeply rooted in history, ritual and tradition. Fathers teach sons the art of chaining attacks with such precision, that they culminate in a crescendo of unstoppable violence. Stalos also carry their tradition in the form of an ancestral weapon. This weapon has been forged to accompany a particular battle art-form. In the darkest hour of Ragnarok, many count on the Stalo's resolve to come to the rescue of the weakest and most downtrodden.

Striker

The Striker Stalo focuses on optimizing the attack chain they are delivering. They work hard to ensure each blow finds its mark and cannot be easily blocked by opponents. Strikers are at their most lethal when lashing out with a flurry of small yet precise series of attacks.

Stalwart

The Stalwart Stalo has refined the art of group warfare. They are sought after for shield-walls as their skills are of great benefit to the entire warband. Most allies will fight close to the Stalwart in order to benefit from his expertise and techniques.

Keeper

The Stalo known as the Keeper invests himself into the ancestral relic of his forefathers. Part warrior, part forge master, he hones the relic's properties to accentuate his fighting style. He understands its past, allowing it to guide his fighting style into something truly synergistic with his weapon.

	STRIKER	STALWART	KEEPER
Trait	Physical	Mental	Spiritual
Active	Twin Strike	Cloned Manoeuvre	Touch of the Hallowed Ancestors
Passive	Stubborn	Aura of Peace	Attuned Weapon
Skill	Perception	Sense Motive	Ancestral Weapon

Cross-Archetype Active Powers: Maiden of Ratatosk	Repeating Perfect Parry (Perfect Parry) [Amplify Echo Amplify]	Fylgia's Pride (Vengeful Parry) [Amplify Cannibalize Amplify]	Presence of the Ultimate Shield Maiden	Fylgia's Scorn (Cleansing Attack) [Amplify Cannibalize Weapon]	Repeating Regenerating Attack (Regenerating Attack) [Amplify Echo Proficiency]	Cross-Archetype Active Powers: Fardrengir
Repeating Vengeful Parry (Vengeful Parry) [Amplify Echo Amplify]	Stance of the Blood Brotherhood	Cleansing Attack	Disarm	Recuperating Blinding Strike	Stance of the Cascading Winds	Repeating Hamstring (Hamstring) [Amplify Echo Proficiency]
Fylgia's Sanctuary (Unearthly Resilience) [Area Maintain Area]	Riposte	Cleansing Block	Disarming Parry	Versatile Combat Manoeuvre	Destroyer of Crowds	Fylgia's Kiss (Catharsis) [Range Combo Amplify]
Presence of the Invincible Shield	Vengeful Parry	Aggressive Assault	ACTIVE POWERS	Lunging Attack	Flying Charge	Presence of the Ultimate Warrior
Fylgia's Splendour (Throw Dirt) [Amplify Amplify Echo]	Precision Attack	Strike Weapon	Roll into Position	Flanking Attack	Sly Stance	Fylgia's Rallying Strike
Repeating Furious Onslaught (Furious Onslaught) [Amplify Echo Proficiency]	Stance of the Violent Avalanche	Misery Likes Company	Formulating Attack	Evasive Manoeuvre	Stance of the Spring of Inspiration	Repeating Trip (Trip) [Amplify Echo Amplify]
Cross-Archetype Active Powers: Blacksmith	Presence of the Weapons Master	Fylgia's Touch (Channeling) [Combo Range Amplify]	Presence of the Wind Warrior	Fylgia's Grace (Purge Vulnerability) [Area Amplify Area]	Repeating Throw Dirt (Throw Dirt) [Amplify Echo Amplify]	Cross-Archetype Active Powers: Sceadugengan

Cross-Archetype Passive Powers: Maiden of Ratatosk	Insistence for Humiliation	Dance of Autumn	Companion in Life	Constitution	Desperation	Cross-Archetype Passive Powers: Fardrengir
Favour Defense	Fuelled by the Crowd	Resistance to Blindness	Stout	Bastion	Cornered Ferocity	Insistence for Momentum
Aura of Influence	Insight	Cerebral Warrior	Insistence for Advantage	Martial Prowess	Die Hard	Fellowship of the White Hare
Companion in Death	Spirit Warrior	Insistence for Humility	PASSIVE POWERS	Insistence for Subtlety	Combat Manoeuvrability	Companion in Destiny
Drive Back	Protector	Quick Draw	Insistence for Time	Combat Awareness	Precision	Fleet Footed
Insistence for Blood	Might	Misery Loves Company	War Planner	Keen Senses	Agility	Nimble
Cross-Archetype Passive Powers: Blacksmith	Favour Offence	Tactical Advantage	Companion in War	Dark Consultation	Insistence for Darkness	Cross-Archetype Passive Powers: Sceadugengan

Cross-Archetype Skills: Maiden of Ratatosk	Ancestral Weapon	War Tactics	Endurance	Sense Motive	Repair Equipment	Cross Archetype Skills: Fardrengir
Verbal Manipulation	Omens/Portents	Lore: Personas	Repair Equipment	Lore: Locales	Etiquette	Intimidate
Endurance	Riding	Athletics	Sense Motive	Perception	War Tactics	Omens/Portents
War Tactics	Repair Equipment	Ancestral Weapon	SKILLS	Intimidate	Repair Equipment	Ancestral Weapon
Etiquette	Brawling	Survival: Urban	Endurance	Survival: Wilderness	Athletics	Riding
Infuse	Navigation	War Tactics	Repair Equipment	Endurance	Drinking/Wenching	Lore: Personas
Cross Archetype Skills: Blacksmith	Craft	Etiquette	Perception	Ancestral Weapon	Escape	Cross Archetype Skills: Sceadugengan

New Game Concepts

Pronouncing a Curse

The Viking sagas are filled with heroes and villains pronouncing curses that have a lingering effect. A curse that sticks can only be manifested by someone in the most dire of circumstances driven to great emotional distress. In order to pronounce a curse one must meet 2 criteria from the list below:

- Have at least a total of 4 spiritual runes in Stun, Wounds, Death and Drain piles
- Facing imminent and unavoidable defeat on an important quest
- Facing imminent death
- Pronouncing the curse on a recurring foe who has caused emotional or physical injury more than thrice
- Know your victim personally for many years

The Norn may evolve this list as they see fit. If someone is cursing an item, the Norn should use the Creature Reliquary skill rules. Some possible curses that may be pronounced:

- "May you always walk in Hel's shadow never knowing peace!"
- "By Andvari's scorn, I damn your precious weapon!"
- "May Aegir's wrath swallow you! You will never make landfall in Vinland!"

The scope and effect of the curse are ultimately judged by the Norn.

The individual must be in good standing within the Tapestry of Fate. They cannot be suffering from an afterlife Wyrd penalty (from any activity such as robbing the dead). Once a curse is successfully pronounced, the individual who uttered the curse suffers a -1 to their afterlife Wyrd.

Magic

Verwandlung

Every plant, animal, vale, mountain and stream has a metaphysical essence that can be felt and seen by only a select few trained in the ancient art of Verwandlung. The land spirits known as the Vaettir are masters at Verwandlung magic, and Druids work hard to attain the same level of harmony with the land. Verwandlung magic does not seek to dominate this essence, but instead it works to nurture and coax out the very best from the land. This allows a Verwandliung practitioner to generate a myriad of Alkas whose variety astounds and amazes other magic users who may manage only one type of Alka per realm.

When casting a Verwandlung spell add +1 Focus for every 2 adjacent Alka spaces that surround the caster (+0 to +3). Verwandlung Alka based spells also come with very their own specialized Meta tags which alter the way Alkas behave (Creep, etc...).

New Metas

There are a few new meta tags that are added to the Runic Game System. Some are additions to archetypes and active powers (ie. "Proficiency") and others are added to crafted items (ie. armour only "Deflect"). Those that are added to armour items can be evoked at the time when the Defend action is performed (or in some cases a Counter is played). If someone who is being attacked performs a Defend action while wearing armour that has a defensive meta, then they can play any rune in conjunction with the rune that was played for the Defend action to trigger it. When applicable, a defensive meta may be triggered multiple times.

A "shield" is defined as a weapon where Parry exceeds the DF value.

Absorb

Defensive Meta (can be triggered more than once)

Absorb negates two intensities of a harmful condition that are coming in as a result of an Active power. The meta will not reduce the intensities of pre-existing conditions. Stacking the Absorb meta will negate an additional two harmful conditions (you choose which conditions if there are more than one type). This meta may be played in conjunction with a Counter rune being played. This can only be placed on armour and shields.

Example: Your opponent plays 4 runes in order to activate their Trip Active power with 3 Amplify meta tags. They move up to you and apply 4 intensities of the Impeded condition. You play a Physical rune to counter and add another rune for the Absorb meta effect. Your initial rune counters 1 intensity, your Absorb meta counters another 2 intensities, leaving you to take 1 intensity of Impeded.

Deflect

Defensive Meta (can be triggered more than once)

Deflect triples the total PF and Parry values. This can only be placed on armour and shields. Multiple instances of Deflect increase the multiplier by 3 (ie. x3, x6, x9, etc...)

Dodge

Defensive Meta (can be triggered more than once)

Dodge allows an immediate Wyrd of 2 runes with a Minor Sacrifice +1 (See Wyrd rules on page 363). These runes can be used for dealing with the attack that is currently being resolved. If not used right now, they must be placed into Contingency and declared for defence only. This meta can only be placed on armour and shields.

Eldritch

Defensive Meta

Eldritch triples all existing Evade bonuses and then grants an additional Evade bonus equal to total Parry divided by five, round up. This meta can only be placed on armour and shields. Multiple instances of Eldritch will increase the existing Evade multiplier by increments of 3 as well as adding another Evade bonus of Parry divided by five.

Example: Brynna has Evade 2 and Parry 8. She performs a Defend action and plays another rune to trigger Eldritch. Her defend action with Eldritch grants her 8 Evade (6+2).

Multi

Multi isn't a new Meta but there is a small extension that needs to be added for ranged weapons. Range is increased by +5 hexes for anyone using the Multi meta.

Piercer

Similar to the Weapon meta, Piercer works only with ranged piercing weapons (thrown or shot). When this meta is applied to a range attack, the attack is allowed to damage up to three opponents who are arranged in a straight line (piercing through the first two before finally lodging into the third enemy). By performing a Minor Sacrifice +1, one intensity of the Degeneration condition may be applied to someone struck by the attack. The attacker may not apply more than 1 intensity per victim struck in this way (additional Piercer metas will raise this cap).

Proficiency

Exactly the same as the Weapon meta, however if the weapons being used are self-crafted, then the wielder may also choose to perform a Minor Sacrifice +1 in order to increase the attributes of the weapon by +1. The only attributes that are granted the bonus must already be greater than zero. The bonuses last for the duration of the Active power.

Example: Hagar the blacksmith is wielding a sword (Size: 3, DF: 3, Pierce: 0, Reach: 1) and shield (Size: 3, Parry: 4) which he personally crafted. By activating the Proficiency meta, the weapons not only trigger their weapon metas such as gore, but also gain bonuses to each item attribute: sword (Size: 3, DF: 4, Pierce: 0, Reach: 2) and shield (Size: 3, Parry: 5).

Sight

Your consciousness and perceptions are extended via your Alkas. When you cast {Spell} and {Alka} powers with this meta tag, the spell or Alka may be cast through one of your existing Alkas. These effects check range from the Alka's hex rather than your own location on the battlefield. This helps the caster with line of sight and range requirements. After the new spell or Alka resolves, remove the Alka token that was used as the originating point for the effect.

Multiple Sight metas allow the effect (spell or Alka) to be duplicated and cast from another different Alka hex. The separate effects must choose different targets- if they involve Area or Multi metas, the effects cannot overlap (ie. the same target cannot be hit twice). All Alka tokens used as sources are consumed after the effects resolve.

Stutter

The Alka can be placed ignoring the contiguous restrictions. Each token may have a 1 hex (5') empty space before placing the next token. Multiple Stutter metas will increase the gap by another +1 hex (5'). The gap is not mandatory and may be shrunk as needed.

New Conditions

Charm

[Detrimental]

Counter: Specified in the Active/Passive power that bestows the condition. By default 1 Mental or Spiritual rune per intensity.

Increase Intensity: By Active power.

Decrease Intensity: Play a Mental or Spiritual rune during Upkeep to reduce Intensity by 1 (max. 1 rune per Upkeep)

Max. Intensity Bonus Effect: None

The Charm condition allows someone to sway the victim's disposition towards the friendly and obedient spectrum. The Charm condition is powerful and supernatural in nature, allowing someone to quickly and successfully dissuade the victim from aggression towards them. Further charms will sway the victim towards greater obedience and even devotion.

Intensity	Disposition	Effect
1	Neutral	Won't attack the one who applied the Charm. The victim loses 1 Charm intensity if they 229 are attacked by the one who applied the Charm.
2	Friendly	Won't attack the one who applied the Charm or their allies. Will turn against their old allies. The victim loses 2 Charm intensity if they are attacked by the one who applied the Charm or his or her allies.
3	Obedient	Will follow all non-suicidal orders from the one who applied the Charm. The victim loses 1 Charm intensity if they are attacked by the one who applied the Charm or his or her allies.
4	Slave	Will follow all orders from the one who applied the Charm.

Higher level combatants have a natural resistance to Charm from someone of lower level. Each level difference grants the higher level combatant a free +1 intensity resistance to Charm.

Attempting to Charm someone who is already Charmed by someone else becomes a contest of persuasion. The new Charm effect must successfully apply more intensities of Charm than the victim already possesses.

The Charm condition uses the Possession intensity stack on the playmat. Charm may not be applied on someone with Possession intensity greater than 0. Also someone who is already charmed will immediately cease to be charmed when affected by the Possession condition.

Players may add their own flavour for intent, and the Norn is encouraged to alter the behavioral table above in order to match the request.

Flow

[Beneficial]

Counter: None
Increase Intensity: By power effect.
Decrease Intensity: N/A
Max. Intensity Bonus Effect: Wyrd 1 rune

Some powers grant a partial bonus after a certain condition has been met. This partial bonus is called "Flow". Flow represents someone getting in the mindset for the activity they are performing, slowly gaining momentum and finesse. Each Flow is marked on the "Rage" condition area on the playmat by incrementing it by 1 intensity. The Flow and Rage conditions are mutually exclusive. Any Rage gain will wipe out and replace any existing Flow. While the Rage condition is higher than 0, no Flow may be gained.

After an effect awards Flow intensity, the Flow condition is checked to see if it has reached or exceeded the maximum intensity, if it has, then the Flow triggers. A trigger means that the combatant Wyrds 1 rune and Flow is reduced to 0 intensity. Any one action may never produce more than 4 Flow. Triggering Flow multiple times in a single combat round has repercussions (consult the Wyrd section on page 363).

Example: Vali the Stalo has two Passive powers (1 extra instance is infused on his armour) that grant Flow when an opponent is attacked from behind, and another power that grants Flow when an opponent is knocked back. Vali circles around behind an opponent and attacks using an Active power that also knocks an opponent backwards. The attack results in his opponent being knocked back by 1 hex (the opponent didn't counter). Vali gains 3 Flow from the attack (2 from attacking from behind and another 1 from knocking his opponent backwards). He plays a rune to move into the opponent's back arc once more followed by another attack. This time the opponent counters the knockback, so Vali only gets 2 Flow. It is enough to trigger Flow, it resets to 0 and Vali gets to Wyrd 1 rune immediately.

New Effects

Consume

Attribute values such as Focus or Condition intensities may be reduced by 1 in order to gain the specified benefit. The value must be greater than zero in order for Consume to work. If any powers would negate a loss or immediately restore the loss of a condition intensity (ie. a power that does not allow the intensity to drop below 1), then that intensity cannot be Consumed. The Focus points that are Consumed are no longer usable until the end of round. Powers with Consume will specify what value may be Consumed for the listed benefit. The Consume power is treated at {interrupt} speed. The effect lasts until the Cleanup phase unless otherwise specified. A Consume based Passive power may be triggered only once per round unless otherwise stated. Multiple instances of the power, however, will permit more uses per round. A power with Consume which is Amplified does not force nor allow a second Consume to be activated. Nevertheless the Consume benefit is factored into the Amplify multiplier.

The Rage condition behaves in a unique way when Consumed. Consuming Rage when Rage is at maximum intensity (4) will add a +1 intensity to the Curse condition. This Curse condition represents the individual's desire to attack the closest combatant, even if they are allies. This curse intensity will reduce to 0 if for the duration of an entire combat round the combatant did not attack or receive any damage.

The term "Consume" is also extended to Alkas. When an Alka token is Consumed, it disappears and the Alka effect is transferred onto the combatant.

Shade Active Powers

Shade powers work differently based on your Shroud condition intensity. If the Shroud condition intensity is 1 to 2 the "light" effect is used, if the condition intensity is 3 or 4 then the "dark" effect is used. If the Shroud condition is at intensity 0, then the runes are treated as unbound and may be used only for generic actions. Shade powers may never be maintained. Some light and dark effects have their own power sub-type (ie. {spell}). However if a sub-type is not explicitly stated, then it is treated as a {Manoeuvre}. Shade effects with Defend actions trigger as {interrupt}.

Shadow Passive Powers

Shadow powers work differently based on your Shroud condition intensity. If the shroud condition intensity is 1 to 2 the "light" effect is used, if the condition intensity is 3 or 4 then the "dark" effect is used. If the Shroud condition is at intensity 0, then the Shadow Passive powers provide no benefits.

Snare Active Powers

{Snare}: The snare power places an adjacent persistent token on the battlefield. It may be placed in an occupied space. Anyone passing over it or standing in its effect radius will spring the trap and suffer its effects. By default a snare is single use, has a 2 hex (10') area of effect and it lasts past the end of round (like Alkas). This power requires that the individual carry at least 1 crafting material. The individual doesn't need to use up any of the materials, so long as they possess at least 1 for {snare} powers will work. A snare has a level equal to the combatant's level plus the instances of the Hunting/Trapping skill rank. Area metas will create an area effect for the snare, affecting anyone within 2 hexes (10') of the snare per Area meta. The individual setting the snare will never be affected by their own snare, nor can they trigger it. By default every combatant will be aware of the snare. A snare may be placed in an adjacent hex that is occupied by a combatant, instantly springing its effect. However adjacent enemies may interrupt the placement of a snare by playing any 1 rune as an {interrupt} (similar to countering spells and ranged weapon attacks).

Vaettir Bond

The Vaettir are entirely spiritual beings and the land they oversee is subsumed by their being. A Vaettir may assume physical form in order to interact with the physical beings who inhabit the region. Usually the forms available to a Vaettir tend to terrify the mortal populace, making the option less desirable for amicable exchanges. Vaettir have another tool at their disposal, however; they may choose a worthy and willing mortal to bond with. Forming the bond and breaking the bond requires the consent of both parties. Once bonded, both the Vaettir and the steward gain benefits.

A bond with a Greater Vaettir confers the following to a willing steward:
- The Vaettir knows the location and health of their steward at all times.
- It takes 2 damage to move a rune down a pile on the playmat. Any leftover damage is discarded (5 damage using the middle wounds track, will result in a rune moving from Essence to the top zone of wounds)
- You gain a free Catharsis effect during Upkeep as the Vaettir looks after you.
- Bond Curse *

A bond with a Lesser Vaettir grants the following:
- The Vaettir knows the location of their steward at all times.
- Heal +1 per Upkeep
- Bond Curse *

* Bond Curse: You gain a Curse condition with a +1 intensity per major taint upon the land *(example: Jormundgand's breath lingering in the fishing outpost after he comes up out of the depths to explore the kraken farm on the south shore of the Bay of Ice)*. For each intensity in the cursed condition, the steward performs an Ultimate sacrifice. Take note of these runes, as they only return when the areas have been cleansed.

New Powers and Skills

Denizens of the North introduces many new powers and skills that accompany the new playable archetypes as well as the Norn controlled denizens.

New Active Powers

Armoured Reflex

Metas:	[Amplify Amplify Amplify]
Type:	{Interrupt}
Description:	You defend subconsciously and brace yourself for impact.
Combat Effect:	Against the current attack, gain +2 Physical PF and reduce any knockback by 4.
Out-of-Combat Effect:	When not under duress, you can easily catch something thrown at you

Beckon Vanagard

Metas:	[Amplify Amplify Maintain]
Type:	{Alka}
Description:	The ground becomes verdant and all colours become vibrant.
Combat Effect:	Perform a Major Sacrifice +1 to create an Alka of 2 hexes that grants an immediate Wyrd +1. See page 363 for more details on Wyrd.
Out-of-Combat Effect:	You may restore life to dead vegetation!

Clone Power

Metas:	[Range Range Range]
Type:	{Spell}
Description:	You look deep into another combatant's soul, seeing their inner being.
Combat Effect:	Clone an Active power belonging to another combatant [Counter S]. It must be a power you are aware of, either having witnessed it, or having knowledge of it by some other magical means. Until the Cleanup phase, the rest of the runes in-Hand bind themselves to this effect instead of their regular effects. You also shift in Initiative by +/- 1 position.
Out-of-Combat Effect:	You can read another being's surface thoughts by performing an Ultimate Sacrifice +1. A random memory may also be learned by performing an Ultimate Sacrifice +1.

Cloned Manoeuvre

Metas:	[Range Range Amplify]
Type:	{Manoeuvre}
Description:	You are extremely adept at copying an ally's technique. You also have the ability to temporarily teach others how to perform certain complex actions.
Combat Effect:	While adjacent to an ally, you copy and bind a Manoeuvre they performed earlier this combat round. You bind the cloned Active power to another rune you possess In-Hand. The binding lasts until end of turn so this power may not be maintained. An Amplify meta tag allows you to bind that power to another rune In-Hand. If instead you perform this power with a Minor Sacrifice +1, then you bestow to a

willing adjacent ally, one of your Manoeuvres that is bound to a rune in your In-Hand pile. They choose a rune from their In-Hand pile and it becomes bound to your power until the end of the current combat round. An Amplify meta tag allows them to bind that power to another rune in their In-Hand pile.

Out-of-Combat Effect: After watching someone successfully complete a skill check, you gain a +1 bonus on your next attempt with that skill, if completed within minutes of the viewing.

Death Strike

Metas:	[Amplify Amplify Amplify]
Type:	{Manoeuvre}
Description:	Your fighting technique revolves around dealing devastating blows that end fights quickly.
Combat Effect:	You perform an Attack action against a foe who is healthy (no runes in the Wounds piles). The attack receives a bonus +3 DF and +2 Pierce. Once the attack has been declared on a valid and healthy defender, it will go through regardless even if the defender damages themselves with an interrupt effect.
Out-of-Combat Effect:	You carry yourself with an aura of mystery and danger. Perform an Ultimate Sacrifice +1 to gain a +2 bonus to an Intimidate skill check.

Defying Leap

Metas:	[Amplify Amplify Amplify]
Type:	{Manoeuvre}
Description:	Your ability to leap and strike devastating blows borders on the unfathomable.
Combat Effect:	You may leap a number of hexes equal to your Physical Trait times your Rage intensity. This is not a Move action and your max height achieved may be as high as the maximum distance allowable. The destination must be an unoccupied hex.
Out-of-Combat Effect:	Your leaping distances are doubled.

Field of Poppies

Metas:	[Amplify Amplify Maintain]
Type:	{Alka Spell}
Description:	The ground erupts in red poppy flowers as conditions melt away.
Combat Effect:	Create an Alka of 4 hexes that negates 1 intensity from a given condition and grants the one who consumed the token an immediate free Movement of 1 hex. When affected by this Alka, you choose a condition, and its intensity is reduced by 1 whenever a token is consumed.
Out-of-Combat Effect:	You may create seeds for edible plants (cucumbers, tomatoes, lettuce).

Field of Quagmires

Metas: [Amplify Amplify Maintain]

Type: {Alka Spell}

Description: The ground liquefies and turns into a bobbling and misty swamp of quicksand and icy slush.

Combat Effect: Create an Alka of 4 hexes that imparts +1 intensity to the Impeded condition and +1 intensity to the Blind condition. Combatants on or adjacent to this Alka are considered to be in water.

Out-of-Combat Effect: You can reshape earth and stone to create tunnels (10' sphere per minute).

Field of Thorny Vines

Metas: [Amplify Amplify Maintain]

Type: {Alka Spell}

Description: The ground erupts as dense thorny vines that grow to 10' in height. The thorns are excruciatingly painful.

Combat Effect: Create an Alka of 4 hexes that deals +4 Physical damage with 4 Pierce and also deals +1 Mental damage.

Out-of-Combat Effect: When you move through rough terrain (thick underbrush or deep snow) your movement remains unimpeded.

Flare

Metas: [Amplify Amplify Proficiency]

Type: {Interrupt}

Description: Your body erupts in an unavoidable flash of elemental energy.

Combat Effect: Perform a Weak Defend action with a +1 bonus and +1 or -1 to the intensity of the Aura condition.

Out-of-Combat Effect: When you face imminent danger you gain +1 rank to Perception skill checks.

Frenetic Charge

Metas: [Amplify Amplify Weapon]

Type: {Manoeuvre}

Description: You feel like a cornered animal and charge wildly against your aggressors.

Combat Effect: Perform a Move action with a +2 bonus, you can pass through opponents (move through their hexes). If you are Bloodied, at maximum intensity Rage, and have not attacked this opponent during this combat round, you can perform a Weak Attack action with a +1 bonus on each opponent you pass through. You cannot end your movement in the same hex as another combatant.

Out-of-Combat Effect: Whenever you are facing impossible odds, you may perform an Ultimate Sacrifice +2 to gain a +1 bonus to a skill check.

Furious Bestial Mauling

Metas:	[Amplify Amplify Cannibalize]
Type:	{Manoeuvre}
Description:	Your rage, shapechange and gaping wounds prove to be a lethal cocktail for your foes.
Combat Effect:	Perform an Attack action while at maximum Rage, Bloodied and Shapechanged. The attack gains a bonus +4 DF, +2 Pierce and 1 hex knockback. You may perform a Minor Sacrifice +1 to reposition yourself by 1 hex (5').
Out-of-Combat Effect:	When you become angry, you may reveal your bestial side by partially shapechanging. This sight grants you a +1 on Intimidate skill checks. However depending on the social encounter, such a display can attract unwanted attention.

Fylgia's Rallying Strike

Metas:	[Amplify Cannibalize Area]
Type:	{Manoeuvre}
Description:	In the heat of battle, you ensure that your blows help to better position your allies.
Combat Effect:	Perform a Weak Attack action and grant yourself and all adjacent allies a +/- 1 shift in Initiative. Area meta tags increase the range for valid allies.
Out-of-Combat Effect:	When helping someone else on a skill check, you may perform an Ultimate Sacrifice +1 in order to give them a +1 bonus. The recipient may only be aided by you in order to benefit from this bonus.

Gate Hrokkvir

Metas:	[Amplify Maintain Range]
Type:	{Gate}
Description:	You bring forth a massive tree to fight for you.
Combat Effect:	Gate a Hrokkvir with +6 Levels.
Out-of-Combat Effect:	You can move vegetation at a rate of 10' per minute. At dweller level 30 or more, the vegetation can move at the same speed as your movement rate.

Geyser of Living Water

Metas:	[Amplify Amplify Maintain]
Type:	{Alka}
Description:	The ground erupts as a font of water floods the battlefield.
Combat Effect:	Create an Alka of 4 hexes that Heals +6 and Recovers +4. Combatants on or adjacent to this Alka are considered to be in water.
Out-of-Combat Effect:	You may create water at will (1 ounce per minute)

Healing Stance

Metas:	[Amplify Amplify Amplify]
Type:	{Stance}
Description:	The stance fills you with positive energy that permeates your body as well as your actions.
Combat Effect:	While in this stance, any healing you confer or receive gains a +2 bonus.
Out-of-Combat Effect:	You have a positive effect on those around you. Spirits remain high long after others would have succumbed to depression and despair.

Howl, Heart of Fury

Metas:	[Amplify Cannibalize Area]
Type:	{Spell}
Description:	You instill fury in the hearts of those around you.
Combat Effect:	Bestow Rage +1 intensity and Heal +4. Unwilling subjects can counter the effect by playing a Spiritual rune.
Out-of-Combat Effect:	You can spread your infectious foul mood upon others.

Improvised Attack

Metas:	[Amplify Cannibalize Range]
Type:	{Manoeuvre}
Description:	In a rage, you grab the nearest available object to pummel your foes.
Combat Effect:	While you are under the Rage condition you grab any inanimate object(s) within reach. The total damage from the objects is equal to their size plus your Physical trait. The object size must respect equipment rules in relation to your size plus half your Physical trait. The improvised items are unwieldy and have a reach of 1. You may attempt to use another combatant as a weapon, but you must perform a sacrifice based on their size in relation to you. If their size is equal to or smaller than you, then it is a Minor Sacrifice +1, and if they are larger than you, it is a Minor Sacrifice +2. After you pay your sacrifice cost, they may counter the attempt by playing a Physical rune if they are smaller or the same size as you, or any rune if they are larger than you. You may throw your improvised weapon(s) if you play a Range meta. Objects smaller than you can be thrown 6 hexes and objects larger than you can be thrown 3 hexes. At maximum Rage the ranges double.
Out-of-Combat Effect:	When angered you don't know your own strength. For feats of strength you transform your Void rune into a Physical rune for the duration of the skill check.

Infused Strike

Metas:	[Amplify Amplify Proficiency]
Type:	{Manoeuvre}
Description:	You strike a blow which unleashes a power which was stored within your instrument of death.

| Combat Effect: | Perform a Weak Attack action and a Minor Sacrifice +1 in order to trigger an Active power of one equipped item. The Active power triggers after the attack resolves and may not receive any meta tags. Amplifying this power will increase the attack, the sacrifice cost and will trigger the power one extra time (always without meta tags). |
| Out-of-Combat Effect: | When activating your magic items for their powers, you gain a 25% bonus in their effect. |

Invincible Sprint

Metas:	[Amplify Amplify Amplify]
Type:	{Manoeuvre}
Description:	You have an uncanny way of avoiding Alkas.
Combat Effect:	Perform a Move action and ignore 1 Alka token (which is not consumed).
Out-of-Combat Effect:	When faced with extreme temperatures, your comfort tolerance is double that of an average man.

Lead the Charge

Metas:	[Amplify Amplify Cannibalize]
Type:	{Manoeuvre}
Description:	Your rage, shapechange and gaping wounds harden your resolve when leading the charge against the enemy.
Combat Effect:	Perform an Attack action with a +1 damage bonus while at maximum Rage, Bloodied and Shapechanged. You gain added defences against the next attack against you this combat round: PF +1 to both Mental and Spiritual damage.
Out-of-Combat Effect:	You exude an aura of confidence when leading others into dangerous situations. Gain a +1 skill bonus when attempting to convince others to follow your lead.

Ley Lines of Power

Metas:	[Amplify Amplify Maintain]
Type:	{Alka}
Description:	The ground glows as magical energy seeps out.
Combat Effect:	Create an Alka of 4 hexes that grants a bonus to the next spell cast of +1 Focus, a free Range meta and Recover +2.
Out-of-Combat Effect:	Concentrate in order to detect the presence of magic within 5'.

Mesmerizing Gaze

Metas:	[Amplify Range Amplify]
Type:	{Manoeuvre}
Description:	Your unearthly skills allow you to sway another combatant's actions.
Combat Effect:	You Charm another combatant by +1 Intensity [Counter: M]. The satisfaction grants you Heal +2.
Out-of-Combat Effect:	Grants a bonus +2 to a Verbal Manipulation skill check if an Ultimate Sacrifice +1 is paid.

Mimicry

Metas: [Range Maintain Maintain]

Type: {Spell}

Description: Your body magically changes shape to copy another combatant's appearance. You copy all physical traits including smell and sound.

Combat Effect: Heal +4 and change your appearance to become identical to that of another combatant [Counter P]. The copied combatant must have a similar shape and size. Clothes and equipment are copied in appearance only. Equipment is treated as mundane (non-magical) and you may choose not to "equip" it (treated as worn/carried inventory). If the copied combatant is within 2 hexes of you, then an Active power or attack directed at you may be redirected to the combatant you copied. Someone attempting to target you may pay 1 Mental rune plus 1 Mental rune per 10 of your levels to reveal you as the duplicate (reveal lasts until the next Cleanup phase).

Out-of-Combat Effect: You get a +2 bonus to your Disguise checks if you perform an Ultimate Sacrifice +1 and no one is watching you.

Mount's Synergy

Metas: [Amplify Amplify Amplify]

Type: {Stance}

Description: You and your rider are one.

Combat Effect: When you activate any Active power that has a Move action or Attack action, you may bestow either (both) to your rider. If you assign either a Move or Attack action to your rider, you both Heal +1 per action assigned.

Out-of-Combat Effect: You have trained with your rider and can engage in complex communication with one another at an empathic level.

Needle Storm

Metas: [Amplify Area Area]

Type: {Spell}

Description: Your body magically spawns and expels hundreds of hard and sharp pine needles.

Combat Effect: Deal an amount of Physical damage equal to your size to all enemies surrounding you. The radius of effect is 4 hexes.

Out-of-Combat Effect: Your blood has the same consistency as sap. It also regenerates almost instantaneously when lost.

Obliterating Blow

Metas: [Amplify Amplify Weapon]

Type: {Manoeuvre}

Description: You channel your rage and pain into fierce punishment.

Combat Effect: If you are at max Rage and are Bloodied, perform an Attack action with +3 P DF, +2 Pierce and 1 hex knockback [Counter: P]

Out-of-Combat Effect: Any physical action that requires shoving or pushing results in double the distance.

One With the Land

Metas:	[Amplify Amplify Amplify]
Type:	{Verwandlung Spell Stance}
Description:	You open a bond with the land around you. The land's essence flows through you and visa versa.
Combat Effect:	While entering this stance your life force flows into the land, perform a Major Sacrifice +1 and then gain PF +2 vs. Physical, PF +1 vs. Mental, and PF +1 vs. Spiritual. During the Upkeep phase the land's life force flows into you, Heal +2.
Out-of-Combat Effect:	If you close your eyes and concentrate, you can project your visual awareness up to 50' in any direction.

Oyenstikker

Metas:	[Maintain Maintain Maintain]
Type:	{Shapechange}
Description:	You shape change into a giant dragonfly.
Combat Effect:	Shapechange into a dragonfly. You lose your weapons and armour (absorbed into new form) but you gain: Flight, Parry +1, Move +4, unarmed Attack actions gain a bonus DF +5 P and Heal +4 during Upkeep. Your size remains unchanged. Base movement and unarmed attack damage is calculated based on size. All Active and Passive powers remain unchanged (Passive powers need to be applied to new attributes). Once shapechanged, another combatant may equip you with one Accessory item.
Out-of-Combat Effect:	Turn into a giant dragonfly at will.

Pained Strike

Metas:	[Amplify Amplify Weapon]
Type:	{Manoeuvre}
Description:	Your fury increases as you focus on your pain.
Combat Effect:	Perform an Attack action, if you are Bloodied, gain Rage +1.
Out-of-Combat Effect:	Gain a +1 skill bonus on Physical skills while you have at least 1 rune in Drain.

Pilfer

Metas:	[Amplify Amplify Amplify]
Type:	{Manoeuvre}
Description:	You snatch something and run away.
Combat Effect:	You perform a Move action and take an item from another combatant (armour may not be taken unless amplified 4 or more times). Unwilling combatants may resist by playing a Physical rune. These actions may be performed in any order. Each Amplify meta tag increases both the movement and the quantity of items stolen.
Out-of-Combat Effect:	Grants a +2 bonus to Feather Fingers skill checks if an Ultimate Sacrifice +1 is paid.

Pinecone Bombardment

Metas: [Amplify Area Area]
Type: {Spell}
Description: Your body magically spawns and expels hundreds of hard and sharp pinecones.
Combat Effect: Deal 4 Physical damage to all enemies who surround you. The radius of the area is a number of hexes equal to your half your size.
Out-of-Combat Effect: You may cause your skin to toughen to the texture and density of tree bark.

Presence of the Invincible Shield

Metas: [Amplify Area Area]
Type: {Stance}
Description: You show your allies how to block incoming blows.
Combat Effect: Those affected gain a +2 Parry. Cannot be granted with the Area meta to someone already in a stance.
Out-of-Combat Effect: You are sought out by young warriors looking to improve their combat skills. If you train someone of lower level for a day, you may receive up to 50 Skatt in payment (stacks with other such skills).

Presence of the Ultimate Shield Maiden

Metas: [Area Area Area]
Type: {Stance}
Description: You have learned how to push yourself in order to achieve the impossible. Your skill demonstrations allow your allies to do the same.
Combat Effect: When someone affected performs a Weak Defend action, they may perform a Minor Sacrifice +1 and they will perform a regular Defend action instead. Cannot be granted with the Area meta to someone already in a stance.
Out-of-Combat Effect: You are sought out by young warriors looking to improve their combat skills. If you train someone of lower level for a day, you may receive up to 50 Skatt in payment (stacks with other such skills).

Presence of the Ultimate Warrior

Metas: [Area Area Area]
Type: {Stance}
Description: You have learned how to push yourself in order to achieve the impossible. Your skill demonstrations allow your allies to do the same.
Combat Effect: When someone affected performs a Weak Attack action, they may perform a Minor Sacrifice +1 and they will perform a regular Attack action instead. Cannot be granted with the Area meta to someone already in a stance.
Out-of-Combat Effect: You are sought out by young warriors looking to improve their combat skills. If you train someone of lower level for a day, you may receive up to 50 Skatt in payment (stacks with other such skills).

Presence of the Weapons Master

Metas:	[Amplify Area Area]
Type:	{Stance}
Description:	You show your allies how properly use their weapons to better attack and defend.
Combat Effect:	Those affected gain a +1 DF and +1 Parry. Cannot be granted with the Area meta to someone already in a stance.
Out-of-Combat Effect:	You are sought out by young warriors looking to improve their combat skills. If you train someone of lower level for a day, you may receive up to 50 Skatt in payment (stacks with other such skills).

Presence of the Wind Warrior

Metas:	[Area Area Area]
Type:	{Stance}
Description:	You show your allies how to move efficiently.
Combat Effect:	When someone affected performs a Weak Move action, they will perform a regular Move action instead. Cannot be granted with the Area meta to someone already in a stance.
Out-of-Combat Effect:	You are sought out by young warriors looking to improve their combat skills. If you train someone of lower level for a day, you may receive up to 50 Skatt in payment (stacks with other such skills).

Projectile Ricochet Technique

Metas:	[Amplify Amplify Amplify]
Type:	{Stance}
Description:	Your deep understanding of projectile weapons (arrows and thrown) allows you to perform "banked" shots.
Combat Effect:	When you apply the Piercer meta tag to an Active power, you may deviate the straight line once during the trajectory. The deviation must start at an opponent who has been struck by the attack, and must continue in a straight line along the new path. An Amplified stance allows more than one new trajectory. The attack may not ricochet back to someone who is already being targeted by this Attack action.
Out-of-Combat Effect:	You have a throwing technique that astounds as your deep comprehensions of object dynamics allows you to perform impossible throws.

Protective Impulse

Metas:	[Amplify Cannibalize Area]
Type:	{Manoeuvre}
Description:	While raging you feel the overwhelming need to protect the allies around you.
Combat Effect:	While under the Rage condition, with intensity 1, 2 or 3 you perform an Attack action on a foe with a +2 damage bonus per adjacent Bloodied ally. Area meta tags increase the radius for valid allies.
Out-of-Combat Effect:	When faced with a chaotic and hostile scene, you spot the innocent and injured with ease.

Reckless Aggressive Assault

Metas:	[Amplify Multi Weapon]
Type:	{Manoeuvre}
Description:	In your zeal you push yourself past your limits in order to unleash a powerful flurry of blows that push back your opponents.
Combat Effect:	Perform a Minor Sacrifice +2 to perform an Attack action with 2 hexes (10') Knockback. The opponent may reduce the push by 1 hex per Physical rune played.
Out-of-Combat Effect:	You are especially gifted at boasting. In fact, no one is better at it than you!

Reckless Bull Rush

Metas:	[Amplify Multi Amplify]
Type:	{Manoeuvre}
Description:	When attempting to bowl someone over, you have little concern for your well-being.
Combat Effect:	Perform a Minor Sacrifice +2 to perform a Move action and push an opponent by 4 hexes (20'). The opponent may reduce the push by 1 hex per Physical rune played. Hitting multiple combatants with the Multi meta requires that they be within reach (factor in the reach bonus granted by Multi meta).
Out-of-Combat Effect:	When engaging in competitive feats of strength, you have an edge by being able to push yourself past the breaking point. Perform an Ultimate Sacrifice in order to gain a +1 bonus. You may only perform one such sacrifice per skill attempt.

Reckless Feral Pounce

Metas:	[Amplify Amplify Amplify]
Type:	{Manoeuvre}
Description:	When unencumbered, you are particularly adept at jumping out of harm's way.
Combat Effect:	If you do not wear armour and do not wield weapons, perform a Minor Sacrifice +2 to perform a Defend action with a +6 Parry.
Out-of-Combat Effect:	While afflicted with a curse, your body fights against the magical taint with fervour. The harmful effects are lessened by 33%.

Reckless Lunging Attack

Metas:	[Amplify Multi Weapon]
Type:	{Manoeuvre}
Description:	In your rush to beat someone up, you push yourself past your physical limits.
Combat Effect:	Perform a Minor Sacrifice +2 to perform a Move action and an Attack action (in any order).
Out-of-Combat Effect:	When in a competitive race to reach an objective, gain +1 Move.

Reckless Raging Attack

Metas:	[Amplify Multi Weapon]
Type:	{Manoeuvre}
Description:	You wound yourself in your quest to attain inner fury.

Combat Effect: Perform a Minor Sacrifice +2 to perform an Attack action and gain +1 intensity in the Rage condition.

Out-of-Combat Effect: When faced with poisons, your body has a higher tolerance than most granting you extra resistances.

Reckless Wounding Attack

Metas: [Amplify Multi Weapon]

Type: {Manoeuvre}

Description: In your zeal to punish your opponent, you strain your body past its limits.

Combat Effect: Perform a Minor Sacrifice +2 to perform an Attack action, also applying the Degeneration condition with a +1 intensity [Counter P].

Out-of-Combat Effect: When performing hard work for an employer, your zeal and dedication usually catches the employer's attention and appreciation.

Rider's Synergy

Metas: [Amplify Amplify Amplify]

Type: {Stance}

Description: You and your mount are one.

Combat Effect: When you activate any Active power that has a Move action or Attack action, you may bestow either (both) to your mount. If you assign either a Move or Attack action to your mount, you both Heal +1 per action assigned.

Out-of-Combat Effect: You have trained your mount to respond to very subtle commands at a distance (whistle, certain arm gesture, etc).

Run to Shadow

Metas: [Amplify Amplify Amplify]

Type: {Manoeuvre}

Description: You run into the shadow's welcoming embrace.

Combat Effect: You perform a Move action and increase the Shroud intensity +1.

Out-of-Combat Effect: If you are startled, you subconsciously reposition yourself to the most defensive position. During the Initiative setup phase of the combat (before the first round of combat begins), you get to perform one free Move action. If multiple combatants have this ability, then the movements are resolved in Initiative order.

Shade of the Abyssal Current

Metas: [Amplify Amplify Amplify]

Type: {Shade}

Description: You interchange light and darkness, confusing everyone upon the field of battle.

Light Combat Effect: After you get attacked you may exchange places with another combatant within 2 hexes. Unwilling subjects may counter the exchange by playing a Physical rune. {Stance}

Dark Combat Effect: After you perform an Attack action you may exchange places with another combatant within 2 hexes. Unwilling subjects may counter the exchange by playing a Physical rune. {Stance}

Out-of-Combat Effect: When telling outlandish lies that are diametrically opposed to the true facts, you gain a +1 bonus to Verbal Manipulation.

Shade of the Blustering Blizzard

Metas: [Amplify Amplify Amplify]

Type: {Shade}

Description: You embrace both the light and the darkness in order to fuel your evasion.

Light Combat Effect: Perform a Weak Move action, Shroud +1 {Manoeuvre}

Dark Combat Effect: Perform a Weak Defend action with a +1 Parry bonus. If the attacking power has an {Area} meta, then you receive a 33% chance to fully avoid the effect. {Manoeuvre}

Out-of-Combat Effect: Grants extra insight into someone's motivations to engage in violent behaviour.

Shade of the Dark Mother

Metas: [Amplify Amplify Amplify]

Type: {Shade}

Description: You embrace both the light and the darkness in order to keep allies safe.

Light Combat Effect: Shroud +1 on an ally up to 5 hexes away. {Manoeuvre}

Dark Combat Effect: Consume Shroud to gain 4 intensities of Taunt until end of turn. During cleanup reduce Taunt to 0. {Manoeuvre}

Out-of-Combat Effect: Grants an empathic bond with a warband member up to 50' away. Sense the emotions the other feels. There is no need for line of sight.

Shade of the Darkening Sky

Metas: [Amplify Amplify Amplify]

Type: {Shade}

Description: You bring forth the darkness upon the battlefield and shift the light elsewhere.

Light Combat Effect: Exchange places with a willing combatant within 10 hexes. {Spell}

Dark Combat Effect: Create a curtain of darkness that obstructs line of sight. This Alka affects 6 hexes. {Alka Spell}

Out-of-Combat Effect: See in low light conditions similar to a cat.

Shade of the Darting Fox

Metas: [Amplify Amplify **Amplify**]

Type: {Shade}

Description: You embrace both the light and the darkness in order to stay out of harm's way.

Light Combat Effect: Heal +2 and Shroud +1. {Spell}

Dark Combat Effect: Teleport another combatant who is within 10 hexes to an unoccupied adjacent hex. You must have a line of sight to them. Unwilling combatants may pay a Mental rune to counter this effect. {Spell}

Out-of-Combat Effect: Grants additional insight as to how best to avoid a dangerous situation.

Shade of the Enveloping Miasma

Metas: [Amplify Amplify Amplify]

Type: {Shade}

Description: You use the shadow to change reality around you.

Light Combat Effect: Perform a Weak Move action and you may pass through enemies. For every enemy you pass through, you may strip them of 1 intensity of the Shroud condition [Counter M]. For every intensity stripped, you may increase your Shroud intensity by +1. You may not run through an opponent more than once. {Manoeuvre}

Dark Combat Effect: Perform a Weak Move action and you may pass through allies. Every ally you run through may gain +1 Shroud if they perform a Minor Sacrifice +1. {Manoeuvre}

Out-of-Combat Effect: Grants you the ability to successfully mediate an argument by bringing both viewpoints towards a common point. You gain a +1 bonus to Verbal Manipulation checks when dealing with such situations.

Shade of the Enraged Serpent

Metas: [Amplify Amplify Amplify]
Type: {Shade}
Description: You use the contrasts of light and dark to inflict maximum punishment upon your foes.
Light Combat Effect: Perform a Weak Attack action and gain +1 Shroud intensity if you are adjacent to two enemies. {Manoeuvre}
Dark Combat Effect: Perform a Weak Attack action with damage bonus equal to your Shroud intensity. {Manoeuvre}
Out-of-Combat Effect: Grants a +1 to Disguise skill checks when you attempt to impersonate someone you have known for a week or more.

Shade of the Endless Mind

Metas: [Amplify Amplify Amplify]
Type: {Shade}
Description: You illuminate the mind while stealing the darkest and most violent of thoughts.
Light Combat Effect: Perform a Weak Attack action that also deals 1 Mental damage. {Manoeuvre}
Dark Combat Effect: Lose 2 intensities of Shroud to grant a Wyrd +1 to yourself or an adjacent ally. Consult page 363 for more on Wyrd. {Manoeuvre}
Out-of-Combat Effect: When performing a Verbal Manipulation skill check, you may impose a difficulty increase in order to attempt a much more drastic swing in their reaction should you succeed.

Shade of the Fallen Jarl

Metas: [Amplify Amplify Amplify]
Type: {Shade}
Description: You understand your environment as well as the foes you face. Using the contrasts of light and darkness, you visualize what needs to be done moments before you execute.
Light Combat Effect: Perform a Move action and gain +1 Shroud intensity if you end your movement adjacent to two enemies. {Manoeuvre}
Dark Combat Effect: Perform a Minor Sacrifice +1 to perform a Weak Defend action with a bonus Evade +1. {Manoeuvre}
Out-of-Combat Effect: Grants insight into someone's weaknesses and vulnerabilities.

Shade of Night and Day

Metas: [Amplify Amplify Amplify]

Type: {Shade}

Description: You use the strengths of both light and darkness when executing your manoeuvres.

Light Combat Effect: Perform a Weak Attack action and then switch places with any adjacent combatant [Counter P]. {Manoeuvre}

Dark Combat Effect: You Charm another combatant by +1 Intensity [Counter M]. The effect may target someone up to 10' away (2 hexes). {Manoeuvre}

Out-of-Combat Effect: While standing in a deep shadow, you observe your surroundings and may gain a +2 bonus to Perception if you perform an Ultimate Sacrifice +1.

Shade of the Toxic River

Metas: [Amplify Amplify Amplify]

Type: {Shade}

Description: You syphon off both benevolent and malicious effects on others, and feed it to the shadow.

Light Combat Effect: Perform a Weak attack and reduce the intensity of a condition by 1 on yourself or adjacent combatant [Counter M]. {Manoeuvre}

Dark Combat Effect: Perform a Move action and reduce the intensity of a condition by 1 on yourself or adjacent combatant [Counter M]. {Manoeuvre}

Out-of-Combat Effect: Studying a toxic poison at a distance, you understand its effects.

Shade of Malevolence

Metas: [Amplify Amplify Amplify]

Type: {Shade}

Description: Your mastery over the light and dark allows you to play with afflictions as if they were game pieces on a Hnefatafl board.

Light Combat Effect: Inflict Vulnerable intensity +1 [counter M] and Recover +4. {Manoeuvre}

Dark Combat Effect: Perform a Minor Sacrifice +1 to perform a Weak Attack action and transfer 1 intensity of a condition from yourself onto another adjacent combatant [counter M]. {Manoeuvre}

Out-of-Combat Effect: Gain a +1 skill bonus when assisting someone else in making poison.

Shade of Piercing Eyes

Metas: [Amplify Amplify Amplify]

Type: {Shade}

Description: Those who dabble in your domain become easier to coerce.

Light Combat Effect: Inflict Shroud intensity +1 [counter M] to someone within 5 hexes (25'). {Manoeuvre}

Dark Combat Effect: Inflict Charm intensity +1 [counter S] to anyone within 5 hexes. {Manoeuvre}

Out-of-Combat Effect: Gain +1 skill bonus on Verbal Manipulation checks when dealing with criminals or other undesirable people.

Shade of the Lost Ship

Metas:	[Amplify Amplify Amplify]
Type:	{Shade}
Description:	Your knowledge of the shadows allows you to strike and retreat out of range.
Light Combat Effect:	Perform an Weak Attack action with a bonus +2 Reach or +10 Range. {Manoeuvre}
Dark Combat Effect:	Perform a Weak Defend action with a +1 Parry bonus, followed by a Weak Move action. {Manoeuvre}
Out-of-Combat Effect:	Grants an extra skill success when throwing small objects such as hand axes.

Shade of the Treasure Hoard

Metas:	[Amplify Amplify Amplify]
Type:	{Shade}
Description:	You cannot control your avarice. The shadow lends you a hand when relieving others of their prized possessions.
Light Combat Effect:	If you stand behind your opponent, perform a Weak Attack action and steal a non-equipped item (such as a pouch of coins) [Counter P] from an adjacent combatant. {Manoeuvre}
Dark Combat Effect:	Perform a Minor Sacrifice +1 to perform a Weak Defend action and steal an equipped item (such as an axe) [Counter M] from an adjacent combatant. {Manoeuvre}
Out-of-Combat Effect:	Grants a +1 bonus on Feather Fingers skill checks if an Ultimate Sacrifice +1 is performed.

Shade of Whispers

Metas:	[Amplify Amplify Amplify]
Type:	{Shade}
Description:	Your body darkens or lightens to match your surroundings, granting you a chameleon-like appearance.
Light Combat Effect:	Negate a meta tag being played by an adjacent combatant [counter M] and gain a Shroud +1 if you are Bloodied. {Interrupt}
Dark Combat Effect:	Throw up an illusion that grants a 33% outright miss chance on this attack (one Amplify meta tag grants a 66% miss chance and two Amplify meta tags grant a 100% miss chance). If the attack strikes you, then you perform a free Weak Defend action with a +1 Parry bonus (the meta tags played apply to this effect as well). {Interrupt}
Out-of-Combat Effect:	You can throw your voice up to 30' away.

Soul-bound Strike

Metas:	[Amplify Multi Proficiency]
Type:	{Manoeuvre}
Description:	The attacker uses a weapon that they crafted themselves with exceptional skill and accuracy to deal a mighty blow.
Combat Effect:	Perform an Attack action with a weapon that you have crafted (or assisted in crafting by using any other related skill- infuse, Dvergar engineering, creature reliquary, realm ores), and gain a damage bonus equal to the number of personally crafted items you are equipped with.
Out-of-Combat Effect:	You may recognize a weapon that you have crafted even if it has suffered some wear and tear.

Stance of Darkness

Metas:	[Amplify Amplify Amplify]
Type:	{Stance}
Description:	Your ability to hide is so extreme that parts of you drift into Svartalfheim.
Combat Effect:	You negate an opponent's Keen Senses passive power. Every amplify meta tag increases the instances negated (ex: Stance of Darkness with two Amplify metas would negate 3 instances of Keen Senses from the opponent).
Out-of-Combat Effect:	If you wish, you will be the last one noticed in social situations.

Stance of the Blood Brotherhood

Metas:	[Amplify Amplify Amplify]
Type:	{Stance}
Description:	Your graceful manoeuvres amplify incoming positive energy.
Combat Effect:	Healing you receive is boosted by +2 per Flow intensity.
Out-of-Combat Effect:	Your success inspires others to greatness. Following your successful skill check in a given action, one ally gains a +1 bonus when attempting the same action. Their attempt must immediately follow your attempt.

Stance of the Cascading Winds

Metas:	[Amplify Amplify Amplify]
Type:	{Stance}
Description:	Your movements increase in finesse, culminating in a dazzling display.
Combat Effect:	Gain +2 Move per Flow intensity.
Out-of-Combat Effect:	Your repetitive actions are exponentially more fruitful the longer you perform them without stop.

Stance of the Spring of Inspiration

Metas:	[Amplify Amplify Amplify]
Type:	{Stance}
Description:	Your movements help centre your mind. You can see clearly, anticipating the

intentions of others.

Combat Effect: Defend actions gain +2 Parry per Flow intensity.

Out-of-Combat Effect: You gain a +1 skill check bonus when performing a skill you successfully completed in the last 24 hours.

Stance of the Violent Avalanche

Metas: [Amplify Amplify Amplify]
Type: {Stance}
Description: Your strikes increase in ferocity with each falling blow.
Combat Effect: Attack actions gain a +1 DF and a Reach/Range +1/+5 bonus per Flow intensity.
Out-of-Combat Effect: You increase your aptitude in a skill the longer you perform it. Gain a +1 skill bonus on a skill you have already failed today. This does not allow you to instantly repeat a failed skill check.

Stand of Domination

Metas: [Amplify Amplify Amplify]
Type: {Stance}
Description: Another's violence fuels your rage.
Combat Effect: While the stance is in effect you may Heal +1 during the Cleanup phase. After an adjacent enemy attacks, you get to increase the Rage condition by +1 intensity and the stance ends (return the rune to Essence).
Out-of-Combat Effect: You have an authoritative air about you, giving you a bonus in leadership situations.

Stand of Impunity

Metas: [Amplify Amplify Amplify]
Type: {Stance}
Description: You are very expressive on the battlefield.
Combat Effect: While the stance is in effect your Attack actions gain +1 Knockback. When your Rage intensity increases, you may shift +/-1 in Initiative and the stance ends (return the rune to Essence).
Out-of-Combat Effect: You have a way with words and posture giving you an edge when negotiations begin to break down.

Stand of Presence

Metas: [Amplify Amplify Amplify]
Type: {Stance}
Description: You bask in a moment of calm and rejuvenate yourself.
Combat Effect: While the stance is in effect your Attack actions gain +1 Reach. When your Rage intensity decreases, you may perform a Move action. After the Move action, the stance ends (return the rune to Essence).
Out-of-Combat Effect: During tense negotiations that eventually result in success, you have a knack for drawing out extra concessions.

Stand of Punishment

Metas: [Amplify Amplify Amplify]

Type: {Stance}

Description: You take great joy in pushing around your opponents.

Combat Effect: While the stance is in effect you may gain a DF +1 P bonus on your Attack actions. After you successfully push an opponent backwards, you Heal +2 per hex pushed. After the Heal effect, the stance ends (return the rune to Essence).

Out-of-Combat Effect: You have extra talents when it comes to management of slaves and maintaining their obedience.

Swallow

Metas: [Maintain Multi Maintain]

Type: {Manoeuvre}

Description: The attacker opens their mouth and attempts to swallow another combatant.

Combat Effect: If your opponent is half your size or smaller, perform a Weak Attack action with an unarmed attack, apply the Impeded condition +1 [Counter: P] per size difference between you and the defender. If the Impeded condition is not reduced to 0 then the defender is considered swallowed and must reduce the Impeded to 0 in order to get out. While you maintain this ability, during Upkeep apply both the Impeded condition +1 [Counter: P] and the Degeneration condition +1 [Counter: P] per size difference between you and the defender. You cannot perform Defend actions against someone you have swallowed. You can however perform unarmed generic Attack actions against someone you have swallowed (see page 96 in the *Core Rulebook* for more on generic actions).

Out-of-Combat Effect: You can swallow small inedible objects such as keys without suffering any ill effects (3 size categories smaller). The maximum number of small items that can be swallowed in this way is equal to your level divided by 5. You may also regurgitate any of those items at will.

Throw Weapon

Metas: [Amplify Multi Piercer]

Type: {Manoeuvre}

Description: You throw a weapon at your enemy.

Combat Effect: Perform a ranged Attack action with +10 (+50') Range. The attack must involve throwing a weapon.

Out-of-Combat Effect: You may throw small items with impeccable precision.

Touch of the Hallowed Ancestors

Metas: [Amplify Range Area]

Type: {Spell}

Description: Your ancestral weapon answers your call.

Combat Effect: Heal an amount equal to half the QR of the Ancestral Weapon.

Out-of-Combat Effect: Your Ancestral Weapon may be teleported back into your hand if you perform an Ultimate Sacrifice +1. The sacrifice cost increases to +2 if the weapon is no longer in your line of sight.

Trample

Metas: [Amplify Amplify Amplify]
Type: {Manoeuvre}
Description: You charge through smaller opponents dealing damage as you go.
Combat Effect: Perform a Move action, you can pass through opponents (move through their hexes). If you are not wielding any weapons, are larger than the opponent, and have not attacked the opponent this combat round, you can perform a Weak attack action with a +4 DF on each opponent you pass through. You cannot end your movement in the same hex as another combatant.
Out-of-Combat Effect: You can travel over difficult terrain without any movement penalties.

Trap—Incapacitation

Metas: [Area Area Area]
Type: {Snare}
Description: You place a trap on the ground that blinds your prey.
Combat Effect: Set a snare that imposes +1 intensity to the Blind condition [counter: P]. The intensity is boosted by +1 per 5 snare levels.
Out-of-Combat Effect: Traps set with your Hunting/Trapping skill are very hard to detect, imposing a +1 Perception difficulty.

Trap—Lacerations

Metas: [Area Area Area]
Type: {Snare}
Description: You place a trap on the ground that bloodies your prey.
Combat Effect: Set a snare that imposes +1 intensity to the Degeneration condition [counter: P]. The intensity is boosted by +1 per 5 snare levels.
Out-of-Combat Effect: Traps set with your Hunting/Trapping skill are designed for multiple captures of small animals. After small prey is caught and automatically dragged elsewhere, the trap resets and is designed to mask the scent of previous captures and incapacitations/kills.

Trap—Spikes

Metas: [Area Area Area]
Type: {Snare}
Description: You place a devastatingly dangerous trap on the ground.
Combat Effect: Set a snare that deals Physical damage equal to half the snare level. It also has Pierce equal to the snare level.
Out-of-Combat Effect: Your snares can be miniaturized without sacrificing functionality.

Trap-Tangle

Metas: [Area Area Area]
Type: {Snare}
Description: You place a trap on the ground that tangles up your prey.
Combat Effect: Set a snare that imposes +1 intensity to the Impeded condition [counter: P]. The intensity is boosted by +1 per 5 snare levels.
Out-of-Combat Effect: Your Hunting/Trapping skill may snare creatures that are larger than you.

Trapper's Stance

Metas: [Amplify Amplify Amplify]
Type: {Stance}
Description: You prepare yourself for trapping efficiency.
Combat Effect: When you set a snare, your snare level is increased by 2.
Out-of-Combat Effect: You can place your traps very subtly, hiding them in plain sight. You easily trick onlookers by pretending to pick up something you dropped while your other hand places and activates the trap.

Twin Strike

Metas: [Amplify Multi Weapon]
Type: {Manoeuvre}
Description: Your mastery allows your companions to mimic your movements.
Combat Effect: You perform a Weak Attack action. Once it is complete, you grant an ally within 3 hexes (15') the ability to perform a free Weak Attack action against any one combatant you targeted. The ally's attack receives no meta tags, but does trigger all relevant Passive powers that they may possess.
Out-of-Combat Effect: When working as a group, any prolonged tasks you undertake are completed in half the time so long as you push yourself (you perform an Ultimate Sacrifice +1). The other members of the group do not need to pay the Sacrifice cost.

Unleash the Beast

Metas: [Amplify Amplify Maintain]
Type: {Manoeuvre}
Description: Your fury causes your body to grow for a short period of time (unless you focus on maintaining the effect).
Combat Effect: Gain a size +1 and heals you receive are boosted by +2.
Out-of-Combat Effect: If a Passive ability allows you to shapechange based on some condition, then outside of combat you may freely assume that form without meeting the prerequisite condition.

Venomous Bite

Metas: [Amplify Amplify Amplify]

Type: {Manoeuvre}

Description: Your bite injects poison into your prey.

Combat Effect: When wielding no weapons, perform an Attack action that deals no damage and inflict +1 intensity to the Degeneration and Impeded conditions.

Out-of-Combat Effect: You have a bile sack which produces poison that can be extracted for other uses. If you use it to poison a drink, the victim must Wyrd a Physical rune per 5 of your dweller's levels. Failure to do so will place the victim in an unconscious state for 4 hours. Failure to draw any Physical runes will result in death.

Weapon Stance

Metas: [Amplify Amplify Amplify]

Type: {Stance}

Description: The combatant is keenly aware of how to maximize the use of their weapons and shields.

Combat Effect: While in this stance, weapon and shield DF and Parry values are increased by +1 if they are already greater than 0. The stance affects both weapons if dual-wielding. A two handed weapon gains a +1 Reach (+5 range) bonus as well as the DF and Parry bonuses.

Out-of-Combat Effect: You show off your skills in a way that attracts positive attention, granting you favour when seeking employment.

Wild Shape

Metas: [Maintain Maintain Maintain]

Type: {Transform}

Description: You transform into a bestial form that is kindred with your soul.

Combat Effect: Choose a Norn-approved non-human creature (denizen) that has no affiliation with Niflheim. This form is fixed permanently. If it has "base level" then you must pay this cost as you transform: perform a Minor Sacrifice for every base level. You gain all Active and Passive powers as well as skills in the new form (re-bind your Essence runes to the new denizen templates- the Norn may allow you to alter these bindings per casting if you have them pre-prepared). All your equipment and items merge into the new form and no longer confer any benefits. Suggested Norn approved shapes: any Familiar from the *Core Rulebook*, any Mount from this book.

Out-of-Combat Effect: Turn into this shape at will.

New Passive Powers

Alka Kinship

Type: {Enchantment}
Description: Your magic is living and obeys your every command.
Effect: As you pass through your own Alkas, you may choose to ignore the effect and the Alka token is not consumed.

Alka Tenacity

Type: {Enchantment}
Description: Your Alkas are so tenacious that they circumvent defenses.
Effect: Your Alkas that deal damage now have Pierce +4 per instance of this passive power. Pierce will adapt based on the type of damage being dealt (Trait).

Archer's Sight

Type: {Feat}
Description: You apply your inner magic to bolster your ranged attacks.
Effect: During Upkeep, Consume a point of Focus to gain a +5 Range bonus until end of turn. You may consume any and all Focus that you have.

Archer's Third Eye

Type: {Feat}
Description: You apply your inner magic to your next ranged attack.
Effect: While declaring a ranged Attack action, you may Consume 1 Focus in order to add 2 points of Mental damage to that Attack action.

Artisan's Pride

Type: {Enchantment}
Description: Your pride in your craftsmanship bolsters morale.
Effect: During Upkeep, you Heal +1 per equipped item that you personally crafted (or assisted in crafting by using any other related skill-Infuse, Dvergar Engineering, Creature Rreliquary, Realm Ores). If you perform a Minor Sacrifice +1, you may heal an adjacent ally instead.

Assassin's Reflexes

Type: {Feat}

Description: You are skilled at striking first.

Effect: During Upkeep, you may shift your initiative up (earlier) by 2 positions.

Attuned Mount

Type: {Feat}

Description: You may respond to your rider's actions.

Effect: If your Passive powers state that you get an effect based on something you do (or your current state), you may use the rider's action (or state) to fulfill the Passive power's conditions.

Attuned Weapon

Type: {Feat}

Description: You have chosen to improve your skills with one specific weapon type (pole-arms, swords, axes, hammers, shields or bows).

Effect: Gain +1 DF and +1 Parry while wielding the weapon type of choice. You must make a permanent choice when you acquire this power. Examples of weapon types: slashing melee (axes), blunt melee (clubs), pierce melee (spears) or ranged (bows).

Aura of Peace

Type: {Enchantment}

Description: You surround yourself in a calming aura that heals the wounds of friends and foes alike.

Effect: During Upkeep you may gain a +1 Intensity to the Aura condition. Your Aura condition has the inverse effect, healing instead of dealing damage. You are also affected by the Aura.

Brawler of Spring

Type: {Feat}

Description: Your brawling technique applies to the battlefield.

Effect: Attack actions gain a +1 DF bonus per 2 ranks in the Brawling skill.

Builder's Glory

Type: {Enchantment}

Description: You learn how to humiliate your opponents by exalting the quality of your wares.

Effect: If you strike someone who wears/wields damaged equipment, you deal +2 damage per broken piece of equipment. See "Damaged" equipment on page 131 of the *Core Rulebook*.

Burrow

Type: {Feat}

Description: You can dig and move through frozen ground as if it were water. You move the dirt behind you so your passage is closed off in your wake.

Effect: While you move through earth/stone/ice, you may only perform Weak Move actions. Movement granted by Active powers is cut in half.

Champion of Summer

Type: {Feat}

Description: Your strength and dexterity aid you on the battlefield.

Effect: Gain +1 Move per 2 ranks in the Athletics skill.

Crafter's Promise

Type: {Feat}

Description: You are intimately familiar with your crafted items, knowing how to turn at the last second in order to avoid damage.

Effect: Your equipped items are harder to destroy. They gain a +4 QR when being targeted for damage.

Deflect Aggression

Type: {Feat}

Description: Your demeanour convinces opponents to seek out other victims.

Effect: When you perform a Defend action, you may perform a Minor Sacrifice +2 in order to apply 1 intensity Blind condition upon your attacker [Counter: M]. The Blind condition is only applied after the attack has been fully resolved.

Equipment Mastery

Type: {Feat}

Description: You may wield larger items with great ease.

Effect: All items equipped by you are considered to be 1 size smaller for purposes of calculating encumbrance.

Fae-Kin

Type: {Enchantment}

Description: If you abstain from using any weapons or armour which normally interferes with your body's magical nature, you gain added spell power.

Effect: If you equip no armour and wield no weapons, you gain +1 Focus. You gain an additional +1 Focus every 7 levels.

Faithful Mount

Type: {Feat}

Description: You and your rider are working in perfect synergy.

Effect: If your rider gains 1 or more rank in the Aura condition, you are exempt from the effect. If you gain the Aura condition, your rider is exempt from the effect as well.

Harbour Grudge

Type: {Feat}

Description: It is more difficult to quell the anger in your heart.

Effect: Any effect that attempts to reduce your Rage condition intensity has its effect reduced by your ranks in the Short Fuse skill.

Hover

Type: {Enchantment}

Description: You may will your feet to rise up off the ground by a foot. You now move on an air cushion allowing you to run over water, hot coals or broken rubble without being affected by the surface below.

Effect: You levitate a foot off the ground and ignore any terrain penalties that would be applied. You still get affected by Alkas and must climb when there are inclines greater than 45 degrees (Hover doesn't help with inclines of greater than 45 degrees).

Hunter's Cunning

Type: {Feat}

Description: You are specially trained in the trapping arts. When you place a trap you move into the optimal position to place the next one in the series.

Effect: When you place a snare you may perform a Weak Move action afterwards.

Hunter's Heart

Type: {Feat}

Description: You apply your hunting expertise when you attack your foes.

Effect: During Upkeep, Heal +1 per 2 ranks in the Survival:Wilderness skill.

Insistence for Advantage

Type: {Feat}

Description: You gain momentum as you disarm your opponent.

Effect: Gain +1 Flow when your Attack action (Active power) results in an opponent becoming disarmed or their equipment getting damaged.

Insistence for Blood

Type: {Feat}

Description: You gain momentum as you pierce your victim.

Effect: Gain +1 Flow when your Attack action (Active power) results in an opponent's Degeneration condition intensity rising above 0.

Insistence for Darkness

Type: {Feat}

Description: You gain momentum as you hinder your opponent's perception.

Effect: Gain +1 Flow when your Attack action (Active power) results in an opponent's Blind condition intensity rising above 0.

Insistence for Humiliation

Type: {Feat}

Description: You gain momentum as you knock your opponent off balance.

Effect: Gain +1 Flow when your Attack action (Active power) results in an opponent's Vulnerable condition intensity rising above 0.

Insistence for Humility

Type: {Feat}

Description: You gain momentum as you push your opponent, forcing them backwards.

Effect: Gain +1 Flow when your Attack action (Active power) results in an opponent being pushed backwards.

Insistence for Momentum

Type: {Feat}

Description: You gain momentum as you cut at your opponent's legs.

Effect: Gain +1 Flow when your Attack action (Active power) results in an opponent's Impeded condition intensity rising above 0.

Insistence for Subtlety

Type: {Feat}

Description: You gain momentum as you bloody your opponent.

Effect: Gain +1 Flow when your Attack action (Active power) deals damage to a combatant from behind.

Insistence for Time

Type: {Feat}

Description: You gain momentum as you time your strikes for the most opportune moments.

Effect: Gain +1 Flow when you shift a position in the Initiative order.

Invoker's Charity

Type: {Feat}

Description: Every time you invoke the power of a magic item, you may invest a part of yourself into the effect in order to bolster it.

Effect: After invoking a magic item's active power, you may perform a Major Sacrifice +1 in order to trigger one of the three listed Meta tags (except Maintain and Open).

Iron Beast

Type: {Feat}

Description: You focus your rage and channel it into a wide attack arc, clawing those around you.

Effect: Consume Rage to grant your next Attack action a free Multi meta and +1 Reach.

Iron Fist

Type: {Feat}

Description: Your power surges as you embrace the rage that boils in your heart.

Effect: Consume Rage to grant your next attack +1 DF and Degeneration +1.

Iron Hide

Type: {Feat}

Description: Your exterior hardens as you embrace the rage that boils in your heart.

Effect: If you are Bloodied, Consume Rage to gain either +3 PF P or +2 PF M or +2 PF S the next time you are attacked.

Learn Power

Type: {Feat}

Description: You are a devoted thane who learns from his master.

Effect: When you first acquire this Passive power, you must choose 1 Passive power that your master knows and substitute it for "Learn Power". You may not learn a power that is bound to the master's Void rune.

Mighty Arm

Type: {Feat}

Description: Your keen eye and strong arms allow you to make devastating ranged attacks.

Effect: On an Attack action with a ranged weapon (shot or thrown), gain +1 DF and Pierce +2.

Niflheim's Boon

Type: {Enchantment}

Description: You are fueled by the powers of the nether realm. Magic is re-energized by Niflheim's essence running through you.

Effect: Gain Focus +1 per 3 runes in Drain.

Niflheim's Celerity

Type: {Enchantment}

Description: You are fueled by the powers of the nether realm. Your body accelerates from the nether taint in your blood.

Effect: Gain Move +1 per rune in Drain.

Niflheim's Embrace

Type: {Enchantment}

Description: You are fuelled by the powers of the nether realm. Niflheim's grasp on your soul allows you to see and react to all dangers you face.

Effect: Gain Evade +1 per 4 runes in Drain.

Niflheim's Might

Type: {Enchantment}

Description: You are fueled by the powers of the nether realm. Your strength is amplified by your black blood.

Effect: Gain DF +1 per rune in Drain.

Oppose the Crowd

Type: {Feat}

Description: You thrive when surrounded by foes. Your ability to avoid damage is proportional to the number of enemies around you.

Effect: Gain PF +1 vs. Physical per 4 adjacent foes.

Raging Bear

Type: {Feat}

Description: Rage consumes you and your body shape changes into a giant bear.

Effect: When you hit max rage, you may shapechange into a giant bear. You lose your weapons and armour (absorbed into new form) but you gain: Quadruped, Size +4, Reach +2, Physical PF +4. Base movement and unarmed attack damage is calculated based on size. All Active and Passive powers remain unchanged (Passive powers need to be applied to new attributes). Once shape-changed, another combatant may equip you with one Accessory item. If your Rage intensity drops below 4, you may choose to revert to your original form.

Rider of Lightning

Type: {Feat}

Description: You have a bond with your mount.

Effect: While mounted, gain PF +1 per 2 ranks in the Riding skill.

Rider of Thunder

Type: {Feat}

Description: You have a bond with your mount.

Effect: While mounted, grant your mount a +1 Move bonus per 2 ranks in the Riding skill. Double the bonus if the mount has the quadruped ability.

Rune of Divine Blessing

Type: {Rune Enchantment}

Description: You are watched over by a higher power's grace which functions through a rune that has been tattooed on your body.

Effect: Gain +1 PF vs. Spiritual damage if you perform a Minor Sacrifice +1 during Upkeep.

Rune of Leadership

Type: {Rune Enchantment}

Description: You are tattooed with a rune that shields your mind from external influences.

Effect: Gain +1 PF vs. Mental damage if you perform a Minor Sacrifice +1 during Upkeep.

Rune of Scrying

Type: {Rune Enchantment}

Description: A rune that has been tattooed on your body allows you to read the mind of those who have been affected by your spells.

Effect: When you target another combatant with one of your spells, they reveal all their Active powers to you [Counter M].

Rune of the Darkstitched

Type: {Rune Enchantment}

Description: Your body has been wracked by the dark rune magic of the Svart Alfar, transforming it into an abomination.

Effect: All of your sacrifice costs are increased in category (Minor sacrifices become Moderate sacrifices and Ultimate sacrifice +1 becomes Ultimate sacrifice +2). When you receive damage, before applying any defences, up to 10 points per rune in Drain are reflected back upon the source of the damage (ie. attacker). You still take the damage and the attacker may perform Defend actions against this damage reflection.

Seeker of Winter

Type: {Feat}

Description: Your endurance gives you an advantage on the battlefield, allowing you to act when the time is right.

Effect: During the Upkeep phase, move +/-1 position in Initiative per 2 ranks in the Endurance skill.

Selective Spirit

Type: {Enchantment}

Description: Under certain conditions your soul becomes enraged and territorial, preventing hostile spirits from entering your body.

Effect: When possession is being self-applied and you are bloodied with a rune in Drain, no hostile spirits may enter your body. However spirits with an insane or autonomous disposition may enter your body.

Shadow of Illicit Deeds

Type: {Shadow}

Description: When you stand in shadow, dark tendrils reach for your enemies. When you stand in light, the shadow never truly leaves your side.

Light Effect: The first time each combat round that you are affected by an Active power with an Area meta, your Shroud intensity increases by +1.

Dark Effect: When you are attacked with a melee weapon, after resolving the damage you may Consume 2 Shroud to snatch the weapon from your attacker [Counter: P].

Shadow of Faith

Type: {Shadow}

Description: When you stand in shadow, it protects you as a beloved child. When you stand in light, the shadow is drawn to your violence.

Light Effect: If you are Bloodied, after you perform a standard Attack action, perform a Minor Sacrifice +1 to increase your Shroud intensity by +1.

Dark Effect: Consume Shroud to gain a +2 Parry bonus until end of round.

Shadow of Hvergelmir

Type: {Shadow}

Description: When you stand in shadow, your illness washes away. When you stand in light, the shadow obscures you from danger.

Light Effect: During Upkeep, if you are Bloodied, your Shroud condition increases by 1 intensity and you Recover +2.

Dark Effect: During Upkeep, Consume Shroud to reduce a condition intensity per 4 ranks in Sneak, Feather Fingers and Verbal Manipulation.

Shadow of Memory

Type: {Shadow}

Description: When you stand in shadow, it guides your strike towards your opponent's psyche. When you stand in light, the shadow becomes your armour.

Light Effect: If you are struck a second time during a combat round, your Shroud condition increases by 1 intensity.

Dark Effect: Consume Shroud to convert 2 points of damage on your next attack from Physical to Mental. You may increase the amount of damage converted by 1 additional point per Minor Sacrifice +2.

Shadow of Niflheim

Type: {Shadow}

Description: When you stand in shadow, your movements are quick and lethal. When you stand in light, the shadow hungers for blood.

Light Effect: After you deal a killing blow, you may perform a Major Sacrifice +1 to increase your Shroud condition by 1 intensity and perform a Weak Move action.

Dark Effect: Consume Shroud to gain a +1 bonus to DF per 3 ranks in Sneak, +1/+5 bonus to Reach/Range per 3 ranks in Feather Fingers and +1 bonus to Parry per 3 ranks in Verbal Manipulation.

Shadow of the Ice Raven

Type: {Shadow}

Description: When you stand in shadow, you draw upon penumbral powers. When you stand in light, magic floods through you.

Light Effect: During Upkeep, if you are maintaining an Active power, you may Consume Shroud to gain a +1 Focus for the remainder of the combat round.

Dark Effect: Consume Shroud to add a free meta tag to your next Active power. The meta tag must be a valid one for the Active power.

Shadow of the Ice Wolf

Type: {Shadow}

Description: When you stand in shadow, you draw upon penumbral powers. When you stand in light, you lunge like a hungry ice wolf.

Light Effect: During Upkeep you may Consume Shroud to perform a Move action with a +1 bonus.

Dark Effect: Consume 2 Shroud to exchange a rune in play with a rune in hand. If you choose a rune from a rune chain that is providing an ongoing effect, the effect must be reassessed when the rune from In-Hand is swapped into the chain (the root effect or the metas may change). The Void rune may never participate in the swap.

Shadow of Youth

Type: {Shadow}

Description: When you stand in shadow, its caress mends your wounds. When you stand in light, the shadow beckons for you to enter.

Light Effect: If you are Bloodied, after you end a standard Move action, perform a Minor Sacrifice +1 to increase your Shroud condition by 1 intensity.

Dark Effect: During Upkeep, Consume Shroud to Recover +2 and Heal +4. You Heal an additional +2 if you are Bloodied.

Spiritual Discretion

Type: {Enchantment}

Description: Your soul is fuelled by immeasurable conviction. When foreign spirits enter your body, you convert them into benevolent and subservient spirits.

Effect: When receiving a level of Possession, you may perform an Ultimate Sacrifice +2 in order to force the spirit into having a "benevolent" disposition. It will still act on its own accord with any runes afforded to it, but its actions will be for the good of the possessed individual.

Stand of Deliverance

Type: {Feat}

Description: Your self-sacrifice enables you to shake off the cobwebs of conflict and pain.

Effect: When entering or exiting a stance, you may perform a Moderate Sacrifice +1 to reduce a condition that affects you by -1 intensity. This can only trigger during the Action phase.

Stand of Haste

Type: {Feat}

Description: Your dexterity increases as you rely on your trusty stances.

Effect: When entering or exiting a stance, you may perform a Weak Move action. This can only trigger during the Action phase.

Stand of the Four Winds

Type: {Feat}

Description: Your tactical prowess increases as you rely on your trusty stances.

Effect: When entering or exiting a stance, you may perform a Minor Sacrifice +2 to shift your Initiative position by +/-1. This can only trigger during the Action phase.

Stand of Victory

Type: {Feat}

Description: Your aggression increases as you rely on your trusty stances.

Effect: When entering or exiting a stance, you may perform a Minor Sacrifice +1 to make a Weak Attack action. This can only trigger during the Action phase.

Striker

Type: {Feat}

Description: Your fighting style allows you to strike foes who would otherwise be beyond your reach.

Effect: Gain Reach +1 on all melee Attack actions. If wielding a ranged weapon then you gain a Range +5 bonus.

Stubborn

Type: {Feat}

Description: Your manoeuvres are driven by your stubborn persistence.

Effect: Your Active powers that cause an effect requiring a counter become more difficult to counter. In addition to the counter cost, the defender must also perform a Minor Sacrifice +1.

Summon Forge Beast

Type: {Enchantment}

Description: There are creatures that have powers which are similar to that of a blacksmith's forge. Some of those creatures have a desire to help in the creation process. Such beasts are rare and usually found in the more mythical realms upon the branches of the world tree. The Blacksmith can attract such a beast by being in the correct realm, or next to an Alka of that realm. Such a beast becomes friendly and will aid the Blacksmith in the crafting and infusing process, as well as act as a faithful thane.

Effect: Gain a forge beast thane at level 3. If you already have this thane, then multiple instances of this Passive power boost the level by another +3.

Summon Mount

Type: {Feat}

Description: You attract a "mount" type thane such as a Golden Boar or Silver Stag.

Effect: Gain a mount thane at level 3. If you already have this thane, then multiple instances of this Passive power boost the level by another +3.

Tactical Pause

Type: {Feat}

Description: You delay your actions and watch for an opportune time to strike.

Effect: During Upkeep, you may shift your initiative down (later) by 2 positions.

Temper Rage

Type: {Feat}

Description: You can force yourself to ignore your allies when at max rage.

Effect: While at max Rage, you may perform an Ultimate Sacrifice +1 in order to avoid attacking allies for 1 combat round.

Timely Mount

Type: {Feat}

Description: You and your rider time your movements perfectly.

Effect: During Upkeep you may move your Initiative marker 1 space above or below your rider's Initiative marker.

Titanic Size

Type: {Feat}

Description: You grow at an astounding rate, but cannot benefit from any magical items as they are incompatible with your special physiology.

Effect: Size +1 and gain another Size +1 every 5 levels. You may never equip any magic items.

Trail Blaze

Type: {Enchantment}

Description: While you move, you may extend an Alka that you have already placed on the battlefield.

Effect: While moving, you may perform a Minor Sacrifice +1 to drop an Alka adjacent to an Alka you have already placed on the ground. For each Minor Sacrifice performed, you get to place 1 Alka on an adjacent hex. This Alka must be adjacent to another Alka you placed earlier.

Trap Master

Type: {Feat}

Description: You apply your knowledge of traps when designing them.

Effect: Add +1 level to your traps per rank in the Hunting/Trapping skill.

Trapper's Companion

Type: {Feat}

Description: You are aware of the traps of your allies and can avoid taking damage even when caught in the area of effect.

Effect: When in the area of a friendly trap's effect, you may elect to negate the effect/damage upon yourself.

Tribal Blood

Type: {Enchantment}

Description: You are bound by blood to your warband members. Any harm to your companions amplifies your battle prowess.

Effect: If an ally has died in the last few minutes, gain DF +1 on Attack actions and a Parry +1 bonus on Defend actions. This bonus scales by the number of allies who have died recently (maximum +6/+6).

Verdant Size

Type: {Feat}

Description: You grow and drop roots, sacrificing mobility for size.

Effect: Size +2, Move -1 and can only perform Weak Move actions. The +2 Move gained from the +2 Size is diminished by the -1 Move penalty.

War Planner

Type: {Feat}

Description: Your phenomenal warfare experience allows you to anticipate the movements of others, so that you may better adjust your plans.

Effect: During Upkeep, you may shift +/- 1 in Initiative per 2 ranks in War Tactics.

Zerkir Chest Bump

Type: {Feat}

Description: You run and jump at your opponent, chest first.

Effect: During Upkeep, Consume 1 Rage to perform a Weak Move. At your destination, knockback an adjacent combatant by +2 hexes [Counter P], and then perform another Weak Move.

Zerkir Weapon Toss

Type: {Feat}

Description: Your rage is so overpowering that you throw anything you hold at your opponents.

Effect: Consume 1 Rage. On your next attack with a melee weapon, you may throw it with a +5 Range bonus and with +1 Knockback. The weapon bounces against your target, back into your hand. The Multi meta may not be used in conjunction with this power.

New Skills

Ancestral Weapon
[Difficulty +2, Spiritual]

Some weapons hold such great importance that they do not pass into the afterlife. Their purpose is to serve the living and as a result, they pass onto to a worthy heir after their owner's demise. This special inheritance is not considered a transgression upon the deceased or the afterlife. After the previous owner is cremated, their ashes are bound into a new ore ingot and forged into the weapon. This skill imparts the knowledge of how to bind the ashes to the ore, as well as the process involved in adding this new ingot to the existing weapon. As the weapon passes from owner to owner, each owner's ashes are imbued into the weapon.

The weapon has a very high QR, however the wielder can only gain access to a certain amount of the item's powers and abilities. A dweller or denizen starting out with such a weapon benefits from a QR equal to half the wielder's level (minimum 7). This QR is further boosted by +10% per wielder's Disir level. The size of the weapon is 3 or the Reach attribute, whichever is greater. The attributes of the weapon are defined by the craft skill table (see page 329). QR is spent to improve the attributes and metas of the weapon. Every Additional instance of this skill grants 1 automatic counter to being disarmed per round as well as a virtual +2 QR versus having the weapon damaged.

This weapon is considered to be crafted by the wielder so long as it has been wielded by the wielder's ancestor or the wielder has leveled their dweller twice while using this weapon exclusively.

As the wielder increases in level so does the QR. Every 2 levels gained will grant 1 unused QR to the Ancestral Weapon. This QR can be utilized for new attributes using the Craft skill rules.

If such a weapon is found the Norn will determine the used and unused portions of QR as well as the attributes of the weapon.

The loss of an Ancestral Weapon is a real travesty for the Stalo. If it cannot be recovered, then reforging is the only other option. A reforged Ancestral Weapon loses the Disir level bonus since the ancestry line has been reset.

Animal Shapeshift

[Difficulty +2, Spiritual]
[Amplify Amplify Maintain]

This skill cannot be attempted without at least 1 rank. Over the span of seconds, the individual changes their shape (Shapechange rules) into one of the three predetermined animals. When gaining a rank in this skill, the dweller or denizen chooses 1 small animal from each of the three major biomes: air, water and land. A common selection would be: sparrow, trout and ferret.

The dweller or denizen retains all of their powers and skills in this new form and uses the physical attributes granted by the new form. Perception and Wilderness Survival grant bonuses to the dweller's skills. Human speech is possible in the new form.

To use this skill in combat the combatant must play a rune. Additional runes may be played as meta tags in order to boost the effect. Every additional rune played grants a +1 bonus to Move, DF or Parry.

Table 1: Animal Shapeshift Table

Animal Type	Size	Move	DF	PF	Parry	Perception	Wilderness Survival
Air	1	4 (flight)	1	0	0	+1	+2
Water	1	4 (underwater swimming)	1	0	4	+1	+2
Land	1	2 (quadruped)	1	0	2	+3	+2

Appraisal
[Difficulty +0, Mental]

This skill is used to assess the item attributes as bestowed via the Craft skill. Every success will reveal 5 QR worth of attributes. Even without this skill, repeated use of an item will eventually reveal its crafted attributes (infused effects are assessed using the Lore:Arcana skill). In addition this skill allows someone to assess the local market value for goods and services. This assessment is very accurate and takes into account current economy, perceived availability and demand. Extra successes on Appraisal can be converted to bonuses on a subsequent Negotiation skill check. Every 3 successes in Appraisal can be converted to 1 success on the Negotiation skill check.

Brew
[Difficulty +1, Mental]

The Brewing skill allows one to create potions, tattoo inks and ointments. These are single use items whose effects are either instant (single combat round) or last for a longer duration. The effect's potency is defined by the consumable's total QR. Every success above a difficulty of 1 adds extra craft successes to the QR of the potion or ointment.

Total QR = Base QR + Extra Craft Successes

Table 2: Brew Consumable Table

Type	Duration	Base QR
Potion	Instant effect (one combat round)	6
Ointment	Lasts for the scene (whole combat)	0
Tattoo	Lasts for an adventure (game night)	-6

In order to create the potions, a number of raw materials (herbs) must be prepared before the skill attempt is made.

Table 3: Brew Raw Materials Table

Total	QR Raw Materials Required		
	Potion	Ointment	Tattoo
1	1	1	1
2	2	4	8
3	3	9	27
4	4	16	64
5	5	25	125
Etc…	Etc…	Etc…	Etc…

One or more effects may be added to a potion or ointment. One effect may be stacked many times so long as the QR allows for it. Listed below are the types of effects that can be brewed into the consumable and how they trigger:

Table 4: Brew Effects Table

QR	Effect	Potion	Ointment & Tattoo
1	Heal +1 (immediate effect)	Heal immediately	Heal triggers during upkeep
4	Remove 1 Intensity from a condition	Immediately remove the condition by the intensity	Condition intensity is reduced during Upkeep
1	Recover +2	Recover immediately	Recover triggers during upkeep
1	Grant Attack actions +1 P DF	Next Attack action	Grants the bonus to the first Attack action of the round
3	Focus +1	Next spell	Grants the bonus to the first spell cast each round
1	Grant Parry +1	Next Defend action	Grants the bonus to the first Defend action of the round
2	Grant PF +1	Next time you are attacked	Grants the bonus to the first time you are attacked in the round
4	Grant an Evade +1	Next Defend action	Grants the bonus to the first Defend action of the round
2	Omens / Portents skill rank +1	Next Omens / Portents skill check	One Omens / Portents skill check per combat round (or every check if tattoo)

The Norn may allow some other types of consumable effects which aren't listed in the table above. A lot of caution and consideration needs to be given before creating consumables that grant Passive powers or Condition intensities.

If you gain a benefit from a consumable, you cannot use a second consumable that grants the same benefit. If you do use a consumable that grants the same benefit, the new benefit is negated. The original benefit must wear off before it can be re-applied with another consumable.

See page 345 for rules on consumable rules.

Example: Anund the Druid has a Brew skill of 2 and Destiny 4. He wishes to make a potion of focus and health. He has 4 successes (3 from the Wyrd and 2 from the skill ranks minus the difficulty of the brew skill). He will need to boil 10 ounces of esoteric herbs within a small cauldron filled with water. The resulting potion has a QR of 10 (6 base +4 from the success). He spends 6 QR on focus and 4 QR on healing- this results in a potion that instantly Heals +4 and grants +2 Focus for the next spell.

Capture Memories
[Difficulty +2, Mental]

This skill allows you to read the mind of another being within 15'. If the target is awake, half of their Mental trait is added to the skill check as a difficulty modifier. Half of the victim's Mental Trait is added as a difficulty modifier. Failure indicates that the victim has resisted your probe and is now aware that someone is trying to probe their mind. For every success, you can view 4 memories from that being's life. Every success above 2 allows you to pick one specific memory and probe it further. An example of a specific memory is "the time you met king Harald for the first time". The the further probe could reveal details such as the topic of conversation with the member of the Blotskadi who was in the room.

Craft

Table 5: Craft Success Table

[Difficulty +0, Mental]

Crafting allows someone to create an item that could be of use in combat or in everyday life. Someone attempting the Craft skill with zero ranks limits an item's quality rating (QR) to 2. Crafting requires materials and tools. The exact number of consumable materials needed and the tool quality required can be found in a table below.

Skill Check Result	Crafting Result
Success	Item successfully created
Failure by 1	Item created, but with "damaged" state
Failure by 2 or more	Junk

The crafting process is handled by a skill check. The individual performing the crafting attempt declares what they wish to create and then sets the quality rating (QR) of the attempt. The QR becomes the difficulty rating (DR) of the skill attempt. The QR declared cannot be higher than the limitation imposed by the tools being used. The amount of crafting materials are consumed and the skill check is made. Success means that the item of the specified QR has been created. Failure by 1 means that the item created is "damaged", and a failure by 2 or more means the item crafting attempt failed. There are no benefits to scoring additional successes (although some powers and skills may override this).

The crafting process has a few requirements. Chief among them are the right tools and the raw materials. The tools are generalized, and do not take into account leather or fur vs. wood or metal ores. However the quality level of the tools is a very important factor that influences the quality level of the resulting crafted items and the price of the tools themselves.

Table 6: Craft Tool Table

Tool Quality	QR of Tool	Maximum Crafted Item QR	Price
Basic Tools	1	6	5
Masterwork Tools	6	9	405
Grand Master Tools	9	15	1,125
Dvergar Basic Tools	15	27	3,645
Dvergar Masterwork Tools	27	51	13,005
Dvergar Grand Master Tools	51	99	49,005

Crafting a crafting tool is no different than any other item except in the following ways:

All QR upgrades are spent on allowing it to make items, so no other effects can be added

Dvergar grade tools require the use of realm ores from Nidavellir

A crafting attempt also consumes raw materials (crafting materials) such as leather, wood and iron ore. The materials are also generalized for use with any type of final product. When a crafting attempt is being made, the number of crafting materials that are required and consumed (regardless of the success or failure of the crafting attempt) is determined by the QR of the desired item. The rule of thumb is the QR squared. So a QR 6 item would require 36 crafting materials. All regular crafting materials are considered to be QR 1. Price per crafting material averages 5 skatt.

Once an item is successfully created, the QR can be spent on item attributes. Any unspent QR can remain for infusions (see the Infuse skill on page 334).

A "shield" is defined as a weapon where Parry exceeds the DF value. It is considered its own equipment category when crafting and infusing.

QR Cost	Effect	Type of item that can receive the effect
1	Small non-magical effect (it floats, it is a container, it is combustible, etc...)	Weapon, Armour, Shield Accessory, Miscellaneous
1	Recover +2 (bonus when healing)	Accessory, Miscellaneous
1	Pierce +2	Weapon
1	Heal +1 (bonus when healing)	Accessory, Miscellaneous
1	Physical DF +1	Weapon, Shield
1	Parry +1	Weapon, Armour, Shield
1	Reach +1	Weapon, Shield
2	Range +10 (bow and crossbow) makes an item 2-handed regardless of size	Weapon
1	Range +5 (thrown weapon only) every weapon can be thrown 5 hexes, the first addition of this effect increases throw range to 10 hexes.	Weapon
2	Physical PF +1	Armour, Shield
1	Physical DF +1 (bonus added to {Spell} powers)	Accessory
2	Mental DF +1 (bonus added to {Spell} powers)	Accessory
2	Spiritual DF +1 (bonus added to {Spell} powers)	Accessory
4	Evade +1	Weapon, Armour, Shield, Accessory
1	Move +1	Accessory
3	Focus +1	Weapon, Armour, Shield, Accessory
3	Mental PF +1	Armour, Shield
3	Spiritual PF +1	Armour, Shield
0	First Weapon meta (Gore, Knockdown, Hamstring)	Weapon
1	Second weapon meta (Gore, Knockdown, Hamstring)	Weapon
2	Third (and beyond) weapon meta (Gore, Knockdown, Hamstring)	Weapon
4	Non-Standard weapon meta (Blind, etc...)	Weapon
0	First defensive meta (Absorb, Deflect, Dodge, Eldritch)	Armour, Shield
1	Second defensive meta (Absorb, Deflect, Dodge, Eldritch)	Armour, Shield
2	Third (and beyond) defensive meta (Absorb, Deflect, Dodge, Eldritch)	Armour, Shield
4	Non-Standard defensive meta (Shroud, etc...)	Armour, Shield
0	Add the "Consumable" attribute to the item - 1 use only, destroyed after use, grants a bonus 6 QR to the item	Accessory, Miscellaneous

By default, a created item's size is equal to its QR. The Miniaturize skill can be used to reduce the item's size.

The Miscellaneous category is used for anything that doesn't fit the norm of a weapon, armour or accessory. A longship would be a good example of a Miscellaneous item.

Another item's ore may be reclaimed/salvaged/remade by performing a Craft skill check. The item in question must be a mundane item without infusions, Dvergar engineering or creature reliquaries. The difficulty rating for such an attempt is a quarter of the item's QR. The amount of ore reclaimed is half the item's QR. Realm ore items set the difficulty at half the item's QR and only reclaim ore ingots equal to a quarter of the item's QR.

Example: Annikki the blacksmith has a set of Masterwork tools and a pile of 100 ore. She has 4 ranks in Craft and a destiny of 3. She is going to attempt to make a QR 7 axe. This will require her to use 49 ores. She performs a Wyrd and draws 1 Mental rune and 2 Spiritual runes- a partial success! With 6 successes she manages to create a damaged size 7 axe. Before repairing the item she'll try and perform her Miniaturize skill in order to make the axe more usable and easy to repair. Her Miniaturize skill yields 3 successes, making her QR 7 axe size 4. Now performing a Repair Equipment skill check is only against a difficulty of 4- success again! She needs to pick 7 QR worth of weapon attributes to complete her weapon. She decides on the following: DF 3 (3 QR), Reach 1 (1 QR), Pierce 6 (3 QR), meta: Degeneration (free QR).

Creature Reliquary

[Difficulty +2, Spiritual]

This skill allows the blacksmith to identify a very special part of a creature that may be used to alter and improve an existing item. The binding ritual for the creature reliquary involves incorporating a special creature part (fang, blood, horns, etc) into the item in question. After the six-hour long ritual is complete, a unique consciousness takes hold of the item and it has its own repertoire of powers. The consciousness has a personality and set of powers that it will use to execute its agenda. The table below explains the abilities of the creature reliquary based on it's level:

Table 8: Creature Reliquary Table

Reliquary Level (item QR boost)	Essence/ Destiny	Communication
10 (+1)	2/2	None
20 (+2)	3/3	None
30 (+3)	4/4	Empathy
40 (+4)	5/5	Empathy
50 (+5)	6/6	Telepathy
60 (+6)	7/7	Telepathy
70 (+7)	8/8	Speech

Level of Reliquary: The level of the denizen from which the creature reliquary was taken determines the reliquary level. The minimum level of the creature is 10. It also boosts the item's QR by +1 per 10 reliquary levels.

Essence/Destiny: Every reliquary is treated as a thane that cannot take damage, nor equip any items. It has an Essence (rune bag) and Destiny (draws runes in combat). The first Active power every reliquary gets is "Possess Opponent" and the first Passive Power it gets is "Puppet Master". All other Active and Passive powers are determined by the Norn. Sacrifice effect powers can never be part of a reliquary's repertoire as it cannot take damage.

Communication: Depending on the reliquary's level, it may be able to communicate with the wielder. "Empathy" just transmits emotion to the wielder, "telepathy" is speech which can only be heard by the wielder, and "speech" is verbal communication that can be heard by anyone nearby.

The skill check for this skill works as follows: In order to use the creature reliquary to change the properties of an existing item, the starting difficulty rating is 1 and increases by +1 for every 10 denizen levels of the creature. So a Level 30 creature's reliquary would be a difficulty rating of 6 (1 base + 2 modifier and +3 for 30 levels). No more than one creature reliquary may be added to an item. Success also increases the item's overall QR rating by the amount the reliquary requires. A failure on this skill check will not only result in no effect, but it will also permanently reduce the QR of the item by -1 (Norn should adjust items powers and attributes accordingly).

Once the item is crafted, the Norn will decide the reliquary's personality and motivations. The creature's most passionate vices and virtues will manifest within the item. Whenever an opportunity presents itself where the item may act upon its core desires, it will use the wielder as a proxy. It will use the Possess Opponent power (with Puppet Master) to control the wielder. The item may bestow some of its Passive powers upon the wielder (Norn's discretion). If the item's QR is higher than the level of a dweller or denizen within five feet of it, it may compel the individual at range without requiring the individual to wield it.

During combat it shares initiative with the wielder, and the wielder may choose who will go first. If the reliquary isn't actively trying to dominate the wielder, it will allow the wielder to utilize its powers (player may Wyrd and play the runes for the reliquary). The powers of the Reliquary are different than those infused into the item as only the Reliquary runes may use Reliquary powers.

If a Creature Reliquary receives the damaged condition, lost QR will affect the Destiny and Essence by 1 for each QR lost. A non-hostile Creature Reliquary is considered a Thane.

Dvergar Engineering
[Difficulty +2, Mental]

You may apply "science and wonder" to something you have created using the craft or infuse skill. Be it making an item explosive, steam powered or some relatively super high tech advancement that would seem truly incomprehensible to a Dark Age blacksmith. Some ideas are Frey's folding boat that could fit in a pocket, or Thor's hammer that would return to the thrower. The effect that you add must be approved and negotiated with the Norn. The Norn will work with you to arrive to the proper QR cost of the effect. Dvergar Engineering cannot have any effects that alter the numerical attributes of an item (cannot augment DF for example). The effects that get added must be non-numerical effects, or numerical effects that wouldn't normally be on such an item (ex: afterlife Wyrd bonus). Each instance of this skill allows for one modification to be added. Having two instances of this skill would allow one to put up to two Dvergar engineering effects on an item.

The skill check for this skill works as follows: In order to use the Dvergar engineering, the starting difficulty rating is 1 and increases by +4 for every Dvergar engineering effect already on the item. So an item that already has one Dvergar engineering effect on it would pose a difficulty of 7 (1 base +2 difficulty modifier and +4 from the previous engineering). A failure on this skill check will not only result in no effect, but it will also permanently reduce the QR of the item by -1 (Norn should adjust items powers and attributes accordingly).

Below are some sample effects and sample costs:

Table 9: Dvergar Engineering Wondrous Effect Table

Wondrous Effect	QR Cost
Thrown item will return to the wielder (during the Cleanup phase) Or A damaged item repairs itself (1 hour per QR of the item)	1
Item grants the wearer the Quadruped ability (double move speed but cannot equip any weapons)	2
Item continuously creates thick black smoke (5'x5'x10') obscuring ranged line of sight. Treat as an Alka token that is placed on an unoccupied hex, anyone standing in or passing through disturbs the smoke and the smoke dissipates (remove token).	2
The size of an item is reduced to 1 for purposes of storage (item cannot be equipped while shrunk down)	2
Allow an equipped accessory to shapechange with its wearer (equipped item retains effect) example: an amulet becomes a saddle on the new beast form	2
An effigy can be modified to turn into a weapon (upon command word) with a QR equal to its level (design weapon when Dvergar Engineering is used); Deduct 3 QR from the weapon in order to have this power	3
Weapon no longer deals damage and instead heals anyone struck by it (all DF bonuses boost the healing effect)	3
The item in question can alter the weather in drastic ways: increase or decrease wind speeds and precipitation by +50% every 10 minutes. Or +1 Afterlife Wyrd if item is buried with the deceased (effect doesn't stack)	4
Item grants the wearer the Flight ability (can fly 3' above the ground per dweller level)	4
Grants the item's benefits to anyone who touches the item, even multiple people at the same time (Used for enchanted longships and chariots)	5
Weapon meta triggers automatically. There is no need to play a rune for the Weapon meta. Does not work with the Maintain meta.	6
Weapon deals Mental or Spiritual damage instead of Physical. Pay the QR cost to convert 2 points of Physical damage to 1 point of either Mental or Spiritual. The QR cost must be repaid for every 2 points converted in this way. The defender chooses the damage order to be resolved.	2
Create a pair or triad of "set items" that gain powers when used in conjunction with one another*	*
Secret item, all Lore: Arcana skill checks are penalized by -1 per QR invested into this effect. A failed check will reveal false or no information about the item's true abilities.	*

* Set items must all be equipped in order to unlock the set bonus powers. Each item in the set must give up the same amount of QR in order to create the QR pool for the set powers. No more than 25% of the item's QR may be used in this way. Twice the QR cost taken away from the items will be available for a pool of powers that become available when the items are equipped together. The QR reserved for the set effect may only be used for Dvergar Engineering effects (unless permitted otherwise by the Norn). *Example: If 4 QR are paid for the set (2 from a sword and 2 from a shield), then 8 free QR can be filled with joint set powers.*

Infuse

[Difficulty +1, Spiritual]

The infusing skill renders items magical or useful for a particular type of activity. Infusing an item with a power or skill requires the item in question, as well as someone who possesses the desired power or skill which is to be infused. The power or skill cannot be bound to the Void rune for purposes of Infusion. Keen Aptitude and Cross Archetype Passive powers cannot be infused, nor can any skill that creates or modifies items (craft, brew, infuse, etc...). Neither may powers that scale by level (Fangs, Unencumbered Dodger, etc...) unless permitted by the Norn (see Keen Aptitude rules on page 348). The dweller or denizen that is contributing the power must be a willing participant. Infusing doesn't require crafting tools or materials. The item in question must have some unused QR in order for it to be able to accept an Active or Passive power. An Active power requires 1 QR a Passive power requires 2 QR and a skill requires 2 QR. The difficulty for the Skill check is determined by the number of powers already in the item. By default the DR is 1, and increases by +3 for each power already infused in the item. It is pointless to Infuse the same Passive power more than once since the wielder may only benefit from any one instance of an Infused Passive power (see *Core Rulebook* page 132).

The infusing ritual forces both the blacksmith and the power donor to make an Ultimate Sacrifice +1. If the blacksmith is the power donor, then they must pay both sacrifice costs.

Infusing has a chance of causing an anomaly. An anomaly is an unforeseen arcane side-effect that changes the nature of the item in an unpredictable manner. If the Wyrd results in no Spiritual runes pulled, the item gets a random anomaly (which is usually some negative effect determined by the Norn). Adding an a Passive power to the item with the reverse effect is a good starting point for an anomaly.

Reminder- only equipped items will grant the benefits to the wearer. Simply carrying the item will not trigger any infused Active powers. Skills and Passive powers confer the effect continuously, while an Active power requires the Void rune to be played in order to evoke the power from the item.

The infuse skill also permits someone to rip out an existing enchantment in order to make room for a new one. The difficulty rating of such an attempt is one-quarter the QR of the item. The ritual for removing an Active power takes 1 hour and 2 hours for a Passive power.

Example: A set of lock picks that are QR 2 can be infused with the skill "Lock Picking" in order to confer 1 rank of that particular skill to anyone who wields that item. The skill check difficulty would be 1.

Inner Sanctum

[Difficulty +2, Spiritual]

This skill cannot be attempted without at least 1 rank. This skill allows one to create a mystic abode that is magically shrouded from prying eyes and ears. It takes nothing more than sheer willpower (Ultimate Sacrifice +1) to create the sanctum and shape it to an appearance that is desirable. The size, defences and other features are dictated by the number of successes. The space occupied in the real world is a shrouded 125 cubic feet (to spot a perception check must beat the invisibility rating), however the interior space grows with more skill successes. The duration of the inner sanctum is tied to the Ultimate Sacrifice. The sanctum remains as long as the rune remains in Drain. The player can choose to keep the rune in their Drain pile even when the natural recovery from Drain triggers.

Items, such as furnishings, that are magically created within the sanctum cannot be carried out of the sanctum. Similarly, food grown in the sanctum must be consumed within the sanctum. Any unauthorized visitors must cross a number of Alkas equal to the Defence before gaining access. Crossing this defensive threshold is considered one action and cannot be performed partially. The Druid can define the types of Alkas that trigger on any intruders. At higher levels, the Druid may choose to obscure the exit out of his grove as well. Anyone wanting to leave without permission would have to succeed the required Perception check as well as navigate successfully through the defensive Alkas.

At higher ranks the Inner Sanctum may move. The Druid must perform an Ultimate Sacrifice +2 to perform a movement action. The movement action will move the Inner Sanctum a number of miles based on the rank. The Inner Sanctum may not cross large bodies of water. Any body of water than spans at least 100' may not be crossed. The Sanctum may not scale sheer surfaces such as cliffs, or traverse inclines greater than 70 degrees.

Table 10: Inner Sanctum Table

Number of skill successes	Movement	Invisibility	Defense Alkas	Interior Size	Features
1	0	2	1	1,000 cubic feet	Natural ambient warmth approaching body temperature
2	0	4	2	2,000	Natural magical light equivalent to torchlight
3	0	6	3	4,000	Furnishings of choice *
4	0	8	4	8,000	Earth allowing for gardens to grow at 10x speeds
5	Can travel 1 mile per hour	10	5	16,000	Hidden Exit (Invisibility 9)
6	Can travel 2 miles per hour	12	6	32.000	Hidden Exit (Invisibility 11)
7	Can travel 3 miles per hour	14	7	64000	Natural magical light equivalent to sunlight

*Furnishings created by this skill may not be brought out of the sanctum. All furniture created by this skill are non-magical and mundane in nature (chairs, tables, lanterns, etc...).

Druids are invited to design their groves with structures, streams, forests and gardens. Should a grove be infiltrated the battlefield would be defined by the Druid's layout.

Example: Skallagrim the chieftain is trying to hunt down the Druid who chased away his lumberjacks. Skallagrim has a Destiny of 5 and 3 ranks in the Perception skill. Anund the Druid created his Inner Sanctum with 3 successes. Skallagrim must successfully pierce the invisibility of 7 with a Perception skill check in order to spot the grove. Assuming he is successful, he must run across a threshold of alkas in order to gain entrance. Anund has placed 2 Beckon Jotunheim and 1 Beckon Muspelheim. In all he is receiving 3 levels of Degeneration, 2 levels of Impeded and 1 level of Blind. Any of these intensities may be reduced by playing a Physical rune. Skallagrim has a destiny of 5.

Lock Bash

[Difficulty +0, Physical]

Very much like the Lock Picking skill, except there is no finesse to this manoeuvre. You simply know how to smash intricate metal devices rendering them useless. These ranks may apply to other items of similar nature, not just locks.

Lore: Poison

[Difficulty +2, Mental]

The skill allows you to create poisons and antidotes. The number of successes indicates the strength (QR) of the poison or antidote. The quantity of herbs (crafting materials) needed is equal to the desired QR squared. The QR of the poison is the number of Ultimate Sacrifices the poisoned victim needs to perform every hour. An antidote must be higher QR than the poison that afflicts the victim, and once ingested will neutralize the venom's effects.

Miniaturize

[Difficulty +0, Physical]

You may reduce the size of a piece of equipment which hasn't yet been miniaturized. Each success reduces the size by 1. Once the miniaturization is complete, the item acquires the "miniaturized" attribute.

Peak Performance

[Difficulty +2, Spiritual]

This skill allows you to push past your limits, drawing inspiration from beyond yourself, achieving a truly spectacular result. This difficulty rating of this skill is equal to the runes that you have in Drain. Success means you must perform an Ultimate Sacrifice +1 and your next skill check will gain a +1 skill rank bonus.

Realm Ores

[Difficulty +2, Physical]

Every realm upon Yggdrasil has some spectacular crafting material which, when used by a blacksmith, grants incredible properties to the final product. Instead of using regular Midgard ore, if the item is wholly crafted with a spectacular realm ore, then the listed benefits below will apply to the item. Each ore will increase the item's final QR. This QR increase does not impact the difficulty rating for the craft skill check. The prices listed below are per unit of crafting material.

Ore	Native Realm	Salient Effect
Star Meteorite	Midgard	Highly volatile and explosive material. Any impact causes a shockwave to emanate from the surface (crafting with this material is very time consuming)
Red Gold	Asgard	Enlightened: Focus bonus of +1 per 3 runes in the Stun Pile
Song Wood	Vanagard	Wood Harmonies: Area metas are now +3 hexes instead of +2 hexes
Moon Silver	Alfgard	Sun's Kiss: Item sheds tremendous light (100' radius) and warmth (+35F / +20C degrees)
Mead Iron	Nidavellir	Mead's Helm: While drunk, wearer gains +2 ranks to social skill checks and +1 to Physical DF
Rime Ice	Jotunheim	Ivory Blizzard: Persistent Ice Aura (intensity cannot go below 1)
Shadow Steel	Svartalfheim	Invisible Steel: Cannot be seen while wielded or worn. 100% Concealable unless dropped.
Molten Core	Muspelheim	Fire Fog: Persistent Fire Aura (intensity cannot go below 1)
Snake Hide	Hvergelmir	Snake Sigil: The wielder or wearer of an item created from this ore is place into Rage condition with +1 intensity (cannot be lowered while wearing or wielding)
Death Bone	Niflheim	Hel's Gift: Draugar continuously seek you out

Weapon Benefit	Armour Benefit	QR	Price
The attack from this weapon not only attacks the space occupied by the victim, but also hits all adjacent hexes (hits friends and foes alike)	Every time you are struck by an attack, the damage dealt to you is also dealt to everyone adjacent to you.	4	4
Blood Seeker: when attacking someone who is degenerating, you add +1 intensities of Impeded [Counter: M]	Armour meta "Dodge" benefits increase by +1 runes drawn if the wearer is bloodied	6	12
Undead Bane: when attacking creatures from Niflheim, you add +1 intensity to Degeneration as they burst into fire [Counter: S]	Healing received and delivered boosted by the wearer's Spiritual Trait	6	12
Umbra Bane: each attack to a creature from Svartalfheim deals +1 S damage	The wearer's spells cannot be interrupted.	5	10
Razor's Edge: Weapon Pierce is augmented by the wielder's Physical trait.	Armour negates first 5 points of damage. This reduction cannot be overcome by Pierce or the Vulnerable condition.	5	10
Aggression: All attacks knock back opponents a number of hexes equal to the wearer's Physical trait [Counter: PP]	Wearer grows in size (Size +2)	6	12
Unseen Blade: Attacks apply +1 intensity of the Vulnerable condition before damage is dealt [Counter: M].	Wearer always under 1 intensity of shroud (cannot be lowered to less than 1). Consume Shroud powers fail at Shroud 1.	5	10
Immolation: Attacks apply +1 intensity of the Degeneration condition [Counter P]	All attackers have their weapons receive the "damaged" attribute when they strike the armoured warrior [Counter P]; The armour QR must be higher than the attacker's weapon QR.	6	12
Venom Touched Rune: The attacker may choose to perform a Major Sacrifice +2 to make the attack deal +1 intensity to the Degeneration and Blind conditions	The first detrimental condition received in a combat round gets 1 intensity countered for free	4	8
Hel's Scorn: Weapons deal Spiritual damage	PF vs. Spiritual equal to wearer's Spiritual Trait.	4	8

If several pieces of equipment have the same realm ore, the effects do not stack. Every instance of this skill allows an extra alloy to be added to the mix. For example having 2 instances of this skill allows an item to be created with 2 different realm ores. This skill also grants the blacksmith the ability to break down an existing item and to extract the ore into a usable ingot.

Shields are defined as weapons with Parry greater than DF. They may be treated as weapons or armour for the purposes of Realm Ores. They always qualify as armour, but may also qualify as a weapon if their Reach and DF are greater than zero.

The skill check for this skill works as follows: In order to use the realm ore, the starting difficulty rating is 1 and increases by +3 for every additional realm ore added to the mix. So an item crafted using three realm ores would have a difficulty of 9 (1 base +2 difficulty modifier and +6 from two additional ores). Success also increases the item's overall QR rating by the amount the realm ores require. A failure on this skill check will not only result in no effect, but it will also permanently reduce the QR of the item by -1 (Norn should adjust items powers and attributes accordingly).

Riding

[Difficulty +0, Physical]

To simply ride a mount such as a horse, there is absolutely no need to perform a ride check. However as the circumstances get more complicated, the Norn may require the players involved to perform a check. Good reasons would be to maintain control of a mount as an ambush is sprung, or to carry an extra rider while navigating a dangerous mountain pass during a blizzard. Without any ranks in riding only Weak Attack and Defend actions may be performed from the back of a mount. Spells with adjacent range may not be cast, only with an ability or meta that extends range would spells from a mount be possible. As more ranks are gained, some of these limitations go away.

Table 12: Riding Skill Table

Rank	Benefits	Combat Bonuses
1	Can perform attack actions and spells with no penalties.	Mount gains a +1 Movement bonus.
2	No more skill checks needed when on horseback and performing challenging maneuvers.	Physical damage dealt while on the mount gains a +1 bonus.
3	Can ride a monstrous quadruped.	During Upkeep, the mount may shift its initiative towards that of rider by 1 position.
4	No more skill checks needed when on a flying mount.	Can perform attack actions and spells with no penalties while on a flying mount.

Sacred Wood Binding

[Difficulty +2, Spiritual]

Druids can create and bind a personal wand or staff made from sacred wood. Wands and staves carry their respective properties which are based on the type of wood used. Druids may only own and wield one such instrument at any given time. Creating a new wand or staff irrevocably disenchants the previous one.

Creating a wand or staff requires a skill check against a difficulty of 2 while in possession of the desired type of wood. If the Druid decides to create a Wand (it will always grow/shrink and remain 1-handed), then its QR is equal to 50% of the Druid's level. If the Druid creates a staff (it will always grow/shrink and remain 2-handed) then the QR is equal to 75% of the Druid's level. Using the "Weapon Attribute" table found under the Craft skill, the QR is spent on effects which will be assigned to the staff or wand. The wand is treated as a "weapon" and "accessory", while the staff is treated as a "weapon" and "shield" for the purposes of effect restrictions.

Each type of wood provides a special effect upon the wielder. Some sacred wood effects grant a new meta tag. While the sacred weapon is equipped, it adds another option to the original Active power meta tags listed. Only one meta tag can be activated with a rune played, so if multiple options are available the player must choose one. Negated condition intensities function similarly to the "Resistance to X" Passive powers found in the *Core Rulebook*.

Table 13: Sacred Wood Binding Table

Wood	Effect
Alder	Your spells and Alkas gain the "Sight" meta tag (bound to Spiritual runes) with a +1 Focus bonus per 4 ranks in Sacred Wood Binding
Ash	Both Active and Passive power heal effects boosted by +1 per rank in Sacred Wood Binding
Birch	Ignore 1 hex of knockback per rank in Sacred Wood Binding
Blackthorn	Each round negate 1 intensity of Impeded per 2 ranks in Sacred Wood Binding
Broom	Grants a PF +1 vs. Physical per 2 ranks in Sacred Wood Binding
Cedar	Each round negate 1 intensity of Vulnerable per 2 ranks in Sacred Wood Binding
Elder	While bloodied, gain an extra +1 Destiny per 8 ranks in Sacred Wood Binding
Elm	Your summoned creatures gain +1 level per rank in Sacred Wood Binding
Fir	Grants a +1 rank in Omens/Portents per 2 ranks in Sacred Wood Binding
Gorse	Your spells and Alkas gain the "Stutter" meta tag (bound to Spiritual runes) with a +1 Focus bonus per 4 ranks in Sacred Wood Binding
Hawthorne	Grants Focus +1 per 3 ranks in Sacred Wood Binding
Hazel	Each round negate 1 intensity of Possession per 2 ranks in Sacred Wood Binding
Holly	If wielded at time of death, afterlife pulls +1 per 8 ranks in Sacred Wood Binding
Juniper	Grants a +1 rank in Perception per 2 ranks in Sacred Wood Binding
Mistletoe	Staff or wand acts as a scorn pole with +1 extra successes per rank in Sacred Wood Binding
Oak	Each round negate 1 intensity of Degeneration per 2 ranks in Sacred Wood Binding
Pine	Grants Evade +1 per 4 ranks in Sacred Wood Binding
Rowan	Grants a +1 rank in Survival Wilderness per 2 ranks in Sacred Wood Binding
Willow	Allows perfect sight in complete darkness within +25' per rank in Sacred Wood Binding
Yew	Each round negate 1 intensity of Blind per 2 ranks in Sacred Wood Binding

Short Fuse

[Difficulty +1, Spiritual]

After failing a skill check, you may perform this skill check to try and succeed at the task again. The skill that was failed has the difficulty lowered by 1 for this skill. Performing this skill check requires an Ultimate Sacrifice +1. However a failure on this skill immediately imbues you with violent intent and you gain 4 ranks in the Rage condition.

War Tactics

[Difficulty +1, Mental]

You have training in military tactics. You understand logistics between battles dealing with equipment, morale, pay and upkeep. You're also trained in field strategies like ambushes, terrain, deceit and order propagation. With this skill you are equipped to lead troops consisting from a war-band to the likes of an army.

Norn Rules

This section expands on the rules that have already been presented in the *Core Rulebook*. In this section you will find new rules along with additional explanations and evolutions for existing rules.

Alkas

Alkas figure predominately in the extended world as presented in Denizens of the North. As such, additional clarifications on the nature and behaviour of Alkas is provided below:

- Maintained Alkas are re-cast every Upkeep, growing the area of the Alka. Unless another power permits it, the Maintained Alka needs to originate once more from a hex adjacent to the caster. If there is an occupant on that hex, they suffer the benevolent or malicious effects immediately.

- Each Alka token is considered a single source, so a movement through a path involving more than one bead must be resolved one bead at a time.

- If an Alka would affect more than one combatant, for example two very small combatants that would fit in the same hex, then all valid combatants are affected by the Alka.

- Any malicious effects bestowed by Alkas have counters specified. In the event a counter is not explicitly specified, then the default counter is 1 Mental rune to negate the effect.

- An important distinction to take note of is that some Alkas are simply {Alka} effects while others have the {Spell} descriptor. Focus is only added to Alka effects with the {Spell} descriptor.

- Alkas are not affected by gravity and if placed by someone with flight, the Alka will remain stationary and airborne.

- Alkas can be interrupted like spells and range attacks.

- If the caster of the Alka directs its path towards a Shrouded opponent, then the Norn may rule that the Shroud cost must be paid. If the Alka, however, is declared to surround the caster and a Shrouded opponent is in that area, then the Norn may allow the Alka to resolve on the Shrouded opponent without the need to overcome Shroud. The Norn will use their best judgment in such a situation.

The Passive power **Alka Mastery** from the *Core Rulebook* has been redesigned in order to integrate with many more Alkas and Alka masters like the Druid. The effect is as follows: *"At the end of your Action phase, perform a Major Sacrifice +1 in order to replenish all consumed Alka tokens for the last Alka you played this turn"*. This avoids timing issues during the Cleanup phase as well as tracking an overabundance of consumed Alkas.

Consumables

The Druid archetype introduces consumables such as potions and ointments to the game. During combat, quaffing a potion requires the dweller or denizen to play one rune, and due to the care required, applying an ointment would require the play of two runes. Applying a tattoo would take longer and would have to be done outside of combat.

If you gain a benefit from a consumable, you cannot use a second consumable that grants the same benefit. If you do use a consumable that grants the same benefit, the new benefit is negated. If the initial benefit wears off, it can be re-applied with another consumable. See page 327 for details on the Brew skill.

Example: Anund the Druid applies an ointment that grants heal +4 and Focus +1. He also quaffs a potion that grants heal +2 and DF +5. The cumulative effect is that he heals +4 during upkeep (disregard the potion heal effect, because duplicate effects cannot stack) and gains a Focus +1 for the duration of the combat and gains a DF +5 until the end of the combat round.

Damage- Falling, Burning and Hybrid

Sometimes damage comes from the environment, such as falling off a cliff or being pushed into a fire. In those cases damage ranges heavily depend on the circumstances. Due to the sheer permutations of any given situation, environmental damage is impossible to define. Following some general guidelines may help the Norn determine the possible effects.

Falling Damage

As a general rule of thumb, falling damage starts at 2 damage and doubles every 10 feet. A 50' drop would deal 32 damage (no PF may be applied). The Norn should also allow for a skill check in order to reduce the damage. For falling one could surmise that an athletics skill check would reduce the damage by 5 for every success.

Burning Damage

Similarly stepping into a location of extreme temperatures (heat or cold) would deal an amount of damage based on both temperature, duration and exposure. Walking through a cursed hallway that exudes frost from Jotunheim could be defined as dealing 8 damage for every hex travelled. Stopping to heal would deal another 16 damage per combat round (or equivalent out of combat duration). In the case of fire, the Norn may also add the degeneration condition as the combatant is immolated and combustible materials start to burn.

Hybrid Damage

Sometimes damage is a hybrid of Traits- ie. "Deal 6 Physical damage and 2 Spiritual damage". In these cases the defender (recipient of the damage) will choose the order in which to resolve the damage. They may choose to apply the Spiritual damage first and then apply the Physical damage. In some exceptions an Active power may dictate the order in which the effects must be resolved.

Effective Hit Points

Players and Norns sometimes have a need to assess the durability of a combatant (ie. How much damage it can take before it dies). This concept is called "Effective Hit Points" (EHP). EHP of a dweller or denizen can be calculated by multiplying the Essence value by 3 for the white (hard) wounds track, 5 for the grey (moderate) wounds track, and 7 for the black (easy) wounds track and then adding the Destiny value. So if a player was using the grey wounds track and then had 6 Essence and 4 Destiny, they would have 34 EHP... meaning they take 34 damage with no PF or Defend actions.

Gate Abilities

Additional clarification on the nature and behaviour of Gate powers is provided below:

- Gate powers can be interrupted.
- {Gate Spell} powers would add Focus to the level of the creature.
- Gated creatures start their initiative at the bottom of the initiative chain (last).
- Gated creatures immediately Wyrd their destiny (until their turn, the runes can be used for {Interrupt} actions).
- Gated creatures receive no Upkeep phase the turn they are brought into play.
- Once the rune with the Gate effect leaves the In-Play pile, the Gated creature ceases to exist.

Generic Actions

During combat, players may fall into a mode of playing where they solely focus on the rune symbols they drew and what Active powers they may have at their disposal. Always remind your players that they may play runes for Generic actions allowing them to describe cinematic actions limited only by their imaginations and the scene that the Norn has constructed. For more on Generic actions used as cinematic actions, see page 96 in the *Core Rulebook*.

Standard Action

Denizens of the North adds a Generic action descriptor called "standard". It means a non-Weak action. So a standard Attack action would be a non-weak Attack action.

Flight

Flying creatures move at the same rate as they would move on the ground. Quadrupeds that obtain flight capabilities will move at double their base movement rate while in flight.

Focus

Focus as described in the *Core Rulebook* may increase the numeric values in a spell. Additional clarifications on the application of Focus are provided below:

- As stated in the *Core Rulebook*, Focus boosts the numeric values in Active powers with the {Spell} descriptor. If the active power has more than one source, Focus may be split across the sources.
- Focus can also be used to decrease numeric values that appear in spells.
- As stated in the *Core Rulebook*, Focus may not increase effects that grant focus or inflict condition intensities.
- Focus cannot increase the drawing of runes (Wyrd effects).
- Focus added to {Gate Spell} effects increases the creature level
- Focus added to {Alka Spell} effects increase the number of Alka tokens

Foraging for Raw Materials

Some play groups may not want to interrupt the flow of play to accommodate the Blacksmith, Druid and others that need raw materials to create magic items.

A player can simply state: "wherever we go, I will be on the constant lookout for crafting/brewing materials". The Norn would then judge the environment and the time constraints (if any) and use one of the columns in the table below. A rune would be Wyrded at the end of the game session to determine how much was found and picked up.

Table 14: Foraging Results

Rune	Sparse Terrain	Average Terrain	Bountiful Terrain
Physical	3	8	20
Mental	1	6	15
Spiritual	0	4	10

Speaking in broad generalizations, most locales in the far north would be considered sparse terrain. The rest of Midgard would be considered average terrain, and a few specific niches could be considered bountiful Terrain. The values found are cut in half if the adventuring group was under very tight time constraints (round up).

Haugbui

No rest for the wicked! An interesting possibility Norns can entertain is to afflict a player's dweller with the Haugbui curse when they die. Possible reasons would be a very important personal goal hasn't been achieved while alive, or excessive barrow looting has damned the dweller to a Valkyrie-free future!

Simply have the player reassign half of their Essence runes (determined at random) to the Haugbui board powers and skills. The original power and skill bindings for these runes are lost. The player plays this hybrid dweller until they resolve what is keeping them bound to this mortal world. Once they are free the Norn may grant a modifier to their afterlife Wyrd. The Norn may conversely damn the spirit to becoming a Lost Soul if things go sour for the Haugbui.

Keen Aptitude

The Passive power called Keen Aptitude is a common occurrence on denizen power boards but it is much less common occurrence on the dweller Passive powers boards- this is by design. When the Norn runs many denizens, Keen Aptitude helps keep play simple and powers become easy to scale. When dwellers gain access to Keen Aptitude, it becomes a rare game-play reward that grants a rare power stacking opportunity. The Norn may stack one Passive power as many times as they please, however, dwellers (players) and thanes are limited to stacking any Passive power only once. The Norn may allow a player to bypass this limitation in some very specific cases. Likewise the Norn may choose to waive this restriction on Thanes who have many instances of this power (ie. Seith Aberration).

Example: Thorvald the half-Troll Ulfhednar has just leveled-up and has picked Keen Aptitude from the Troll-Blood aspect Passive power board. He is a competent warrior who already has the Might and Martial Prowess powers. Thorvald would like to deal more damage, so he chooses Might as the cloned power for Keen Aptitude. He now has two instances of Might and one instance of Martial Prowess making him even more deadly. The next time he gains access to Keen Aptitude, he will no longer be able to choose Might, but he could choose Martial Prowess.

As a general rule, the Keen Aptitude Passive power cannot be used to clone any Passive powers that have their effect scale on level (ie. Fangs, Unencumbered Dodger, Fae-Kin, etc.). Depending on the QR levels of items given out, the Norn may allow a single copy to be made in order to allow unarmed/unarmoured players to keep up to the rate of magic items being handed out. Under some very specific circumstances the Norn may wish to permit a second copy. It should keep pace with the play groupís access to magic items. The Norn's available options are to limit scaling Passive powers to:

> **1 Instance (recommended):** When the original Passive power is chosen from the power board.
> **2 Instances:** From the original Passive power and an accessory that grants the power (infuse).
> **3 Instances:** The Passive power chosen, an accessory that grants the power, and a Keen Aptitude copy.

Longships

Overland travel is very hazardous and the most abundant food sources are found in deep waters. As a result, longships play a very important role for the denizens of Midgard. Every self-respecting Viking warband should be the proud owners of a longship. With a very optimized design, a longship can accommodate 2 crew members for every 3' of usable length. Every crew member has an oar and sits on their own "sea bench"- a personal treasure chest filled with their belongings. Wider ships are designed to reserve the central space for cargo. Those looking to colonize distant shores would be bringing livestock and lumber. The sails are constructed from sheep wool, ochre and horse-fat. The sailing of a longship requires a minimum of 4 crew members. Propulsion could be achieved by sail or oars. Speed is measured in "knots" with 1 knot being equivalent to 1.9 km/h or 1.2 mph. The speeds listed below are for travel under average weather conditions. The absence or presence of favourable wind can affect the speed by as much as +/- 50%.

For those who wish to buy a longship, the options are as follows:

Table 15: Buying Longships Table

Longship Type	Crew Capacity	Speed	Damage / Weaponry	Essence / Durability	Manoeuvrability	Extra Capacity	Stability	Price
Kravi–size: 12 (30'); QR 12	24	7 knots	24 / 0	12 / 0	45 degrees	0	0	8,000 skatt
Snekkja–size: 27 (75'); QR 16	54	8 knots	64 / 0	16 / +5 PF	90 degrees	+3	+1	12,000 skatt
Skeid – size: 43 (120'); QR 24	82	10 knots	96 / 8	24 / +15 PF	90 degrees	+5	+2	18,000 skatt

The dwellers will most likely encounter those from Outer-Midgard. Their ships are presented below for comparison.

Another factor that Midgard longships have over their foreign counterparts is that they can navigate shallow water (3' or deeper). Besides the canoe, crusader ships require at least 12' of depth.

Longship Type	Crew Capacity	Speed	Damage / Weaponry	Essence / Durability	Manoeuvrability	Extra Capacity	Stability
Skraeling Canoe – size: 8 (16')	16	2 knots	16 / 0	4 / 0	135 degrees	0	0
Crusader Cog – size: 27 (45')	54	5 knots	54 / 0	13 / 0	45 degrees	0	0
Crusader Galley – size: 43 (90')	82	4 knots	86 / 0	21 / 0	45 degrees	+6	0

Building Longships

Longships come in many different sizes and configurations. The Craft skill is used in the construction of longships, requiring tools and materials, resulting in a finished product and QR total. The time required is usually 4-6 weeks. Once the QR has been determined, the points will be spent on the "Ship Attribute" table below. Every point spent will automatically increase the ship size by the listed amount.

Table 17: Foreign Vessels Table

Effect	Size Boost	QR Cost
Speed: Boost speed by 1 knot. When using a combat grid and miniature ships, it represents a +1 hex of movement.	+1	1
Weaponry: Ship damage gains a +4 Pierce.	+1	1
Durability: PF +5 vs. Physical damage.	+2	1
Manoeuvrable: Normally a ship can only rotate a maximum of 45 degrees per rune played. This ability allows the ship to rotate an extra +45 degrees per rune played.	+1	3
Stability: Automatic +1 success on checks vs. capsize.	+2	2
Capacity: Add an extra 10 cubic feet of cargo space.	+3	1

By default, a ship's Size is 6 and its Speed is 1 knot. All effects stack on top of the default values.

The final QR determines how much damage the ship can deal and withstand. Every QR adds +4 damage when used to ram a sea creature or ship. Similarly, every QR adds 1 rune to the ship's rune bag (maximum 24). The final size of the ship determines the ship's crew capacity. Simply multiply the Size by 2 to determine the crew capacity.

Market value selling price is 75% of QR x 1,000 skatt.

Naval Battles

Embarking on naval travel comes with its own dangers, ranging from sea monsters to raiding vessels. If naval combat were to occur, the Norn may choose to resolve it in any number of ways. The dwellers may wish to use cinematic/generic actions to attempt fleeing the threat. The Norn should compare the ship's speed and manoeuvrability to the threat's ability to catch up in order to conclude the result. If the dwellers choose to fight or cannot escape then combat can be resolved in a few ways. The most common technique involves sailing up along side another ship, securing the two ships with grappling hooks and then boarding. Similar tactics could be applied to deep sea monsters. Master navigators will use their intimate knowledge of their ship to perform even more cunning and devious manoeuvres in order to wreak havoc on the enemy. Possible options:

Purely naval: The only combatants are the ship and naval enemies

Crew only: The dwellers, their thanes and the crew fight the crew of the other ship or sea monster(s)

Hybrid: The ship is treated as movable terrain and crew combat is the main focus

For combat purposes, abstracting crew members may be desirable. For rules on conducting massive battles, please see the "Mass Battles" section on page 357. This section could also be applied to massive naval battles involving dozens of ships.

Controlling the ship is heavily abstracted so that the games focus more on cinematic flavour rather than the technical aspects of sailing. Interacting with the ship requires someone on the ship to spend a rune to perform any of the following actions:

Movement: The ship moves in a straight line a number of hexes equal to its Speed (can move less)

Turn: The ship may rotate up to its maximum Manoeuvrability rating (can rotate less)

Anyone with at least 1 rank in Navigation could perform any of the following actions as well:

Ramming Damage: The ship can be driven into another ship or sea monster in order to deal damage. Ramming damage can be done only once per combat round and requires at least 5 hexes (25') of movement. The ship deals damage to the recipient and applies the Weaponry attribute if greater than 0. A ship cannot take Mental or Spiritual damage and it immune to conditions. When Physical damage is dealt, the ship uses the same Wounds track that was chosen for the adventure. The Norn may judge that a portion of the damage spills over to all crew members of the defending ship.

Capsizing Attack: Your ship can be rammed into the side of another vessel in an attempt to capsize it. Your ship must be of equal size or larger. Your ship's bow must strike other vessel's port or starboard. Half damage is dealt and the defending vessel must attempt to resist the capsize.

An attack, storm or monster may threaten to capsize your vessel. Resisting a capsize works as follows: The captain of the ship (the crew member at the rudder) performs a Navigation skill check. The skill check is usually based on the Physical trait and receives free successes equal to the Stability attribute of the ship. The opposed difficulty is either set by an arbitrary DR in the case of a storm or monster, or set by an opposed Navigation skill check by the attacking vessel's captain.

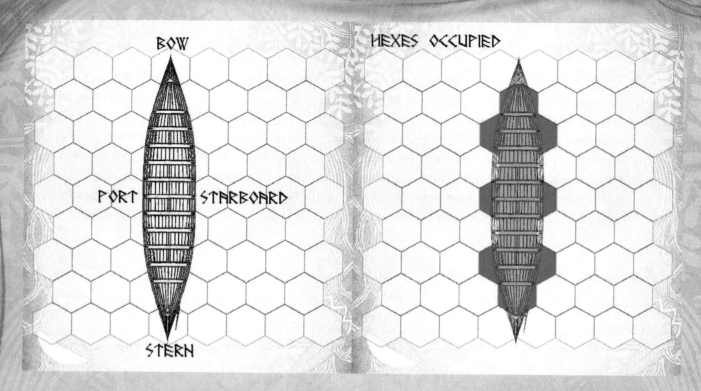

Whenever a skill check is required for piloting the ship, the default skill is "Navigation" (unless otherwise specified).

Magic Items

Assessing Magic Items
The Appraisal skill is used in not only determining the value of an item, but also the assessment of an item's crafted attributes. The Lore: Arcana skill allows someone to determine the magical properties of the item, which includes effects from Infuse, Brew, Sacred Wood Binding, Dvergar Engineering, Creature Reliquary and Realm Ores. As the Norn reveals the attributes and magic powers, they should ensure that the last effects to be revealed are Creature Reliquary followed by any Infuse anomalies.

Magic Items for Denizens and Thanes
Denizens and thanes can use any runes to activate magic item Active Powers. Denizen equipment restrictions are the same as those for dwellers, however thanes may only equip accessories. Some non-humanoid shaped denizens may be challenged in how many weapons they can wield given limbs that may not be able to hold items (ie. Wings, etc). In those cases the Norn may allow (at their own discretion) the denizen to benefit from more than one equipped accessory.

Destroying Magic Items
A damaged item may be destroyed outside of combat. It must be smashed and pulverized by a series of consecutive blows from a higher QR item. The Norn may judge that magic items over QR 30 need special instructions for their ultimate destruction. These instructions may be a small quest in itself.

Giving out Magic Items

The players could be comfortably equipped with items with QR equal to half their level. So a level 15 could have a set of QR 7 equipment, and a level 20 can have a set of QR 10 equipment. The good Blacksmith is capable of creating slightly better items with QR ranging from 50% to 75% of level. A very strong level 20 craft blacksmith could provide someone with 4 items of QR 15 quality. The table below helps to summarize the equipment curve. The last column adds up 4 average items that a typical dweller or denizen could equip (2 weapons, 1 armour and 1 accessory).

Table 18: Suggested Magic Equipment Table

Level	Average 1-item QR	Powerful 1-item QR	Total Avg Equipped Gear QR
10	5	8	20
20	10	15	40
30	15	23	60
40	20	30	80

Although rare, it is possible to find an item with unused QR. Wyrd 2 runes and consult the table below to determine if there are any unused QR:

Table 19: Magic Item Unused QR Table

Wyrd Result	Unused QR
⬜⬜	0
⬜⬜	0
⬜⬜	0
⬜⬜	1
⬜⬜	2
⬜⬜	3

Buying and selling magic items should not be a common occurrence. Most magic items hold special meaning in the eyes of their owners and carry a history with them. When there is a market for magic items, they are usually sold for an amount of Skatt equal to the QR squared x 10. A QR 7 item would sell for 490 Skatt. This will fluctuate based on the merchant and the health of the market in the area.

Limited Knowledge of Magic Items

At the Norn's discretion, dwellers may be limited to what they can harness and exploit from a magic item. The reasoning may be that despite holding a legendary sword, the dweller doesn't have the wisdom required to utilize the full potential of this exquisite blade. The same reasoning can be extended to Blacksmiths creating items. The rule of thumb that could be used is: limit the amount of QR usable by the wielder/crafter to 75%. Meaning a level 12 dweller may be wielding a QR 15 axe, but they cannot benefit from more than 9 QR worth of attributes/infusions/etc...

Extending this to crafting, a Blacksmith may create an item with a significant amount of QR, but the amount that could be used for crafted attributes and infused powers would be limited to 75% of the Blacksmith's level. This would create an item with unused QR that could later be used by a higher level blacksmith.

Managing a Business or Community

Since the onset of Fimbulwinter, eternal night and unrelenting winters have torn the social fabric of Midgard. Towns and villages in the interior were the first to crumble. These communities hunted animals for the first few months, but the increasingly cold temperatures forced the animals to the coast where the climate was more forgiving. This forced those living in the mountainous interior to abandon their towns and migrate to the coast. Those living on the coast sustained themselves with hunting and fishing, but the added refugees strained the food and wood supply. Long range lumber foraging expeditions did not fare well, as many did not return. Some were ambushed and captured by slavers, others were attacked and killed by large and hungry predators.

Within the first two years, most larger coastal centers crumbled from their own weight. High demand and consumption of both firewood and food was the main reason. Compounding that, the all-too-common scenario of densely packed houses with desperate people were a volatile situation... a powder keg waiting to explode.

Some of those who left the towns and villages found themselves at the mercy of roving bandits and slave traders. The others established new homes in the unoccupied corners of Midgard. The First Age saw the population decline as the weak and vulnerable died off.

The start of the second age saw the emergence of warlords, those who capitalized on the chaos and carved out a kingdom for themselves. They weren't shy to buy slaves in order to achieve their goals. Others made their fortunes by stockpiling food and wood and selling it at exorbitant prices. The success of the warlords and their outposts began a movement where people came back into community life. Only those with something to offer, something of value, were admitted into the outposts. With the promise of food and shelter, these warlords could exact a tax over their new subjects.

A time may come when the dwellers establish a business or even an outpost of their own.

Running a Business

A dweller may begin play with an operational business that has survived the First Age of Ragnarok. It is even conceivable that a dweller may have established a business capitalizing on some market demand for a particular good or service. The following rules will aid a Norn that is tasked with managing the profits and losses of such a business. After all, the dweller is most likely an adventurer that wishes the business to run itself while the they are away on grand adventures.

Table 20: Business Profits

Wyrd Result	Profits
⬜⬜	+25%
⬜⬜	-100%(Disaster*)
⬜⬜	+75% (Innovation*)
⬜⬜	+50%
⬜⬜	-25%
⬜⬜	-50%

*Innovation: the staff have discovered a way to optimize the business and the monthly profit baseline has increased by +75%. The Norn is encouraged to detail the innovation they have found.

*Disaster: the business is in big trouble, a rival has attacked it and has possibly taken it over. The business requires immediate attention or it is lost forever. The Norn should add other possible disaster scenarios based on the story.

The Norn should ask the player to present the nature of the business and the staff that he would have on hand. Part of the initial role-play will determine the size and profitability of the operation. The Norn will have the final say on any aspect pertaining to the business. The player can also design methods of communication with their business while they are gallivanting on adventures. For example employing a runner may be a way of keeping in touch with the business, as well as a good way to have a runner come and deliver the monthly profits to their owner.

When an adventurer gets money every month from a store or business they own the Norn can consult the table below to see how it is doing. The Norn should draw two runes per month of operation.

The dweller should keep track of how much money remains in the business in case negative profits (loss) eats into the reserves. Operational costs can be abstracted and don't need to be managed. In the interest of simplicity the dweller should only apply monthly profits or losses.

Example: A player has started a chicken farm after inheriting a bunch of live chickens and discovering an abandoned grainery. He and the Norn discuss the operation, the setup costs, the required staff and the local demand for eggs and chickens. Their conclusion is that the farm can net him 20,000 skatt per month in profits (after covering all operational expenses). He has no capital saved up, so he hopes his first month will be profitable. A loss will mean he loses staff and inventory requiring the Norn to reassess the monthly profit baseline.

Establishing an Outpost

Should the dwellers find themselves leading a throng of refugees, they will need more than charismatic leadership skills to care for the flock. If the Norn needs to determine the composition of the followers, the table on page 140 in the *Core Rulebook* can be used. Any instances that seem inappropriate could be substituted with additional instances of "thrall". Finding a suitable location for an outpost becomes the first pressing question. The Norn may consult the runes to randomly generate the surrounding riches (known or unknown). The terrain wealth table below outlines the possible outcomes for the site. Some resources may only become apparent after some additional exploration. The Norn may also allow players to perform Survival: Wilderness skill checks with positive results resulting in multiple draws for terrain wealth.

Table 21: Terrain Wealth

Wyrd Result	Average r-item QR	Powerful r-item QR	Total Avg Equipped Gear QR
⬜⬜	Sustain 50 people	Sparse Terrain	None
⬜⬜	Sustain 100 people	Sparse Terrain	None
⬜⬜	Sustain 500 people	Sparse Terrain	None
⬜⬜	Sustain 1,000 people	Average Terrain	1,000 skatt value/month
⬜⬜	Sustain 5,000 people	Average Terrain	5,000 skatt value/month
⬜⬜	Sustain 10,000 people	Bountiful Terrain	10,000 skatt value/month

The "crafting materials" column references the information in the "foraging for raw materials" section above (see page 348).

The wealth column results are never immediately apparent. Discovery requires further exploration which would take from several days to several months.

The next step involves the construction of the outpost. The Norn may allow the foraging and construction efforts to be group effort, thus scaled by all able-bodied members of the outpost.

Outpost Considerations:

Shelter: How will you build your homes to protect your citizens from the deadly elements?
Heat: What will you burn to keep warm? Will you have enough furs from hunting and trapping?
Food: Who can hunt and who can fish? Can the fishing efforts be bolstered by longships?
Security: Will ramparts and palisades be built? How about an ice trench?
Sanitation and health: How are the sick cared for? How will waste be managed?
Death and burial: How will the dead be honoured? Spare wood for funeral pyres or carve out crypts?

The Norn and the players should work together in establishing the costs, logistics and construction of the outpost. The players should be encouraged to draw out their new town, flesh-out their followers and assign a name to their new home.

Once it has been built, monthly operations are summarized in three separate rune pulls on the "outpost events" table below. The first 2-rune pull describes how much the town has managed to stockpile. The next 2-rune pull presents the dwellers with a major event. The third 2-rune pull introduces a minor event that helps shape the town's legacy. The major and minor events are way to advance the town's status, history and character. If the dwellers are present, then they can role play the events. Conversely, if they are away from their outpost when the events occur, they could receive news of what has transpired in their absence.

Table 22: Outpost Events

Wyrd Result	Resources Harvested	Major Event	Minor Event(s)
⬜⬜	Business as usual, the population is satisfied with your rule.	A denizen of renown comes to visit your outpost.	More refugees arrive at the town (population growth +10%).
⬜⬜	Blessings from the higher powers, all collected materials are +50%.	A mysterious artifact is found. It has a profound impact on the outpost and/or its populace.	Outpost is attacked and your town suffers casualties (population loss -10%). Reduce loss for well designed defenses.
⬜⬜	Bountiful harvest, all collected materials are +25%.	Monster(s) rampage through the outpost. Perhaps they came from the countryside or some sorcerer inadvertently opened a portal to another realm.	A major blizzard besieges the outpost for most of the month making it impossible to leave/reach. If insufficient food and wood reserves exist, morale diminishes.
⬜⬜	Food stocks have degraded, reduce the food sources level by one category.	An Einherjar or Son of Muspel come to the area. They are on a quest for their liege.	Someone steals some valuable assets from the outpost (longships, stockpiles, etc).
⬜⬜	Crafting material has become more sparse (degrade the terrain quality- Sparse terrain becomes barren).	Druids have discovered a way to improve the land (upgrade the terrain type by one level maximum "bountiful").	A massive influx of refugees arrive at the gates (population growth +20%).
⬜⬜	Wealth resources have run out.	Merchants come to setup a market in your outpost. Taxation revenue increases by 15%.	A sickness ravages the outpost (population loss -10%).

The other statistics that both players and the Norn may choose to track are the happiness index and taxation. Depending on the relationship between the lords of the outpost (dwellers) and the populace (denizens), taxation may be something that is instituted in order to cover costs that relate to outpost infrastructure.

The players should keep track of their material stockpiles, population and wealth. The Norn should track the outpost's notoriety as passing travelers carry news.

Mass Battles

Sometimes battles break out where individual unit powers are irrelevant. There are simply so many combatants that the battle must be resolved at a macro level. Each side of the battle should abstract 1 or more units and represent them with a single rune. Each army's Essence would be the sum of those runes. Runes are chosen at random and placed in an army Essence bag.

Example: King Erik Blood Axe is facing Hakon the Good's army, with 800 units under Erik's banner and 1,000 under Hakon's. The Norn could assign 50 units per rune. One side would have 16 runes and the other 20. These runes are placed into their respective bags and they become each army's Essence attribute.

The Destiny would be determined by the level of the commander, the state of the army and any Norn assigned mitigating factors. The default minimum Destiny is 1.

Table 23: Army Destiny Modifiers Table

Factor	Destiny Bonus
Commander	+1 Destiny per 10 levels
Rested and fed	+1 Destiny
Blessing of a high power	+1 or more Destiny

Example: Both kings are level 28, granting them a Destiny of 3 (1 base +2 from the commander bonus). King Hakon's army is tired after crossing the sea, but Erik's forces are rested as they await the invasion so Erik's army is boosted to Destiny 4.

Each army must bind their Traits to different Active powers. Bind 1 Active power per Trait. Choices should be made based on the composition of the army. Duplicate choices are not permitted.

Table 24: Army Active Powers Table

Druids and Galdrs [Amplify Amplify Maintain] Heal +2

Maidens of Ratatosk and Sceadugengan [Amplify Amplify Amplify] Parry 4 {defend action}

Berzerkirs and Ulfhednars [Amplify Amplify Amplify] Deal 2 Physical damage {attack action}

Fardrengir and Seithkonas [Amplify Amplify Amplify] Deal 1 Mental damage

Blacksmiths and Stalos [Amplify Maintain Maintain] Attack actions gain +1 damage bonus

Skalds and the Godi [Amplify Amplify Amplify] Deal 1 Physical damage, or 3 Physical damage if Bloodied {attack action}

Example: King Erik's army is reinforced by his wife's witches from the north. His entourage are skalds and ragers. His army binds Physical runes to Fardrengir and Seithkonas, binds Mental runes to Skalds and Godi and binds Spiritual runes to Berzerkirs and Ulfhednars.

Each army must bind their 3 Traits to different Passive powers. Bind 1 Passive power per Trait. Duplicate choices are not permitted.

Table 25: Army Passive Powers Table

Horses: Move +1

Spectacular Weapons: DF +1

Spectacular Armour: PF +1 while not Bloodied

Magic: Pierce +2

Nature Affinity: Heal and Parry effects are boosted by +1 when Bloodied

Luck of the Divine: perform an Ultimate Sacrifice +1 to Wyrd 2 extra runes (usable once per combat round)

Example: King Erik's army binds Magic, Luck of the Divine and Nature Affinity.

Combat is resolved assuming both armies are within striking distance of each other, so no positioning is required. Initiative is set as usual, and both sides slug it out dealing damage to each other's Essence bags. Active powers will be used most of the time, but any rune can also be used for a Generic Attack action (deal 1 Physical damage), Generic Defend action (block 1 Physical damage) or Generic Move. As the battle drags on, fatigue sets in and mistakes are made. The Norn should either boost attack or penalize defense in order to break any stalemates.

If an army chooses to disengage and flee the battlefield, they must have an overall superior movement rate. By default each army has a Move of 3. Army Passive powers can boost this. Every rune played grants 3 move (plus any bonuses). If 12 hexes of distance are achieved then the army has retreated successfully.

The Norn should feel free to add more modifiers based on terrain or other battlefield details.

Summon Rules – Thanes & Mounts

In the *Core Rulebook* you will find several "Summon" Passive powers. It isn't stated explicitly, but you can split up your thane levels for more than one thane. If you have 15 levels of effigy, they could be split over two effigies: a level 6 effigy and a level 9 effigy for example.

Also for thanes that grow in size with level such as the effigy, it is reasonable to allow the player to limit the size of the effigy. For an organic thane such as an animal it would be less likely, but for something manufactured and animated, the Norn can use their discretion.

Vikings did not have a military force that was mounted. Cavalry tactics didn't exist, but that is not to say warriors did not know how to fight from atop a mount. In Fate of the Norns: Ragnarok, both dwellers and denizens may end up with mounts both mundane (horses) and mythical (drakes). Mounts should be handled much like thanes. If they are involved in combat, then they get a level assignment and in turn get an Essence bag and an assigned Destiny. Unless they are a special thane granted by a Passive power, they will only be able to perform generic actions. Should the Norn choose, the mount will also have an initiative tile assigned to them.

For a creature to be considered as a Mount it must be larger than the rider. In some cases the Norn may suspend this requirement due to special situations and/or considerations. Denizens designated as "mount" types have Active and Passive powers that create a powerful synergy with a rider.

The advantage to having a mount in combat is that it allows the dweller to use the mount's runes for movement while retaining their own for other actions. Mounts also permit a rider to wear better armour since the encumbrance penalties will be ignored. The down side of a mount is that it will most likely be of lower level than the dweller and may die quickly in a combat that has a lot of area type damage.

For those players who wish to keep increasing the level of their mount after taking all possible "summon" Passive powers available to them may, at the discretion of the Norn, gain access to the new mount Passive powers board (see below). If access is granted and the dweller has exhausted all summon possibilities of a particular kind, when they level up they may choose to unlock a passive power on the Extra Mount Passive Power Board. The board cells with "Summon" allow a dweller to gain an increase in a particular summon they already have. Other bonuses are types that are conferred to the mount. Norns should not grant access to this board while a mount's level exceeds its rider's level.

Summon	Mount PF +1 P	Summon	Mount PF +1 P	Summon
Mount DF +2 P	Summon	Mount PF +1 P	Summon	Mount Parry +2
Summon	Mount DF +2 P	**Extra Mount Passive Power Board**	Mount Parry +2	Summon
Mount DF +2 P	Summon	Mount Heal +2 during Upkeep	Summon	Mount Parry +2
Summon	Mount Heal +2 during Upkeep	Summon	Mount Heal +2 during Upkeep	Summon

Prepared Powers

The combat system aims to create a very competitive environment that is based on a strong foundation of first round balance. This is achieved by ensuring combat begins without any side having an unfair advantage. However, there may be some compelling narrative reasons as to why some individuals may begin combat with some powers already activated. For example some game groups may wish to eschew the game balance and allow an Ulfhednar who was in wolf form prior to hostilities breaking out, to begin combat with the Maintained power already placed In-Play. This is a valid option, which may be extended by allowing every combatant who was maintaining an active power to begin with 2 runes already in play on round 1 (the active power and a maintain meta). In exchange, the combatant would draw 2 less runes on the first round of combat.

Building upon this rule, if a combat breaks out as a result of a very specific action, then the individual who precipitates the action would be placed at the top of the initiative chain. That individual would pre-draw the runes required for the action into their In-Hand pile and then be forced to play them for the action when they lead off the combat. The runes that were pre-drawn would reduce the initial Wyrd by that amount.

Example: Vanadis the Seithkona attempts to cast Shrink upon the merchant after the negotiations go sour. This action is very hostile and will precipitate a combat. Vanadis looks through her Essence bag and takes the rune bound to the Shrink power. This rune is placed In-Hand. She then draws 1 less rune when drawing runes for the first round of combat. When her action phase rolls around, she is obligated to cast the Shrink power on the merchant. She may add as many meta tags as she wishes.

Projectile Weapons

A certain level of abstraction is utilized when dealing with projectile weapons. There is no need to count arrows and likewise there's no need to count throwing daggers, axes or javelins. When purchasing thrown weapons and ammunition, the Norn may wish to sell a "bundle" that is sufficient for a combat. This approach eliminates any need for bookkeeping and overhead that would slow down a combat unnecessarily.

Portals to Other Realms

How do portals between worlds come about? Alkas are created by the proximity of two realms. Should Alkas be amplified sufficiently, then a rupture can occur allowing an opening to form between both realms. If a dweller or denizen has the capabilities to cast an Alka Active power with five Amplify metas, then they can open a temporary portal to another realm. Eight Amplify metas would be enough to create a permanent pathway between two realms.

This kind of magic carries significant risk. A portal is much more permeable than an Alka. As such, much more of the realmís essence will pour through... not to mention possibly hostile denizens from beyond! Great care should be taken with each portal created as the destination is truly random within the chosen realm.

Sizes Beyond Massive

There will be some creatures like the Borghild which are moving battlefields. Norse myths are full of massive giants and we present some rules for the truly colossal!

A combatant will take up more than 1 hex when they get to size 6. Beyond that please consult the table to see how many hexes they will occupy:

Table 26: Sizes Beyond Massive Table

Size	Hexes occupied
6	2
10	3
14	4
18	5
22	6
Etc...	Etc...

For many multi-hex creatures, their anatomy and ability to turn would allow them to originate an attack from any hex which they occupy. When they complete a move, or are receiving an attack, care should be taken to define which hexes are front facing and which are rear facing- all adjacent hexes should be split 50/50 between front and rear facing.

Occupying more than one hex on the combat play-mat does not imply that the multi-hex combatant would be struck more than once by an Alka or a spell with an Area meta. Under some particular circumstances, however, the Norn may choose to allow the combatant to be struck more than once due to size. The application of double or triple effect should be used judiciously.

At a certain point smaller occupants can start sharing the same hexes as a larger creature. The general rule of thumb is that if the creature is 3 or more sizes larger than you, then you can occupy the same space as that large creature (either standing beneath it, or on top of it).

A very large creature may opt to target ALL occupants sharing his location (same hexes) as the target of a physical attack. This should be limited to once per combat round since the creature would have to move in an awkward fashion to achieve this. Again the Norn could allow for multiple such attacks per round under certain conditions. Treat the creatures in the same hex as adjacent or within reach of a weapon when adjusting an Active power to work with this rule.

Example: If a size 22 Borghild walked over and stood over several smaller enemies, one Attack action could strike all enemies within the shared hexes. These enemies would have to be size 19 or smaller.

At a certain size differential, the larger creature starts to receive penalties when attempting to strike a tiny target. The Norn should grant a temporary situation based Shroud intensity to a smaller target when the attacker is 8 sizes or greater. The Shroud intensity should be considered at 4 when the size differential is 16 sizes or more. This Shroud bonus would be only applied against the specific attack and not marked on the combatant's playmat.

Starting Dwellers off at Higher Levels

Some sagas may have the Norn asking players to make dwellers that are higher level than the usual starting range of level 8 to 12. In those cases, starting wealth and life-path rune pulls should be scaled up. The rule of thumb that the Norn can use is a multiplier that is applied every 3 levels. Up until level 12, all dweller generation tables are used as presented in the *Core Rulebook*. At level 13 to 15 the table benefits are doubled to represent life experience and wealth accumulation. At level 16 to 18 the amount should be tripled; so on and so forth.

Non-numerical benefits should also be scaled. Being higher level means the dweller has had extra life experiences which may grant added benefits such as extra allies on the connections table.

Shapechanged and Transformed

With the advent of new player archetypes, the possibilities of mixing and matching different shapechanges and transformations becomes more prevalent. It is important to point out that if you are already shapechanged, then performing another shapechange overwrites the previous one. Likewise, if you are transformed, then the new transform overwrites the previous one. If you are transformed, and then you shapechange, then that is a legitimate stacking effect.

Animal-shaped beings would have a very hard time wearing equipment that isnít specifically crafted for them. When a dweller or denizen shapechanges or transforms into a bestial form, all of their items merge into their new form and they are considered to have no equipped items. The items that suit such a form are usually an accessory and to use it effectively the combatant must drop the item before the shapechange/transformation and then pick it up in the new form. This would require the playing of a rune to pick up and equip the accessory. Alternatively an ally can bestow the accessory when the ally shapechanges/transforms, deferring the rune payment to the ally. New shapes that permit quadruped movement are at odds with equipped weapons. Should a special shape grant the quadruped ability and allow for weapons to be equipped, the movement bonus granted by quadruped wouldn't be applicable unless the combatant's limbs are free.

Transformed dwellers retain the Void rune bindings (Active power, Passive power and skill).

Simple Tactics Runic Game System (STRGS)

Some play groups may not want to play with a hex grid and miniature figurines. For those types of games, certain concepts may need to be generalized. Below are a list of concepts and a simple mechanic on how to translate more tactical powers to more generalized effects.

Range & Area of Effect

STRGS abstracts range, positioning and area of effect into 3 categories: Adjacent, Near and entire Battlefield. This replaces the typical ranges and areas calculated with hexes or 5' increments. STRGS allows term near to be defined by each individual play group. When setting up a scene, the Norn will decide if combatants are near to one another or not.

Power Conversions

All powers that are adjacent remain adjacent

All powers that have range (or area) are considered to have a range/area of near

Any adjacent powers that get a Range or Area meta will become near

Any near powers that get a Range or Area meta will become battlefield

Alkas are considered to cover the area adjacent to the caster (Amplify metas will allow greater coverage)

Item Conversions

All unarmed attacks and 1-handed melee weapons (for human size) are treated as adjacent

All 2-handed melee weapons (for human size) are treated as near

All ranged weapons are treated as battlefield

Power Effect Conversions

Some powers have effects that are highly tactical in nature. Below is a conversion chart that converts a tactical effect into a much more narrative-friendly effect.

Tactical Power	Narrative Power
Any power that pushes or pulls an opponent	Push someone out of near range or pull someone into near range.
Movement bonus	Receiving a move bonus of any kind changes weak move actions into regular move actions.
Weak move action	You may change your relative location to someone else by 1 level (example: battlefield becomes near or near becomes adjacent).
Move action	Place yourself anywhere on the battlefield.
Alkas	Alka effect hits everything nearby.
Amplified Alkas	Alka effect hits everything on the battlefield.

Wyrd

Anyone drawing more runes than their allotted Destiny in a single combat round stresses their body, mind and soul. It is not something ordained by the Norns and the price gets steeper with every incremental transgression. As a global rule, drawing one extra rune from a power that may allow you to Wyrd +1 causes no harm. The harm begins when two or more extra runes are drawn. Consult the table below for the mandatory Sacrifice costs. All of the costs are cumulative. Drawing 4 runes would cause a total of one minor, moderate and major sacrifice.

Table 27: STRGS Power Effects Conversions Table

Extra Wyrd	Sacrifice				
	None	Minor	Moderate	Major	Ultimate
2		+1			
3		+1	+1		
4		+1	+1	+1	
5		+1	+1	+1	+1
6		+1	+1	+1	+2

Drawing 7 runes or more keeps compounding the Ultimate Sacrifice.

New Lifepath Tables

During dweller creation many players and Norns may choose to use the tables from the *Core Rulebook* spanning from page 138 to 144. These tables are useful when the play group wishes to quickly draft up a background for their dwellers. Below are a new set of extended tables in order to build a deeper and more engaging randomly generated back-story.

Early Life

The Early Life table helps place a dweller in the world. It also gives them a family connection as well as two critical events in their lives. These key events should be elaborated upon by the player and the Norn should encourage players to build up a colourful story around both events. The Norn may choose to impose limits to the player defined back-story to ensure that it fits within the parameters of the Norn's world.

The "Early Life" table should have a separate rune pull for every column.

Rune	Birth Place	Family	Defining Event	Scarring Event
	Norrland	Orphaned	You were recognized for a great deed that elevated your reputation	Childhood rival
	Jamtland	Orphaned	You have had tremendous success in the romantic arena	Almost died in a natural disaster
	Helsingland	Orphaned	You made a great friend who always looks out for your wellbeing	Close friend was declared an outlaw
	Uppland	Orphaned	You had a childhood pet with whom you went on great adventures	Forced to leave home
	Svealand	Estranged from your family	Many years ago you came into great wealth	Lover was abducted
	Gotaland	Estranged from your family	Reputation: your heroic deeds have spread far and wide	Mercilessly beaten and robbed
	Smaland	Estranged from your family	You saved someone's life, and a higher power rewarded you	Had to pay a weregild to settle a intra-family feud
	Skane	Estranged from your family	You brewed an especially legendary cask of mead	Close friend murdered
	Zealand	One surviving parent/sibling	You overcame a strange illness that claimed the lives of many	Failed at a critical task that greatly impacted your life
	Jutland	One surviving parent/sibling	Defeating a criminal organization you came upon a far reaching plot	Personal integrity was besmirched in front of important people
	RanRike	One surviving parent/sibling	You received a good omen from a Voelva pertaining to your future	Accused of a crime you did not commit
	Vestfold	One surviving parent/sibling	During your travels you discovered a wondrous place	Witnessed a deeply dark and disturbing magical event
	Rogaland	Two surviving family members	You have endeared yourself to someone with great power	Implicated as the main reason your warband was defeated
	Hordaland	Two surviving family members	Something you did has attracted the attention of a higher power	Witnessed a traumatizing predatory assault
	Sogn	Two surviving family members	You saved your town from disaster, the townsfolk are eternally grateful	Raised by an abusive parental figure
	Trondelag	Two surviving family members	A magical effect has left your body with an indelible benefit	Trauma induced psychotic episode that negatively impacted your reputation
	Halogaland	Three surviving family members	Several people owe you favours	Someone with great means wants you to suffer
	Shetland	Three surviving family members	Someone died and left you a map to a hidden "treasure"	Lost a non-vital body part
	Orkney	Four surviving family members	The killing or sparing of someone's life has set your moral compass	Lover was killed
	Alba	Five surviving family members	A Godi is forever in your debt, granting you blessings in a domain	You witnessed something you shouldn't have
	Hibernia	Six surviving family members	You were able to witness the wonders of a realm outside Midgard	A blow to the head has left you with extensive memory loss
	Strathclyde	Seven surviving family members	An important choice you made resulted in an ally and an enemy	You suffered a great betrayal
	Northumbria	Eight surviving family members	Someone you admire has shown you a life path you have chosen to follow	Pregnancy- your partner left you
	Svalbard	Nine surviving family members	You found true love	You have offspring that harbours ill will and resentment towards you
	Islandia	Family lineage can be traced back to a dynastic ancestry (choose how many family members are alive)	A higher power has blessed you with omens, granting you purpose	Personally lost a very important family heirloom

Brushes With Power

The Norn may wish to have the dwellers assume a more heroic role. The back-stories below were designed to build and amplify tension in an already dangerous world. Heroes know people in high places and the longer their lifespan, the more significant their interactions become. Many of the referenced characters can be found in the "Legends and Villains" chapter (page 14). For every 10 years of their lives, the dweller should Wyrd 1 rune and

Rune	Civil	Royal	Divine
ᛏ	You met an important merchant that returned from Miklagard. You may purchase a rare item.	You visited the court of King Aethelstan in Winchester. Gain a social contact from the Witenagemot.	While fulfilling a bounty on an outlaw's head you burned down a saw mill. The local land Vaettir has chosen to bless you for clearing this blight from her lands.
ᚲ	You angered a local Angel of Death who now has refused to bury you when the time comes. She has also put out the word to her sisters in the adjoining petty kingdoms.	Your visit to the port of Winchester has resulted in an altercation with crusaders. Edmund the Just wants your head.	You witnessed horror upon the high seas- a glimpse of the terrifying Jormungand which leaves you mentally and emotionally scarred.
ᛒ	During a raid on the Baltic sea you gained the respect of a local tribal chief. He owes you a debt.	While playing the game of braids in King Bjorn Eriksson's mead hall you win some wagers and his respect.	Svalms the Dvergar has hired you to fetch some special ores from Finnmark. Upon return you are rewarded handsomely.
ᛜ	During your travels to far eastern lands you managed to offend Baba Yaga's sensibilities. You receive a peculiar curse.	King Bjorn Farmann has mistakenly identified you as an assassin sent by King Erik Bloodaxe. You find no quarter in his lands.	Odin the wanderer has marked you as a promising hero. Since that day your encounters have become increasingly challenging and deadly.
ᛗ	You crossed paths with Einar of the Storjunkari and his witches. They read the bones and prophesied that your paths would cross again under very different circumstances.	You performed an errand for the late King Harald Fairhair. His eldest son, King Erik Bloodaxe, remembers your good deed.	You helped a Jarl who is strategic to Farbauti the Muspeli Jotun. He rewards you with a torch which will never consumed nor extinguished.
ᛞ	While you were in Islandia, Erik the Red engaged you in an athletic competition. You beat him and he has been habouring a murderous grudge ever since.	You were asked to deliver an ultimatum from the court of Northumbria to Alba. The news infuriated Constantine and he grudgingly spared your life, promising death if you should ever re-enter his kingdom.	You trespass into the sacred cave of Pohjola and witness the presence of Skoll and Hati. Fright drives you away and you are unsure what to do with this knowledge. Many would kill those with such information.
ᛖ	Erik the Frost Bear saved your life while your ship was adrift and damaged after a storm. You owe him a favour and you know he'll be back to cash it.	While traveling in a far north you came across Queen Drifa and her elite warband. You provided her a map of the south in exchange of a map of the north.	Angrboda visited you in a dream, revealing Loki's predicament and she promised a reward so vast you considered it even if your allegiance was to the gods.
ᛟ	Long ago you visited Islandia's eastern shores. There you met an ulfhednar price named Halfdan Ingvarsson. He didn't like your presence in his ancestral lands and he chased you off with his warband.	While visiting the Danevirke, some in your group went missing. As you searched for their whereabouts you were chased off by hostile emissaries working for King Gorm the Old.	An Einherjar hired a legendary but drunk Fardrengir. He asked the Fardrengir to lead him to a secret cave. Hours later you hired the same Fandrengir for more coin but for a different task. The drunk took you instead of the stingy Einherhar. Now the Einherjar wants your head.
ᚺ	While in Ath Cliath and making arrangements for a ship bound for Norveig you med Ingrid the Wanderer. She shared many tales of far away places which ignited your wanderlust.	On the way through Jutland you saved a caravan from bandits. You escorted it to the Danevirke and discovered that the caravan carried much needed supplies. King Gorm the Old personally thanked and rewarded you.	Thor found you camped out in the ruins of a shrine dedicated to the Rime Jotun Hrungnir. He was unsure whether to thank you or kill you! Had to smashed the shrine, or had you come to pay homage. Your sharp wit and quick tongue saved you that day.
ᛃ	After being awarded a job contract by a petty king, you were ousted and replaced by Hildolfr's mercenar-ies. Demanding justice, you were threatened and run out of town by the leader of the Battle Wolves.	While in Ath Cliath you attended a banquet in King Sitric's honour. You displeased your host and he had you arrested. During your rigged trial you were stripped of title and re-branded as a slave.	The Vanir goddess Freya took pity on you while you pined on an object of your desire. She helped you, then marked you with with a blessing that will help you in fulfilling your next desire.
ᚾ	While visiting Evingard on business you met with Karl Ingvar. He was pleased with your wares and sense of humour and looks forward to your return.	While in the Great Isles you met Hakon the Good on a hunting trip. You learned more about the Harald Fairhair family tree as well as the politics and scheming.	In an effort to keep warm on the island of Svalbard, you were forced to build a makeshift shelter from ice and snow. The next morning you found the mark of Bergelmir on a block of ice. He has shown interest in you... for good or ill.
ᛈ	Getting lost on the eastern side of Islandia, you met a welcoming druid named Ivar Iron Root. You fell prey to his ensorcellment and were temporarily turned into a soft slave. You barely escaped with your life.	Months ago your wanderlust led you to the Northern reaches of the Baltic sea. There you met mistress Louhi of Pohjola. She was pleasant until you tried to enter the sacred caves. She became very angered and hostile and you thought it best to leave.	In order to give the dead a proper burial, you engaged in ferrying the deceased from the Shetland islands to Alba's coast where an Angel of Death awaited your arrival. Along the way a wave capsized your boat condemning the dead to the depths. Ran, Vanir goddess of the sea has taken notice of your unintended sacrifice to her.
ᛁ	You met a mountain of a man named Leif the Mountain Shaker. You both got drunk and proceeded to rampage across the countryside.	While in Ath Cliath you gained audience with King Sitric. He had heard of your great exploits and tasked you with hunting his enemy- the Hibernian clans.	While were hunting in the forests of Helsingland, two wolves joined in the hunt. They corralled the prey in your direction. When you slew the prey, you dedicated one of the killed to Geri and Freki. Soon afterwards two ravens were seen in the skies above. Odin has taken notice of your deeds.

consult the "Brushes with Power" table below. The first 10 years would result in a civil relationship, the next decade a royal relationship and the following decade a divine relationship. Older dwellers would restart the cycle at "civil" and repeat. For example a 42 year old dweller would Wyrd 4 times on the table, noting a result from the civil column, followed by the royal column, then the divine column and finally the civil column once more.

Table 30: Brushes With Power Table

Rune	Civil	Royal	Divine
ᚤ	Years ago you attempted the trade route to Miklagard. On the way your ship was intercepted by Koschey the Deathless. You lost your cargo and barely escaped with your lives.	While being high-profile prisoners of the crusaders you had a brief moment to interact with Emperor Otto the Great. He spoke briefly while assessing your worth for an exchange of hostages with King Gorm the Old of the Danevirke.	One of your past jobs was to guard the causeway to your chieftain's crannog. The relief to your shift never came, but you stayed steadfast for 3 days and night. Heimdall took notice and left you gift beneath the causeway.
ᚢ	You were hired by a n aspiring merchant named Magnus Magnusson. He wanted to you to prospect a new mining operation and report back with your findings.	While returning from Islandia to Jutland you stopped in the Faroe Islands. Trondur i Gotu was overjoyed with your gifts of fine lumber. You were treated to a feast and unforgettable bardic tales.	You discovered an ancient temple to Gulveig. Despite her death, you felt her presence. The next few nights were filled with dreams of the legendary Fafnir's Treasure.
ᚦ	You were captured by the Crusaders and brought before one of their tribunals in Francia. You were convicted for the "crimes" of your ancestors and sentenced to death. Luckily you managed to escape before the execution.	In a very important and daring trading expedition you ventured to the south, into Outer Midgard, to an exotic city called Roma. There you met with Pope John XII and his conclave while trading in fine northern goods. Due to your refusal in becoming a grossly underpaid lackey, he scuttled the entire trade deal.	You were on the trail of an outlaw. He had been responsible for arson, theft and pranks to different communities along the Sogn coast. When you finally caught and surrounded him your were taken aback by his arrogance and sharp tongue. He managed to talk you into letting him go and after he left you discovered that you had been pickpocketed! Could it have been Loki himself?
ᚨ	Olaf Hoskuldsson, a prosperous merchant of the Laxdal region of Islandia hired you to import important goods from Skiringssal to Laxdal.	While visiting Kalevala you met the local hero Vainamoinen. You experienced first hand the prosperity that the Sampo has brought to his lands.	Many years ago you were at the back of an army that was marching upon Svalbard. Suddenly, out of the darkness, a titanic wolf maw swallowed up half the army in one gulp. without second thought, the rest of the army fled from Fenrir.
ᚱ	A storm blew your ship off course, stranding you at Iona abbey. The Abbott extended his hospitality so long as you renounce your pagan beliefs while under his roof.	Many years back King Harald Fairhair sent his son Erik Blood Axe to the far north. You accompanied him on a mission to kill Rognvald the sorcerer king. In his dying breath, Rognvald pronounced a powerful curse upon Erik's entire warband.	A decade ago your quest took you to see the Dvergar named Fjalar and Galar. The item you would need crafted would require the hearts of several prominent Jarls. This was only the first ingredient. Deciding that the price was too steep, you abandoned the quest. It haunts you to this day.
ᚾ	While you visited south western Islandia, you met a man named Thorsteinn Ingolfsson. He had invited you to attend the very first Althing which was to occur many months later.	King Bjorn Eriksson lost a longship race to you and your crew. He took it very badly and ordered your ship burned. To this day you avoid his kingdom in fear of a lingering grudge.	An elite warband was being formed by queen Drifa. You enlisted and passed the training. The first quest took you to Jotunheim to meet with the mighty Rime Jotun Thrym. His objective was challenging and you were grievously wounded requiring several months of recovery.
ᚲ	Your travels took you far west to Gronland. While there you were continuously harassed by the fearsome Skraeling. Their Angakkuq demanded your retreat or surrender.	King Bjorn Farmann received word of your benevolent deeds within his kingdom. He summoned you to his court to thank you personally.	After getting separated from your adventuring party you wandered the wilderness without food nor water. After several days, delirious, you stared up into the sun. You saw the branches of Yggdrasil beyond the clouds and atop them a celestial eagle looking down upon you. The vision guided you safely home.
ᚹ	You met Vergeisa the Fire Wolf and retrieved an important relic for her organization. She paid you handsomely and offered you membership in her secret organization.	You met King Erik Bloodaxe while he was sailing about Norveig shoring up support for his claim for the crown. Your slow and indecisive answer has placed you in his bad books.	During a voyage west from the Great Isles you came upon a glowing figure hovering over the water- a Lios Alfar. The beauty and emotions you felt in that instant blotted out your memories from the following week.
ᚷ	While travelling from Islandia to Gronland you saw a longship manned by Draugar and Haugbui. You retreated due to a lack of a combat ready crew.	You performed a favour for a local Karl and he owes you a debt of gratitude.	While exploring the catacombs beneath an ancient stone temple you discovered a nightmarish presence- a Svart Alfar. The experience kept you awake and distraught for several nights.
ᚠ	After defending a town from an invasion, the corpses were piled high. A representative from the shadowy Blotskadi organization came to ask if they could take away the corpses for you.	While traveling through East Anglia you decided to hunt deer in a walled-in glade. Little did you know that the glade was sacred to Hakon the Good. He has now set a warband upon you.	You had a near death experience and as you looked over at your blood brother's soul escaping his lifeless body, you witnessed the full glory of Kara the Valkyrie as she embraced his soul.
ᚹ	You visited Trondelag and spent a night with an exotic woman. It turns out she was the local chieftain's wife and now he wants you dead.	King Harald Fairhair's sons have been slaughtering one another for some time. You were seen at one such slaughter and in the eyes of the surviving sons your allegiance has been mistakenly set to the defeated pretender king.	While experimenting with unknown magics you inadvertently opened a portal to Muspelheim. On the other side, an amused Laufey, the Muspeli Jotun of arcane secrets. She wiped your mind of this magic, telling you that you weren't ready for it.
ᚬ	Draw 2 more times on this column	Draw 2 more times on this column	Draw 2 more times on this column

Dweller Relationships

Every pair of players may choose to pull a pair of runes to see how they know each other. The circumstances of their relationship and the current state of affairs are determined by 2 separate rune pulls. If some seemingly contradictory pairs are pulled such as "Good Friends" and "Mistrust", then the players are challenged to come up with a reason why their good friendship has taken a recent downturn. If players feel uncomfortable role-playing any results that result in dweller tension, the Norn should allow them to re-Wyrd the rune.

Table 31: Dweller Relationships Table

Rune	Circumstance	State
	Drinking buddies	Mistrust
	Related: distant family	Anger
	Employer / employee	Platonic affection
	Good friends (or lovers?)	Mutual respect
	Have gambled together	Whimsical
	Travelled together	Curious
	Saved the other's life	Looking forward to collaborating together
	Were robbed by the same criminal	Indebted
	Made a bet, will travel together until someone wins the bet	Bound in purpose
	Both are teacher and student, exchanging wisdom	One person waiting on the other to fulfill some bargain
	Entered into a legal agreement that is mutually beneficial	Enjoyment of each other's company
	Employed to spy on one another by rival/competing organizations	Oath to protect one another
	Both survivors of a massacre	Pushing each other to ever greater epic deeds
	Prisoners who escaped together	Rivalry
	Both worked together building a longship or a mead hall for a community in need	Fear and/or Uncertainty
	A common omen stitched both destinies together	Greed
	Shared reverence for same (or similar) divine power(s)	Jealousy
	Paid off a weregild for the other's misdeeds	Shared plans for achieving a specific goal
	Hunting the same prey (monster, outlaw, etc...)	Enemies: keeping friends close, but this particular enemy even closer
	Running away from the same danger	Desire for power or to overthrow unjust power
	Met at a wedding	Shared wanderlust and desire for exploration
	Met at a funeral	Religious or spiritual connection
	Woke up together after a heavy night of drinking (possible memory blackout?)	Mystery
	Fighting over the ownership of an item of value	Regret
	Extended History: Return the Void rune to the bag and Wyrd 2 more times	Misery

Fafnir's Treasure Addendum

The blight that has caused the zombear infestation and the corruption in the surrounding lands comes from a gaping sinkhole up in the mountains. At the bottom of the 3,000 foot drop is a contraption that was built by the Dvergar for Hel. She received this infernal device as a gift when she ascended to the throne of Niflheim. This device is a powerful multipurpose weapon that keeps even the most powerful beings at bay with its devastating effects.

Hel's Needle
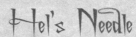

Miscellaneous
Size: 15
QR: 72

Helís needle is a bone spire surrounded by 3 smaller bone altars. The main spire is roughly 40′ tall and houses 3 alcoves. Each of the altars has the following items on them:

Altar 1: Sword, Shield, Tool

Altar 2: 24 runes

Altar 3: Small statues representing 6 rulers of 6 realms: Odin, Aegir, Surt, Bergelmir, Ivaldi, and Hel

As one can surmise, the items placed in the alcoves have an effect on how the machine operates. An alcove will only accept items from a given altar.

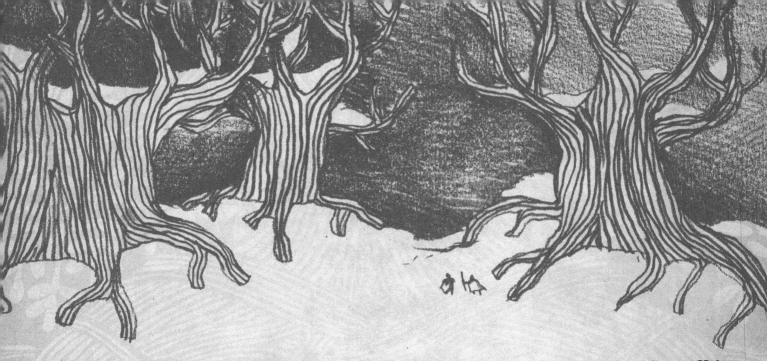

There are many combinations, but one is the root cause of the damage that was brought upon the land: *sword, Dagaz, Hel.*

What happened was that a hunter from Evingard stumbled across the sinkhole and his curiosity got the better of him. After descending to the bottom, he tried using the device. It was his combination of items that unleashed the essence of Niflheim upon the land, killing smaller animals and tainting larger ones such as the polar bears.

In order to reverse the effect, the players need to either return the device to Niflheim, or trigger some self-destruct mechanism. Other creative solutions may also exist.

Shield, Othala, Hel: Machine teleports back to Niflheim

Sword, Mann, Surt: Machine self-destructs (Hel may have an override)

Shield, Hagalaz, Jotunheim: Surround the device in a snowstorm (1000' diameter) that slowly fills the sinkhole (1í per minute)

The Norn may decide other adventurers have preceded the group and have been trying to fool with this powerful artifact. For example, some of the combinations could have been:

Sword, Jethe, Hel: Summon a dozen Draugar to come and terrorize the land

Tool, Fehu, Hel: Summon some magic item that was buried with someone who has descended into Niflheim

Tool, Mann, Ivaldi: Machine becomes a Hraesvelgr (see Denizens chapter in Lords of the Ash)

There are literally hundreds of possible combinations. The Norn is encouraged to create some in the event players wish to use this dangerous device for possible personal gain.

Saga: Cornerstone of the World

This very short saga builds on the locale in Islandia known as Evingard (see *Fafnir's Treasure book*). This saga will take 2-6 dwellers of level 11-13 on an adventure that will have them solve a mystery in the mines north of Evingard.

The Cornerstone of the World

> *Blood as my ink, bone as my quill,*
> *I leave my last words upon these walls...*
> *Agustin the Miner*

The Cornerstone of the World is a short saga that is designed for an evening of adventure. The story begins in the outpost of Evingard (see the Fafnir's Treasure book for full details on this remote outpost) as the players are hired by the owner of a once very lucrative mine. For many years this mine has created much wealth and has drawn many to Evingard in search of fortunes. The owner of the mine is a man that goes by the name of Magnus. He has as much sway in Evingard as the Ulfhednar chieftain known as Ingvar. Magnus hires local talent as management, and buys slaves to work the mines. In the past he has made trips to Ath Cliath in order to get the hardest workers that King Sitric's slave trade has to offer. On the same trips he would offload the fruits of his mines, creating obscene amounts of profit.

Evingard is situated next to one of the most important sites in all of Midgard: the Cornerstone of the World. This is where the world tree Yggdrasil holds up the realm of mankind. At this location, the barriers between worlds are thinnest. The essence of many other realms seep into Midgard via the Cornerstone of the World. This has resulted in the mountain range north west of Evingard becoming a melting pot of potent magic, Alkas and portals to other worlds.

Magnus discovered these wonders and has been seeking increasingly more exotic ores as he digs deeper and deeper into the mountains. He mines iron ore as a cover, but his real desire is to extract ores from Vanagard and Jotunheim as well as other exotic locales. Using brokers, Magnus sells those ores at exorbitant prices to blacksmiths who wish to create something truly unique. Some say the blacksmiths are disguised Dvergar who are creating items for besieged Asgard. Magnus ensures that the sales cannot be traced back to him so competitors will not flock to the Cornerstone of the World.

Every so often the miners broke through a wall and stumbled into a natural cavernous chamber beneath the mountains. That is when Magnus would relocate and reassign the miners to other duties while his trusted advisors would look for signs of natural alkas and portals into other realms.

A month ago the mine started having problems. The hundreds of slaves who work the mines appeared to have started a revolt. It turns out that the last natural chamber they uncovered in the depths contained a sealed portal into another realm. As procedures warranted, Magnus' reconnaissance team looked at ways to open the portal. In the process they released some denizens from the serpentine realm of Hvergelmir. These serpents and their magics impregnated the miners with the dreaded snake sigil.

All land in Midgard is presided over by a guardian spirit called a Vaettir. A Vaettir's power is proportional to the land size they govern. The Vaettir that oversees the north eastern part of Islandia is a great dragon named Dreki. Vaettirs are known to choose mortals to bond with and elevate them into leadership positions. Two generations ago, Dreki chose Ingvar as his bond. When a Vaettir thrives, so does the land and the bonded leader. Likewise when a Vaettir is sick, the land withers and the leader weakens.

The snake sigil from Hvergelmir has caused a sickness in the great Vaettir Dreki. For the last month Ingvar has been terribly ill and Evingard has been hammered by unending gale force snow squalls. Ivar the druid will approach the group when they are en route to the mines and ask that they deliver a healing elixir to Dreki.

The saga is broken down into scenes called vignettes. The Norn will select which vignettes and the order in which they will be presented to the players. Adventures between vignettes can be handled in summary form, or played through in detail.

VIGNETTE 1: The walk to the mines

> This path has been trodden by the tears
> and indignation of many trampled nations...
> Agustin the Miner

The walk from Evingard was well patrolled and well-guarded when the mine was operational. Now it has been reclaimed by the forces of nature and its denizens. Since the trek takes the dwellers inland and up into the mountains, the temperature drops noticeably. The average temperature in Evingard is -25 degrees Celsius. The road and the mines have the temperature plunge to -35. Anyone not dressed appropriately, such as wearing winter furs will suffer from exposure. Exposure results in Destiny being penalized by -1 while affected by the cold. The penalty is removed if exposed to continuous warmth for one hour. The trail is no longer heavily travelled, so it has accumulated 4' of snow. Anyone not wearing snow shoes or skis will only be able to perform weak move actions.

Snowshoes and skis counter the movement penalties caused by deep snow. However skis also confer a +1 movement bonus when moving in a straight line and an additional +1 if moving downhill. Skis apply a -1 penalty when moving uphill.

While trekking towards the mine, the dwellers may be attacked by hungry giant wolves. If the dwellers are careful to mask their presence with a successful Wilderness Survival [3P] check, they may avoid the wolves. Anyone with Animal Empathy may try to dissuade the wolves [4S]. There will be a number of level 9 wolves equal to the number of dwellers minus one. There is also an alpha wolf that is level 11. The wolves have adapted to the deep snow and do not suffer from movement penalties.

VIGNETTE 2: Lost in the wilderness

Escape from this infernal existence is not an option.
Hungry beasts, the winter's icy grasp and despair are our jailers...
Agustin the Miner

If the dwellers get lost or run off into the wilderness, they will run into a few interesting scenarios. If they were running away from danger, or were genuinely lost, then they will run into Ivar the Druid. If they were purposely wandering away from the mines, they will face some fearsome foes. These lands are so hostile that even the hunters from the nearby lodge are reluctant to wander into these lands. Every hour in the wilderness has a 33% chance of having a hostile encounter. When an encounter occurs, wyrd 1 rune and consult the following table:

- = *Pack of wolves (level 10) numbering one more than the previous pack encountered*
- = *Snow Serpent is level 9 with a bonus +2 levels per dweller in the adventuring group. It also gains +1 level per previous encounter with a snow serpent.*
- = *Pack of level 14 trolls numbering half the number of dwellers (round up). There will be +1 trolls per previous encounter with trolls.*

VIGNETTE 3: The Entrance to the Mines

As I tread under the gallows gate, the ravens take a break
from their feast to mock my daily march into the darkness....
Agustin the Miner

Once the dwellers arrive at the mine they are greeting by a very bleak scene. The remnants of the outdoor slave camp looks completely abandoned and iced over. The camp looks like it accommodated over 500 shift workers at one time. Tents, wooden racks and bags of personal effects litter the camp. If the players decide to loot the camp, the return is minimal. The ice is hard to crack, and the reward is literally a few Skatt per dozen camps. The entrance to the mines are are huge. The opening is 200 feet wide and 80 feet high. Outside the opening are very large piles of worthless stone. Each of the dozen piles is roughly 300 feet tall, indicating the depth and scale of this operation. The reinforcing beams for the entrance have been turned into the hangman's gallows. No fewer than 50 frozen corpses sway in the wind as a murder of crows stands watch at the highest of the supporting rafters. As the adventurers approach the entrance, the crows begin to caw in unison. This is an opportunity to perform an Omens and Portents check. The dwellers make out the melody of a childhood song being recited by the crows. Consult the following table for the results of an Omens/Portents skill check:

1 success = Something isn't right, there is a melody to their caws, but you cannot decipher anymore

2 successes = The childhood song is about a hermit who refuses to see or accept the world around him... you will meet someone who refuses to deal with reality

3 successes = The end of the song deals with the hermit's wife, she has sickness that needs to be cured before she can help her husband... you will need to heal someone who can make things right

4 successes = The cure she needed required gathering many ingredients that no one was willing to seek... Your quest will take you to several important places that will test your wits and heroism

Inside the cave are many makeshift homes, probably those that belonged to the taskmasters and managers of the mine. All of the buildings are abandoned and seem to have already been ransacked. A successful Perception skill check will reveal some loot and added information:

1 success = You find paperwork pertaining to the mine. anyone with the Read and Write skill can ascertain that the mine was extracting a carriage worth of iron ore every 6 hours.

2 successes = You find some hidden compartments in the homes that contain money and items of value. 200 skatt worth of loot per player is discovered.

3 successes = You find a letter from Magnus (dated 2 months ago) to the foreman stating that slave rebellion is unacceptable and all means should be used in order to quash it. He also questions the scale of the rebellion, finding it hard to believe that all of the slaves have turned.

4 successes = You find a scroll that recounts the last days of a guard that barricaded himself into one of the houses... "they scratch at the doors, sniffing around like dogs. some move on all fours as if possessed by some bestial spirits. They have no regard for those who surrender, devouring every man's still beating heart. I implore the gods to intervene, but my spirits dampen with every passing hour". The last occupant of the house looks like he was dragged out, as a trail of bloody scratch marks will attest.

5 successes = You find a magical item.

VIGNETTE 4: The Flooded Hallway

> We hear sounds that no man or beast could make—
> whispering, gnashing, shrieking, in our ears or is it in our minds?
> Dismissing our protests, our slavers insist we dig deeper...
>
> Agustin the Miner

The main passageway that leads from the taskmaster village and into the deeper mine passes by some equipment and storage rooms. The storage rooms look like they were used to hold the extracted ore at one time, but now the room is empty. A perception check at moderate[3] difficulty will reveal that some of the ore can be found hidden under some dirt, and it is iron ore. The store room contains: pick axes, rope, shovels, lanterns (but very little flaming oil), candles, empty crates and barrels. There are also some cabers that are used to reinforce tunnels. Out in the hallway are two wagons that would have been used to transport the ore.

As the main passage begins to descend, the dwellers are confronted by a complete flooding of the passageway. The flooded section is very long, roughly 300'. To swim to the other end requires an unlikely[5] swim skill check. This natural challenge will only be overcome by careful planning and ingenuity. The dwellers can use their powers, skills and anything they picked up to overcome this challenge.

VIGNETTE 5: The Trapped Undertaker

Like blood from a fresh gaping wound,
my dreams are seeping out into my dismal and pathetic life.
Yesterday I heard that they quelled a revolt on the lower levels, but I saw no bodies.
Lord help me, I think I'm losing my mind...
Agustin the Miner

Deep within the mines is a chamber that looks completely barricaded from the inside. The barricade was put up in a way that the heavier objects that are stacked high fall on anyone trying to clear through it. It takes five Athletics skill checks to clear the passage. The difficulty to clear it without taking damage is hard [4] and clearing a section and setting off a trap is moderate [3]. If a trap is sprung, anyone within 15' of the barricade take damage equal to 4x the attempt (first trap deals 4 damage, next trap deals 8 damage, so on and so forth). Within the room is one of the mine's undertakers named Lut. He isn't an Angel of Death, but has a healthy respect for Hel. Lut fears that those breaking into the chamber are the infected slaves. He prefers to hide than engage in open combat. If the dwellers are going to break through, he buries himself leaving a small hole for air (perception[2] to detect his presence). If he feels like he is going to die, then he will put up a fight as a level 6 grizzled warrior. However he is very sympathetic to anyone not visibly infected by the Hvergelmir parasites. He will tell his tale to anyone who will listen.

He was hired a few months ago to bury the slaves that had been worked to death. For the disposal of corpses, he would use mine shafts and chambers that the miners had already mined dry. He would love to get back to Evingard in order to resume his apprenticeship to the Angel of Death named Jadvyg. He promises that anyone who helps him escape will receive a proper burial when the time comes.

VIGNETTE 6: The Cannibals

Madness has broken out in every mine shaft, and I cannot tell how much of this blood is my own. Despite my pleading, my companions have insisted on eating the Zesh of the fallen... .

Agustin the Miner

The miners and taskmasters that have been infected by the snake sigil do not harm one another; instead they seek out the un-infected. The curse forces them to spread the infection to as many as possible. They fight with a bestial ferocity with the goal of dropping opponents into an unconscious state. Those who fall unconscious are bitten repeatedly by those already infected in order to spread the curse. To the casual observer it would seem that the victim is bitten by a cannibal, however those who scrutinize the scene will observe that the infected open their mouth just above the victim, and then the spawn of Hvergelmir that live within the infected writhe out through the mouth and burrow their way into the new host. The resulting wounds appear as though the victim had been bitten and chewed on from all exposed sides.

Snake Sigil: Those that are infected carry writhing snakes within their body. Upon death, the snake will burst out of the corpse (same combat round, added at the end of initiative) and attack the dwellers. The snake's level depends on how long it has gestated within the host. Those that are more recent take on half the host's level and those that have matured within their host have a level that matches the host's level (1 week or more).

When the infected attack, they enter the rage condition with a +1 intensity per Upkeep. They all have the Furious Cohort power that allows them to work together, even at Rage intensity 4. When they stand over an unconscious foe, they will spend a rune to impregnate the victim. An impregnated victim immediately suffers enough spiritual damage to place 1 rune in the Drain pile. The Snake sigil curse is represented by a +1 intensity on the Curse condition. Every 2 days the curse increases by +1. While suffering from the Snake Sigil, runes in Drain do not recover over time. In fact whenever the Snake Sigil increases by +1 intensity, the victim must make an Ultimate Sacrifice +1. At intensity 1 the victim still retains some of their previous personality, but they have an impending bestial nature that threatens to consume their being. At intensity 2 they lose control around anyone who isn't infected, wishing to infect them at all costs. If left alone, they still retain enough humanity to allow them to try and find a way to cleanse themselves of the impregnation. At intensity 3 all control is lost and they are fully subservient to the voices in their head. It is said that Nidhogg communicates to his spawn in this way. At intensity 4 the serpents within their host grow to full maturity. If at any intensity the host dies, the serpents leave the host and seek out a new host (a serpent may play any rune to attempt to enter a new host by burrowing through their flesh) and the defender can play any rune to counter the attack.

VIGNETTE 7: The Writhing Hall

I cannot participate in this folly but how can I resist? The voices are so loud...
Agustin the Miner

The Snake Sigil changes the victim's psyche suppressing inhibition and any sense of ethics or civility. The sigil has a way of amplifying the more primal and instinctual behaviours in the victim. Deep within the mines is a room where a lot of the infected miners and task masters have congregated for carnal activities. There are literally hundreds of bodies that are packed into a room that is too small to accommodate so many. As the adventurers approach, the first impression they have in the darkness is that the floors and walls are moving. However upon a successful Perception check of difficulty Moderate[3] (Hard[4] if the group doesn't approach with any lights), they will notice that the room is filled with writhing naked bodies.

The infected within the room do not notice the adventurers unless actively provoked. They are so self-consumed, that a Perception check from them is heavily penalized (Hard[4]). However any aggression from the adventurers will have a handful of cannibals break out of their lust filled embrace and attack the dwellers (Moderate[3]). The dwellers will be quickly overwhelmed if they don't take quick action in taking any fights out of this chamber. If a fight breaks out, every round, more cannibals will join the fight (Easy[2]).

Round 1:   A number of level 6 cannibals equal to the number of adventurers.
Round 2:   1 level 9 cannibal
Round 3:   2 level 9 cannibals
              subsequent rounds the numbers keep increasing by +1
Round 7:   1 level 12 cannibal
Round 8:   2 level 12 cannibals
   so on and so forth...

This hall isn't here to be conquered by the players, but rather a glimpse into the magnitude of the problem. It also reveals to the players that the infected cannot be starved out, as the sigil keeps their bodies alive for as long as the serpent needs to grow.

VIGNETTE 8: The Dreyri (Bats) Over the Causeway

I have Zed from the monsters who were once my friends.
I stumble in the darkness like a drunk without a home.
Lord I feel something stirring within the pit of my stomach...

— Agustin the Miner

ne of the chambers has a wide open ceiling that houses a large population of Dreyri (blood sucking bats). They will be attracted by any light sources, with a flock of level 12 equal to the number of light sources. The dwellers will need to set contingency actions in order to strike as their tactics involve moving in and attacking and then moving out of melee range. For ranged attacks, good light sources will be needed. A typical torch provides 20 feet of reliable visibility.

Below the causeway is a natural lake. Should anyone plunge off the edge they will be effectively removed from combat unless they have a waterproof light source as well as ranged capabilities while treading water. While in water:

- Play a rune to stay afloat
- Only weak Move actions

(unless at least 1 rank in the swim skill)

VIGNETTE 9: The Spiders in the Bowels of the Earth

Quick sharpen the stone so it can taste your Zesh! No! What am I doing?
Why do my hands move of their own accord??
Listen, let's discuss this— PLEASE...

— Agustin the Miner

n this area, a number of level 9 spiders equal to the number of dwellers lie in wait of a meal. The web traps are difficult to see, requiring a Perception skill check at Hard[4] (-1 difficulty per light source). As soon as someone is trapped or interacts with the webs in any way, the spiders attack.

The chamber provides a glimpse into the fate that has befallen the great Vaettir Dreki. Inscribed upon the walls are the final messages by Augustin the mad miner. As the spiders were drawn to his final and fleeting life force, he managed to scribe the following testament: "My ancestors come to claim me, I hear their ghostly hissing. I leave here my last testament... The soul of the mountain is crying out to me in voices of many colours. They hunger for the mountain's soul. I hear their gnashing teeth tear the mountain's flesh. They wish to bring blood back to their earthen homes. Their abyssal homes in the heart of the mountain. They have sealed the other worlds... it is too late. I wrap myself in the webs and await the monstrosity that grows within me..."

VIGNETTE 10: The Corrupted Well Chambers

The sensations are maddening, pure ecstasy...
Agustin the Miner

There is a honeycomb pattern to these series of chambers and the sum of the chambers is known as the Cornerstone of the World. They are all linked in a circle, and the walls are made from tree bark rather than stone. The wood is impervious to the elements as it is part of Yggdrasil (QR 100). Verwandlung magic is amplified in these rooms (all Verwandlung spells get a free amplify meta tag).

The awesome power that radiates off of Yggdrasil allows for very potent Omens and Portents skill checks. Performing a check at the Cornerstone of the world will reveal more than just the immediate quest. The Norn should reward extra successes with hints that allude to the next adventure. Any successes will result in some vivid imagery:

1 success = The wells are portals into other realms that hang upon the cosmic tree
2 successes = A curse was muttered as a powerful artifact was placed
3 successes = The wells have been corrupted and everyone who attempts to pass through gets infected with the Snake Sigil
4 successes = The curses act as a jail for a powerful soul which is imprisoned below

Each chamber is roughly 60 feet in diameter. At the center of each chamber is a well that originally had bas-relief carvings which identified the world it links to. Currently the bas-relief carvings are covered in dried blood that has caked into a very serpentine shape. Emerging from the well is a plethora of vines and branches, rising up to touch the ceiling. If one were to search the vegetation (Perception[3]), they would find a powerful artifact that has been used in a ritual that causes the portal to infect anyone who passes through. Each cursed portal is powered by a magical item that sets the difficulty to resist the curse. The higher the QR the tougher it is to resist the curse. Yggdrasil has a reflex to envelop any powerful sources of magic. The artifact found is tied to each individual well.

REALM	ARTIFACT	GUARDIANS
Asgard	Bifrost Ring	Gold Effigy
Vanagard	Bag of Sustenance	Kraken
Muspelheim	Molten Rod	Fire Skui
Jotunheim	Frost Mauler	Troll
Alfgard	Call of the Ancients	Willow Wisp
Svartalfheim	Visage of Blood	Shadow Skui
Nidavellir	Blood Mail Coat	Snow Serpent

Removing the artifact shuts down the curse that has hijacked the portal. The denizens found in each chamber are afflicted with the sigil and are unquenchably aggressive. There will be one less denizen than there are dwellers, and the denizen level will be 11. After the inevitable combat, the dwellers are free to keep the items found. Removing the items from the chambers also removes the Hvergelmir taint. The blood bubbles and boils, and then flakes off into the air and turns to dust.

Regardless of whether the chambers are cleared, the player should find a mysterious well with a triad of magic rings. They are known as the "Three Norns": Verdandi, Urd, and Skuld. Standing between the rings and the adventurers are three puzzles/riddles. The Norns have ensured that these rings are found by the adventurers- it's part of their destiny. Each ring grants a key power that increases the chances of success during the final confrontation.

SKULD	URD	VERDANDI
QR: 1	QR: 1	QR: 2
Active Power: Catharsis	Active Power: Purge Foreign Spirits	Passive Power: Keen Senses

VIGNETTE 11: The Vaettir's Chamber

I live for the glorious moment when I can birth your children!...
Agustin the Miner

At the lowest sub-level of the caverns and mines lies the physical home of the Great Vaettir Dreki. The cavern floor is covered by thousands of small snakes, causing more mental distress than real physical danger. They emerge from a well that is at the far end of the room. This well was recently created by Nidhogg and leads to Hvergelmir. At the center of the chamber is a huge beast that looks to be a cross between a gigantic serpent and a wingless dragon. It is Dreki but only in body as Nidhogg's corrupting influence has almost completely subverted the Great Vaettir's soul. The curse condition it suffers is different than the Snake Sigil. The curse it suffers is known as Nidhogg's Great Gloom. Nidhogg wishes to convert Dreki into his obedient and subservient liege within Midgard. Surrounding the Great Vaettir are stone monoliths that are the homes of Wight Sovereigns. They have been summoned and bound here by Nidhogg. The Wight Sovereigns act as jailers for the subdued Dreki.

Nidhogg has started to turn the Great Vaettir towards his cause. The Vaettir is afflicted by Possession 4 and has the Great Gloom effect that is represented by the Curse condition at intensity 3. It begins at Possession 4 if none of the wells have been cleared. If at least 1 has been cleared the Possession starts at 3 and if all of them have been cleared then the Possession intensity is 2.

The Wight Sovereigns are working at increasing the Great Gloom to intensity 4. As fate would have it, as the adventurers walk into the chamber, the Wights are minutes away from fulfilling their goal!

Dreki is level 54 with Essence 24 and Destiny 15. Its size is 25.
The wights are level 10 with Essence 6 and Destiny 2. There are as many wights as there are players.

The curse increases as the Wight Sovereigns ravage the Vaettir's soul. There are 100 (+20 per Wight) more points of damage that need to be dealt to the Vaettir in order to increase the Great Gloom curse to intensity 4. The dwellers can heal the Vaettir while killing the Wight Sovereigns before they deal the required damage. Each level of intensity was brought about by tens of thousands of points of damage being dealt, so healing isn't an efficient way to clear the curse.

While the Curse condition persists, the Vaettir is afflicted with the following:
   - Apathy: It cannot fight back
   - Each upkeep phase, Dreki's Possession forces him to summon one level 6 Snow Serpent per level of Possession intensity

Strategy: The Wights will balance dealing damage to the Vaettir and fighting the dwellers. They will initially focus on the dwellers and hope that Dreki will summon enough Snow Serpent reinforcements. Once the dwellers are busy with the serpents, the Wights will resume their assault on the Great Vaettir.

To reduce the intensity of the Curse condition, the dwellers must sacrifice magic items at the Well of Hvergelmir that sits at the back of the Vaettir's chamber. To find out more about the sacrifice ritual, anyone can perform a Lore:Arcana[3] skill check. The ritual cannot be performed during combat because the ritual takes 1 hour per curse intensity. The number of magic items is determined by the curse intensity (magic items are those which have been modified using any of the following skills: Infuse, Dvergar Engineering, Realm Ores, Creature Reliquary).
   - 1 Curse level

If the Great Gloom Curse is allowed to proceed to intensity 4, then the Cornerstone of the World falls and is claimed by the proto-serpent Nidhogg.

Epilogue

If the Great Gloom is cleansed...

Dreki recovers very slowly because the damage has placed a lot of his runes in drain. He then thanks the dwellers and rewards them with a cache of magic items (Norn decides how many items, with a QR half the average dweller level). He will ask the dwellers for help in clearing out the mine of Nidhogg's brood as well as cleansing the wells (if they aren't already clean). As the Cornerstone's wells are cleansed, Yggdrassil's branches begin to regenerate and return into Midgard. Before the corruption came to the Cornerstone of the World, up in the mountain ranges north-west of Evingard, there was a tree that reached up into the clouds. With its return, Dreki's dominion will become the most verdant and vibrant in all of Midgard.

The Great Vaettir will also ask the dwellers to go back to Evingard and engage in negotiations with Magnus in order to close down the mine. Magnus will naturally be reluctant and if push comes to shove, Ingvar the chieftain of Evingard will side with Magnus. Tension may grow as Halfdan Ingvarsson and Ivar Iron Root prepare for violent confrontation. It is in the dweller's best interest to broker a non-violent solution because more claimants are en-route to the Cornerstone of the World. Annikki is leading her marauding warband across the sea in order to secure this very strategic site for the glory of the Vanir. But she isn't alone in her dreams of conquest. Almost every higher power has some emissary en route to the Cornerstone of the World. It will be a short won victory, but for now let the celebrations begin!

If the Cornerstone of the World falls...

Should Nidhogg prove successful, by slaying the dwellers or forcing them to debase themselves by swearing fealty, the Cornerstone of the Word becomes his. This will allow his minions to spontaneously appear anywhere in Dreki's lands (hundred mile radius around the mine). The humans that bend knee in servitude to Nidhogg will be spared, be it dwellers or denizens, and may be converted into Gargangjolp. Anyone afflicted by the snake sigil have a week to live before snakes within their bowels slay the host. Anyone afflicted must remap half of their Essence to powers on the Gargangjolp power and skill boards.

Those who resist will have to retreat and will most likely need to seek help from the most powerful Jarls of Midgard. Evingard will hold up against the tide of serpents, but not for more than a few days or weeks (depending on the defences of the outpost).

Starter Vignettes

In this chapter you will find a few starter vignettes. They are similar to what would be found in the initial sections of a full blown saga. They contain enough information to kick off an epic saga, but will require the Norn to fill in the missing pieces in the later parts of the story. Each starter vignette breaks down the information into eight key sections:

- **Summary**- a quick summary of the overarching plot.

- **Location**- lists the key locales wherein the saga's plot will unfold.

- **Time Period**- sets the time-frame within which the saga should take place. This is important because the starter vignettes span a period of many years. Each saga has outcomes which may greatly impact future sagas.

- **Background**- presents optional background information which help improve the framing of the plot.

- **Main Characters**- presents the list of key denizens that will help propel the plot. Many are described in the "Legends and Villains" chapter (see page 14).

- **Plot:** outlines the start of the saga. The remainder of the plot remains to be filled out by the Norn.

- **Plot Twist**- like any good story, not everything is as straight-forward as it seems. This section puts a hidden spin on the story which may have the players reassessing all of their assumptions.

- **Fallout**- No story is complete without consequences. This section outlines possible ending scenarios and what they could mean to the broader

The time period is set in an important chronology spanning almost 1000 years. It is said that in the year 0, the first man and woman, Ask and Embla were created by the sons of Bor. Ragnarok begins in 930 and some say the end of the world will come before the year 1000.

The Norn should take great care when role-playing the main characters listed in each saga vignette. The mortality of those recurring characters should not be taken lightly because they will feature prominently in future stories. The Norn should use other forms of defeat such as imprisonment, curses and exile. The Fallout sections give hints as to when certain dwellers may shuffle off this mortal coil.

Only the overarching story is outlined within the plot. The Norn should feel free to add violent encounters with brigands, monsters and various deadly challenges throughout the sagas presented below. This will add an unmistakable Viking feel to every adventure.

These starter vignettes are a small part of the overarching story line that covers the period between 925 and 940. The whole story will be revealed in the saga trilogy: *Fate of the Norns: Ragnarok - The Sword Age, The Wind Age and The Wolf Age.*

Rognvald the Sorcerer King

Summary: The dwellers are to accompany prince Erik Blood Axe to Hathaland. There Erik's half-brother Rognvald the Sorcerer King rules with his council of eighty. He has been ordered by King Harald Fairhair to cease his dark arts and to bequeath his rule upon Prince Erik.

Location: Hathaland, Uppland

Time Period: 925-929 (pre-Ragnarok)

Background: It was during King Harald Fairhair's unsuccessful northern campaign versus the kingdoms of Halogaland and Finnmark when he met a beautiful northern witch named Snoefrith. Her mother Svasi came to Harald's hall in Trondelag offering him a gift of fine mead. Harald would later claim that the drink was enchanted with foul Seith magic and will use this as an excuse to banish Snoefrith. That night, the mead made his whole body ache and burn with an unearthly desire for Snoefrith. Svasi ruefully insisted that Harald marry Snoefrith before he could enjoy the

carnal pleasures of her flesh. That night they were married and King Harald remained in Trondelag for four years (circa 901-905). His interests became singular- Snoefrith. During that time he abandoned his ambitions to capture the north and became apathetic to the rest of his kingdom. On the fourth year Snoefrith gave birth to their fourth son, Rognvald. Soon afterwards King Harald's true wife, the queen of Norveig arrived in such a furor that it would strike fear in both kings and gods. The court Skalds attributed the breaking of the enchantment to Queen Gyda's turbulent arrival. Svasi, Snoefrith and her children were all declared outlaws and banished to Finnmark as the king and queen sailed back to Alvaldsnes.

King Harald had many marital indiscretions but most of his high-born bastard sons remained within his court; even assigned various important political or military stations. Unlike his brethren, Rognvald had to fight fight his way in from the outside. When he became of age he traveled to Alvaldsnes to demand his place within the kingdom. He was a troublemaker, starting quarrels with his brothers in order to best them and in turn shame them. Eventually King Harald could not ignore Rognvald's talents, nor his disruptive character upon the rest of his court. He assigned Rognvald to the far eastern front in Uppland because regardless of success or failure, the outcome would be positive. Rognvald would have to face King Bjorn Eriksson of Svealand, a powerful and dangerous foe. If Rognvald should best him, then Uppland would become part of Norveig, and if King Bjorn would kill Rognvald, then the rebel bastard could be laid to rest.

Sometimes the Norns have a sense of humour. Rognvald, in a stroke of insight and good fortune, became the foster son to King Bjorn Erikkson. This brought an end to the Uppland war front. Rognvald declared himself king of Uppand, kept his army, and swore allegiance to the High-King Bjorn Erikkson.

Main Characters:

- *Prince Erik Blood Axe is the eldest highborn son of King Harald Fairhair.*

- *Rognvald the Sorceror King possesses a Death Stone (see page 147) making him immortal so long as he doesn't touch the artifact.*

- *Gunnhild is the consort of Erik Blood Axe. She is a powerful Seithkona who can cast illusions.*

Plot: The dwellers are hired by Prince Erik to join his warband after it was decimated in a bloody battle against a rival kingdom. The dwellers accompany Prince Erik to an audience with his father King Harald Fairhair. The king is old and sickly and confined to his bed. He tells his son about the eastern threat of Rognvald the Sorceror king. Earlier in the day, King Harald had received a message from King Rognvald via a courier. King Rognvald was demanding that the armies of Norveig be withdrawn from Uppland's borders. King Harald is furious and wants the traitor Rognvald driven out or killed. He explains that Rognvald was once a loyal subject, but has now turned against the kingdom.

Prince Erik asks that the dwellers become the scouting vanguard for his army. They are to take a small long-ship and sail ahead of the main fleet. Instructions are given that they must first to go Finnmark in order to retrieve a magical item from a barrow. Then they are to travel overland to Norrland where they will buy vessels and sail down to Hathaland. Rognvald's spies would not expect an attack from the north.

Gunnhild having spent time in Finnmark knows of Snoefrith and of her final resting place. She also knows that Rognvald cannot be killed without first exhuming the Death Stone which has been buried in his mother's tomb. Gunnhild will keep of this information from the dwellers. In her mind they are just hired muscle, not paid to think.

Dealing with King Rognvald is another matter entirely. They ask the dwellers to go to him and keep him distracted and occupied while the main force attacks Hathaland. Prince Erik suggests that the dwellers could pretend to be couriers returning with word from King Harald. Gunnhild cares about results and has no qualms about burning down the town with the dwellers within if it means the goal has been achieved.

King Rognvald will be prepared for subterfuge and assassination attempts. King Rognvald is no fool and expects King Harald to react poorly to his message. He will be in poor health because of the Death Stone's proximity, but his council of eighty sorcerers will fight to the death in order to keep him safe. The best course of action for the dwellers would be speedy diplomacy. King Rognvald will engage in dialogue, but time will run out as Gunnhild will attempt to strike him down with the Death Stone.

Plot Twist: Gunnhild and Snoefrith were rival Seithkonas in Finnmark. Both were equally talented and powerful despite Snoefrith being Gunnhild's senior by many years. Life in Finnmark is tough and many seek an easier way of life in the south. Gunnhild was trapped in a love triangle with two Druids while Snoefrith, with the aid of her mother Svasi had managed to snare the most prestigious man in all of Midgard. This drove Gunnhild to intense feelings of jealousy and hatred. Years later when Snoefrith was outlawed and sent back to Finnmark, Gunnhild rejoiced at her suffering, but eventually the stronger emotion of patriotic sisterhood reconciled the two Seithkonas. Gunnhild went so far as helping raise Snoefrith's children while they were infants. One terrible winter little Rognvald fell deathly ill. They sought all remedies mundane and magical, but it seemed like the Norns had promised Rognvald's soul to Hel. In desperation, Rognvald's grandmother took him to see Drifa, Queen of Svalbard. Queen Drifa took great interest in the child and it was rumoured that he was saved when the queen created a Death Stone in order to chase the Norns away. After Rognvald was saved his family was invited to live with the queen in Svalbard, but Gunnhild was left behind once more. The dark emotions retook her once more. She vowed to sunder Snoefrith's family, and if the rumours were true, she'd take the Death Stone too!

Gunnhild ensured Rognvald would turn against his father. She bolstered his ego while he was jockeying for position within his court. With great cunning, she negotiated the fostering agreement between Rognvald and King Bjorn. With her council, Rognvald formulated the letter to King Harald. To Rognvald, Gunnhild was just the distant but caring aunt, why doubt her motives? Queen Gunnhild would prove to be the master architect of this conspiracy.

Fallout: If Rognvald continues to rule, he will become a very powerful contender for the throne after King Harald's death. If the dwellers side with Rognvald then they have made very powerful enemies of Erik and Gunnhild. They will be banned from the king's council until King Harald's death. If Rognvald is exiled, he will flee to Mirkvid where many sympathetic denizens will grant him shelter. If Rognvald is killed by the Death Stone's touch his sorcerer council scatters and Rognvald's children seek revenge. Earl Einar of the Orkney Islands is the eldest of King Rognvald's sons. He has a sadistic streak and enjoys performing the "blood eagle" torture upon his enemies.

Darkness Falls

Summary: The world the dwellers know is about to change forever. King Harald, the greatest king in Midgard's history is about to die and the dwellers will bear witness to the most cataclysmic event- the devouring of the sun and moon by two celestial wolves. They will watch as the kingdom begins to splinter, and the choices they make will determine their allies and enemies for the foreseeable future.

Location: Alvaldsnes, Norveig

Time Period: 930, the Axe Age begins

Background: Long ago before King

Harald was king, even before he had received his monicker of "Fairhair", he was a man in love. Madly in love with an energetic and ambitious girl named Gyda. She rebuffed his proposals and demanded that he conquer all of the petty kingdoms from Vestfold to Trondelag in order to prove his worth. Harald took up the challenge like a man possessed. He refused to cut or comb his hair until the task was complete. Prior to becoming king of Norveig, he had become known as "Harald the Tanglehaired". Once his quest was complete, he groomed his hair and married his sweetheart.

Controlling such a vast empire required High-King Harald Fairhair to frequently visit the various seats of power. While staying at the various capitals, he fell for various high-born and low-born women. Those of higher rank he married, and those of lower rank he kept as mistresses. The more important unions were to Queen Svanhild Eysteinsdottir of Trondelag and Queen Ragnhild of Jutland. While High-Queen Gyda did not approve, she was pragmatic about the price she had to pay for marrying the most powerful man in Midgard. She passed due to illness a few winters ago.

Main Characters:

- *Prince Alof is the eldest highborn son. His mother is High-Queen Gyda. He has received the best training, court appointments and opportunity. Despite the amount invested into Alof, his father finds him a disappointment. He has been trying to rule the kingdom while his father's health deteriorates.*

- *Prince Hroerek is one of the younger sons. His mother is High-Queen Gyda. He is a dreamer. He has a very idyllic vision of life and ignores anything that may displease him. He has a way of lifting the spirits of everyone in the room when he enters.*

- *Prince Sigtrygg is one of the younger sons. His mother is High-Queen Gyda. Sigtrygg is a cunning and brilliant military leader but fails to grasp even the simplest economic or political tasks. He is cold and emotionless and his decisions are guided by logic as well as battlefield intuition.*

- *Prince Frothi is one of the younger sons. His mother is High-Queen Gyda. He is a shrewd man. He speaks little and prefers to listen to what everyone else may have on their mind. Constantly plotting, he has developed a paranoid streak. So much so that his siblings have started to ignore his warnings, chalking them up to an overactive imagination.*

- *Prince Thorgils is the youngest son. His mother is High-Queen Gyda. A natural diplomat and statesman, most believe that if Prince Alof fails to secure the throne, Prince Thorgils would be the popular choice. However, his inexperience is what plagues his advancement.*

- *Prince Hakon the Good is a lowborn son. His mother was the court drinking wench named Thora Mosterstang. He is very humble and has no expectations about inheriting any position of power within the kingdom. His love and respect towards his dying father is what brought him.*

- *Prince Bjorn Farmann was the eldest from the union between King Harald Fairhair and Queen Svanhild Eysteinsdottir. His father asked that he travel to Alvaldsnes when the time comes. He is very attentive to his subjects and that keeps him busy, but he has made time to come and say farewell to his father.*

- *Prince Erik Blood Axe is the son of King Harald Fairhair and Queen Ragnhild of Jutland. As King Harald's health began to deteriorate, he insisted that Prince Erik remain in Alvadsnes. He has been co-managing the kingdom with Prince Alof in the last year. It is clear that Prince Alof cannot manage it without assistance.*

– **Gunnhild** *is the wife of Erik Blood Axe. She is a smart and powerful Seithkona who looks out for her husband's well being. She never leaves his side and gives council on all matters.*

Plot: The dwellers have become loyal servants of the crown. They go on hunting trips with the princes and hold important roles within their warbands. They are as close to family as can be without being part of the "inner circle". The family is making preparations for the death of the patriarch King Harald Fairhair. He has grown old, his health has deteriorated and he sleeps when he isn't gripped by painful fits. They ask the dwellers to fetch the court Angel of Death but it appears she is away and they must find the next best official. They are also tasked with summoning Harald's various children to his dying chamber. Lastly, they are asked to bring the king's ship to shore and prepare it for the royal barrow.

Each of his children stand around the bed and listen to their father's laboured breathing. Each takes turns saying their farewells and minutes later as High-King Harald draws his final breath, the sky suddenly turns from day to night. Panicked screams can be heard through out the castle and town. Fear grips everyone in attendance. Accusations and speculations are thrown about with abandon. The funeral is delayed as everyone seeks answers. After Voelvas are consulted the truth and gravity of the situation becomes clear- Ragnarok has started, Skoll and Hati have devoured the sun and moon, and Fimbulwinter is coming!

Once the funeral is completed the sons meet in the main hall to discuss succession. Their father had intentionally dragged his feet on naming a successor. The dwellers must navigate intense negotiations, power configurations and offers in order to secure the next monarch. What is clear is that the heir apparent, Prince Alof is not fit for the task. He is also unwilling to share the duties any longer with Prince Erik and his wife Gunnhild.

The Norn should keep track of which monarchs the dwellers are ready to back after several iterations of negotiations and threats. Eventually if a solution is not found, Prince Erik invites his rivals to a longhouse in the woods for further discussions without interruptions from court officials. He proposes a lockdown until an heir is found. High-Queen Gyda's children come as requested, the others are late. Not taking a chance that some of the monarchs in attendance leave, Gunnhild locks the doors and sets fire to the longhouse- killing the immediate bloodline.

New travels quickly and Prince Hakon hurriedly leaves Norveig. Bjorn Farmann declares himself king of Vestfold and begins courting the other parts of the kingdom. Erik and Gunnhild declare themselves as High-King and High-Queen and they begin doing the same.

Plot Twist: The players may feel as though High-Queen Gyda's children may be at the forefront for the crown, but in fact the others are in much better positions to obtain the ultimate title and honour. Their skills are more evenly rounded giving them an advantage.

Gunnhild has sent away the court Angel of Death due to a long standing grudge she holds against King Harald and his Finnmark mistress Snoefrith. She will go to great lengths to destroy anything Snoefrith had touched. Gunnhild is also looking out for her husband's advancement. As High-King Harald grew old, High-Queen Gyda began openly positioning her sons for the throne and actively blocking the other bastard sons from succession. This did not sit well with Gunnhild. She used her alchemy and magic to bring about High-Queen Gyda's demise, and made it look like natural causes.

King Rognvald, if alive, will also make an appearance once King Harald is dead. He may prove to be a serious contender for the throne.

Fallout: Prophesy has played-out. Throughout the course of the saga the dwellers will forge alliances and when the kingdom becomes fractured, enemies will be forged by the choices made. Depending on how everything unfolds, all, some or none of Gyda's children may be deceased. If the dwellers chose Hakon the Good, then their fortunes will be made on the Great Isles. If they choose any other prince then the others will regard them as treacherous enemies. Most will refrain from killing, but Erik and Gunnhild will stop at nothing to achieve their goals- making them the most dangerous of adversaries.

Fimbulwinter has begun. Eternal night and cold sweeps across the land killing people, livestock and hope. Farms fail within weeks and stockpiles become targets of raids. Morality and ethics fall away as survival instincts guide all decisions. The world will never be the same...

The First Althing

Summary: Thorsteinn Ingolfsson has been looking at creating a revolutionary new form of self governance for the denizens of Islandia. Almost all who live upon its shores have fled the monarchy in Norveig. With the coming of Fimbulwinter, however, there is an increased need for a framework that can settle disputes which have become all too common. Rather than letting family feuds escalate to violence, Thorsteinn wishes to try something new. With the help of the dwellers, he will organize the very first Althing.

Location: Althingvellir, Islandia

Time Period: 930

Background: For a generation folks have been coming to Islandia as their homes were turned upside down by Harald the Tanglehaired. Those who came to Islandia were fed up with the monarchy and wanted freedom and self-governance. As they settled Islandia's many inlets and fjords the crowding led to land disputes. Many disputes turned violent without a monarch who could pass judgement. The problem has become endemic in the western part of Islandia due to the mass immigration. Every grievance became amplified with the coming of Fimbulwinter. Thorsteinn Ingolfsson hails from clan Arnar. They were the first to arrive on Islandia's shores and many look to him for wisdom as land owners take the law into their own hands.

For full details on the structure of the Althing, please see page 236 ("Viking Life- Althing" chapter).

For more details on charges and sentencing, please see page 242 ("Viking Life- Justice" chapter).

Main Characters:

- *Njal is a legal expert, second to none in Islandia, but unfortunately he cannot grow a beard. He lives in the southern parts of Islandia, in a village called Bergthorshvol. He has represented many legal cases and has a very strong reputation across the Island. Thorsteinn insists that you bring Njal as it will improve the legitimacy of the Althing.*

- *Hrut comes from an impressive family lineage, a descendant of Sigurd Snake-in-the-Eye and in turn*

Ragnar Lodbrok. He was married to Unn for a very short time. After it was determined that he could not have children (from a local Voelva) Unn divorced him and demanded the return of the dowry. He has demanded to keep the dowry and accuses his ex-wife's family of using witchcraft to drum up false charges. He lives in Hvammur.

- **Unn** is the daughter of Mord Gigja, a very wise man. They live in Saebol and demand Hrut return the large dowry. He has challenged them to a knattleikur (a duel, see below) but they know that without a champion they stand no chance against him.

- **Thorkel** is a leader in the Vathasdal region. His father Thorgrim settled Islandia as a rich land owner and established a large farm with many farmhands who he treated well. When Thorkel travels to the Althing, he brings many farmhands, among them is Skeggi.

- **Skeggi** the farmhand is a valuable and loyal servant of the Thorkel farmstead. He is a hard worker who has recently been rewarded with a silver arm band from his master. He does not want to offend the other farmhands by wearing it out in the open, so he keeps it humbly tucked away with his belongings.

- **Asmund** has recently come to Islandia with his wife Asdis. They are invited to live in the Vathasdal region by Thorkel. Because Thorkel is going to the Althing, Asmund decides to come as well, bringing his wife and four children (Atli oldest son, Grettir youngest son, Thordis oldest daughter and Rannveig youngest daughter).

- **Grettir** is a 14 year old son of Asmund and Asdis. He is disliked by his father Asmund, because he refuses to do chores around the farm. Grettir believes all these chores are beneath him and that he is destined for great and heroic deeds. He is loved by his mother Asdis, because she sees greatness that is being wasted on a farmstead.

- **Olaf Hoskuldsson** is the richest merchant in western Islandia. He is the foster son of Thord and owes most of his success to he inheritance he received when Thord passed away. He is being summoned to the Althing in order to defend himself against Vigdis and her legal claim to her husband's inheritance. He plans on bringing his new sword Fotbitr to the event.

- **Vigdis** is the ex-wife of Thord. Thord was a wealthy landowner who fell out of love with Vigdis and their children. Before he passed he divorced his wife and took a foster son named Olaf Hoskuldsson in order to thwart his wife's claim to the inheritance. She wants what's rightfully hers.

- **Hen-Thorir** is a businessman who has many homes in western-Islandia. He has made many loans and is eager to see how the Althing will help him collect.

- **Skallagrim** is the son of Kveldulf Bjalfason. His son is the infamous Egil, a mountain of a man, who sails about stirring up trouble. He resides in Borgarfjord on the south western end of Islandia. Since he lives close, he will come without reservation. He has no grievances with the locals, but his hatred for King Harald's family runs deep. If questioned about any grievances, he will launch into a tirade about King Harald and the newly self-proclaimed King Erik Blood Axe.

- **Kjartan Hravenkell** is the Godi of Adalbol. He is charged with the care of Freyfaxi, a sacred mare in the service of the god Frey. No one may ride her. Transgression against this religious law is dealt with severely, the punishment ranging from outlawry to a death sentence. He refuses the invitation to the Althing.

- **Arnkell Thorvalds** is a rich owner of a very prosperous lumber mill. His son Snorri is acused of riding Freyfaxi, a sacred mare dedicated to the god Frey. He refuses the invitation to the Althing.

- **Ingvar** *is the ulfhednar chieftain who resides in Evingard. He is unlikely to come due to the troubles that have started at the Cornerstone of the World.*

- **Erik the Red" Thorvaldsson** *may have a few accusers at the Althing. Charges ranging from robbery to murder may be leveled against him. Despite the summons, he will refuse to come, choosing to stay within the relative safety of Hornstrandir. This may spin off into a follow-up adventure for the dwellers.*

Plot: The assembly is to take place in three weeks. There are many preparations remaining, including the personal invitations to the island's chiefs. The dwellers are hired by Thorsteinn to help organize the Althingvellir site as well as summon the heads of every outpost in Islandia. The heads are listed in the "main characters" section above. If the dwellers don't own a boat, Thorsteinn loans them a longship for the job. While travelling to eastern Islandia to invite Godi Kjartan Hravenkell the dwellers find that the town is in an uproar over the desecration of a sacred mare by Snorri Thorvalds. Despite the very appropriate invitation to settle the dispute, all parties involved refuse to attend. If the dwellers choose to stop in Hornstrandir they find a veritable den of vipers and thieves, not a single honourable man in the whole outpost. Grievances in Hornstrandir are settled with the blade and they will laugh and mock the Althing if it is brought up. The dwellers shouldn't be able to leave without a few cuts and bruises as a parting gift from the locals.

The Althingvellir site setup includes a pitch where youths can play knattleikur. It's a local ball game where teams attempt to outscore the opposing side. The other part of the setup is the holmgangr, an area reserved for dueling. Some disputes may forgo arbitration by jury if both sides agree to resolution by holmgangr. A holmgangr pitch is a small island or a raised dais that confines the space used in a duel. Tradition requires that the holmgangr be surrounded by sacred "axe waters", a body over water such as a river or lake, even if it is man made. This requirement may be waived considering it is Fimbulwinter. The participants of the duel negotiate the terms of the contest, as well as the stakes. Some would fight until first blood was drawn, others would allow each dueler three shields. A winner was declared once all three are destroyed. Some claimants may summon a champion in their place if they are incapable of participating in the holmgangr.

Thorsteinn asks the dwellers to assist with judging the many grievances that are brought before the Althing. They are free to refuse the obligation. They may also be hired by some of the participants as legal counsel, helping build a case for their claims and/or defenses.

First Case

The first case is the claim Vigdis brings forth against Olaf Hoskuldsson. She claims that her ex-husband Thord built his fortunes with her help and that this last minute divorce and foster-son arrangement was out of ill will. Olaf's defense is that everything Thord did may be suspect but it was within legal limits of the law.

Second Case

Hrut and Unn level accusations against one another and it takes some time to calm them down. Hrut demands a knattleikur knowing full well that he would beat Unn or her father in a duel. Before the case Unn will look for a champion. Her father Mord will instead look to prove the charge of impotence.

Other cases

The Norn should feel free to add more cases where merchants may be seeking seizure of property after loans have not been repaid. Since the onset of Fimbulwinter, many businesses have failed and debts have become impossible to repay. Hen-Thorir has made many loans and is unmoved by excuses as to why his money cannot be repaid.

Interlude

While the proceedings are unfolding a bunch of youths are playing knattleikur. It is a close game and things heat up as the spirit of competition fills the player's hearts. Things get too physical between Grettir and Skeggi and an argument breaks out. Their teammates restrain them in order to halt the confrontation before it gets violent. As the two sides part, Grettir grabs a leather sack that looks like his but in fact belongs to Skeggi. Skeggi's beloved arm-ring is inside and he disputes the ownership claim. Grettir refuses to acknowledge Skeggi's demand to check the contents of the bag so Skeggi attacks Grettir with an axe. Grettir being the stronger of the two reverses the blow and kills Skeggi.

Third Case

The third grievance is fresh as Thorkel summons Grettir to the Althing. The initial charge is murder, but is reduced to killing after all evidence is presented. No matter what the dwellers attempt, they feel like these events have been per-ordained by the Norns.

Plot Twist: the outcome for Grettir has been predetermined by the Norns. He is to be sentenced to lesser Outlawry for a period of three years. During this time he will be cast out of Islandia, wherein he will perform great deeds and return a legend.

If the dwellers find a way to use divination magic to scry Hrut's past, they will discover that he is under a curse of infertility. After his wedding to Unn he traveled to Halogaland on business and while there he had a marital indiscretion with a Sammi witch named Gunnhild. She found out he was married and placed the curse upon him.

The Norn may choose to involve the dwellers in an on-site altercation by having charges leveled against the dwellers. This would see them stripped of "juror" status and brought before the Althing (and possibly the holmgangr pitch).

Kjartan and Arnkell, despite being no-shows at the Althing will cross paths with the dwellers in the future. This small meeting is a setup for the future encounter.

If Olaf Hoskuldson is forced to use his magic sword Fotbitr, things won't end well.

Fallout: The individuals the dwellers choose to defend will look to them as allies. They will receive invites to their outposts and will be treated as honoured guests. Those denizens that the dwellers rule against will look for revenge. The dwellers may have chosen to stand as proxies in the holmgangr.

The Crusaders March North

Summary: The great Holy Roman Empire was fixated on the barbarian hordes to the far east. The Faith must be brought by word and sword. When the sun was suddenly blotted out of the sky by Skoll, however, strategies quickly changed. Emperor Otto had heard of the Midgard prophesies that had told of wolves devouring the sun and moon. His armies are redirected from the east and are set on a northward campaign into Midgard. The dwellers are captured at the Danevirke and brought south to Quedlinburg in Saxony. There are tortured, interrogated and used as advisers or bargaining collateral.

Location: Quedlinburg, Saxony

Time Period: 931-932

Background: Emperor Otto's northern campaign was never successful. When he attempted naval incursions, Viking longships laid waste to his fleet. When he attempted an eastern flanking manoeuvre through the Baltic tribes, he was furiously repelled. Then finally he mustered a massive force with the aid of Pope John XII and hoped for a successful frontal assault. He had the overwhelming numbers in order to breach the mighty Danevirke, but at the moment of victory Ragnarok began. His frightened army scattered leaving him with ignoble defeat. Ever since he has been looking to capture and abduct persons of renown from Midgard in hopes of learning more about this spectacular event.

Main Characters:

- *The dwellers* are the main focus of this saga.

- *Emperor Otto* is the leader of the Holy Roman Empire that sits to the south of Midgard. His seat of power is in Quedlinburg, Saxony.

- *Aethelstan* is the general that Emperor Otto sends to gain a foothold on the Great Isles.

- *Hakon the Good* is a low-born bastard son of the late High-King Harald Fairhair. He seeks a new home after his bretheren sundered Norveig with their infighting for the throne.

Plot: Unwittingly the dwellers are hired by agents of the crusaders. They are asked to gather reconnaissance information for King Gorm the Old on the crusader formations south of the wall. They are paid an exorbitant amount on the condition that they keep the mission a secret. Once they sneak past the wall and are a mile or so south of the Danevirke, they are ambushed by an overwhelming force and brought to Quedlinburg. After being worked over in the dungeons, Emperor Otto comes to see them. He has many questions about the north: What happened to the sun and moon? Who is responsible? How is it reversed? What is the easiest way for an army to breach Midgard?

If the dwellers prove difficult he keeps them as bargaining chips when nogotiating prisoner swaps with King Gorm the Old. They have time to escape and can slowly make their way back to the Danevirke. It will be a challenge and they may be recaptured because they stand out from the peasants of these foreign lands.

If the dwellers wish to cooperate, Emperor Otto promises their freedom if they help Aethelstan establish a beach-head for the invasion in the Great Isles. If they work in ernest to help Aethelstan establish Wessex, then they are granted freedom. If they give Aethelstan a hard time, then they are incarcerated in Winchester after the beach-head is established.

Plot Twist: If the dwellers choose to go with Aethelstan, they meet up with another "prisoner" from Midgard, Lief the Mountain Shaker. An adventurer who has seen many exotic sites and fought many strange monsters is looking to broaden his horizons. He is genuinely intrigued by the crusaders and their ways. He sees this as an opportunity to learn about these strangers, their customs and beliefs. He feels he has as much to gain from them as they do from him and he will go the distance with Aethelstan. If the dwellers tag along, they will cross paths with Hakon the Good who arrives shortly after the beach-head is established in Winchester.

Fallout: If the dwellers choose to double-cross and escape from the crusaders then the status quo in the relationship is maintained. If they ally themselves with the crusaders then they make friends with two kings and an emperor; the new King Aethelstan, King Hakon the Good and Emperor Otto. Emperor Otto may have some work for them in the south and may ask them to go and spy on margrave Berengar. When word gets out, this will sour any relationships they may already have with the kings of Midgard.

Hravenkell's saga

Summary: The story begins in Evingard. A troubled Halfdan Ingvarsson comes to see the dwellers. The village of Adalbol to the west of Evingard has come under threat. A monstrously giant rampaging bull has cut off access to the town. Recently Halfdan has taken the responsibility of moving lumber from Adalbol to the port of Evingard. This new threat has halted his obligations to Adalbol.

Location: Adalbol, Islandia

Time: 933, the Sword Age begins

Background: The Adventure takes place in the remote town of Adalbol. Two leading families, the Thorvalds (who follow the Aesir) and the Hravenkells (who follow the Vanir) are rivals. The Hravenkells are bovine herders who have lost their only bull in a recent cold snap. The Thorvalds are wood cutters who operate a mill on the fjord. The waters within the fjord are heated by the many thermal springs and haven't frozen over. This allows the water wheel saw mill to continue operations throughout Fimbul-winter.

Kjartan Hravenkell is both chieftain of Adalbol and high-godi of Frey. He is the patriarch of the Hravenkell clan and has worked tirelessly to maintain his clan's dominance in these lands. The Thorvalds clan is led by Arnkel whose business has flourished and has brought incredible wealth and influence to his clan. This has strained relations between both men.

A month prior to the arrival of the dwellers, a spiral of violence would degenerate relations and inflict a terrible curse upon all of Adalbol's inhabitants.

The story begins in a rather sordid fashion, with a marriage sundered by infidelity. Alfhild, the local Angel of Death, and her husband Briedavik were happy. Then a year ago they gave birth to a wonderful but demanding daughter they named Brana. The sleepless nights and stress started to cause rift in their marriage. The breaking point that unravelled their relationship came when Alfhild found her husband in bed with the young girl Vigdis Thorvalds. The ensuing storm would have resulted in Alfhild and Brana leaving town, but chieftain Kjartan worked swiftly to exile Briedavik instead. A community losing an Angel of Death would have had a much more profound repercussion upon Adalbol.

Briedavik's exile did not go well. The cold bit deeply into his skin and he may have died had it not been for the Land Vaettir's intervention. The Vaettir could not bear to watch the suffering and regret that consumed the man. She took pity and transformed his body to that of a man-wolf. The fur would keep him warm, and the new form could allow him to hunt for sustenance. He could repay her by dealing with undesirables within her dominion, namely the Thorvalds who have been clear cutting her forests. Briedavik retained his human consciousness, but it acquired a bestial edge.

Main Characters:

  – **Alfhild** is the Angel of Death, mother to Brana and divorced from Briedavik. Alfhild was very grateful to Snorri for haing saved little Brana from being abducted by a were-wolf. In the process, little Snorri offended the chieftain Kjartan Hravenkell and was sentenced to death. Alfhild cursed Kjartan for killing Snorri. The curse is that he will know no rest while alive or dead. He will succumb to the beast within.

- **Arnkel Thorvalds** is the Snorri's father and head of the Thorvalds clan and owner of a prosperous lumber business. His wife died during childbirth. His lumber mill does very well even during Fimbul-winter since the fjord's heated waters do not freeze. It allows his water wheel saw mill to operate and the river allows for upstream lumber to be shipped downstream without much effort and cost. Arnkel suspects that the land vaettir has it in for him, but he presses on unintimidated. Arnkel despises the Hvravenkell clan for killing Snorri. In revenge he went and killed the sacred mare Freyfaxi. He stole her head to deal a deep emotional wound to Kjartan. Despite the curse of the bull, Arnkel will not relent on his revenge. Whatever the cost, he will see the Hravenkells ruined.

- **Bjorn Hravenkell** is brother to Kjartan the chieftain. He is a devoted brother and the boss at the cow farm. His only bull died a few weeks ago and Bjorn has requested passing merchants to get him a new one. He is ready to pay top coin. There is a lot of tension between his clan and the Thorvalds, but this hasn't stopped him from falling in love with Vigdis Thorvalds. Bjorn was heartbroken when Vigdis had a one-night-stand with Briedavik. After his brother's strange death he inherited a lot of responsibility. Atop his business, Bjorn inherited and needed to manage the leadership of the town, Frey's temple and the duties as head of the Hravenkell clan. He visited the grave every day, even when busy, even if it meant bringing the cow herd with him. One day, one of his cows got pregnant and he still had not pro-cured a new bull. This unnatural pregnancy progressed quickly and days later a young bull was born. It was a menace and grew quickly, propelled by some dark sorcery. Within a week it was double the size of any full grown bull. It turned on everyone and in a murderous rage began killing with abandon.

- **Brana** is the infant daughter of Alfhild and Briedavik. She is abducted by her father when he is in werewolf form and is then subsequently rescued by Snorri.

- **Briedavik** was the stone mason of Adalbol. He became estranged from his wife Alfhild and daughter Brana after a marital indescretion. Briedanik has been exiled from Adalbol for his affair with Vigdis Thorvalds. The land Vaettir known as Byggvir saved his life and he now owes her a blood debt. In a moment of grief and heartbreak, he attempted to abduct his daughter but Snorri Thorvalds intervened. Rather than harm-ing the boy, he let him "save" little Brana. There will be more opportunities to reunite with little Brana.

- **Byggvir** is an old and powerful Land Vaettir. She oversees the entire Adalbol Fjord. She is sympa-thetic to the Norns and the Vanir and hates the Thorvalds for clear cutting the land. She has inflicted various "accidents" upon the Thorvalds in hopes of closing down their booming lumber business. Many have died in the swift currents of the fjord and Byggvir loves to animate the drowned corpses as black skeletons who harry her enemies.

- **Freyfaxi** is the sacred mare dedicated to the Vanir god Frey. The mare brings bounty and fertility to the land so long as she isn't touched by a non-Godi and no one may every ride her. The child Snorri rode her in order to save Brana from the were-wolf (Briedavik shapechanged by the Vaettir). In revenge for the killing of Snorri, Freyfaxi was killed and decapitated by Snorri's father Arnkel Thorvalds. The deed was done in secret so no evidence could point to the perpetrator.

- **Kjartan Hravenkell** is the chieftain of Adalbol and high-godi of Frey. Brother to Bjorn the bovine herder. His prized possession was a sacred mare named Freyfaxi. He has also worked hard to ensure that clan Hravenkell doesn't get superseded by the rival clan of the Thorvalds (the lucrative saw mill owners). When he found out little Snorri rode Freyfaxi, he had no choice but to punish the boy for the desecration he had caused. He chose the harshest punishment prescribed by the law in order to kill the sole Thorvalds son, possibly ending the lineage. This earned him a curse from Alfhild. A few days later someone killed Freyfaxi and did away with the head making a proper burial impossible. This caused Kjartan to sink into an endless spiral of anger, grief and shame. He sat on his throne for three days, brooding, refusing food and drink. On the third day he had turned to stone and had merged with his throne. He was buried and visited daily by his brother Bjorn. Sometimes his brother brought the cows to the burial mound. During one such visit, Alfhild's curse impregnated a cow with Kjartan's soul. He was born within a few days and became a bull with a terrible and violent temperament. He grew to adulthood in a few days and then broke loose, trampling the towns inhabitants to death. He cannot be killed and will eternally rise from the ashes until Freyfaxi's head is found and given a proper burial.

- **Snorri Throvalds** is the only son of Arnkel. His mother is deceased. He was a good teen, with a good heart. One day he saw little Brana being abducted by a were-wolf and he ran to the stables to get a horse. They were all spooked by the beast, only Freyfaxi remained calm. Despite knowing the sacred nature of the mare, he threw caution to the wind and rode after her on Freyfaxi. The mare startled the were-wolf and he dropped the basket with little Brana inside. This allowed Snorri to scoop her up and bring her back to Adalbol. After returning he went to face Kjartan and confessed the truth. Kjartan didn't take the news well and sentenced the teen to death.

- **Vigdis Thorvalds** is the daughter of the lumber magnate Arnkel Thorvalds. She fell in love with Bjorn but had a fight with him over his wandering eyes. In an attempt to make him jealous, she seduced Briedavik and shared a night of passion with him. She went too far, however, sundering Briedavik's mariage to Alfhild and wounding Bjorn much more deeply than intended. She keeps out of the public eye while gossip runs wild throughout Adalbol.

Plot: As the dwellers approach the town they catch a glimpse of a were-wolf bounding through the snow carrying a basket normally used to carry infants. He is too hard to catch and eludes any pursuit. The dwellers arrive in Adalbol to find it dark and quiet. Occasional distant bull or boar-like grunts can be heard. Everyone seems to be indoors and all the lights are off. There are large hoof tracks in the snow throughout Adalbol.

In the first house they enter, the dwellers find Arnkel Thorvalds sitting at his dinner table in the dark. Laid out on the table is the corpse of his son Snorri who looks long dead from having his throat cut. Arnkel is pretty vague about how long he has been sitting there and refuses to end his mourning, telling the dwellers "the shadows are the company I seek in my time of grief".

If the dwellers go to the main hall, they find it abandoned and the high-throne missing. Behind where the throne should have been is a massive gaping hole in the wall- hacked open from both sides by axes. There are drag marks that look like the throne (heavier than it should be) was dragged out in the direction of the barrows.

Most residents are found sitting quietly in their cold and dark homes. If the dwellers interact with the denizens, they find the denizens of Adalbol very cold and emotionless. The townsfolk are not hostile towards the dwellers unless threatened. The townsfolk will share information about the town and the long list of grievances. Each person who harbours a grudge will ask the dwellers to help solve their problems... however they will not help them in doing so.

The solution to Adalbol's problems is the resolution of every grievance.

Plot Twist: Everyone in Adalbol is long dead and have since become Haugbui- Briedavik is the only exception. They also cannot be killed and will rise within minutes of being defeated or even destroyed. Only solving the cycle of grievances will put this town to rest. When the curse lifts, everyone turns to ash with the exception of Briedavik who is crushed by the loss of his daughter.

Fallout: If the dwellers succeed, word of their great deeds increases their legend. Monarchs of Midgard will view the dwellers in the more favourable light when encountered in future sagas. If the town's problems are solved, then Briedavik and the vaettir Byggvir become strong allies. If the curse isn't lifted then Adalbol remains shrouded in gloom.

Reforging the Sun

Summary: The sun has been devoured and some disagree that this should become the new reality. Prophesy states that Fimbulwinter will last only three years and there are organizations who have been working at reforging a new sun that could be launched into the skies above Midgard. It appears that the elite mercenary group known as the Battle-Wolves is the organization that is going to make it happen. They are looking for new members to help accelerate the re-forging process.

Location: Evingard, Islandia and Ath Cliath, Hibernia

Time Period: 933-934

Background: Many would speculate that Hildolfr and Odin are one and the same. If the senior members of the Battle-Wolves know, they remain tight lipped. Regardless, what is important is that Hildolfr's goals are similar to those of Odin, namely the construction of a new sun. Almost no task is too tough for this elite mercenary outfit. As a result they command top coin for their services while working for the most prestigious clients across Midgard. With deep coffers, an extensive network of powerful and connected denizens, they focus their clandestine work on forging a new sun. Despite keeping their work secret, they have faced setbacks as emissaries of the Rime Jotuns have worked to oppose them every step of the way.

The Rime Jotuns are acclimatized to the cold and dark of Jotunheim. Now Fimbulwinter provides them with a clear advantage over the Aesir gods who have been accustomed to a bright and warm lifestyle. The agents of the Rime Jotuns will stop at nothing to bring ruin to Hildolfr's plans. That is why Hildolfr is careful to keep his plans a secret from everyone except his inner circle. The most critical component of the work is the highly paid Dvergar blacksmith known simply as Svalms. His talents makes it all possible, since no mortal would have the knowledge required to forge such an incredible artifact.

Hildolfr came to see him with a hypothetical project- to create an artifact that can generate enough heat to melt the snows of Midgard. Svalms provided an estimated cost and list of materials required, most of which was missing from his forge in Ath Cliath. Hildolfr promised to double the payment if Svalms would keep the project a secret. Svalms began to look for the required materials but the quantities he needed were nowhere to be found in Midgard. Hildolfr decided to secretly help, so Draugstagg was hired as a trusted merchant who could provide the needed materials to Svalms. Draugstagg and Hildolfr would behave as if they were unaware of each other's existence. This would downplay Hildolfr's power and reach and also make the project seem more innocuous to Svalms.

The Cornerstone of the World is a critical and strategic locale in the coming war. He who controls the Cornerstone controls the gateways into other worlds. Portals are quick routes to other worlds, but they are random and unpredictable. As a result, any ongoing operation that requires minerals to flow from other realms into Midgard requires the Cornerstone's predictable gateways. The merchant Magnus Magnusson owed a huge debt of gratitude to Hildolfr for his success. To repay his debt Magnus oversees a pipeline of special crates of ore for Hildolfr (marked with the Othala rune). Magnus manages a mine that digs into the earth surrounding the Cornerstone, extracting iron and copper ore from the earth. This is a cover operation for the real flow of goods that moves from the other realms, through the Cornerstone and into Midgard. The port in Evingard moves the regular crates as well as the ones marked with the Othala rune to Ath-Cliath. There, agents from the Whitesmith's Guild purchase the Othala marked crates from Draugstagg. For more on the Whitesmith's Guild please see page 131 in the "Fabled Markets of Ath-Cliath" section.

On the first night of Ragnarok, Bergelmir, king of the Rime Jotuns, tasked Isaice, a mysterious witch from Jarnvid, with the goal of shutting down any attempts at constructing a new sun. She and her agents have been busy monitoring all major Dvergar forges for suspicious activities. Recently, Svalms in Ath-Cliath has caught her attention.

Main Characters:

- *Hildolfr is the mysterious leader of the legendary Battle-Wolves. He is a strategic thinker, careful planner and efficient executor. Despite his many talents, what he is trying to achieve is so grand that inevitably problems strike at the least opportune moments.*

- *Svalms is an awe-inspiring ultra-talented Dvergar who has assumed human appearance. He is guided by profit and has no stakes in Ragnarok's outcome. It doesn't matter whether the gods or Jotuns win. Like most of his brethren, Svalms sees the Norns as snake oil peddlers whose ëprophecyí is self-fulfilling when the gullible work to make it happen.*

- *Magnus Magnusson is the willing co-conspirator of the secret mining operation in Evingard. His knowledge is limited to what Hildolfr needs him to know. He is happy with the arrangement since his business has seen a hundredfold increase in profits. Much more on Evingard can be found in the Fafnir's Treasure saga book.*

- *The Battle-Wolves Inner Circle can all be found on page 14 in the "Legends and Villains" chapter. These five members manage the most important tasks in the organization.*

- *Isaice is a mysterious woman whose real name remains a mystery. She is the thorn in Hildolfr's side. With the uncanny ability to strike and then disappear, she has waged a relentless assault on the ore pipeline. She has many allies who she uses in order to strike multiple locations at once. Each strike not only delays production, but it also drains the Battle-Wolves' coffers.*

Plot: There are three parts to the story.

Part I

Funds are drying up. The Battle-Wolves approach the dwellers with an offer: if they complete a quest for them, instead of payment, they will be granted membership into the illustrious Battle-Wolves. King Sitric is paying the Battle-Wolves to go and find his daughter Ingrid "the Wanderer". She may soon have a marriage proposal and he needs her back in Ath-Cliath. Time is of the essence because Canute, son of Gorm the Old is coming in two weeks time.

Part 2

Nidhogg the primordial serpent corrupts Dreki the Land Vaettir. This halts all mining in the vicinity of Evingard. See the "Cornerstone of the World" saga on page 374.

Part 3

Isaice has approached Svalms with a higher counter-offer. He must choose sides, and like any self respecting Dvergar, he is looking at the highest bidder. Failure in Part 1 means that the Battle-Wolves cannot afford to raise the payment. Success means that Isaice works to disrupt the mining and delivery at several key points in the pipeline. She also tried to win the dwellers over to her side.

If the dwellers stick with Hildolfr, they get assigned objectives that take them into other worlds. With some key miners unable to complete their assignments, the dwellers must go into Muspelheim, Vanagard and Nidavellir to retrieve some outstanding crafting materials.

Plot Twist: The agents from Jotunheim are ready to pay the unknown Dvergar more in order to sabotage the project. If they find out who it is and the dwellers fail to raise the funds to keep paying Svalms, he turns sides.

If the dwellers have a lengthy conversation with Isaice, she defends her cause by bringing up the many grievances the Jotuns have towards the gods (see "the Writ" in the *Core Rulebook* page 19). She is also ready to introduce them to Drifa, Queen of Svalbard who may hire them as part of her elite guard. Isaice will also reward the dwellers with magical items that will allow them to shrug off the cold and see perfectly in darkness.

Should the dwellers decide to reforge the moon as well, then there are delays that are pre-ordained by the Norns. Inexplicable delays occur until 935.

Fallout: The outcome of this adventure will determine the duration of Fimbulwinter. If the dwellers launch a new sun into the sky, then Fimbulwinter ends and all of Yggdrassil enjoys the wonders of light and warmth. If the project is sabotaged, then the status quo remains and the Jotuns continue to press their advantage in the heavens.

This saga also affects how the higher powers will perceive the dwellers. If the dwellers help Hildolfr with his secret task, then the heavenly alliances are set: the dwellers are allies of the gods and foes of the giants. If the dwellers help Isaice after discovering her motives, then the alliances are inverted. Either way, the dwellers are now major players in the second age of Ragnarok. Their names and achievements will be discussed by beings in the outer realms.

The War for the Sampo

Summary: The kingdoms of Pohjola and Kalevala are on the precipice of war. Mistress Louhi prepares her armies for attack in hopes of recovering the Sampo. Lord Vainamoinen expects the attack and has laid traps for the incoming army. The dwellers are caught in the middle.

Location: Northern Baltic region

Time Period: 933

Background: The full background of the conflict can be found in the descriptions of Mistress Louhi and Lord Vainamoinen in the "Legends and Villains" chapter (page 14). While Vainamoinen was returning with the Sampo Louhi attacked in eagle form. The resulting battle damaged the Sampo, greatly reducing its capabilities. Any more jostling may destroy this fragile relic of power. As a result it is housed in the most secure and guarded locations. Without the Sampo, Kalevala would have succumbed to Fimbulwinter. Instead the country has enjoyed its greatest bounty since its founding.

Main Characters:

– *Louhi Mistress of Pohjola wants her Sampo back. She has a standing army that she will level against Kalevala, as she doesn't want to destroy her birthplace. If push comes to shove, she will loose Skoll and Hati upon the kingdom and its inhabitants.*

– *Lord Vainamoinen Hero of Kalevala is going to do everything in his might to protect Kalevala and keep the Sampo. His powerful song magic will slow an invading army, and the magical beings of Kalevala will ensure that the country has formidable defenses. If he can smash the invaders, then he will counterattack and burn Pohjola to ashes, ensuring an end to this conflict.*

– *Ilmarinen is the master blacksmith credited with the creation of the Sampo. He has devised many traps to snare the incoming army.*

– *Joukahainen is a powerful Skald, second to only Vainamoinen. Joukahainen has many reasons to despise Vainamoinen and has chosen to ally himself with Louhi in the coming war. He plans to counter Vainamoinen's spell songs.*

– *Skoll & Hati are two gargantuan celestial wolves who hail from Jotunheim. They stand a mile tall at the shoulder. The amount of damage they could cause in Midgard is unprecedented. Mistress Louhi's charm magic has bound their loyalty to her.*

Plot: The Sampo is such a unique and powerful device that its destruction would damage humanity's chances of surviving Ragnarok. As such the dweller's primary goal will be saving the Sampo from destruction. The secondary goal will be to keep the kingdoms from war, as the land of Midgard will need the monarchy unified in order to survive the crusader invasion. This is a very difficult task because both sides have a long list of grievances against the other and are reluctant to budge.

The dwellers may also choose to join one side or the other based on their opinion on the conflict thus far. If they do the Norn should encourage them to create tactics for overcoming the opposing side. Pohjola will attack by sea with hundreds of longships. Kalevala will have traps set in the sea that will sink many incoming ships. They will also have incendiary traps set on shore to deal with any warbands whose boats survived the naval traps. Lastly Kalevala has a strong army that will decimate whatever armies may breach their forests. The plan is to then sail north and counter-attack Pohjola who will have very few warbands in reserve.

Plot Twist: Louhi has two new pets which individually are more powerful than a regular standing army. These weapons of mass destruction, once loosed will tear kingdoms to shreds. Kalevala is completely unprepared for the possibility of celestial wolves joining the fight. If they do, all preparations would be for naught against such divine monstrosities.

Fallout: If an amicable solution could be found and both leaders forge a new friendship, then they will be added to the roster in the saga "Rallying the Kings and Queens of Midgard". If a protracted war breaks out, they will disregard anything else occurring in Midgard and focus on destroying one another. If Skoll and Hati join the war, then there is a chance that higher powers will intervene after a few kingdoms have been reduced to dust.

Rallying the Kings and Queens of Midgard

Summary: King Aethelstan's military is conquering the north without much resistance. King Sitric and his Great Isle alliance may not be enough to stop Edmund the Just's advance. Complicating matters, Hakon the Good has launched an invasion of Norveig, looking to claim the throne for Aethelstan's cause. Meanwhile the kings of Midgard, who are divided and fighting each other, will most surely fall. The dwellers must meet with the kings and unite them in the defense of Midgard.

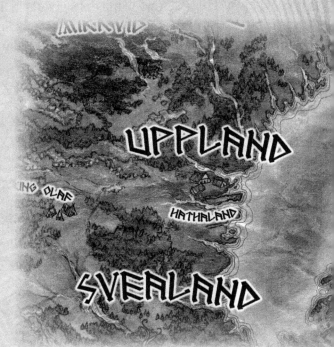

Location: Hathaland, Uppland

Time Period: 934

Background: Each of the kings has an incentive that will spur them to join the Midgard Alliance. Naturally they have their own personal and local problems, so it will take some skillful diplomacy to get the monarchy to see the larger picture. Depending on how the "Darkness Falls" saga unfolded, the power landscape will vary greatly.

Main Characters:

- *King Erik Blood Axe* is the front-runner for the throne of Norveig. He rules from his seat of power in Alvaldsnes. He wants to be crowned at the Throne of Kings.

- *King Sitric Cuaran* is the monarch of Ath-Cliath and Hibernia. He will join if the dwellers bring him the heads of the Hibernian clan chiefs who oppose his rule.

- *King Ragnall* has his seat of power in Jorvik and rules Northumbria. He will join if King Sitric has been recruited.

- *King Gofraid* has conquered Strathclyde. He will join if King Sitric has been recruited and if King Constantine signs a treaty of non-aggression towards Strathclyde.

- **King Gorm the Old** is the lord of the Danevirke. He will join if the other monarchs pledge 50,000 Skatt to his war chest. He knows first hand what the crusaders are capable of.

- **King Bjorn Eriksson** is lord of Uppland and Svealand. He will join for the fun of it!

- **King Rognvald** of Uppland (if alive) will join without question if the dwellers have helped him in the past.

- **King Bjorn Farmann** is the beloved lord of Vestfold. He will refuse to join if King Erik is in the alliance or if he plans to be. King Bjorn would rather co-rule with Hakon the Good than Erik Blood Axe.

- **Queen Drifa** is the undisputed mistress of Svalbard. She has little interest in joining the alliance as her kingdom is so far removed from the conflict. Only if things are going poorly will she join in order to preserve the old ways.

- **King Constantine II** is the monarch of Alba. If he does join the Midgard alliance, it will be temporary. If and when the crusaders gain the upper hand, his armies will strike a lethal blow from behind.

Plot: The kings each want something done for them before they join an alliance. The dwellers will need to undergo a quest to secure each monarch into the alliance. Some will be easier than others. How well the crusaders do depends on how many kingdoms join the alliance. If less than four join, then the cause is lost. Victory is assured only when six or more join the alliance. If some of these monarchs are already dead, then the Norn should introduce new monarchs into the roster.

Plot Twist: Hakon the Good has a secret strategy. He plans to win by bribery instead of force. He comes with many chests of gold and silver which he uses to reward the petty kings who are first to join his cause. He will also enter into agreements where the petty kings will retain control of their lands under Hakon's rule. Those who convert to the New Faith will enjoy lower taxation rates. King Erik has been rather bloodthirsty and oppressive in his quest for Norveig, so many petty kings will see Hakon's approach as the most desirable outcome- making conquest shockingly swift.

When counting how many kingdoms have joined the alliance for purposes of the victory resolution, if Constantine joins and then backstabs, reduce the total count by two to three. This depends on how opportune his moment was when he switched sides.

Kings and Queens are very fickle and their egos must be managed. Depending on who the dwellers recruit first, their jobs may become more difficult if a monarch is offended that they weren't approached earlier. Relationship management will become very important. If the dwellers already have a bad relationship with a certain monarch, then forging the alliance will be more difficult.

Fallout: Should the dwellers take up this quest, they will become mortal enemies to the kings of Outer-Midgard.

The Coming of the Storjunkari

FINNMARK

HÅLOGALAND

Summary: The dwellers are woven into a tale of northern struggle, recognition and redemption. A new power is rising in the north. An omen brings the dwellers to distant Finnmark where they meet a strange young man named Einar. He opens their eyes to a new reality that is coming full circle.

Location: Finnmark

Time Period: 935, the Wind Age begins

Background: The far north of Midgard has always been slandered and ignored by the rest of Midgard. Its inhabitants have been written off and vilified as primitive barbarians or evil witches and sorcerers. It is a land forgotten by time, which is unfortunate as the ancient traditions of this region have maintained the secrets of the first humans who walked upon Midgard. The secrets of creation past, and the secrets of destruction future.

Their dwellings are tents, their villages move with the migration patterns of the reindeer herds. Life is sacred and taking a life while hunting must end in reverence and thanks. They are neighbours to the Land Vaettir and communicate with them more naturally than humans do with speech.

Their magic is not of this world. It taps into the energies of the cosmic tree Yggdrasil and the currents that flow around it. A magic that was born from the first life. An art that only the Orlog can comprehend, and even then, usually it bends and sometimes breaks the mortal mind.

Main Characters:

- *Einar is the vision of the Storjunkari tribes. There are no leaders or kings among the northern tribes. His role would be better described as that of a guide. Einar's purity of spirit has allowed him to become a vessel that guides mankind to their logical conclusion with respect to Ragnarok... a return to how it all began.*

- *Berga is Einar's first wife and speaks for her husband when they must interact with outsiders. Her demeanour may seem strange, perhaps insane, but it is part and parcel of who she is. She has been mistaken as a Seithkona, but in truth, she and her fellow wives are Orlogs.*

- *Kjell is a chieftain in Norrland. He has his prejudices against the tribes of the north, but Einar's group has definitely changed his outlook on their way of life.*

- *Queen Drifa the mistress of Svalbard knows much about the northern culture and lifestyle. Svalbard is very different, it is an extension of Jotunheim rather than Halogaland or Midgard. If the dwellers are in good standing with her, she will impart knowledge about the reindeer cult, nomadic lifestyle and society in Finnmark.*

Plot: The story begins as a new moon rises for the first time in years. It may be as a result of the "Reforging a New Sun" saga (should the dwellers organize a plan to reforge it as well), or attributed to someone else's efforts. Regardless, the moon rises and the dwellers are delivered a powerful omen. They must go to Finnmark, to the ancient shrine of the reindeer. Along the way, they may choose to stop and visit Queen Drifa if they are in good standing with her. While they are there they cross paths with Vargeisa the Fire Wolf. She tells them ominously that her goals will be fulfilled in the coming Wind Age. The dwellers may choose to join her at a later date at the Cornerstone of the World as she travels in search of the seals.

The omen brings the dwellers to an ancient stone shrine, encased in ice. Chipping away at the ice the dwellers find a pictograph recounting the story of Einar's youth. It includes a very prominent moon which grows in every scene. The carvings shows a route south to Helsingland. As the dwellers begin their trip, reindeer come out of the brush and look though they are leading the way.

Traveling south, following the route, the dwellers come across an abandoned tower. After some investigation the dwellers piece together that this was the last known location of Wayland the Artisan. Perhaps some wondrous magic items may still linger behind.

Still further south in Norrland the dwellers cross paths with a prominent Chieftain name Kjell. He recounts how Einar and his tribe looked emaciated from their hurried travels south. They had skipped meals and sleep in order to get to their destination down south. He took pity on them and gave them provisions. Kjell shows the dwellers wood etchings the tribe left behind as thanks. These etchings depict a series of panels:

- *The first shows two worlds, one of darkness and ice, the other of fire and light. In between there looks to be something vaguely serpentine.*

- *The second shows that from the mists in-between the worlds a tree begins to grow. Entwined in the roots is a great wyrm.*

- *The third shows the tree with many more worlds upon its branches and roots. In orbit around the tree are a sun and moon.*

- *The fourth panel depicts the tree in silhouette with an absence of both sun and moon.*

- *The sixth and final panel depict the tree shaking, surrounded by turbulent winds. There are beings of light and dark who surround the entirety of the tree. It appears to be a war between the beings of light and those who look unsettlingly dark.*

If asked about Helsingland, Kjell recounts some history about his neighbours to the south. Thorir Helsing was the founder of Helsingland. He was a good man and he established these lands as a haven for those fleeing King Harald's war with King Bjorn Eriksson. His children, however, were a different matter. Kjell refuses to elaborate. Since Ragnarok, the kingdom has been abandoned, as if everyone just vanished into thin air. Some say the Helsing clan have wandered into Mirkvid.

The dwellers travel to Helsingland, following the reindeer. It appears that Kjell was correct, the kingdom is deserted. The dwellers pass abandoned villages with homes that betray a sudden unexpected departure. Meals are half eaten and signs of uncompleted chores are everywhere. In the capital city, in the King's fort, the dwellers find Einar and his tribe. He stands with arms outstretched to the sky, his wives forming a chanting circle around him, everyone else is on their knees. The moonlight here is polarizing, light and dark in stark extremes, dancing like the flames upon untold candles.

As the ritual ends, the wives speak in riddles when asked any questions. Einar remains silent and content as a wind picks up, tossing around light and dark as if they were leaves.

Plot Twist: The rise of the moon ushers in the third age of Ragnarok- the Wind Age. It is the age where the cosmic tree shakes from the disturbances surrounding it... a wind of scintillating light and unsettling darkness.

Fallout: If you stop and listen, you can hear the Wind Age, it's coming... and it brings the War of Shadow!

Appendix A: Updated Equipment

With the addition of Defensive Metas, the *Core Rulebook* equipment tables are updated.

Armour & Shields	Size	DF	Reach	PF	Focus	Parry	Meta	Cost
Reinforced shield	3					3	Deflect	90
Metal shield	4					4	Deflect	160
Spiked Wooden shield	4	1	1			2	Deflect	160
Spiked metal shield	5	1	1			3	Deflect	250
Tower Defender	5					5	Deflect	250
Bladed Shield	6	2	1			3	Deflect	360
Spiked Tower Shield	6	1	1			4	Deflect	360
Tower Shield	6					6	Deflect	360
Light Armour	3			1		1	Absorb	100
Light Magician's Robes	3				1		Eldritch	100
Medium Armour	4			2			Absorb	170
Medium Ceremonial Garb	4				1	1	Eldritch	170
Medium Graceful Armour	4			1		2	Absorb	170
Heavy Armour	5			2		1	Absorb	260
Heavy Runic Garb	5				1	2	Eldritch	260
Heavy Divine Robes	5			1	1		Eldritch	260
Heavy Nimble Armour	5			1		3	Absorb	260

Appendix B: Pre-Generated Dwellers

In this section you will find six level-8 pre-generated dwellers. They have been designed for immediate play with only one set of runes (split among all six dwellers). Some of their powers have been simplified in order to ensure they are truly pick-up-and-play ready.

Blacksmith

The Blacksmith has talents that many envy. He can create items not only out of metals and stones but also out of wood. He is a master warrior thanks to his knowledge of weapon creation. Blacksmiths are one of the clan's most valued subjects due to religious taboos around looting corpses. Many blacksmiths worship Dvergar, since their crafting skills are the envy of all.

Some master blacksmiths have created artefacts that clans and kingdoms have gone to war over. They are not bound by their forges: once they surpass apprentice levels, they gain the ability to summon a forge beast to their side, allowing them to craft while travelling.

Creating items, ranging from the mundane to the magical, follows a simple set of rules. The process uses the skill system, and may be attempted by those with no ranks in the required skills. The two principal skills are: Craft and Infuse. Craft allows one to create mundane items of great quality, and infuse allows one to add magical properties to an already crafted item.

Exemplar

The Exemplar Blacksmith enjoys time in the forge, but enjoys testing and showing off their creations even more. The exemplar judges his creations on the battlefield against items created by other smiths. He pushes himself to ever higher standards and ideals.

Artificer

The Creator Blacksmith enjoys nothing more than spending as much time and effort in the forge. The focus of an artificer's efforts are to create the most awe inspiring items, far surpassing anything shop owners may be peddling.

Alchemist

The Alchemist Blacksmith is one who explores the esoteric pleasures of imbuing items with magical properties. These items are sought after as they expand and greatly increase the power of the wielder.

	EXEMPLAR	ARTIFICER	ALCHEMIST
ACTIVE	**Weapon Stance** [Amplify Amplify Amplify] While in this stance, weapon and shield DF and Parry values are increased by +1 if they are already greater than 1. {Stance}	**Soul Bound Strike** [Amplify Multi Proficiency] Perform an Attack action with a weapon that you have crafted and gain a damage bonus equal to the number of personally crafted items you have equipped [+4]. {Manoeuvre}	**Infused Strike** [Amplify Amplify Proficiency] Perform a Weak Attack action and trigger an Active power of one equipped item; Minor Sacrifice +1. {Manoeuvre}
PASSIVE	**Builder's Glory** If you strike someone who wears/wields damaged equipment, you deal +2 damage per broken piece of equipment.	**Crafter's Promise** Your equipped items are harder to destroy. They gain a +4 QR when being compared for the intent of destruction.	**Invoker's Charity** When invoking a magic item's power, you may perform a Major Sacrifice +1 to trigger one Meta tags.
SKILL	**Repair Equipment**	**Craft**	**Infuse**

Essence
Your memories
lifeforce & wisdom

 4

Destiny
The effect you can
cause on the world

 2

Level: 8
Size: 4

4 Move **2** PF **4** Parry **4** DF

ACTIVE POWERS

Defensive Stance
Metas: [Amplify Amplify Amplify]
Type: {Stance}
Combat Effect: Protection Factor +1
Out-of-Combat Effect: Your defensive reflexes allow you to roll with any damage, reducing damage (falling, avalanche, etc).

Regenerating Block
Metas: [Amplify Amplify Amplify]
Type: {Interrupt}
Combat Effect: Perform a defend action and Heal +1 and Recover +2
Out-of-Combat Effect: When you avoid a perilous situation, you attract good fortune.

Disarming Parry
Metas: [Amplify Amplify Amplify]
Type: {Interrupt}
Combat Effect: Perform a defend action and disarm the attacker's weapon [Counter P].
Out-of-Combat Effect: You have the uncanny ability to catch and deflect fast moving objects.

Specialized Sundering Blow
Metas: [Amplify Amplify Proficiency]
Type: {Manoeuvre}
Combat Effect: Perform a weak attack action with a +1 Damage Factor and damage an opponent's equipped item [Counter P].
Out-of-Combat Effect: You have a talent for spotting structural weaknesses in crafted items.

META TAGS

AMPLIFY: Double the power effect
MULTI: +1 Reach and strike up to 2 more targets within reach
PROFICIENCY: Unleash your weapon's "meta"effect and you may perform a Minor Sacrifice +1 to add +1 to all weapon attributes

PASSIVE POWERS

Protector: You may perform defend actions for adjacent allies.
Drive Back: Each attack pushed your opponent back 1 hex (5') [Counter P]. You may perform a Minor Sacrifice +1 to move into the hex vacated by the opponent.
Tactician: During Upkeep, you may shift +/-1 position in Initiative.
Stand of Victory: When entering or exiting a stance, you may perform a Minor Sacrifice +1 to make a Weak Attack action. This can only trigger during the Action phase.

SKILLS

Appraisal: You know the relative quality and worth of any crafted item you observe.
Infuse: You may infuse active and passive powers into items. Use the Void rune to trigger infused Active powers.
Craft: You may craft items ranging from weapons and armour to jewelry and transportation.
Repair Equipment: You may remove the "damaged" condition from crafted items.

Crafted Warhammer	Crafted Spiked Shield	Crafted Scale Mail Armour	Mystic Arm Ring
Damage Factor: 2	Damage Factor: 2	Protection Factor: 2	Infused Powers:
Reach: 2	Parry: 4	Meta: Absorb	- Regenerating Block
Meta: Knockdown	Meta: Deflect	(Negate 2 harmful	- Specialized SunderingBlow
(Apply the Vulnerable	(Multiply total Parry and	conditions)	- Stand of Victory
condition)	Protection Factor by 3)		

Druid

Druids follow the way of the woods. Wood is sacred and has a spirit: knowing how to interact with it is a hidden art that goes by the name of Verwandlung and is the sacred property of the druid. Verwandlung involves a hierarchy of different wood that must be fashioned into wands and staves. Wielding the wand or staff made from that wood gives the druid powers associated with that grade of wood. Powers involve and encompass interactions with vegetation as well as with wild animals.

The mightiest of druids become one with the land and have the awe-inspiring power of terra-forming: a druid can change desolate tundra into a verdant mountain range as easily as one dresses in the morning. Druids shun civilization and prefer to dwell in pure nature.

Warden of the Woods

The Warden of the Woods specializes in verdant magic that is both restorative and benevolent. The Druid strives to understand the land and the spirits that dwell within. He understands that he is the drop that wishes to reunite with the sea.

Child of the Stars

Some Druids have the gift of foresight granted to them by their attunement to the heavens. The Child of the Stars gains insight from the constellations and can easily share his knowledge with his allies. He is also an expert brewer of potions and ointments.

Animist

This particular Druid has specialized in the ability to assume animal form. This bestial form is a kindred spirit for the Animist. The special affinity allows them to exemplify the very best from that species.

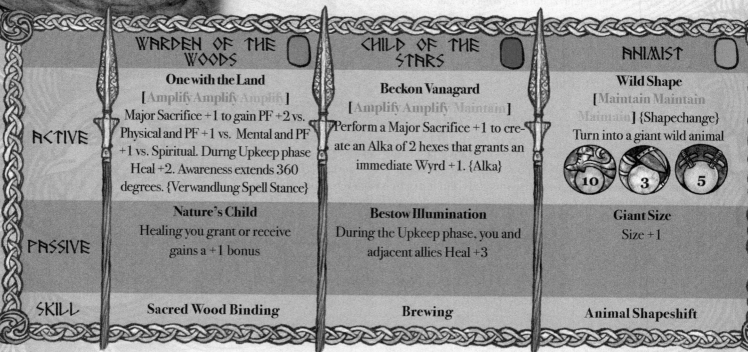

WARDEN OF THE WOODS	CHILD OF THE STARS	ANIMIST
One with the Land [Amplify Amplify Amplify] Major Sacrifice +1 to gain PF +2 vs. Physical and PF +1 vs. Mental and PF +1 vs. Spiritual. Durng Upkeep phase Heal +2. Awareness extends 360 degrees. {Verwandlung Spell Stance}	**Beckon Vanagard** [Amplify Amplify Maintain] Perform a Major Sacrifice +1 to create an Alka of 2 hexes that grants an immediate Wyrd +1. {Alka}	**Wild Shape** [Maintain Maintain Maimain] {Shapechange} Turn into a giant wild animal ⟨10⟩ ⟨3⟩ ⟨5⟩
Nature's Child Healing you grant or receive gains a +1 bonus	**Bestow Illumination** During the Upkeep phase, you and adjacent allies Heal +3	**Giant Size** Size +1
Sacred Wood Binding	**Brewing**	**Animal Shapeshift**

ACTIVE — PASSIVE — SKILL

METHALHUS

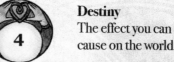

Essence
Your memories
lifeforce & wisdom

4

Destiny
The effect you can
cause on the world

2

Level: 8
Size: 4

Move	PF	Parry	DF	Pierce	Focus
4	2	2	2	2	2

ACTIVE POWERS

Forest's Gaze
Metas: [Amplify Area Maintain]
Type: {Verwandlung Spell}
Combat Effect: Heal 4, and then heal another 4 points when the recipient of this spell performs a move action this turn.
Out-of-Combat Effect: You can magically heal the wounds of others.

Field of Quagmires
Metas: [Amplify Amplify Maintain]
Type: {Verwandlung Alka Spell}
Combat Effect: Create an Alka of 4 hexes that imparts +1 intensity to the Impeded condition and +1 intensity to the Blind condition.
Out-of-Combat Effect: You can reshape earth and stone creating tunnels (10' sphere per minute).

Geyser of Living Water
Metas: [Amplify Amplify Maintain]
Type: {Verwandlung Alka Spell}
Combat Effect: Create an Alka of 4 hexes that Heals +6 and Recovers +4.
Out-of-Combat Effect: You may create water at will (1 ounce per minute)

Field of Thorny Vines
Metas: [Amplify Amplify Maintain]
Type: {Verwandlung Alka Spell}
Combat Effect: Create an Alka of 4 hexes that deals +4 Physical damage with 4 Pierce and also deals +1 Mental damage.
Out-of-Combat Effect: When you face imminent danger you gain +1 rank to Perception skill checks.

META TAGS

AMPLIFY: Double the effect.
AREA: Everyone within 2 hexes (10') are affected.
MAINTAIN: Power may last past the end of the combat round.

PASSIVE POWERS

Fae-Kin: Focus +2 while not wearing armour.
Nature's Child: Healing you grant or receive gains a +1 bonus.
Unencumbered Dodger: Protection Factor +2 and Parry +2 while not wearing armour.
Stout: During the Upkeep phase you may reduce the intensity of a detrimental condition by 1.

SKILLS

Omens / Portents: When the higher powers send signs, you know how to interpret them.
Survival, Wilderness: You know how to survive in the harsh unforgiving wilds (forage for food and shelter).
Brew: You have the knowledge of how to brew potions and ointments.
Sacred Wood Binding: Your specially prepared sacred staff grants you perfect night vision. The vision distance is 25' per rank in this skill.

Sacred Staff Spear
Damage Factor: 2
Pierce: 2
Reach: 3
Meta: Knockdown
(Apply the Vulnerable condition)

4 Recovery Salves
Reduce a condition intensity by 1 per Brew rank.

6 Healing Potions
Heal +6 per Brew rank.

Verwandlung Magic
Nature magic that benefits from conduits to other realms. For every 2 adjacent Alkas, you gain Focus +1

INGRID

Fardrengir

The Fardrengir is a travelling soul and a seasoned hunter. She will not stay in a town too long. Her need for adventure, exploration and nature will keep her on the move. The Fardrengir is a master of the wilderness. Many travellers seek the Fardrengirís guidance in their trek. She can safely navigate even the most difficult terrain. She works towards harmony with all beasts of nature, but that does not diminish the hunter inside her heart.

Fardrengir usually travel with animal companions that are possessed by the realm spirits of Yggdrasil. The companions have consciousness far more evolved than a regular animal. They serve as mounts allowing the Fardrengir to cover vast distances in very little time.

Farvaldr

The Farvaldr is consumed with wanderlust. They cannot stay in one place for long and through their travels, they have become masters of the wild. Their survival instincts are second to none. Farvaldr are trap specialists, having the ability to rig a lethal trap from almost anything found in the wild. The most successful bounty hunters are the Falvaldr, also known as Striders. Their competition affectionately call them ìspidersî rather than "Striders".

Dyrvaldr

An animal lover at heart, the beast master attracts special mounts with whom they forge an unbreakable bond. They train with these loyal thanes in order to hone their mesmerizing and synchronized manoeuvres. What they achieve together is much more astonishing than what they muster on their own. Depending on the Dyrvaldr's goals, they will choose the right mount that will compliment the skills and powers they require.

Geirvaldr

The Geirvaldr is the spear master. A hunter who specializes in bows and thrown weapons. The celerity and dexterity of their arms shocks and astonishes onlookers. Besides their uncanny accuracy, the Geirvaldr has the ability to draw and launch an astonishing number of projectiles- be it with bow or javelin.

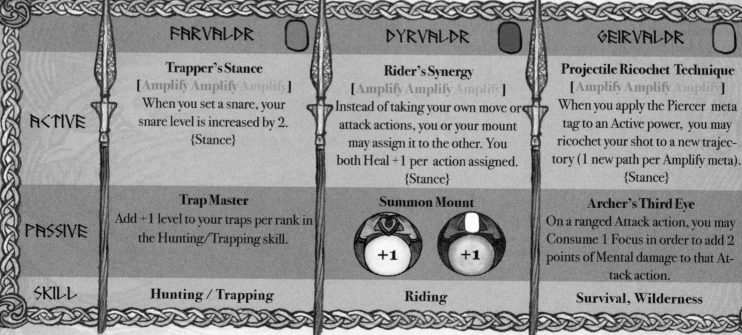

	FARVALDR	DYRVALDR	GEIRVALDR
ACTIVE	**Trapper's Stance** [Amplify Amplify Amplify] When you set a snare, your snare level is increased by 2. {Stance}	**Rider's Synergy** [Amplify Amplify Amplify] Instead of taking your own move or attack actions, you or your mount may assign it to the other. You both Heal +1 per action assigned. {Stance}	**Projectile Ricochet Technique** [Amplify Amplify Amplify] When you apply the Piercer meta tag to an Active power, you may ricochet your shot to a new trajectory (1 new path per Amplify meta). {Stance}
PASSIVE	**Trap Master** Add +1 level to your traps per rank in the Hunting/Trapping skill.	**Summon Mount** +1 +1	**Archer's Third Eye** On a ranged Attack action, you may Consume 1 Focus in order to add 2 points of Mental damage to that Attack action.
SKILL	**Hunting / Trapping**	**Riding**	**Survival, Wilderness**

 Essence
Your memories
lifeforce & wisdom

 4

 Destiny
The effect you can
cause on the world

 2

Level: 8
Size: 4

Move 4 DF 2 Pierce 2 Focus 1

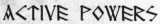

ACTIVE POWERS

Trap Incapacitation
Metas: [Area Area Area]
Type: {Snare}
Combat Effect: Set a snare that imposes +1 intensity to the Blind condition [counter: P]. The intensity is boosted by +1 per 5 snare levels.
Out-of-Combat Effect: Your traps are very well hidden making them especially deadly.

Trap-Spikes
Metas: [Area Area Area]
Type: {Snare}
Combat Effect: Set a snare that deals Physical damage equal to half the snare level. It also has a pierce equal to the snare level.
Out-of-Combat Effect: Your snares can be miniaturized without the need to sacrifice functionality (palm sized).

Hamstring
Metas: [Amplify Multi Piercer]
Type: {Manoeuvre}
Combat Effect: Perform a weak attack action with a +1 damage bonus and inflict Impeded with +1 intensity [Counter P].
Out-of-Combat Effect: You move quickly through water and deep snow.

Regenerating Attack
Metas: [Amplify Multi Piercer]
Type: {Manoeuvre}
Combat Effect: Perform an Attack action and Heal +1 and Recover +2 to self or adjacent.
Out-of-Combat Effect: The suffering of others fuels your inspiration and resolve.

META TAGS

AMPLIFY: Double the effect.
AREA: Everyone within 2 hexes (10') are affected.
MULTI: Add +5 hex (25') range and up to 2 more targets.
PIERCER: Hit two targets who are in a straight line.

PASSIVE POWERS

Tactical Advantage: During Upkeep you may perform a free move action.
Quick Draw: You may exchange equipment or draw more ammunition without having to play a rune.
Summon Mount: You attract a silver stag or golden boar companion (skill taken twice- level 6, size 6).

 2   2  12   1   2 3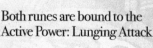

Both runes are bound to the
Active Power: Lunging Attack

SKILLS

Riding: This skill allows you to perform complex manoeuvres while riding.
Animal Empathy: You have an affinity with wild animals, knowing how to calm in the inner beast.
Tracking: Few can hide their tracks from your expert tracking skills.
Hunting / Trapping: Your skills allow you to find game trails and your traps can catch both large and small prey.

Hunter's Bow
Damage Factor: 2
Pierce: 2
Range: 10
Meta: Gore
(Apply the Degeneration condition)

Eldritch Ring
Focus +1

Snare (Traps) A snare has a level equal to your level plus the instances of the Hunting/Trapping skill rank. You are immune to your own traps and cannot trigger them. Anyone else within the effect radius sets off the trap.

Sceadugengan

NOTT

Sceadugengan are known as the "dark walkers". They begin their lives as rogues, living a life of theft, fraud and murder. Life's ambition drives the rogue to obtain the most for the least amount of effort. Their motto is ïwhen all else fails, steal and backstabî. But while in pursuit of increasingly better concealment, pilfering and assassination techniques, they eventually fall upon the dark lore of the Svart Alfar. This pursuit takes them down a dark road where their psyche and spirit erode and are replaced with greed, envy and lust. Their growing powers are fed by the shadows and darkness, encouraging a penumbral existence. This lore and techniques transform the rogue into a Sceadugengan. The darkness becomes their play-thing. The general population of Midgard is easy prey for seasoned dark walker. Many seek out the Sceadugengan for their clandestine talents and offer lucrative contracts. The Sceadugengan's powers stem from the dance of light and dark. Despite an adoration for the Svart, the powers of shadow also require the Lios. Some of their powers will take on a life of their own, transforming their very nature to capitalize on the surrounding light and darkness.

Thief

The Sceadugengan that is driven by greed seeks the path of the thief. Wealth is a motivator, but the thrill of the score is what truly excites her. It is said that in Svartalfheim you can have your sword plucked right out of your hand without even knowing it. The Thief studies the techniques that allow her to secretly pilfer personal effects, even in the heat of combat. No one's possessions are safe when a Sceadugengan Thief is around.

Assassin

Most Sceadugengans' actions are beholden to their shady moral compass. However the darkest of those belong to the assassins. They are the ones who have embraced their talent and bliss when choking out the flame of life. The combat style that they bring back from the shadow involves the least amount of strikes in order to murder their quarry. Those who are the best in this discipline also melt away after the deed is done, so as to avoid any blame.

Scoundrel

While the other Sceadugengan pride themselves at stealth, the scoundrel prefers to hide in plain sight. Their mightiest power is their disarming charisma. Replacing the need for nimble fingers and instead relying on flattery, charm and pure presence, the Scoundrel can spin almost any situation into a favourable one. The Svart lore they covet has trained the scoundrels in the art of using others to do their dirty work.

	THIEF	ASSASSIN	SCOUNDREL
ACTIVE	**Pilfer** [Amplify Amplify Amplify] You perform a Move action and then take 1 item from another combatant [Counter P] (any order) {Manoeuvre}	**Death Strike** [Amplify Amplify Amplify] You perform an Attack action against a foe who is healthy (no runes in the Wounds piles). The attack receives a bonus +3 DF and +2 Pierce. {Manoeuvre}	**Mesmerizing Gaze** [Amplify Range Amplify] You Charm another combatant by +1 Intensity [Counter: M]. The satisfaction heals you +2. {Manoeuvre}
PASSIVE	**Quick Draw** You can exchange equipment and ammunition without playing a rune.	**Assassin's Reflexes** During Upkeep, you may shift your initiative up (earlier) by 2 positions.	**Deflect Aggression** After a Defend action, you may perform a Minor Sacrifice +2 to apply 1 intensity Blind condition upon the attacker [Counter: M].
SKILL	**Feather Fingers**	**Sneak**	**Verbal Manipulation**

Essence
Your memories
lifeforce & wisdom

4

Destiny
The effect you can
cause on the world

2

Level: 8
Size: 4

4	4	6	2
Move	Parry	DF	Pierce

ACTIVE POWERS

Shade of Night and Day
Metas: [Amplify Amplify Amplify]
Type: {Shade Manoeuvre}
Light Combat Effect: Perform a Weak Attack action
and then switch places with any adjacent combatant
[Counter P].
Dark Combat Effect: You Charm another combatant
by +1 Intensity [Counter: M]. The effect may target
someone up to 10' away (2 hexes).

Shade of the Darting Fox
Metas: [Amplify Amplify Amplify]
Type: {Shade Spell}
Light Combat Effect: Heal +2 and Shroud +1.
Dark Combat Effect: Teleport another combatant who is
within 10 hexes to an unoccupied adjacent hex. You must
have a line of sight to them [Counter M].

Cleansing Block
Metas: [Amplify Amplify Amplify]
Type: {Interrupt}
Combat Effect: Perform a weak Defend action with a
+1 bonus and reduce a condition that afflicts you (or
adjacent) by 1 intensity.
Out-of-Combat Effect: Your danger sense allows you
to reposition yourself before combat.

Shadow Strike
Metas: [Amplify Multi Weapon]
Type: {Manoeuvre}
Combat Effect: Perform a Minor Sacrifice +2 to
perform an Attack action and apply +1 intensity to the
Shroud condition.
Out-of-Combat Effect: You have very quick reactions to
sudden events.

META TAGS
AMPLIFY: Double the power effect.
MULTI: +1 Reach and strike up to 2 more targets within reach.
WEAPON: Unleash your weapon's "meta" effect.
RANGE: Adds 10 hexes (50') to range powers.

PASSIVE POWERS

Blend into Shadow: During Upkeep you may increase your Shroud condition by +1 intensity.
Precision: Your attacks gain Pierce +2.
Brutalize: Your first attack action applies +1 intensity of the Degeneration condition [Counter P].
Shadow of Youth:
> Light Effect: If you are Bloodied, after you end a (non-weak) Move action, perform a Minor Sacrifice +1 to increase your Shroud
> condition by 1 intensity.
> Dark Effect: During Upkeep, Consume Shroud to Recover +2 and Heal +4. You Heal an additional +2 if you are Bloodied.

SKILLS

Verbal Manipulation: You can talk others into doing stuff they would not normally do.
Sneak: You know how to move about undetected.
Feather Fingers: This skill grants you a five-finger discount.
Escape: You can slip out of any restraints that are placed upon you.

2 Cruel Daggers
Damage Factor: 3
Reach: 1
Meta: Gore (Apply the
Degeneration condition)

Dark Bracers
Parry: 4

Meta: Deflect (multiply your
PF and Parry by x3)

Light/Dark Powers
While Shroud is 1 or 2 you are
in the "light". While Shroud is
3 or 4 you are in the "dark".

SOLBLINDI

Stalo

The Stalo is the master of controlled combat manoeuvres. It is said that Odin himself taught the first warriors the ways of the Stalo, and throughout the centuries these skills have been passed down through the chosen bloodlines. The Stalo arts are deeply rooted in history, ritual and tradition. Fathers teach sons the art of chaining attacks with such precision, that they culminate in a crescendo of unstoppable violence. Stalos also carry their tradition in the form of an ancestral weapon. This weapon has been forged to accompany a particular battle art-form. In the darkest hour of Ragnarok, many count on the Stalos resolve to come to the rescue of the weakest and most downtrodden.

Striker

The Striker Stalo focuses on optimizing the attack chain they are delivering. They work hard to ensure each blow finds its mark and cannot be easily blocked by opponents. Strikers are at their most lethal when lashing out with a flurry of small yet precise series of attacks.

Stalwart

The Stalwart Stalo has refined the art of group warfare. They are sought after for shield-walls as their skills are of great benefit to the entire warband. Most allies will fight close to the Stalwart in order to benefit from his expertise and techniques.

Keeper

The Stalo known as the Keeper invests himself into the ancestral relic of his forefathers. Part warrior, part forge master, he hones the relic's properties to accentuate his fighting style. He understands its past, allowing it to guide his fighting style into something truly synergistic with his weapon.

	STRIKER	STALWART	KEEPER
ACTIVE	**[Amplify Multi Weapon]** Perform a Weak Attack action. Immediately after, grant an ally within 3 hexes (15') a free Weak Attack action against any one combatant you just targeted. {Manoeuvre}	**Cloned Manoeuvre** **[Range Range Amplify]** After an ally performs a manoeuvre, copy and bind it to 1 rune in your In-Hand pile. It is usable until end of turn. Perform a Minor Sacrifice +1 to invert the effect. {Manoeuvre}	**Touch of the Hallowed Ancestors** **[Amplify Range Area]** Heal equal to half the QR of the Ancestral Weapon [4]. Perform an Ultimate Sacrifice +1 to teleport your ancestral weapon back into your hand. {Spell}
PASSIVE	**Stubborn** The cost to counter your powers, is increased. The defender must also perform a Minor Sacrifice +1.	**Aura of Peace** During Upkeep you may gain a +1 Intensity to the Aura condition. Your Aura heals instead of dealing damage (includes you).	**Attuned Weapon** Gain a +1 Damage Factor and +1 Parry while wielding the Ancestral Weapon.
SKILL	Perception	Sense Motive	Ancestral Weapon

Essence
Your memories
lifeforce & wisdom

4

Destiny
The effect you can
cause on the world

2

Level: 8
Size: 4

Move	PF	Parry	DF	Pierce
4	2	2	4	2

ACTIVE POWERS

Destroyer of Crowds
Metas: [Amplify Multi Weapon]
Type: {Manoeuvre}
Combat Effect: Perform an Attack action with a +1 damage bonus per 2 adjacent foes.
Out-of-Combat Effect: You can move gracefully through thick crowds without slowing down.

Stance of the Cascading Winds
Metas: [Amplify Amplify Amplify]
Type: {Stance}
Combat Effect: Move actions gain a +2 bonus per Flow intensity.
Out-of-Combat Effect: Repeating your skills improves your chances at success.

Flying Charge
Metas: [Amplify Multi Weapon]
Type: {Manoeuvre}
Combat Effect: Perform a Move action and a weak Attack action (in any order).
Out-of-Combat Effect: Your superb ability of ambushing foes allows you to trick and trap someone in social environments as well.

Lunging Attack
Metas: [Amplify Multi Weapon]
Type: {Manoeuvre}
Combat Effect: Perform a Weak Move action and an Attack action (in any order).
Out-of-Combat Effect: You are especially good at pouncing, allowing you to surprise and ambush your prey.

META TAGS

AMPLIFY: Double the power effect.
MULTI: +1 Reach and strike up to 2 more targets within reach.
WEAPON: Unleash your weapon's "meta" effect.
RANGE: Adds 10 hexes (50') to range powers.
AREA: Adds a 2 hex (10') radius to the effect.

Flow
When you attack from behind you get +1 Flow. Mark this on the "Rage" condition on your playmat. When Flow reaches 4, draw a rune and reset Flow to 0.

PASSIVE POWERS

Insistence for Subtlety: Gain Flow when your Attack action deals damage to a combatant from behind.
Combat Manoeuvrability: During Upkeep you may perform a free Move action.
Die Hard: During Upkeep you may Heal +1 and Recover +2
Martial Prowess: While equipped with a weapon, your Attack actions gain a +1 damage bonus.

SKILLS

Sense Motive: You can detect the real intensions behind someone's actions and/or words.
Ancestral Weapon: Your family's ancestral weapon has been passed down for generations.
Perception: Your senses are very acute, giving you the ability to perceive hidden items or imminent danger/ambush.
Athletics: Your athleticism allows you to perform physical feats which elude others.

Ancestral Spear
Damage Factor: 3
Pierce: 2
Reach 3
Meta: Gore (apply the Degeneration condition)

Scale Armour
Protection Factor: 2

Meta: Absorb
Negate 2 harmful conditions

419

HAGAR

Berserkir

A Berserkir is a warrior who is blessed with the anger of the gods. In this rage, he loses all control and becomes a killing machine, striking down foes with the strength of twice four men. They have no need for armour, since neither iron nor fire can touch their skin while in this feverish rage. People have tried calming the fires within a Berserkir consumed with Modr by pushing them into vats of ice-cold water, but the water was turned to steam by the fiery anger of the Berserkirís breast. Throwing naked women in the path of a Berserkir has also failed to calm the heavenly rage.

In some cases, a Berserkir has been known to transform himself into a mighty bear. After the rage wears off, the warrior is in a weakened state for a time. It is said that a king sent five Berserkirs to conquer a neighbouring kingdom and they accomplished their task, slaying all of the opponentís armies.

This rage is spiritual in nature, since it is a lesser form of what the god Thor possesses.

Juggernaut
Berserkirs that personify the oncoming storm are known as Juggernauts. They are a purely destructive force that believe the best defence is a strong offence. Most will utterly decimate an opponent before they can mount an effective attack. Those that survive the initial onslaught find themselves on their heels, facing an aggressor that will eventually spell their doom.

Dreadnought
Berserkirs that are blessed with rage cannot be touched by fire or steel. Dreadnoughts strive to become the most indestructible forces of nature. Their resolve is unwavering and their body is immovable. Most foes retreat knowing that killing a Dreadnought is an almost insurmountable challenge.

Ursen
Berserkirs that embrace their bear form choose to follow the path of the Ursen. They use their form to gain every advantage over their opposition- size, speed, power and ferocity. Ursen use their tremendous reach to great advantage, swatting opponents about the battlefield.

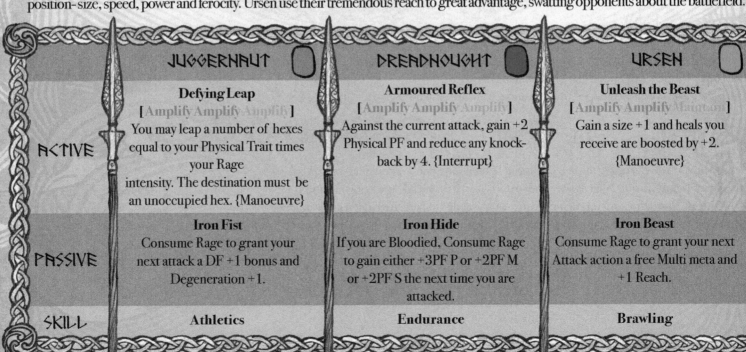

	JUGGERNAUT	DREADNOUGHT	URSEN
ACTIVE	**Defying Leap** [Amplify Amplify Amplify] You may leap a number of hexes equal to your Physical Trait times your Rage intensity. The destination must be an unoccupied hex. {Manoeuvre}	**Armoured Reflex** [Amplify Amplify Amplify] Against the current attack, gain +2 Physical PF and reduce any knock-back by 4. {Interrupt}	**Unleash the Beast** [Amplify Amplify Maintain] Gain a size +1 and heals you receive are boosted by +2. {Manoeuvre}
PASSIVE	**Iron Fist** Consume Rage to grant your next attack a DF +1 bonus and Degeneration +1.	**Iron Hide** If you are Bloodied, Consume Rage to gain either +3PF P or +2PF M or +2PF S the next time you are attacked.	**Iron Beast** Consume Rage to grant your next Attack action a free Multi meta and +1 Reach.
SKILL	Athletics	Endurance	Brawling

420

Essence
Your memories
lifeforce & wisdom

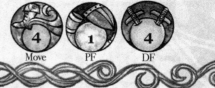

4

Destiny
The effect you can
cause on the world

2

Level: 8
Size: 4

4 — Move
1 — PF
4 — DF

ACTIVE POWERS

Raging Charge
Metas: [Amplify Amplify Amplify]
Type: {Manoeuvre}
Combat Effect: Perform a Move action and
apply +1 intensity to the Rage condition.
Out-of-Combat Effect: You are a natural
wrestler. On a failed Brawl skill check, perform
an Ultimate Sacrifice +1 to try again.

Reckless Power Attack
Metas: [Amplify Multi Weapon]
Type: {Stance}
Combat Effect: Pay a Minor Sacrifice +1 to
perform an Attack action with +3 damage
Out-of-Combat Effect: You can push yourself
past your limits

Lunging Attack
Metas: [Amplify Multi Weapon]
Type: {Stance}
Combat Effect: Perform a Weak Move action
and an Attack action (in any order).
Out-of-Combat Effect: You are especially
good at pouncing, allowing you to surprise and
ambush your prey.

Stand of Presence
Metas: [Amplify Amplify Amplify]
Type: {Stance}
Combat Effect: While the stance is in effect
you gain a Reach +1 on your Attack actions.
When your Rage intensity decreases, you may
perform a Move action. After the Move action,
the stance ends (return the rune to Essence).
Out-of-Combat Effect: After tense
negotiations that eventually result in
success, you have a knack for drawing out
extra concessions.

META TAGS

AMPLIFY: Double the power effect
MULTI: +1 Reach and strike up to 2 more targets within reach
WEAPON: Unleach your weapon's "meta" effect

PASSIVE POWERS

Constitution: During the Upkeep phase, Heal +1 per itensity of all conditions that affect you.
Drive Back: Each attack pushed your opponent back 1 hex (5') [Counter P]. You may perform a Minor Sacrifice +1 to move into the hex vacated by the opponent.
Bastion: When you are facing 2 or more adjacent foes, gain +2 Protection Factor
Raging Bear: Upon reaching Rage intensity 4 you may shapechange into a giant golden bear (gain, Size +4, Reach +2, Protection Factor +4 and quadruped movement)

 16   4   5

SKILLS

Brawling: You are a skilled brawler, using your whole body as a weapon.
Intimidate: Use your menacing presence to cow others into compliance.
Endurance: You can push yourself well past normal limits before succumbing to exhaustion.
Short Fuse: After failing a skill check, you may perform this skill check to try and succeed at the task again.
The skill that was failed has the difficulty lowered by 1 for this skill. Performing this skill check requires an
Ultimate Sacrifice +1. However a failure on this skill immediately imbues you with violent intent and you gain
ranks in the Rage condition.

War Axes
Damage Factor: 2
Reach: 2
Meta: Hamstring
(Apply the Impeded condition)

Leather Armour
Protection Factor: 1

Meta: Absorb
(Negate 2 harmful conditions)

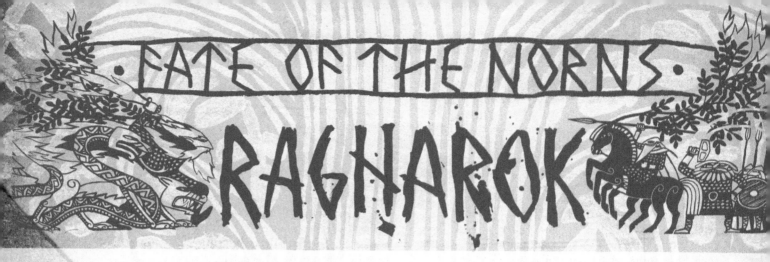

Get a **set of Nordic Runes** that are colour coded
for the **Fate of the Norns: Ragnarok game!**

www.fateofthenorns.com

Fate of the Norns: Ragnarok
SAGA - FAFNIR'S TREASURE

Fate of the Norns: Ragnarok
CORE RULEBOOK

FATE OF THE NORNS

**Fate of
the Norns:
Ragnarok**

**LORDS OF
THE ASH**

coming 2015

PENDELHAVEN PUBLISHING

CPSIA information can be obtained
at www.ICGtesting.com
Printed in the USA
BVOW10*1028161016
464689BV00035B/3/P

9 780994 024008